Obsession

The Middleton Series
Book 1

Lisa Lang Blakeney

Writergirl Press

LISA LANG BLAKENEY

Love reading novels featuring hot alpha men who fall for smart women? Then join <u>MY VIP MAILING LIST</u> at https://LisaLangBlakeney. com/VIP and get a FREE book just for joining!

Copyright © 2024 Lisa Lang Blakeney.
All rights reserved.
Published by: Writergirl Press

FOLLOW ME
Follow me on Facebook
Join my Fan Group
Follow me on Amazon
Follow me on Bookbub
Follow me on Instagram

License Note

This book is a work of fiction. Any similarity to real events, people, or places is entirely coincidental. All rights reserved. This book may not be reproduced or distributed in any format without the permission of the author, except in the case of brief quotations used for review.

The author acknowledges the trademarked status of products referred to in this book and acknowledges that trademarks have been used without permission.

This book contains mature content, including graphic sex. Please do not continue reading if you are under the age of 18 or if this type of content is disturbing to you.

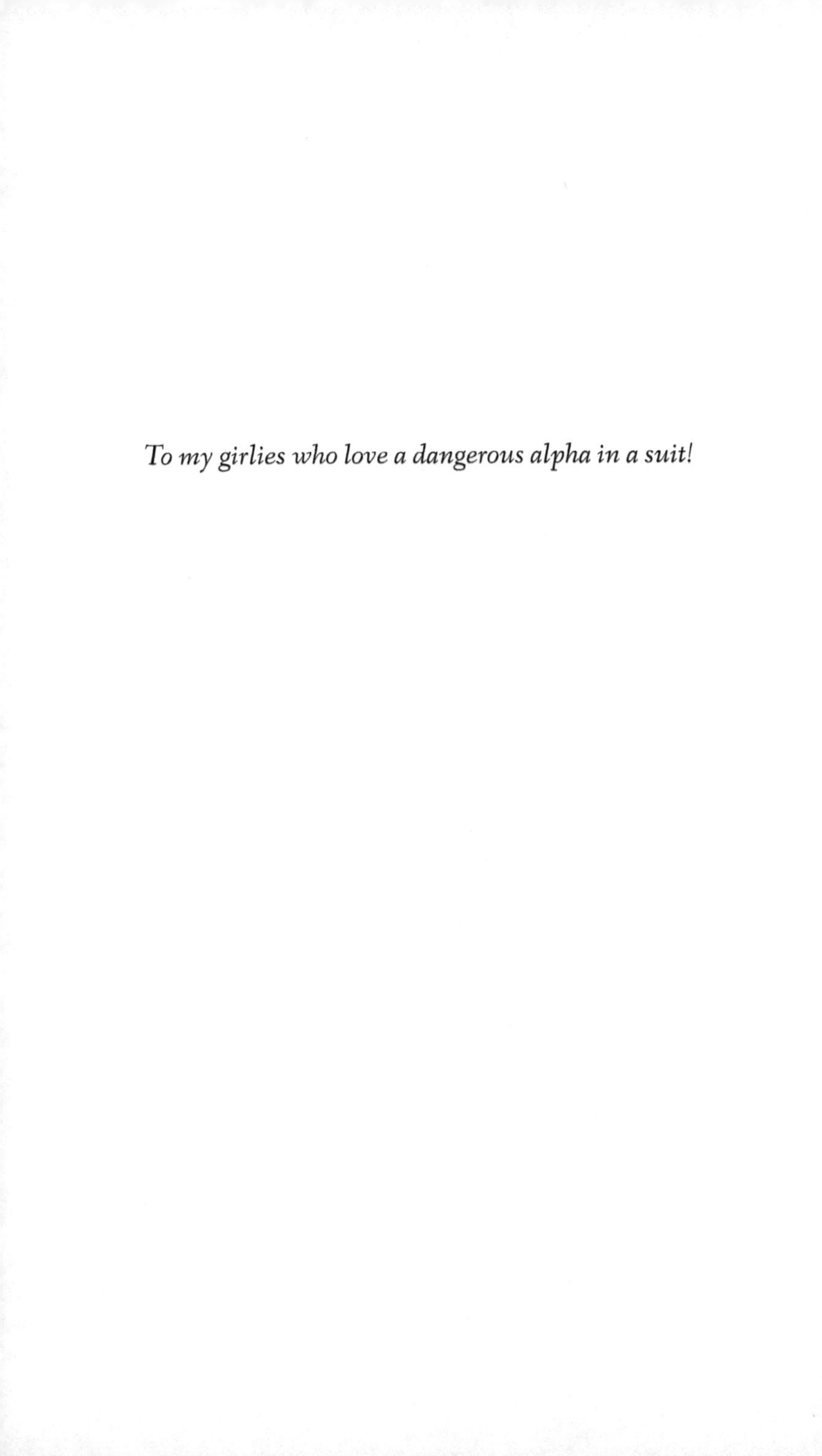

To my girlies who love a dangerous alpha in a suit!

Books By Lisa

****Discounted Book Bundles****
Ultimate Masterson Book Bundle
Ultimate King Brothers Book Bundle
Ultimate Nighthawks Book Bundle
Ultimate Alpha Book One Bundle

The Masterson Series
Devour this addictive series about the possessive bad boy,
Roman Masterson, who falls hard and fast for the girl he's
promised his family to protect.
Masterson
Masterson Unleashed
Masterson In Love
Masterson Made
Joseph Loves Juliette

Masterson Next Generation Series
The crazy hot fruit doesn't fall far from the tree. Dive into
this second generation of Masterson men!
Knox - Knox & Gigi

Bronx - Bronx & Karma
Seven - coming soon

The King Brothers Series
Dive into this series of interconnected standalones featuring 3 alpha hot brothers and the women they lay claim to without apology.
Claimed - Camden & Jade
Indebted - Cutter & Sloan
Broken - Stone & Tiny
Promised - All King Brothers

The Nighthawk Series
Sexy, smart sports romances set in the professional world of football. All standalones.
Saint - Saint & Sabrina
Wolf - Cooper & Ursula
Diesel - Mason & Olivia
Jett - Jett & Adrienne
Rush - Rush & Mia
Freak - Freak & Willow
Brick - Brick & Kaya
Dak - Dak & Katrina

Valencia Ice Mafia Series
Hot hockey romances set on the college campus of Valencia City University.
Neo - Neo & Violet
Shane - Shane & Kennedy
Bass - Coming Soon

The Middleton Series
(Club Blue Whiskey)

Dark, age-gap, romantic suspense trilogy, set in the underbelly of Los Angeles featuring dangerous billionaire Hunter Middleton and the object of his obsession, Megan.

Obsession

Submission

Possession

MASTERSON

Meet Alpha Roman Masterson
Free For A Limited Time!

"Our passion is incredibly intense. The connection between us borders on the possessive. Our feelings are absolutely forbidden. The question now is...what the fuck are we going to do about it?"

DOWNLOAD NOW

Available exclusively through this link.

Chapter 1

Table 21

MEGAN

I stare at the body of a man sprawled in the middle of the alleyway.

Trash bags in hand, I stand there frozen, not knowing whether to go back inside and pretend I saw nothing or casually walk past the body and dump the trash bags in the dumpster.

The answer is beyond obvious.

I quietly step back inside and close the door. Locking it, I drop the key on the kitchen floor and kick it under one of the metal counters before calling out to Billy, the line cook, "Well, damn, the door's locked."

Billy's large afro peeks from behind the wall where he's been taking his break. "Where's the key?"

I squint at the long key holder attached to the wall as if I've suddenly gone half-blind. "I don't know. Should've been hanging right here."

Billy stares at me.

I stare back.

"What're you looking at me for?" I say, mustering up an annoyed voice. "I can't produce another key out of my ass." When he leers at my behind, I flip him off with a quick grin. "Tell Ralph to throw these out when he comes in the morning. He knows where the extra key is. I've got to start my shift."

As I dump the bags next to the door and walk away, I call out, "Stop staring at my ass, Billy, and go call your pregnant girlfriend."

I don't have to look at him to see the guilt on his face before I push the door open to walk into ear-splitting music that almost vibrates in my bones. People are screaming and laughing as sweaty bodies grind and dance against each other with loose movements, the strobe lights working the crowd, and the DJ swaying with the beats.

I slip through the go-between of the bar, nodding to Harry, who quickly hands over a drink to a waiting customer before hurrying away for his break.

"Megan!" comes a familiar shout of my name, and I turn to smile at the greasy-looking man, one of my oldest patrons.

"You want the regular, Charlie?" I ask, seeing that his hand is empty.

"Make it two," He lifts his fingers to show me the number before shouting loudly over the music, "For me and my girl!"

His girl turns out to be a familiar-looking face from the neighborhood with badly dyed lavender hair, fake lashes that look like they hurt, and a body clearly built on a surgical table. I feel sorry for Charlie, but I'm not going to hurt Cookie's chance of landing a score. She's got two kids to feed at home and Charlie probably has a week's pay burning a hole in his pocket.

So I smile, "Well, good for you!"

They both disappear into the crowd, and I already know where Cookie is leading him.

"Poor bastard," a man sitting close to me comments.

I wipe down the counter, shrugging, "At least he'll go home a happy man."

"With a lighter wallet."

I just grin.

What I've just witnessed over the last ten minutes is par for the course. The Blue Whiskey Lounge isn't your average nightclub. The reason why my salary is pretty good is that the kind of clientele this place attracts isn't the safest or the classiest, so we're well compensated for the risk involved.

That's not the first sex worker I've seen pretending that she's just a party girl looking for a good time. And that's not the first dead body I've seen in the alleyway behind this club, and it probably won't be the last. The first time, I was foolish enough to call the police, but now I know better. Last time, it nearly cost me my hard-earned scholarship.

Nobody will bother me here as long as I keep my head down and focus on my work. The midnight shift isn't the best or safest, but it's the highest-paid one. And if I want to make rent for a one room apartment in the seediest part of Los Angeles and be able to afford groceries, I have to gamble with my safety. Those are the breaks.

I notice as one of the servers approaches me, "Two whiskeys and scotch for Table 21."

My hand, which is already reaching for the glasses, freezes in mid-air before I deliberately relax it. I cast a quick look in the direction of the table and see three men sitting there in expensive suits. After six months of working in this club, I already know that Table 21 is reserved for special clients. The kind you really don't want to mess with.

One of the men is facing me, and when I look over at

the table, he looks up and meets my gaze head-on. His piercing grey eyes leave me breathless with fear. This man is no stranger to violence.

I quickly look away and start preparing the drinks. Handing them over, I warn the pretty server under my breath, "Don't linger for tips."

I watch her leave and wonder if she'll be smart enough to listen to me. She won't be the first fool to be attracted to power dressed in designer clothes and then pay the price for it. When I see one of the men grab her ass under the short skirt, I tense up. Then I see the smile on her face and I close my eyes in regret and pity.

This one won't last.

I turn my back and go back to work. Unlike other dance clubs, The Blue Whiskey stays open after the clock strikes three a.m. The music dies down, and most of the people who still want to dance the night away move on to other clubs in the district. Conversations become hushed, and shady business dealings begin.

From three in the morning, for the next few hours until sunrise, The Blue Whiskey is at its most dangerous. I have never met the owner of this club, and I never intend to meet him, although I've heard about him. The dude runs a tight ship. So tight that even the LA police department turns a blind eye if a man is shot in his club or lies dead in the adjacent alleyway. A man with that kind of influence is not someone anyone like me should get to know.

I busy myself with preparing drinks as the sounds in the room become more muted. I keep my eyes down, and my flirtatious smile (which is part of my job description) fades away.

An hour ticks away, and I look up, between orders, towards Table 21. The men are still sitting there. Two of them are clearly drunk, but the third one, the one in the tailored power suit with the grey eyes, is stone-cold sober. The glass of whiskey is in his hand as he gently swirls the liquid. Once again, he notices that I'm watching, and he looks back at me.

He has a head full of dark hair, almost jet black under the flashing lights, and he arches a sharp brow at me, the corner of his lips quirking up at what he clearly perceives as my interest.

I lower my gaze.

I'm not blind.

The man is sex on a stick.

But I have an exam tomorrow, and I can't take that exam if I'm too busy lying next to the dead body out in the alleyway.

The door of the kitchen opens and the manager, Steve, walks out frowning. "Megan, why do we have extra servers tonight?"

"What?" I glance at him. "We have eight like every night. What do you mean?"

"Sally is still on the roster," Steve scowls. "She said you told her to work overtime."

I blink, "What? I didn't–"

I pause when I look up to see Sally leaning towards one of the drunk men who lifts her skirt and stuffs a few dollar bills in the lining of her panties.

My heart nearly stops. "I didn't tell her to work overtime, but I think she's working that table."

Steve immediately looks to his right, and he goes still before hissing, "Has she lost her fucking mind?"

But he doesn't move to go toward her; he just stands there and watches as the other man grabs a willing Sally who has hundred-dollar bills peeking out from her low-cut top and her crotch. Her cheeks are flushed, and she looks a little tipsy.

"What do we do?" I ask quietly.

But Steve's face is white with fear as he stares at their sober companion. "We ain't doing shit. She's fucked. Oh, fuck."

One of the men grabs Sally's skirt, and I can hear a ripping sound. My heart nearly stops in its chest. No matter how I planned to stay out of any altercation over at Table 21, I can't watch something like this unfold.

The giddy smile on Sally's face has disappeared, and she suddenly looks frightened as she pushes the man away. My heart is pounding as I realize that Steve isn't going to do anything. A familiar fear rises up in my throat and I try to block out a memory that seems to be overlapping with the scene playing out in front of me.

"Steve, do something!" I hiss in alarm, but Steve is just frozen solid.

Sally is screaming now, trying to stop them from groping her, and bile rises up in my throat as I whisper, "I'm sorry."

I can see Steve turning towards me, his voice sounding confused. "What?"

But I block it out, grabbing two full bottles of wine and sliding through the go-between. I hear Steve calling my name in a panic, but I can't stop myself. "Megan–"

The grey-eyed man watches me in interest as I stride over, my face set. He hasn't lifted a finger to help Sally, who is screaming hysterically as she tries to escape his disgusting companions.

If I die, I die.

At least I won't have to pay rent once I'm dead.

There's always an upside to every situation.

I've already reached them, and without stopping, I lift up one heavy bottle and smash it down on the head of the man in front of me. He goes down, crumpling to the floor. His companion sees me and sneers, reaching out to me.

"I don't think so, fuck face," I growl, ignoring the other bottle in my hand and kneeing him in the crotch.

His scream is the best sound I've heard all day. When he joins his companion on the ground, I make it a point to kick him in the balls again.

Sally is crying, trying to fix her ruined clothes, and I scowl at her, "What are you doing standing there like an idiot? Run!"

Her eyes widen, and then, for the first time, she actually obeys me, sprinting towards the front door and out. No one tries to stop her. The first man that I hit with the bottle grabs my ankle, and I stumble forward onto the table. The grey-eyed asshole sitting there, watching me in amusement, blinks when my flailing hand hits him, and I spill his entire drink on his suit.

His small smile disappears, and out of nowhere, I see the men sitting on the surrounding tables jump to their feet. I freeze when I realize that there are more than ten guns pointed in my direction while I lay splattered on a table, my face nearly at crotch level with this stranger who is still watching me.

The entire club has gone silent at this point, and even the man who had grabbed my ankle is frozen in fear. Grey-eyes tilts his head slightly, and two of the men put back their guns and move forward. I hear grunts from behind me and then a pained moan, and I realize they're dragging away his companions from the table.

I swallow, asking in a meek voice, "If I move, will they shoot me?"

He stares at me and then the corner of his lips quirks up again. "Would you like for them to shoot you?"

His voice is raspy and deep, and a shiver runs down my spine at the sound. This time, it's not just fear. I can feel my lower muscles tighten in a spasm of need that I didn't anticipate, and horror washes over me at my reaction.

"No," I squeak and then quickly add, for politeness's sake, "Sir."

I see a dark emotion move behind his eyes, and it's almost hypnotizing. "Bang, bang."

I don't know if he's teasing me or if it's a directive for someone in the room, so my mouth turns dry. "Excuse me?"

His hand suddenly reaches out and puts a finger under my jaw, tilting my head back to face him. My heart is pounding so fiercely that I wonder if he can hear it.

"You ruined my suit."

I blink at him, "What?"

He gestures towards his suit. "How will you pay me back for the damage?"

"It's a suit," I say slowly. "You're going to shoot me over a suit?"

He gives me a steady look.

A smart idea would be to apologize, beg for forgiveness, and swear on everyone's life but my own that I will pay for dry cleaning. However, the fact that to him, his suit is more valuable than my life is pissing me off. So, I don't do the smart thing.

I do the stupid thing and say, "It's not my fault your hand was in the way."

From behind me, at the bar, I hear Steve moan, "Megan, no!"

But I've already said it.

And since I've already aggravated the lion, there's no

harm in going out with a bang. So, I glare at the man and say, "I'm not sorry, and your suit is ugly. Now, at least you have a reason to throw it away."

I hear a thump on the ground and wonder if Steve has passed out. The adrenaline running through my veins is pushing away the fear.

"My life is shitty enough," I say to the man. "Go ahead and shoot me. At least I know I saved a girl's life in the process. What did you do? Sit in your expensive suit and watch her get assaulted! What kind of man even does that? And you know what else?"

I don't know why I can't shut my mouth, but it's like I'm on a roll. Perhaps, if I piss him off enough, he'll just shoot me quickly and get this over with. I hope he doesn't dump me out back, though. I deserve at least a small funeral.

"What?" he asks in a dangerous tone, his voice silky and rubbing against my nipples, making them ache under my shirt. "Do go on."

"I'm glad I ruined your fucking ass suit!"

The man stares at me, and then he smirks, his thumb coming to rub my lower lip, as he murmurs, "You have quite a mouth on you, don't you?"

This is the part where he's supposed to shoot me dead. Why isn't he telling them to kill me?

"What's your point?" I try not to let my fear show.

The look in his eyes tells me he's almost considering it, but he doesn't say anything for a long moment that seems endless. Finally, he mutters, "I think I've scared you enough for today."

I freeze, and this time, my voice is small, as if my brain has suddenly remembered the situation I'm in. "So, you're not going to kill me?"

His smirk is lazy and spells all kinds of trouble. "Over

my ugly suit? Didn't you say that now I have a reason to throw it away?"

I wet my dry lips and mutter, "I just said that to hasten the killing process."

He blinks, "Do you want to die?"

"No?"

"Okay, then." He jerks his chin, and the men suddenly put away their guns and move back to their seats as if nothing had ever happened.

I'm still frozen in my position, and the man says smoothly, "Do you need some help getting up?"

My muscles feel stiff, and I get to my feet slowly. It's then that I register the shaking in my hands. The adrenaline is fading away, only to be replaced by the stark realization that I nearly just got myself killed.

"Um—" I stare at him, and he looks at me with a small smile. "I can't afford to pay for your dry cleaning."

I should be thanking him for not murdering me, not reminding him of his ruined suit, but his lazy question takes me aback. "Oh, do they not pay you enough here?"

I glance back at where Steve is lying unconscious, and I mutter, "They pay me, okay."

"I see."

My eyes feel wet, and I blink.

His smile disappears as I rub my eyes.

"I have to..." I take a step back slowly. "I have to go cry now. I'll replace your drink in a minute."

And with that, I dart off into the kitchen like a speeding bullet, relieved that at least I'm still breathing.

Chapter 2

Campus Visit

MEGAN

It took me three days to emotionally recover from the incident, but now I'm without a job. My manager was displeased that he almost shitted himself and fired me. My rent is due in two weeks, and I have just enough cash for a few groceries. In other words, I'm fucked.

I shuffle to the bathroom and wash my face, not even bothering to look at myself in the mirror any longer than I have to. My tangled curls are in a high bun, and my poorly done blonde highlights are growing out and are as clear as day. I really shouldn't have let Naomi mess with my hair to practice for her cosmetology class, but when your roommate gets you extra packs of Ramen as a bribe, you kind of have no choice.

My wide-set, almond-shaped eyes look exhausted and bruised as I mutter at my reflection, "This is why nobody wants to date you. Ghosts have a better chance of getting a hit on Tinder than you do."

I still have a few lectures to attend today before I can go

home and start my job search again. On my way back, I plan to drop off my résumé at a diner near my house and at a local bar.

I have headaches, so I take two ibuprofen from my bag and pop them into my mouth. My hand hesitates on the half-eaten banana, but I save it instead for lunch.

I sleep my way through Art History and fumble through ceramics. Fortunately, since I frequently participate in classes, the teachers don't bother me today. But then again, I look like death warmed over, so they're probably taking pity on me. It's when I'm hurrying out of class that I bump into a hard male chest.

"Oh shit, sorry!" I immediately crouch down to pick up the notepad that I had been in the process of stuffing in my bag.

"Megan?"

The familiar voice makes me go still, and I look up. Ricky Tomlinson, with his hipster good looks, was a guy I had a massive crush on a few months ago. The outcome of that crush was less than amusing.

"Ricky, what's the holdup?" Comes another familiar voice, and I wonder if today is the day when all of my bad karma is going to come to bite me in the ass.

I don't have time to move away because a fake-tanned hand slides across Ricky's chest from behind just then, and a curvy brunette (a Kim Kardashian wanna-be) snuggles into his side. Her eyes widen in mocking laughter. Yeah, karma is after my ass. It's Ashley.

"Oops, sorry, Megan, I didn't mean to interrupt. Were you about to suck Ricky's dick again to prove how much you adore him? I'm sure you don't need a private room for that. After all, it's not like everyone here hasn't seen you do it."

Her words make me flush in humiliation, but I force

down my feelings, refusing to give in to the taunt. "Maybe you can give me some tips. I heard some guys bragging about it in the parking lot behind campus."

Ashley's face turns a bright red. "Excuse me?"

I put the notepad into my bag and zip it up, keeping my tone deliberately casual. "I'm sure nothing is wrong with your hearing. By the way," I fling the bag over my shoulder. "You need to ease up on your suction, according to one of those guys I overheard. You get a little needy. Nobody likes that."

When Ricky snickers, Ashley flushes. "What the fuck are you laughing at? She's obviously lying!"

I shrug. "Just wanted to be helpful. I believe in returning favors."

Since we're in a crowded hallway, she can't do anything to me, but knowing Ashley, I'll have to watch my back for the next few weeks. I quickly slip away, feeling only a glimmer of satisfaction at getting back at her because I know for a fact that the video she leaked out is still circulating amongst people.

My hands tighten over the strap of my bag, and I force myself to regulate my breathing. Having a panic attack in the middle of the University would just give room for more rumors. I don't need that.

I'm nearly at the gate when I see a shiny black car parked across the road from the main gate. It's not the car that bothers me, but rather the two men leaning against it, studying the students. A bad feeling crawls over me, and I immediately turn my back toward them.

I'm usually not that paranoid, but ever since the incident at The Blue Whiskey, I cannot help but feel that I won't be forgiven that easily. I decide to climb over the fence behind the college. I've nearly reached the corner when I hear a voice. "Miss Taylor?"

I freeze and then peek over my shoulder, my hand tightening on my bag. Both men are standing behind me. One is a stocky man with olive skin who's not much older than me if I had to guess, and the other is an older man with thin, pale skin and grey hair at the temples. They're both wearing casual suits, which is an odd look for campus, and they study me. "You are Miss Taylor, right?"

"I uh, no? No." I try to infuse some confidence in my voice.

"Then why did you stop when we called you Miss Taylor?"

I blink and slowly say, trying to think of a reasonable response, "Because I thought you said Miss Tayla."

The two men exchange a look between them before they look back at me and assert, "You're Megan Taylor."

I take a step back, saying cautiously, "I can see why you think that, but I'm not Megan. Megan Taylor is taller than me and really pretty. I'm Tayla. It's a family name."

It's the most ridiculous lie in the world, and I'm unsure if they're buying it. I just need to find a moment to run. If that asshole wanted me dead, he should've done it in the club three days ago. I've changed my mind now. I don't want to die anymore.

I see the younger one take out his phone to check something, and I'm about to make a run for it when the older guy grabs me without warning.

"This is her," the first one says, holding his phone next to my face. "It looks just like her."

"It does not!" I protest, trying to pull away.

"It's definitely her," the other man says dryly.

"If you try to kill me, I'll scream," I promise. "I've been

told that I have a very shrill voice, and I'm also a biter. I'll bite your fingers off." I infuse a bit of fake confidence in my voice, which sounds more like a squeak. "Try me, bitches."

The two men wince. "God, you're mean."

The stocky one gives me a long look, basically rolling his eyes. "We're not here to kill you, so calm down."

I immediately go still. "How do I know you're not lying?"

He blinks, a little confused, and glances at his companion. "How do we prove that?"

"By letting me go?" I suggest, hopefully.

"Nice try, kid," the older man holding me snorts. "This isn't my first day on the job."

"We're here to find out why you haven't been showing up for work," the first one says, smiling at me. Okay, he looks less like one of *The Sopranos* when he smiles. Then, his statement registers with me, and I give him a stunned look.

"Say that again?"

"The boss sent us to make sure you were okay," he replies. "Let her go, Lars. I don't think she's going to run now."

I rub my arms from where Lars grabbed me, and I glare at him. "Why'd you have to be so rough, Lars?"

Lars just grunts.

Turning away from the rough old guy, I look towards his companion. "Steve sent you?"

"Steve?" The man looks baffled. "No, I just told you the boss sent us."

I lift my brows. "Does the boss have a name? Who is he? You are from the club, right?" I'm growing a little confused now and just a bit wary.

The two men exchange another look and then the first one says, "Yeah, Mr. Middleton sent us. He owns the club.

He's the boss, and apparently, you haven't shown up to work for the last three days."

I look at the two of them. "The owner sent you to check up on a missing bartender?"

I'm pretty sure that I've never met this Mr. Middleton. Of course, I know of him. Who doesn't? He's the most eligible bachelor in town. At thirty-five, he's the CEO of Middleton Financial Group and owns a multitude of businesses in the city, including additional locations of the club Blue Whiskey, which are spread out all over the country.

But once again, I've just heard his name. I've never seen a picture of him. From what I know, he dislikes public appearances, social media, and the press. I heard that he once destroyed an entire tabloid because they tried to get a hold of his pictures and sell them. He has people who speak for him at conferences, but he rarely does.

I never really thought I would ever meet him, despite working in one of his establishments. I didn't even know he knew I existed. So it's a little odd that he sent two of his... I mean, I can only call them henchmen, even though the young one is a little cute now that I'm over my initial paranoia.

"I don't understand." I stare at the nicer one. "I thought I was out of a job."

He gives me a quick grin. "Is that why you've not been coming in? You should've at least come back for your salary, but you're not fired, Miss Taylor. In fact, you're supposed to show up for your shift tonight."

Lars just grunts.

I wonder if he has a maximum amount of words he can use daily and just exhausted them, talking to me.

"So, I still have a job?" I repeat, making sure I'm not imagining this whole thing.

"Yes."

"And he knows what happened there?"

"He does."

"And I'm not in trouble?"

The sort of cute one bursts into laughter. "Absolutely not."

Despite the events that have taken place in the club, it has been the only source of my livelihood. I know what it's like to have nothing and dig out of the trash to eat, so when my eyes fill up, it's Lars who now looks uncomfortable.

"Wait -"

"I'm not crying," I sniffle. "It's just these damn allergies."

I wipe my eyes, sniffle, and start walking away. "I'll come for my shift. I'll be on time. You tell Mr. Middleton he's the best!"

Who said rich men were assholes?

I know he's got a reputation in the club, but maybe that's just exaggerated.

As I exit the campus, leaving behind the two baffled henchmen, I think to myself that Mr. Middleton might not be as horrible of a boss as I had imagined him to be.

So maybe he's not a completely deranged psychopath.

I suppose only time will tell.

Chapter 3

The File

HUNTER

"The Caller brothers have been dealt with," Lars announces.

I study the body hanging from a rope around his wrists, his face bloody.

"And what about Isaiah?"

"Dead," Parker adds. "There were torture marks on him, so we know they grilled him for information."

When neither of them adds anything further, I lift a brow. "Where is he?"

"They shot him in the alley behind the club. We reviewed the security footage, and it seems that one of the bartenders saw the body."

I blink in mild surprise. "The police weren't called?"

"Well, she opened the door, and she didn't step outside when she saw the body. The new cameras we installed in the kitchen last week show her locking the door and kicking the key under the counter."

Amusement flickers in my chest upon hearing that.

"Who was it?"

I already have a feeling that I know who it is, but when the two men exchange a look, my answer is confirmed.

"The bartender we tracked down today at the college."

My memory goes back to the young woman who looked at me with such reckless eyes, even as she had quaked in her shoes. She was like a hissing kitten, afraid for her life but baring her fangs at me.

"Did she give any clarity on why she hasn't been back at work?"

"Not really. I think it surprised her that she still has a job," Parker replies.

I'm not typically a man who is easily intrigued by a woman or by anyone, but the way she rushed forward to defend her coworker, just seconds away from me slitting the throats of those two men, has left a lasting impression in my mind.

"Are we sure that the Caller brothers killed Isaiah?" I move back to the topic at hand, gesturing towards one of my bodyguards to cut down the body.

Parker nods. "We found his wallet on one of them. We also went to his clinic. It was trashed. Looked like a break-in."

"Isaiah didn't keep my records on hand, which is probably what they went looking for," I say slowly. "But murdering him in my backyard is a challenge being thrown at me. The Blue Whiskey has to remain neutral territory. Find out who hired those two. This wasn't just a random act of violence on their part."

I watch Lars and Parker leave and then look at the bodyguard. "Dispose of this one and send word to Mr. Romero that his daughter got her justice."

He nods, and I go to my office, contemplating this new

turn of events. Isaiah was my personal physician. To be kidnapped, tortured, and killed on my turf is highly disrespectful and bold. Somebody is trying to make a statement, but who would be stupid enough to go against me?"

I glance at the wall clock.

It's close to midnight.

I wonder if that little bartender returned to work.

There's a knock on my door.

"Come in," I call out.

It's Steve, the bitch ass manager I hired a little less than a year ago.

"Well?" I study him.

Steve looks ready to piss himself. "Megan called to let me know she's coming in tonight."

"I see."

When he hesitates, I give him a cool look. "If you have something to say, spit it out."

Steve is sweating like a pig at this point. "She's a real good worker. All the customers like her, and she knows how to keep her head down. Also, she's in college right now and —"

Irritation flares in me. "I didn't call her back to work to flay her alive, but since you're in such a chatty mood today, tell me about her."

I don't offer him a seat.

It amuses me to see him shake in his shoes.

I've never really liked Steve. He has this slimy feel to him, but the place has been running smoothly, so I can sacrifice my personal feelings.

"She, uh - She's been here for six months now. It was a rough start, but she figured things out pretty quickly. She always opts for the night shift because it pays well."

Steve is talking so quickly that his words are stumbling over each other.

"Why'd you fire her?"

He stares confused at me for a moment. "I didn't fire her, but I suppose I should have?"

"Are you asking me or telling me?"

"I can give you her employee file to look over, sir, but she's a good worker."

"You already said that."

"Yeah," Steve stammers and his face turns a shade of clammy grey. "She's kind of indispensable."

I arch a brow in a mild threat. "Since when do you decide whether someone is indispensable or not?"

If he throws up on my carpet, I'm going to wipe it with his face.

"No, no. I meant... I wasn't trying to..."

"Give me her file and get out," I tell him, beginning to get annoyed with the fearful look on his face.

Steve is quick to obey, and I lounge in my chair, looking through the brave little Megan Taylor's file.

Her eyes have a captivating look to them. They are deep set, framed by long black lashes, and are so mesmerizing that one could be hypnotized by them. But they have a guarded look to them as well, and while she's smiling in her resume photo, the smile doesn't reach those unforgettable eyes.

"I wonder what you had to survive," I murmur to myself. I've seen that look in people's eyes before.

In all my thirty-five years, I've never had a woman challenge me like this. It was almost as if she was daring me to kill her and yet terrified I would do so. I purposefully don't interact with the staff except for management, so I've never met her before. I doubt I would have forgotten her face if I had.

Entertaining little thing, I muse to myself as I go through her cover letter.

"Let's see whether you really do come back to work today."

I'll be waiting.

Chapter 4

A Girl's Got To Eat

HUNTER

When I bought The Blue Whiskey, the first thing I did was tear down the original building and rebuild it. It seemed like the perfect place to set up my operations. I needed a home base for my network in Los Angeles, and a club was the best front.

Despite being a nightclub, the building is built like a fortress for my protection. The whole club is sectioned into different portions. The ground floor contains the bar and the dance floor, while there are private rooms on the first floor that are paid for by the hour. My office is on the second floor in the back of the club, next to the offices for my bodyguards and other side ventures.

LA is a party city, but all that glitters is also tainted by dirt. The number of gangs and criminal factions in the city has grown at an exponential rate. Havens like The Blue Whiskey allow members of those groups to meet openly with an unspoken rule of no bloodshed. The few times that rule has been broken, the consequences have been dire for those individuals.

I have been sure to be ruthless in enforcing the rules, which is why most will always toe the line. After all, I have a reputation to uphold as Los Angeles's underworld mediator. The sole man who can help negotiate disputes or help make a problem disappear.

Because that's what I do.

I fix problems and make them go away by using whatever means necessary. However, while I play the role of the puppeteer in the underground world, I have my own set of rules and morals that I live by.

The people who work in any of my establishments are under my protection. I also have strict rules in place about how the staff is supposed to be treated. The Blue Whiskey is my base of operations in LA, but I don't interfere in the running of the place. I trust the people I hire. So, to see the way the manager that I hired personally, refusing to step in when a server was being assaulted out of fear for his own safety had my blood boiling. I gave him ample time to step in, but it was the hissing kitten who did so, fangs bared, armed with expensive wine.

Obviously, Steve has to go, but I need to hire a replacement for him before I get rid of him. Fortunately for me, I have my eye on a petite woman with deep, honey-kissed skin and a penchant for justice and violence.

As people dance and grind against each other, I make my way around the dance floor toward one of the open-mouthed booths. I can see my security team mix into the crowd and take up discreet places around me. However, I'm not interested in them.

I have a clear view of the bar, and just as I had predicted, Megan slips in to relieve the bartender they call

Harry. From across the room, I watch her chatting with the clientele, smiling at them as they keep finding excuses to talk to her. But I can see how tired she looks. Her eyes give it away. I'm learning that Megan's eyes may always tell me the truth.

I track her every movement, and I notice one of the customers getting a little fresh with her as she turns around to prepare his drink. My eyes narrow, and my body is automatically moving toward them when I go still. She's stepped away in a deliberate act and slides his drink across the counter to him. While it's smart of her to remove herself from the situation, it bothers me to see her have to smile at that little fucker.

I glance towards Lars, who's sitting at a table close to me. He's worked with me the longest and understands my non-verbal gestures. He immediately stands and strides over to the bar.

Megan sees him and blinks.

Her eyes widen as he grabs the customer, who had been trying to feel her up, by his collar and throws him at the bouncer's feet. The bouncer is quick to respond as he further drags the man outside. The whole thing happens in under five seconds, and Megan is left staring.

Lars returns to his seat, and I see Megan looking around the room. Suddenly, as if she senses my gaze, she meets my eyes.

The color drains from her face once she recognizes who I am.

I lift my hand and crook a finger in her direction, silently ordering her to come here. The flash of quick defiance in her eyes is so fascinating to watch, and then her jaw tightens before she deliberately looks away. It's been years since somebody turned down an order from me. Under the flicker of anger that flares within me, there's also a subtle curiosity.

She's really going to make me go over to her.

When I stand up, my team looks confused. They're not used to me approaching a woman or an employee in my club...ever. I typically wait for people to come to me. I shake my head at them discreetly before making my way over to the bar. Megan is serving a skinny-looking man with tattoos all over his face when she looks at me and freezes.

"When I tell a woman to come over to me, she usually obeys," I say to her.

Although the music is deafening, she hears my words, and her pretty eyes turn into slits, "Congratulations, that's quite an achievement."

The corner of my lips quirks at her response. "I see you've decided to come back to work."

Her face turns stiff at my casual statement, and she gives me a wary look. "Yeah, well, a girl's gotta eat."

She clearly doesn't want to engage with me, so I don't force her. Taking up a seat at the bar, I just watch her work. However, her movements have become somewhat stilted, and she keeps throwing nervous glances in my direction. I just order my usual whisky and sip it occasionally, watching her. The people sitting around me move away, giving me wary looks, and I'm left alone at the end of the bar.

There's a rhythm to her movement, and when she realizes that I have no intention of bothering her, she begins to relax. The crowd at the bar grows thinner as the music slows down, and when Megan is between orders, I ask, "What do you think of my suit?"

She gives me a wary look. "Why?"

I shrug, bringing the glass of whiskey to my lips, my eyes

on her. "You had such strong opinions on my last one. So, I thought I'd ask."

Her face flushes as she sucks her teeth. "You know that was an accident. And your henchmen, I mean friends, pointed guns at me. I'd say we're pretty even at this point."

My lips twitch as I shrug. "Maybe. So tell me," I tilt my head towards the club dance floor. "Why work the late night shift at a club? It's not like you don't know the kind of crowd that comes here."

She picks up a large bar rag and starts wiping down the marble bar top. "Are you including yourself in that?"

"You seem to have a lack of self-awareness," I muse, my eyes taking in the angry glitter in her eyes. "I haven't seen you here for the past few days. I thought you quit."

"I didn't quit!" She snaps at me in a low voice. "I thought they fired me after the fiasco with you."

"Were you told that you were fired?" I ask, curious.

"No," she mutters, and I hear a hint of guilt in her voice. "But I was sure they would, so I didn't show up."

When she looks up at me, her eyes are all fired up, "The only reason they didn't fire me is that I have a good boss."

"You mean, Steve?" I ask in a stilted tone.

"No." Her movements are becoming more aggressive as she wipes the counter with an intensity as if she's determined to remove every stain there's ever been from it. "Mr. Middleton. He personally sent people to check if I was okay. One of them is here tonight. I only came back because of him. He's a decent boss."

My hand is limp as I stare at her, baffled by her misdirected praise. My orders had been to make sure she came back willingly or to drag her back here kicking and screaming. It's probably better that she doesn't know the last half of it unless I want to remove the proud glint in her eyes.

It's difficult not to smirk as I ask, "Have you ever met Mr. Middleton?"

"No," she mumbles. "There's no need for all of that."

"No need?" I respond. "If he's such a great employer, do you not plan on thanking him?"

She gives me an incredulous look. "Why would I put my hand in the lion's mouth?"

I chuckle softly. "I thought he was a wonderful boss."

Megan stops what she's doing and frowns at me. "Why am I even talking to you about this? You nearly got me fired. Go away."

She finishes wiping down the counter, and I watch her as she throws the cloth away, wash her hands, and dry the batch of freshly washed glasses.

"You look like a college student," I say as if I hadn't just read her entire file a few hours ago.

"I am," she says tersely. "So, stop talking to me. It's a waste of your time."

With that, she moves away, and for the rest of the shift, she makes sure to stay at the other end of the bar.

I'm not insulted.

I have to admire a woman who trusts her instincts because I am definitely someone to stay away from.

The advantage of having her back to me for most of the shift is being able to watch her pear-shaped ass move at warp speed. She waits on customers, pours the drinks, rings them up at the register, and cleans up the bar top in record time. She knows what she's doing. She's good at it.

I don't usually date women. My style is more along the lines of fucking them until they can't walk and then having my driver take them wherever they want to go next. But my usual pool is filled with simpering women who are satisfied with the jewelry and branded gifts as a thank you for their time. They praise me in an attempt to stroke my ego, fuck me for a night, and then usually try their best to get my attention during the rest of the week while I ignore them. To be honest, I'm bored with the whole routine. But never have I come across a mouthy little thing like Megan. So far, she amuses me.

In another world, she might be a woman I'd be interested in seeing for more than one night, but I don't have the patience or interest in something that complicated. Instead, I'm thinking Megan might just be management material and the perfect person to replace Steve at least for the time being.

The fact that she hasn't realized who I am is probably going to work in my favor. It'll give me the time to observe her so that I don't make the same mistake I made with the dimwit.

Plus, I have to admit, it's kind of fun to play with her like this. I'm starting to think that she's the most interesting person I've met in a long while, and in my business, that's saying a whole hell of a lot.

I don't typically have...a lot of fun.

Chapter 5

Did You Just Spank Me?

HUNTER

The past few days have been similar to the first one. Instead of spending time at my usual Table 21, I choose the same bar stool daily to interact with Megan.

She does a fantastic job of avoiding me, which tells me that the girl has some experience in avoiding unwanted attention. However, at the same time, she's quite skilled at diffusing explosive situations. She just has a way of handling people, even drunk people.

By spending time like this, I've also confirmed to myself that handing over the reins to Steve was a mistake, considering the kind of crowd that frequents this club. He's lazy, among other things. He hasn't figured out yet that I've decided to watch the ongoings of the club because he's barely ever on the ground floor. Megan is the one running everything once her shift starts. Yeah, I'm going to need to make some changes.

"Fucking weasel," I murmur to myself three days later

as I study the security cameras in my office and catch Steve slinking off with a purple-haired girl into his office.

So, that's why he wanted Megan to stay so desperately because she does his job for him.

"Parker," I pick up my phone. "Come to my office and bring Lars with you."

When the two men enter, I give them a steady look. "I want a background check done on Steve. A thorough one. I also want to know whom he's talking to, who he's meeting, and what he usually does over the course of a day."

Parker glances toward the cameras. "You thinking of firing him?"

"Something like that," I say darkly.

"I also want one of you to do a background check on Megan. Look for the same things. Who her crowd is, where she comes from, what she does in her free time, and who she's close to here in the club."

While Lars doesn't exactly react, Parker suddenly grins. "I can tell you what she's good at. Excuses. You should've seen the way she tried to convince us she wasn't whom we were looking for."

Lars nods, grunting, "Vicious little thing. Threatened to bite me."

Out of my entire security team, Parker and Lars have been with me for the longest. Parker was barely legal, and Lars didn't talk much at first when they started, but they were both here long before I became Hunter Middleton, the billionaire, the philanthropist, and the business owner. The two of them could easily start a security company of their own but instead, choose to work exclusively for me.

"I want to know why she didn't report Isaiah's body and why she chose to lock the door and hide the key," I tell them because it's something that has been bothering me.

Isaiah's murder was meant as a personal attack on me, and so it's something that I'm still looking into until I get the answers I want. I've begun hearing rumors of a man going around calling himself The Executioner. I'm still searching for a connection between the two. I don't believe the Caller Brothers have the balls to do something like this on their own.

"She doesn't look like the type to cause trouble," Parker says, shrugging. "More like she decided she didn't want to get involved. But I can try to get close to her. She seems to like me a little bit."

When Lars shoots him a questioning look, Parker grins. "Like me, tolerate me, whatever."

I didn't give it a moment's thought before, but now I study Parker with a side eye and wonder if Megan finds herself attracted to his type with his pretty boy looks. He's closer to her age than I am.

"Don't get too close to her," I say in a warning tone, and Parker just winks at me.

"I'll become her best friend," he quips. "Poor girl looks like she won't even trust a rock."

I don't see the humor in that comment, but I leave it alone... for now.

When they leave, I decide to step out for a smoke. I'm trying to shift to e-cigarettes, so I use the back entrance of the club to step outside.

Since it's early March, it's not quite hot yet, and there is still some frost in the air. It's still shy of midnight, and I lean against the side of the wall, trying to get used to the disgusting synthetic aftertaste of the cigarette. There is still an unopened real pack in my coat pocket, but I try to resist temptation.

As my thoughts drift back to the pretty-looking

bartender who eyes me as if she expects me to suddenly attack her at any second, my lips curve.

Getting to know her is like trying to pacify an angry kitten. I don't know why she continues to remind me of one, but she does. Maybe it's the way she looks at me, her eyes hostile and her tone cautious. Most of the questions she answers for me are of a yes and no variety. And for a split second, my mind wanders to a dark side where I imagine having her in a compromising position where still, her eyes are hostile, but her tone isn't cautious–it's desperate.

I adjust myself at the crotch and chastise myself for spending so much time on the club floor when I have a thousand other things I should be doing. Of course, I wouldn't be spending so much time here if I wasn't trying to assess Megan's qualities as a potential manager. *Yeah, me hanging around here is a business management decision.* With the current situation, I need a more hands-on approach in hiring somebody to run this place. Otherwise, I would get a thousand resumes, which would result in a thousand more Steves, and nobody wants that.

"Listen, you piece of trash," Megan's voice floats outside to me, and I stir in interest, wondering which poor bastard is getting a verbal lashing from her this time.

She's actually not that far from me when I turn my head. She's standing at the edge of the alleyway, talking to a man who is clearly drunk.

"I've told you five times to keep your hands off me. Otherwise, I'll chop them off. And while I'm at it, I'll chop off your little dick, too, and stuff it up your ass. Don't think I've not done it before. You think you're the first asshole to piss me off?"

Her tone is fierce, but from where I'm standing, I can see her hands shaking as the man advances. It takes me a second to realize that she's simply trying to scare the man off by putting on a tough front.

She must have just arrived to work her shift. Her back is to me, and I watch in interest to see how she deals with the drunkard. My smile fades, however, when I see the man grab her shoulders and shove her into the alleyway.

"You've got a smart ass mouth, bitch," he slurs as he pushes her.

My body begins to move on autopilot as I stride over to the alleyway. Megan is nursing her wrist as she scrambles back, a fierce look in her eyes as the man advances, stumbling. Her eyes are darting here and there to find a makeshift weapon, most likely.

I don't care what his intentions are or how drunk he is. I grab him by the shoulder, and when he turns around, I punch him in the gut, making him crumble to the ground.

Megan's eyes widened at seeing me. "Y-You!"

The man is howling in pain as he scrambles away. I can't stand filth like him and have the urge to kick him in the gut a couple more times, but I have to stop myself from beating him to a pulp. I have a feeling that my feisty little bartender wouldn't be so comfortable with the sight of the man's blood splattered all over the concrete.

So, I let the man escape.

"I thought you were going to chop his dick off," I ask, as I crouch down next to her, gently taking her wrist to check the damage.

"I was getting around to that," she mutters, but I can see the fear still in her eyes. "Why are you following me? Is this because of what happened with your suit?"

She's clearly terrified, but not enough to stop her from babbling.

"I'm not that petty of a man," I assure her as I

continue checking her wrist. "You twisted it, but nothing an ice pack won't fix. I don't suggest working with it today."

Megan makes a face. "I don't have a choice."

"Why?"

"My rent is due, so I can't afford to take any more days off. Any more questions, Sherlock?" she quips.

She takes her hand back from me and tries to move her wrist. All the blood drains from her face at the slightest movement.

"I'm sure your boss isn't going to dock your pay," I tell her. "It's a work injury."

She scoffs, "I once twisted my ankle because a delivery guy side-swiped me on his bike, and my boss docked me a full day's pay because I showed up an hour late. He still made me work that whole day, too. So, no, I'm not going to take that chance."

I feel a hint of irritation at her story. Did that rat bastard Steve make her work after an injury and still not pay her? I may have some questionable people in my club as patrons, but I don't run a damn dump.

"Why didn't you complain to the senior management?" I ask, helping her stand up.

"And say what?" Megan sneers. "He might be smart with money, but I've heard rumors about Mr. Middleton. He's ruthless."

"What's so scary about him?"

"As if you don't already know."

"Humor me."

"Rumors are that he's killed at least three people in this place. It's like one of those open secrets we all know and don't discuss. I wouldn't do this job if I weren't so desperate."

The last part is a whisper, clearly not meant for my ears but said aloud.

She tries to move away from me, but I keep a firm hold on her. "Come on. I'll put some ice on that."

"I can manage." She struggles with me. "Where's your little boy band with the guns? They're probably looking for you right about now."

I ignore her snide comment. It seems that the more nervous she gets, the more mouthy she gets. I wonder why it makes me grin every time she says something that would piss off any other man in my position.

Did she really just call my security team a boy band?

I escort her out of the alleyway, away from the kitchen entrance, and her feet stop as she hesitates. "Where are you taking me? The kitchen is right there. There's ice in the kitchen."

"To my office."

"To your what?" She tries to pull her hand away from me again. "Listen, dude, I know all about stranger danger, and you can bet your sweet ass I'll scream if-"

Her words die down when I decide enough is enough, and in one swoop, I pick up her curvy ass and toss it over my shoulder like a bag of potatoes. I knock all the air out of her in the process, which is probably why she doesn't scream right away, but she begins to struggle with me, and my brows lift at the inventive curse words leaving her lips.

"You son of a snake! You demented fuckwad! Put me down."

I enter through the backside of the club, and she wriggles in my hold. Her resistance is lighting a fire inside of me, which is giving me the deep urge to give her juicy ass a quick smack, but I don't.

At least not yet.

"This is illegal! You can't just kidnap me! Help!"

I see one of my bodyguards step out at the sound of the ruckus, blink several times, and retreat back into the security office.

"Enough," I scold her. "You're disturbing people."

She makes a choking sound now, pounding on my back with her undamaged wrist.

"Disturbing people? You're fucking kidnapping me! Let me go. I swear I'll pay for that suit! I'll even buy you a new one! You don't have to go this far!"

Her shouts are increasing in volume, and I lift my hand and smack her on her ass, the loud cracking sound making her freeze. I suck in a silent breath, imagining the imprint I may have made on her rounded flesh through her pants.

"Did you just spank me?" she asks in a horrified voice.

I don't have to answer because we've already reached my private office, and I stride inside, dumping her (not so gently) on the three-seater leather couch. Then I go to the mini fridge to retrieve a cold compress.

My back is still to her when I say in a dangerous voice, "If you so much as think of escaping, I can do far more than just spank you."

The rustling movement behind me goes still, and when I turn around, Megan is sitting meekly on the couch, her eyes wide and her cheeks flushed.

Now, isn't that an interesting sight? I muse.

"This is the Blue Whiskey," she mumbles softly, looking around as I approach her. "Why do you have an office here?"

I don't respond, sitting on the coffee table in front of her and pressing the cold compress against her wrist. She whimpers and tries to pull her hand away.

"It'll help with the swelling," I say sternly.

She looks agitated and fearful as she looks around her, and I wonder if she will figure it out. I know she's a smart person, so she probably will. It'll just take a moment for it to all register.

The door of my office opens, and Parker pokes his head in. "Hey, boss, we heard some screams – Oh, hey."

He beams at Megan, who stares at him. Then she looks back at me, and her eyes widen as comprehension dawns in the emotive pupils of those eyes of hers.

"Oh, fuck," she curses, slamming the cold compress to the floor. "You're the boss? My boss? Mr. Middleton?"

"Megan." I pick up the ice pack and hand it to her again. "I'm not going to tell you to put this on your wrist again."

Her eyes are like a doe caught in the headlight of a ten-wheeler as she says the only thing she can while she continues to process this new information about me.

"Fuckity, fuck, fuck."

Chapter 6

But I'm A Bartender

MEGAN

My hands are shaking as I close my eyes, praying to whichever deity will listen to me to make this entire scene dissolve into just a terrible nightmare. But when I open my eyes, Mr. Middleton is still watching me. The corner of his lips quirked up.

"I can explain," I say without thinking.

I wonder if there's any way to weasel my way out of this. A few minutes ago, I called him a ruthless murderer. I even told him how many.

To his face.

Oh, dear God.

"Get me the first aid kit, Parker," he says with a strange emotion dancing in his eyes as he looks at the man who had come looking for me at my college.

When the door closes behind Parker, Mr. Middleton asks, "Explain what?"

"Um," I try to wriggle my hand away from his grip, even

as the spasms of pain make me want to cry out. "I don't know. My idiocy? Look, please don't fire me or kill me."

"I have no plans of doing either," he claims as he presses the cold compress around the swelling in my wrist, his touch surprisingly gentle.

"Then I'm not in trouble?" I ask cautiously.

He lifts his gaze to mine, and his icy steel gray eyes turn my mouth dry. Up close like this, I can see his evening shadow clinging along his defined jaw, offering a blend of danger and attractiveness to anyone who dares admire it.

"In trouble for what?" he asks, and I snap my mouth shut, refusing to offer him reasons on a silver platter.

When I don't say anything, he gives me an amused glance. "So you do know when to stop talking? That's good to know."

My face burns in both mortification and insult.

Parker returns and walks inside, grinning at me, as he hands over the first aid kit to Mr. Middleton.

"Hurt yourself, did you?"

"Get out, Parker," Mr. Middleton snaps.

Perhaps I expect everybody to regard this man with a certain amount of fear, which is why my jaw nearly drops when Parker doesn't leave but instead makes a face and speaks again.

"Come on, I'm just trying to be nice. I just want to be her friend. She's the nicest bartender in here."

"Get out before I throw you out," Mr. Middleton says, not even looking in his direction as he takes out a heavy-looking roll of gauze.

I stare in Parker's direction, and he just winks at me, making a hand telephone, mouthing 'Call me.' I sneer at him as he walks out. However, I don't escape unscathed because when I look back at my boss, he's staring at me with an unreadable expression.

I don't know where to look, so I look down at my hand, squinting my eyes in concentration. The look of irritation on his face and the gentleness of his touch doesn't match. He wraps my wrist with great care and by the end of it, I can't so much as bend it.

"I can't work like this," I say with great dismay, lifting my hand and studying his workmanship.

"You're not going to work today," he says, closing the small first aid box and heading over to his desk. He takes a seat in his oversized office chair, places his hands on the table, and watches me with little effect.

Panic fills me as this whole thing is making me uncomfortable. "You said I wasn't fired."

"You're not," he replies calmly.

He reaches across his desk and picks up a file, opening it. It gives me the time to take a really long look at him. Describing this man as handsome is an injustice. In his slate grey suit, which is probably worth ten times my yearly salary, he has this distinguished yet dangerous air about him. He's tall and fit, and while his strongly sculpted face is expressionless most of the time, I've noticed that his eyes are the key to figuring out his mood.

"If you're done gawking at me, you can take a seat," Mr. Middleton gestures towards one of the empty chairs across from his desk.

"I wasn't–" I try defending myself, but he just watches me with raised brows.

"Are you going to sit down, or should I pick you up and carry you over here as well?"

His threat has the intended effect, and I hurry to sit across from him.

I catch a glimpse of the file he's holding and realize that it belongs to me. He has my employee file open in front of him. Most people would read the information on their computer screens; interestingly, he's printed it out.

"Where have you worked before here?" he asks, leaning back in his chair and studying me.

"Um," I try to gather my thoughts, but it's a little difficult to focus on anything when he watches me with that intense gaze of his. My lower abdomen tightens when he holds my eyes, and I sink my teeth into my lower lip, trying to snap out of it. Lusting after this psychopath isn't what I should be doing right now.

"I worked–It was a bakery. I've worked as a barista at a coffee shop and as an assistant manager at a bakery."

"Why didn't you include those positions on your resume?"

Because they fired me from both places.

I try not to grimace. "I didn't think it was relevant."

"Is that so?"

I feel like I've been called into the principal's office.

I squirm in my seat and for some reason, I get the feeling that Mr. Middleton is enjoying my discomfort as if he almost "gets off" on it.

"Have you considered a managerial position?"

"Excuse me?" I blink at him.

He sets down the file and studies me. "To be more precise, your current manager's position."

I stare at him in stunned silence.

My brain begins to work at some point, and I say, sounding stupid to even my own ears, "But I'm a bartender."

"I'm aware of that." Mr. Middleton gives me a steady look. "But starting tomorrow, I want you to start training another employee to take your position. I want you to become the floor manager."

"But that's Steve's job."

"And now it will be yours."

"That's a full-time position," I say in a panicked voice. "I can't work full time. I have to go to college as well."

"I'll make it a part-time position for you," Mr. Middleton says, unbothered. "It'll be a trial position for three months, so you know."

I hesitate, "I don't think-"

"The pay is double what you're earning now."

Double the pay?

I immediately reconsider.

"I've always wanted to be a manager."

He smirks at my quick response. "At least I know what motivates you now."

He leans back in his chair. "You can go home for the day, but I expect you to start interviewing potential hires tomorrow, so come in early."

I stand up quickly, a little dazed by what's happening.

I've just turned around when he adds, "And Megan-"

I look over my shoulder to see him looking at my attire. I don't think there's anything wrong with my faded jeans and cropped sweater, but he has a look of disapproval on his face.

"Wear something appropriate for your new position."

"It's not like your establishment is the Four Seasons Hotel or something," I retort in a snarky tone.

When he just gives me one of his flat looks, I shut up. I'm learning quickly that those kinds of looks from Mr. Middleton don't bode well for anyone...even me, his new manager.

"I'll figure it out," I mutter, telling myself not to provoke the man.

I can feel his eyes on me as I leave his luxurious-looking office, and it's only when I close the door behind me that I acknowledge my wildly beating heart. Aside from the slight incident of him carrying me, he has been nothing short of professional, and yet, the way he looks at me is almost like a dangerous beast eyeing its prey.

My core moistens at the memory of the way he spanked my ass in one smooth movement.

Jesus, that man has red flags written all over him; I scold myself. Don't even think of him like that.

He's too damn old for you, anyway.

"So, he just offered you a job? Like out of nowhere?"

My hand moves in deft strokes as I draw Naomi's features with the charcoal in my hand. "Yeah, and can you stop moving your face, please? You're throwing me off!"

My roommate and best friend shifts on the couch, striking a suggestive pose and grinning. "Paint me like one of your French girls, darling."

"I swear to God, Naomi," I growl. "This is for my assignment."

However, I have already lost momentum, so I crumple the paper and throw it in with the rest of the pile in the corner behind me.

Our apartment is a one-bedroom piece of crap. The living room (if you can call it that) is tiny, as is the kitchen. Over the past two years, we've raided garage sales and fixed up tossed-aside pieces of furniture to fill our tiny home. The whole place is a mix and match of assorted colors, but it's home.

Naomi stretches her lithe body across the couch. "I can't sit still. You know I can't. Just draw somebody from memory or a TV show or something. I've had five expressos since this morning. I am incapable of sitting still."

I glance at the vintage wall clock I found at a yard sale last year. I still have a few hours before my first shift as the new part-time manager of The Blue Whiskey.

"If this works out, and the pay is good, we can move to a better place," I murmur. "God, I really want to leave this hellhole. Mickey is a fucking pervert of a landlord."

Naomi is still in cosmetology school, but she works at a salon nearby. She doesn't make much money either, but it's enough to pay her share of the rent and manage some savings (at least that's what she tells me). She stands to her feet, and I watch her rummage for eggs in the fridge. I stare at her and contemplate just how much we are the complete opposite of each other.

Naomi is playful, whereas I'm usually safe. I barely style my natural coils, whereas she wears a different hairstyle on any given day. A red wig on one day or long braids on another. She looks like a fucking supermodel most times and is also the complete opposite of me with her flirty personality. She's a people person. I, on the other hand, don't like people much.

"I want a condo," she muses, looking for a pan in the pantry. "With glass windows that overlook the city. And a water bed. I definitely want a waterbed."

My hand is idly sketching some broad features with my charcoal piece, and I ask, "What do you want a water bed for? Do they even still make those?"

She looks over my shoulder, winking at me. "Have you ever had sex on a water bed?"

I look up at her. "It can't be that good."

She wiggles her ass at me. "You remember Johnny?"

"The guy from the coffee shop?" I ask, trying to recall Johnny's face.

"Ooh, yeah." Naomi cracks two eggs into the pan. "He had this massive water bed. The boy reached places in me nobody's reached before, do and it's not like his technique was good. The bed kept moving. And so he kept going deeper."

She lets out a large chef's kiss. "Best sex of my life. It's a pity he got back together with his ex, or I would have definitely gone back for more, provided he still had that water bed, of course."

I groan at the thought of phenomenal water bed sex.

"My dry spell is never going to be over. I need to get laid."

The sizzling of the eggs reaches my ears, and I hear the toaster click to indicate that the toast is done. My fingers are still moving over the textured paper as the face I'm drawing begins to get a few more features.

"The last time I tried to get with someone, it was a fucking disaster," I recall.

Naomi brings her plate to our chipped coffee table and sits down on the carpet, her expression heavy. "It still pisses me off. Ricky is a fucking asshole. He needs to grow a pair."

"I saw him the other day, and that bitch Ashley," I tell her, focusing on shading the piercing eyes on my paper. "She brought up the video again."

Naomi's hand freezes in mid-air. "What?"

I try to shrug, but even six months have done nothing to mute the humiliation I've had to endure.

"That bitch!" I can hear the fury in my friend's voice.

I channel my anger into my art piece. "I gave back as good as I got, though. You would have been proud."

"I told you back then that you should've just kicked her ass when she leaked that video of you!"

I look up at Naomi, my own jaw tight. "You know I can't do that. I don't want to lose my scholarship. There's just one more year, and then I'm done."

I look down at the face that I've drawn, and, to my shock, it's a familiar one.

Naomi probably notices my expression, and she leans over. "What is it?"

When she sees the face, she lets out a whistle. "Fuck. He's hot."

"That's my boss."

Her jaw nearly drops. "The one who-"

I nod mutely.

I've captured Mr. Middleton's intense eyes, the cutting edge of his jaw, the slick hair that he always has pushed back.

I let out a rushed breath. "I should toss this."

"Are you kidding?" Naomi retorts. "It's freaking fantastic. And you have class right after your shift at eight in the morning. Just put it in your bag. You have to submit it. It's not like he'll know."

That's true.

I carefully seal the page in a file and tuck it into my bag. Then, I can just put it in my locker at work and head to campus.

"By the way, can I borrow some of your clothes? I'm supposed to dress the part for this new position, but I barely have money for rent this month, much less a nicer outfit."

Naomi stares at me, a gleam in her eyes. "Oh, this is the moment I was waiting for. Let me dress you, Cinderella."

"What? No!" I scramble back. "Absolutely fucking not!"

"Come on." Naomi abandons her dinner, grabbing me by the leg as I try to run to her room.

I try to shake her off, but she attaches herself to my leg. "I did a great job on your hair! Let me dress you!"

"No!" I shout, trying to push her off.

"Don't be a bitch," she wrestles me to the ground. "I got groceries this month, and you owe me! Besides, I need a model for my class, too. I just need a few pictures."

"I don't want to." I struggle. "You dress like a whore!"

I'm exaggerating, of course.

"Well, maybe if you dressed like one, you would get laid once in a while!" she retorts, pushing me back and running like a track star to her room.

"I don't even know if my ass can fit into your clothes," I say, now regretting that I even asked her.

"All my bottoms have a lot of stretch. You'll be fine."

I get to my feet and follow after her, "I'm telling you. I don't want you to-"

"I'll cover the remaining part of your rent." She dangles the bait in front of me, her brows waggling. "Let me dress you and take a few pictures for my class."

I pause at the doorway. "You promise?"

"I get paid in a week." Naomi narrows her eyes. "I'll cover your share."

I press my lips together before saying reluctantly, "If you make me look like a hooker, I'll kill you."

"Pretty Woman was a hooker."

"This is real life, Naomi."

Her sinister smile makes me whimper.

"Exactly."

Chapter 7

Learning The Ropes

MEGAN

I don't see Steve when I walk in for my shift, and I'm about to reach the staff locker room when I see a familiar face.

"Well, if it isn't *Miss Tayla*," Parker grins mockingly.

"You were some strange man on a college campus approaching me. When are you going to let that Tayla thing go?"

"Never, that shit was funny. Where are you going?"

"To put my bag away in my locker," I say as if it's obvious what I'm doing because it is. I try to walk around him because he's blocking my path, but he's an immense guy, much to my annoyance.

"Boss wants to see you," he says with a smirk.

"You enjoy annoying the hell out of me, don't you?"

"Yeah, I do. Now come on, the boss wants to see you."

"How can he want to see me when I just got in? At least let me put my stuff away."

"Sorry, Miss Tayla." Parker puts his hands on my shoulders and turns me around.

"Stop calling me that," I say in irritation.

"But that's who you introduced yourself as," he chuckles.

"Has anybody ever told you how annoying you are?" I glare over my shoulder at him as he opens a door that even employees aren't allowed through.

"Constantly," he says cheerfully, urging me through the door.

"I can walk by myself." I shrug off his hands, annoyed.

"Fine." He doesn't look fazed by my small outburst. "The boss is waiting for you."

To his credit, he stops following me but continues to watch me from the middle of the hallway. Having no choice, I knock on Mr. Middleton's door.

"Come in."

His voice is curt, and for some reason, my stomach does a complete somersault.

When I open the door, I freeze.

He's standing in the middle of his office, half-naked.

"I – I can come back," I try to get the words out as my eyes are drawn to the ripples of his defined chest. If I thought he looked good in a suit, he looks mouthwatering without one.

"Are you done looking?" He drawls. "Hand me my shirt."

I feel numb as I look around blankly for a shirt, only to see a freshly pressed one hanging from the coat rack. I stumble towards it, eyes toward the ground, and drop my bag in the process.

I've just grabbed the shirt when I hear him say in an intrigued voice, "What is this?"

"What?"

When I turn around, he's holding the laminated file that holds the charcoal drawing I made of him just a few hours ago. Dammit, it must have spilled out of my bag.

My heart climbs into my throat as horror fills me. "No, wait! Don't look at that!"

I dart towards him, one hand holding the shirt, the other aiming at the file, but he holds it over his head, just out of my reach, studying it.

"It's a remarkable likeness," he comments as I slam into him in an attempt to get the file back, my face hot with embarrassment.

"Please give it back!" I half-demand and half-beg, mortified. But he stands still, tilting his head back to inspect my sketch.

"There are situations when I believe that college is a waste of good money, but you're quite talented. I just didn't know you had a habit of drawing me. But you should know, I don't particularly appreciate you putting my face out there. Anonymity works to my benefit in my business."

Without thinking, I put one hand over his chest as I reach up on my toes to grab the picture. It's just then that he looks down at me, and I realize our position. My face goes slack, and I find myself unable to move. My eyes are drawn to his full lips, which are inches from mine. His breath wafts over me with the scent of fine whiskey and, I think, mint.

He also looks taken aback, but his eyes narrow, and the air between us suddenly becomes charged with electricity. I find it hard to breathe, unable to move back, and suddenly, my own body is not mine to control.

"You're treading in dangerous waters, Miss Taylor," he warns in a thick voice, his free hand curling around my waist in a grip that has me gasping. The way he says my name has my core contracting in need.

His eyes move to my mouth, and I can hear a small voice in the back of my head screaming for me to move, but my body isn't listening. A pair of sexy lips are moving lower toward mine, and my heart is racing desperately in both fear and anticipation.

"I don't have a habit of fucking my employees," he whispers seductively against my mouth, our lips not touching.

I instantly feel the dampness in my panties even as the crushing humiliation makes me immobile.

Did he just imply?

I push him away, rebuking the intensity of my attraction to this man. "I wasn't suggesting anything, Mr. Middleton. I just want my sketch back."

"You mean my sketch?"

He doesn't look at all fazed by this exchange between us on the surface, but his eyes are damn near communicating that he plans to devour me. This isn't some college boy who'll beg me to suck him off. No, this is a man who'll have me down on my knees with a single word.

I don't fuck my employees.

His words echo back in my head, and I snap out of my sudden shell-shocked state. Falling under this dangerous man's spell and into his bed is probably the worst thing I could do. This job is simply a means to an end. I work to eat and pay for school, and that's it. That's all it could ever be.

"I wasn't hitting on you!" My words are furious. He's making assumptions about me without any valid reasons. "And that sketch is for my art class. I demand that you give it back."

"Why would you draw me of all people?"

"I – There's no particular reason." I stumble over my

words. "I don't know. I mean, I had to draw somebody, and so I just drew you. Give it back."

"I don't think so," his words slither out of his mouth like a snake. "I just told you. I don't like my picture–"

Panic begins setting in.

"But I'll fail the course if I don't hand this in today. Look, I'm sorry, I'll never draw you again. I swear. I just - I need to use this one. I don't have to name it anything. No one will ever know it's you. Please."

I hate begging.

I detest being forced into a position where I have to toss away my pride and beg so desperately, but people love putting me in that position for some reason. They love tearing away at my self-respect until I'm groveling at their feet. Everyone in my life has done that to me so far except a scant few.

Why did I expect this man to be any different?

Mr. Middleton frowns as he looks at me, and there's a strange emotion in his eyes. "You don't have to get that upset. Here."

My hands shake as I snatch back the drawing and hold it against my chest. I feel cold all over, and suddenly, I want to leave, but he's holding me by my shoulders and guiding me to the couch, ordering me to "Breathe."

I shake off his touch. "I'm fine. I'm okay. Like I said, I need this for my class."

"I get it." He lowers his voice as if he's attempting to calm down a frightened child. "It's fine."

"I won't draw you again."

My heartbeat is slowing down as I glance at him. How can I explain to somebody like him what it's like to live in my shoes? He would never understand why something so slight in his eyes could have me so panicked. I can't afford to make one misstep in school...hell, in my life. Every decision I make matters.

"It's a good drawing. Do you mind if I look at it again?" He holds out his hand as he simultaneously asks the question. I suppose it isn't really a request but more of a demand, so I reluctantly hand over the sketch again. "Why is it so important?"

I suppose his question is straightforward and may be warranted based on my overreaction, but I feel like I've explained myself enough. Of course, I realize that a man like him won't take no for an answer, so I purse my lips and reply, "It's for a mid-semester project. The top five students can present some of their work in an art exhibition next month. I need to win it."

We all have to hand in five pieces each and this is my last. Usually, the charcoal sketch isn't looked at as carefully as the earlier submissions, which is partly why I drew it so hastily, but I still have to hand it in with the rest of my work. An incomplete would disqualify me.

"Which exhibition?"

"Do you even know anything about art?"

"Which exhibition?" He repeats with less patience.

"There's one at The Box Gallery next month," I huff.

"I see."

He hands me back the file, and I hold it tightly, watching him warily as he shrugs into his shirt and buttons it up.

"You can put it back in your bag."

He picks up his tie and wraps it around his collar. His calm behavior settles me and I move towards my bag and quietly tuck in the file and zip it up as if it's a secret government file that I've hidden from an enemy faction.

"Sorry about that," I say, realizing that my overreaction

must have made me just look like some unstable, crazy person. It's not a good look for someone who's just been made part-time manager of a club filled with unsavory characters most of the time.

He glances over his shoulder at me, and our eyes lock. "You don't need to apologize, Miss Taylor."

I try to ignore the flip my stomach makes when he drawls out my name like that. God, I really don't know what to make of this man. My opinion of him keeps changing.

"Take a look at these." He gestures towards a stack of files.

I walk over to his desk and see that it's a bunch of resumes.

"These are for the bartender positions?"

"Yes."

"Who prints out resumes anymore? We could have done this all electronically," I say, blurting out what is quite obvious to me but may not be to someone at least ten years my senior.

"You're going to interview all of them today," he orders without acknowledging my rhetorical question. "That's why I told you to come in early. Select one on the spot and begin training them. You will still be working the bar for a week or so until they get the hang of it, but you'll be handing over a bulk of the work to this new person."

I hesitate, and when I look him square in the eyes, I suddenly remember what his chest felt like under my hands. It takes an enormous amount of struggle to keep my voice steady.

"I feel like I need to ask this. I don't understand your thinking. Why do you want me to take on the manager's position? I don't have this kind of experience, and Steve is actually kind of good at it," I lie.

I'm having second thoughts about accepting this position if I have to interact with Mr. Middleton like this constantly. When I was just a bartender, I never met the man. Now, we've become way too familiar with each other in a short span of time.

The look he gives me chills me to the bones. It's as if putting on the shirt changed his entire demeanor. He's all business now.

"You should keep in mind, Miss Taylor, that I'm not accustomed to my employees questioning my decisions."

I blink and stare at him in confusion. The man switches between moods like I do on day two of my period.

"Fine," I say, refusing to be offended by his tone. "I'll interview them."

"As if there was any other appropriate response," he mutters in a deep voice as I fling my bag on my shoulder and exit the office.

Diana is a sharp-eyed brunette with two years of bartending under her belt. She seems to be pretty friendly and knows enough about different drinks that I decide to go with her. I hate to admit this, but a part of my hiring decision is based on the fact that she's pretty enough to get good tips from patrons but not quite pretty enough to cause drama like our previous server did. She should be a perfect fit for The Blue Whiskey.

My shift is quiet and as the hours tick by, I still don't see Steve anywhere and I have to wonder where he's gone. While Mr. Middleton did offer me his job, and I'm slowly accepting that I actually may have a knack for this, I have to wonder whether Steve was fired or 'disposed of'. For a place like this, it's a legitimate concern.

"You good?" I ask Diana, although I'm only asking out of courtesy. She definitely knows her way around a bar and is doing a good job so far. She's not the type of employee I need to babysit whatsoever. "I need to check something in the back."

"Yep, I can handle it."

"Cool."

I leave Diana to work the bar and go check the shift schedule. Maybe Mr. Middleton moved some things around on the calendar, and Steve wasn't scheduled to work today.

"Heard you got promoted," Billy says casually as he flips some burgers for the people seated in one of the back booths.

"Yeah, and?"

"About damn time."

I have to grin at the club's line cook as he stares at my ass. I think he actually means the compliment but ruins it with his gross ogling of my backside.

"How's Brianna doing?" I ask, reminding him about his girlfriend. A girl I've met on numerous occasions.

"Hanging in there." After plating the burgers, Billy pulls the bell for the servers to come to get the order. "She hates being pregnant. Let me know if I can get an extra shift next month, boss. I need the money. Diapers and shit."

"Let me talk to Ralph," I tell him, scribbling it down on the schedule notes. "I think he wanted some days off next month, so I'll put you in for his shifts."

"Thanks, doll. You're a real one."

Billy then moves towards me and lowers his voice, "Did you hear about Steve?"

I go still. "What about him?"

"I heard the big boss called him into his office, and then, like ten minutes later, he was dragged out into the alley. Ron was on a break, and he saw the whole thing. They beat the shit out of him."

"What?" I freeze. "Why?"

"Dunno." Billy shrugs his shoulders. "Maybe he didn't like that you were taking his job and said some slick shit."

I knew there was a possibility that Steve would lose his job but then again there was always the chance that he'd be moved to the earlier shift and I work the late one. I don't know. I guess that was wishful thinking. Maybe deep down I always knew that this was going to end badly once I accepted the job.

"I didn't steal the job from him, Billy," I say defensively. "They told me it was available and asked if I wanted it. I didn't ask questions."

"You don't have to explain yourself to me. You know the kind of place this is. Steve must've stepped on some toes. Don't have nothing to do with you." He adds a bag of fries to the deep fryer. "But I'll tell you one thing, doll, you'd better be careful. I know the money's good here, but it's not worth your neck."

Billy makes a valid point.

"Then why are you sticking around?" I ask, filling in the schedule on the whiteboard.

It's a rhetorical question, but Billy answers it anyway. "I want my kid to have a good life, you know. My old man was a right bastard. Treated me like shit. We never had any money, and he used to take out his anger on me with that fucking belt of his. I don't want that for my kid, and this is the best job someone like me is ever going to get."

I smile bitterly. "I guess both our fathers were pieces of shit then. It was hell for me, too. My dad threw me into the street when I was ten and made me beg on my knees to be let back inside. It was like a game for the asshole, and his wife was even worse. She liked making me eat scraps off the kitchen floor. Kinky bitch. I hope they both rot in hell."

When Billy doesn't respond to my overshare, I wonder if the little glimpse into my childhood was too explicit for him. "You okay?"

My question becomes stuck in my throat as I see Billy standing in front of me with wide eyes and a nervous face, looking behind me. As I follow his gaze in damn near slow motion, my blood turns cold when I see Mr. Middleton standing there watching us.

And he's furious.

Chapter 8

Background Check

HUNTER

It was my lack of supervision that allowed a man like Steve to mismanage my club. I got too relaxed, which is why I won't be making the same mistake with Megan.

The private booth on this floor has a clear view through the glass window, although it's tinted glass meant for people inside to view the entire club, but not the other way around. On the other side, it looks like a mirror.

I make a few calls as I often do in my office, but I spend much of the evening watching Megan show the new bartender the ropes. She looks nothing short of professional, but I keep recalling what she felt like pressed against me.

There had been this confused heat in her eyes as if she didn't quite know how to handle her own emotions. That served as my first indication that my mouthy little kitten isn't very experienced. She's too young for my taste. I prefer women my own age who know their way around a dick and how to please a man in bed without much instruction.

Megan would need to be taught.

I gently rub my bottom lip with my thumb as I gaze at her figure. It might not be a completely unenjoyable experience teaching her. I have to wonder what she'd be like with my cock inside of her.

Will her prickly attitude fade when I feed it to her?

Will she be demanding in bed or totally submissive?

My new manager is quite the little puzzle. It's a pity I can't check and see. All I'd need is one night, but romantic relationships of any kind with each other are off-limits to employees of the club. It's my own rule, which I have no intention of breaking. What example would I be setting if I did?

I see her leave her post to go back to the kitchen, and curiosity has me following her when she doesn't return. And that's when I overhear the words '...made me beg on my knees.'

The words before and after register for me as well, but imagining Megan, fiery, smart-mouthed Megan, having her self-respect stripped from her at any age makes me grind my jaw for some reason.

It's an unsettling image.

It's the cook who notices me first, and I can see the shock on his face as he recognizes me. At one time, I thought my identity was a complete secret from all that work here, but I guess I'm not surprised that he knows. He's been working here for a couple of years now. He'd be an idiot not to have figured it out by now.

However, when Megan looks over to see me standing there, I can see a wave of nausea covering her face.

"What? Why are you here? This isn't your office."

Like most of our interactions, the inappropriate words just burst out of her, but I don't respond. I have to get my temper under control. I cannot believe what I just heard, and it's in my DNA to want to do something about it, mainly because it's...her.

The cook slinks off, leaving her alone with me. He knows his place, which is probably why he's been working here so long.

"I was updating the shifts," she says, her voice cautious. "Billy needs some extra work."

When I say nothing, she looks alarmed. "If I did something wrong, just tell me. Don't just stand there glaring like you want to reprimand me."

It's the abrupt response that drags me back to reality. Megan has respect for process but not for authority, and that shit isn't going to fly.

I force my voice to be normal. "You keep forgetting that I'm your employer."

"No, I don't. How can I? You and your minions remind me everywhere I turn."

I ignore her rebuttal and focus my attention on her clothes. It's the easiest thing to focus on since I don't want to address the real issue. She's not dressed like she normally would be for work. She's a laid-back kind of girl who tends to wear jeans that fit her ass like a glove and slightly distressed tees. Tonight, though, her outfit is more like a sexy secretary. She's wearing a fitted collared top and pencil skirt and has on much more makeup than I've ever seen her wear. It doesn't seem like a look she would put together. It's as if someone dressed her up like their own personal Barbie doll.

"I told you to wear something appropriate for your new position."

She looks down at her blue button-up blouse and black pencil skirt.

"What's wrong with this? It's professional."

I walk over to her and reach out to touch the fabric of her blouse. "It's too tight, and it's tacky."

When her eyes widen, I wonder if she's going to have a snarky comeback, but she snaps her mouth shut and glares at me.

At least she's learning.

"Why didn't you buy something new and branded?"

An outfit more befitting of you.

"Because designer brands cost money," she says slowly as if talking to a five-year-old.

I should be offended.

"And I don't have money," she continues.

She's enunciating each word down to the syllable.

Brat.

The urge to pull her over my knee is overwhelming, and I have to curl my fist and remind myself that she's only a college kid who works for me. I need to be careful.

"Tomorrow afternoon you're going shopping. There's a look I want Blue Whiskey management to have, and you don't have it."

"Uh, there's a Blue Whiskey look?" Her eyes turn wide as saucers, and she sputters. "What does that even mean? Half the clientele here are drunks, and the other half are criminals. It's not like they're going to check the collar of my shirt for the brand name. All they want is the alcohol and the shitty bar food."

I'm still disturbed by her earlier childhood revelation, and when she defies me so openly, I step towards her, my voice prickly. "I think I've made myself clear. I'll see you tomorrow at the club in the afternoon."

The flash of her sulky expression tightens my jaw. I'm glad there are witnesses around to prevent me from grabbing her by a fistful of her hair and slamming my mouth down on hers. That slight pout that vanishes just as soon as it appears is etched into my brain for the rest of the night.

"I have classes until four," she counters. "And I can't afford branded clothes, sir."

The brat almost curtsies when she refers to me as sir. Interesting how my dick likes it. I've never met a woman who gets under my skin as quickly as she does.

"Did you just call me sir?"

"Would you prefer, mister?"

"After your classes then," I tell her sternly, refusing to look at her sassy, painted mouth, which is a vibrant red. "And you might want to control that cheekiness, or I might just forget that you work for me. If you want to act like a brat, I know how to deal with one."

Her lips part in shock with that same confused desire, but I leave, my blood humming in need. This time, I go straight to my office, my pants feeling uncomfortably tight, and I choose not to lay eyes on her for the rest of the night...for her sake and mine.

Lars shows up after Megan's shift is over. I'm not sure whether I'm annoyed or relieved that the file he hands me is light.

"There's not much on her," he shrugs. "She was fired from the last two places she worked because a man showed up. He kept harassing her there until the workplaces let her go, but they confirmed that prior to those incidents, she was a good worker."

"Who's the man?"

"Could be an ex-boyfriend or something, but the description I got was of a man much older than that."

"What did you find about her family background?"

"Once again, not that much. Her father had an affair,

and then her mother was out of the picture. Father married his mistress, and they had a child together. The kid lived with them."

"The kid?" I say with a warning, not because Lars is wrong, but because I don't want to hear it. I don't need to hear that I've had a hard-on for a *kid* all fucking night.

Lars corrects himself. "The young lady lived with them until she was eighteen but was in and out of the hospital until then. Her father has a ton of gambling debts, though, and her younger half-sister is eighteen now. It doesn't seem as if she's not in touch with any of them."

I open the file and skim the medical reports attached.

"Abuse," I murmur. "They abused her in that house."

I glance at Lars, who looks unaffected, but his eyes hold a wealth of anger. He doesn't talk about it much, but I know that Lars came from an abusive household back in his country. If I suspected this was her background, I would have made Parker look into Megan instead.

"She got a scholarship at State Arts College," I say loudly, my lips curving. "How interesting."

Lars knows why I'm amused, but he doesn't comment on it.

"You think that's why she came here?" he finally asks.

"I doubt it," I respond. "She doesn't know anything about me."

The file shows that Megan doesn't have much of a social life.

"There is one thing," Lars says hesitantly. "It seems that Miss Taylor came close twice to losing that scholarship. It might not be relevant, but the first time was the first week she started here. There was a shooting in the club, and she called the police."

I remember that incident. It was about six months ago,

and at the time, Megan's name had come up, but I'd been too busy doing damage control to worry about one lone bartender. I had been under the impression that Steve had fired the person who called the police.

So, it was this troublemaker.

Why am I not surprised?

"For somebody who keeps her head down, she sure gets dragged into a lot of things," I comment. "What about the second time?"

Lars hesitates to tell me the next thing. "I don't have any hard evidence of this, but I believe just before Miss Taylor joined us, there was an incident at her school."

"What kind of incident?"

"A video got leaked of her. Word reached the administration, and they wanted to expel her. But from what I've gathered, the boy involved in that video is a Senator's nephew. So, the video remained in private circles, and the university let it go."

"What kind of video?" I ask cooly.

Lars doesn't know or doesn't want to say, but I have an idea. It seems that Megan's trust issues are not baseless at all, and now I have a better understanding of why she ignored Isaiah's body in the alley. Our deep dive into her life hasn't revealed anything remotely suspicious, so I close the file.

"Well, it doesn't matter," I set the file down. "She seems smart."

"You're thinking of recruiting her permanently?" Lars questions, looking surprised. "Doesn't she seem a bit young?"

"I could have made the same argument for Parker years ago," I smile sharply. "I just want to test her first. She uses her wits, and I need somebody like that on the floor when I conduct the real business of this club."

When Lars leaves, I pick up a different file that has been on my desk for a while.

It's a 'request'.

I study the picture of a broad-shouldered, fully tattooed man with a mean look in his eyes. The White Snakes have been looking for him for a while. Figures they would come to me.

"You're in trouble, Marco." I tap the table lightly.

Picking up the phone, I dial a familiar number. The person on the other end who picks up after two rings answers.

" Exalt Logic. Who can I connect you to?"

"The blue room."

There's a pause on the other end and then the cheerfulness of the receptionist changes and her voice turns terse. "Understood."

I'm connected to another person who asks, "Who are you looking for?"

"Marco Delan from the White Snakes. I need all sightings, all online activities, and phone records."

"Understood. We'll have them delivered to you in two days, Mr. Middleton."

I cut the call and put Marco's file aside. Taking this job could go completely left for me, but this is what I do. If I don't handle it, then there's chaos on the streets.

I stare at the beady eyes in the photo before I stack it on top of my 'handle' pile.

"You'll get what's coming to you soon, Marco. Hope you're ready."

Chapter 9

A Fool In Love

HUNTER

It's noon when I wake up in my bed, alert. The room is dark without a shred of light, and I stay in bed, closing my eyes to experience the silence wrapping itself around me. Reluctantly, I decide it's time to get up, so I pull on some sweatpants and make my way to the kitchen to put on a pot of coffee.

My entire penthouse is decorated in shades of black, white, and grey, and often times it's hard to discern where the lines of one thing begins and another ends. Yet, as I cross the living room, I see a figure huddled on the long couch. I stare at it and then notice the tuft of brown hair peeking out from under the comforter.

Frowning, I make my way over to the couch and kick the dangling arm. "What the fuck are you doing here, Vaughn?"

Vaughn Gunn is one of my oldest friends and the most likely of my small circle of friends to break into my home...and live to tell the tale.

He stirs and mutters something unflattering under his breath.

"What the fuck was that?" I ask dangerously.

He opens one eye and glares at me. "Let me sleep. Why are you even awake at this time?"

"Go sleep at your own damn house." I yank the comforter off, and he falls onto my ten-thousand-dollar area rug.

"I'm not even bothering you, you asshole," he howls, making a half-hearted attempt to pull the blanket back on his body.

"Last time I checked, this is my house, and you were not invited to visit. Now get the fuck up. I'm not going to ask you again."

"Shelly kicked me out," he finally explains after his first cup of coffee at the island counter of my kitchen.

"How did she kick you out when it's your house?" I demand to know, annoyed that Vaughn has given this woman so much power over his life.

"She's mad because I refused to rescind the prenup," he says wearily. "Look, I talked to Christian, and he advised me against it. She had no problem signing it when we got together, but now suddenly, after three years of marriage, she suddenly has an issue with it?"

Christian Lee is a lawyer and another old friend of ours.

"The man has a point." I lift up my mug and take a sip of the hot liquid. "Why the hell are you arguing with her over your money? I don't understand why you're in this marriage if you're not happy."

"I was happy," Vaughn says tightly. "We were happy, but suddenly, there were all these issues. I just don't know where they came from. I feel like there's something I'm missing."

It's true that a man in love is the last person to know, perhaps because he's desperate not to acknowledge the truth.

"You should hire an investigator to look into this," I say, studying my friend.

The sharp look Vaughn shoots at me makes me shrug.

"Security is what I do."

"Security work and investigative work are two very different things."

"I know what you're trying to say, but that's not it. I would never invade Shelly's privacy."

"You know she's hired one to look into you, don't you?" I ask coolly.

Vaughn just falls silent.

I sip my coffee again. "You can either close your eyes, or you can do something about it. We are all here to help you, but if you want to act like a fool over her, that's up to you."

"I married this woman because I loved her," Vaughn hisses, setting his mug down firmly on the granite. "I'm nobody's fool."

"No," I correct him in an unbothered voice. "You married her because she told you she was pregnant, and then she very conveniently lost the baby two months after the wedding."

"I'll pretend you aren't insinuating what I think you are," my friend says as he gives me a lethal look, the vein in his forehead twitching. "You wouldn't understand what it's like to love somebody, Hunter, and I can't imagine you ever will. You're a fucking block of ice. No offense."

"None taken." I casually sip my brew, my eyes on him.

"When I met Shelly, I was done. She was it for me. Even before she got knocked up, I always knew that she was the endgame. Nothing matters aside from her."

I shrug because Vaughn is a hopeless romantic. Me? Not so much.

"Then rescind the prenup," I tell him.

When he doesn't say anything in response, I give him a steady look. "Your silence is speaking volumes, old friend. You know it, and I know it. She's after your money. I don't know what changed these past few years, but now it's about the money, and I would bet that the moment you rescind it, she will ask for a divorce."

"Does your honesty always have to be so brutal?" Vaughn asks with a miserable look on his face.

"You have to figure this out," I tell him. "Clinging on to someone who doesn't want you is disgraceful."

"You can be a shitty friend at times," Vaughn growls at me.

"Yeah, well, you knew what you signed up for when you decided to crash at my place." I glance at the clock on the microwave. "I have to go."

"Where're you going?" Vaughn stares at me. "My life is fucking falling apart, and you're just leaving?"

"Take-out menus are in the left-hand drawer, and there's ice cream in the freezer," I say over my shoulder. "Come to the club later and get drunk."

That I can do for him.

"I don't want to get drunk!" Vaughn complains. "I want to talk about this. I need your advice."

"Next, you'll want to braid each other's hair and watch the latest season of Real Housewives," I retort as I walk towards the bedroom to get changed. "Not happening."

"That's a legendary franchise!" Vaughn scoffs indignantly, but I've already closed the door.

As I take a shower, I wonder what the hell I'm doing. I've got the Marco thing to handle, the Isaiah issue to address, not to mention a million other things to do. Taking out my new manager to shop for clothes is ridiculous, almost as absurd as Vaughn not rescinding that prenup of his. I should've just given her a credit card and told her to buy something appropriate for herself.

Why am I personally overseeing her shopping? What is it about Megan Taylor that makes me do things that are completely outside of my norm? And why are random images of her trying on figure-flattering clothes flashing in my head and making my dick swell?

I've got to stop this. Dwelling too much on why I have these thoughts is only encouraging me to have more. As I button up a new light blue Armani shirt, I look at my reflection in the mirror.

This life, this luxury, came at a heavy price. I lost everything to be pushed to the edge of stealing a container that was filled with expensive medical equipment. I made my first paycheck with that.

That one dark evening when I made a calculated decision, desperate for a change, and for revenge, it altered my life. All those people in the neighborhood who used to look down on that scraggly boy with arms so thin that they looked like they could break at a touch, now fear me.

I put on a contrasting silk tie, my eyes seeing the image of that defiant boy in front of me. I bled, I cheated, I stole. I did everything to drag myself out of that life of despair and to get revenge on the men who stripped me of my only happiness. And now, I'm sitting on the throne, looking down at all those miserable assholes who used to beat me whenever they saw me.

I still have the scars on my back. Literal scars. I've always had the option of getting them surgically removed, but I choose not to. They're a reminder of my roots in case I ever get too comfortable. This empire was built on the blood of the people who took my family from me, and I don't ever want to forget that.

Shrugging on my suit jacket, I take one last final look at myself in the mirror before leaving.

Remember who you are, Middleton.

No distractions allowed.

Or this could all go away like poof.

Chapter 10

You Can't Be Here

HUNTER

Megan doesn't show up for our planned shopping excursion, making me completely toss out the whole 'no distraction' talk I just had with myself. I'm annoyed. I'm not used to people, especially my employees, not listening to me.

It's...odd.

Maybe she thinks I'll give up because I view this shopping trip as something inconsequential but clearly Megan doesn't know me. When I decide on something, it's going to happen one way or the other, even if it's something I have no fucking business doing.

"Go to State Arts College," I tell Parker. "It seems we'll have to pick up Miss Taylor ourselves."

The freeway is always busy but Parker has a knack of finding a path through even the worst of traffic jams. Defensive driving is one of his superpowers. By the time we reach the university, the students are piling out.

"Park across the road," I instruct, watching the gate.

I can see a few envious glances towards the sleek BMW we're in, but I don't focus on the students. My eyes narrow in on one single figure with a head full of lush curls who is approaching the gate.

My head tilts when I notice the limp. Megan isn't walking *but dragging a leg behind her.*

"What's wrong with her?" Parker asks, also seeing what I'm seeing. "You want me to check?"

I don't answer him as I exit the car, striding towards her as if I'm on autopilot, my trench coat flapping behind me as I walk in brisk movements.

The crowds of students have already departed, and there are only a few stragglers. Megan hasn't noticed me, but as I get closer to her, I see that her right cheekbone looks bruised, and her hair is not purposely styled wildly but is a little disheveled.

"Did you lose a fight or something?" I ask, as she nearly jumps once she notices me.

"W-What?" She stares at me uncomfortably. "What are you doing here? You can't be here."

"Why can't I?"

"Because this is where I go to school."

I ignore her words as I use my hand to tilt her chin up, studying her face. Megan's got a delicate facial structure with expressive eyes and high cheekbones, one of which contains a purplish-looking bruise.

"Did you at least win?" I ask her slowly, not totally understanding my irritation at the sight of the mark.

She looks at me with an obstinate look in those luminous eyes of hers. "This is nothing."

I study her.

Her reaction is so familiar it's almost startling. It's what

I used to say to people after I got my ass handed to me when I was a kid.

"So, you didn't just get into an altercation?"

"No." Her cheeks betray her and are colored in embarrassment. "Now, will you please let me go? You and your friends really have to stop showing up here. It's borderline stalkerish."

Even with all her sass, the size of Megan's entire face is comparable to the span of my hand and it reminds me just how young and petite she is. It would be so easy to break her.

"So, who was it?" I ask, deciding not to let this go. Normally, I wouldn't concern myself with people's personal issues. Hell, I basically just told one of my best friends to fuck off this morning, but there's something about this fiery art student that I just can't ignore.

She struggles with her backpack, and I can see that it's difficult for her to walk and carry it at the same time. I don't hesitate to wrench it from her and throw it in Parker's direction, who's followed me out of the car.

"Hey!" Megan protests in alarm. "That's my bag."

"Put it in the car," I order Parker, and when he walks away, I turn my attention to Megan. "You didn't answer my question."

"What question?" She asks in a distracted manner, her eyes on her bag. Her tone is almost mournful as she mumbles, "My sandwich."

"What?"

She glares at me. "My sandwich is in the bag. I was going to have that for lunch."

She's upset over a sandwich?

Now that I look at her, I see that she has curves in all

the right places except on her face. Her cheeks look a bit hollowed.

Does this girl eat?

"Who hit you?" I force her to pay attention. "I won't ask a fourth time."

"Oh, good," she says sarcastically. "Because it's annoying when you repeat yourself."

"I'll go find out myself."

Megan instantly grabs my forearm and it doesn't escape me that this is the first time she's initiated any physical contact with me.

I like it.

"Look, it's just a small matter between friends. Things like this happen all the time. I'll cover it with makeup so nobody will see it at work. I promise not to ruin the Blue Whiskey brand, okay?"

It makes sense that she thinks I'm annoyed because I don't want her bruise on display at the club, but the sight of it bothers me...period.

I feel someone watching me, and when I look up behind Megan, I see a small group of students watching me from the steps of a building with a wide staircase anchored by two large stone pillars. They're studying me with curiosity, but my eyes focus on two in particular. I can sense their hostility from all the way across from here. I bet they have something to do with why my new manager suddenly has a limp and a bruise.

One of them is a brunette wearing tiny scraps of clothing and too much makeup. One could almost call her attractive, but I've seen her type so many times that she does nothing for me. For some reason though, she looks irritated as her eyes move between me and Megan.

The guy next to her has his arm around her waist, but

he's scowling. I don't know what prompts me but I lower my head until my lips are right next to Megan's ear and I murmur softly, "You're one of my people which means you're under my protection. If you were smart, you'd give me names, and I'll take care of them for you."

Even as I say that, my eyes are on the boy radiating anger across the yard. I can see his eyes flash when I lean into Megan's personal space. I don't hear what Megan is saying in response because I meet the boy's baby-blue eyes, and I smile mockingly.

He flushes in fury.

Satisfied that I've annoyed him, I turn and place my hand on the small of Megan's back, "Let's continue this discussion in the car."

"Did you hear what I just said?" she asks, her tone a little demanding. It amuses me how she keeps forgetting that I'm *her* boss.

"I wasn't listening," I say, unconcerned.

"I have to go home first." She tries to wiggle away from me, and I sigh.

"Either you get into the car, or I carry you into the car. Which option do you prefer?"

I find myself hoping that she'll test me. I wouldn't mind lifting her heart-shaped ass over my shoulder in front of every nosy kid on this campus, but fortunately for her, she's not that brave. Clearly not wanting to make a scene, she obediently gets in the car. I've got to admit I'm a little disappointed. I would have rather had the scene.

As I slide in after her, I meet Parker's gaze, jerking my head towards the group of college students still watching us. I watch him lift his cell phone and snap a discreet picture of them.

I didn't lie when I said that Megan is one of my people.

If I can't even keep an employee like her safe, why would anyone trust me to take care of the big jobs?

"Seriously, why are you here?" Megan looks uneasy, and I wonder if she's going to attempt to jump out of the driving vehicle. I wouldn't put anything past this woman at this point.

"You didn't show up today like we discussed." I look out the window at the passing scenery.

"Show up for what?"

Did she seriously forget about shopping with me? Most women would jump at the chance.

"Your shopping trip?"

"There is nothing wrong with the way that I dress. My clothes are clean and totally appropriate for the bar, *sir*." She sounds completely offended, and I press my lips together to prevent myself from smiling. A man could get used to being called sir from a mouth like hers.

"Regardless of what you may think about my club, it's a fine establishment with a certain reputation," I say coolly. "Your clothes need to reflect that. Be grateful that I'm not making you pay for them out of your own salary."

"I remember when I was just a bartender and didn't even know what you looked liked. Remember those good ole' days?" she sneers.

As she glowers at me, I give her a careful look. "Keep up that attitude, and I might consider docking your pay for the outfit you are definitely buying. Rent is due soon, isn't it?"

She immediately shuts up.

Moments later, Megan frowns when we drive up to a cluster of tall white buildings. "This isn't a shopping center."

"That's very insightful," I say plainly. "This is the hospital."

"I'm fine. I don't need to get checked. It's just a scratch, seriously."

I turn my head towards her and am about to protest until the look on her face stops me in my tracks. She looks utterly terrified.

"I'm not going in there," she says firmly.

"You have to get your leg looked at as well as that bruise on your face," I tell her, my tone even.

"No medical insurance."

"The club will cover it."

But Megan shakes her head in quick, desperate movements, pressing herself against the door. Her voice is shaking, and her normally defiant eyes are wide and terrified. When I look into them, I don't see any trace of my fiery manager.

"Boss," Parker sounds tense. "Lars can patch her up at the club."

When I meet Parker's gaze, I see that he has a concerned expression on his face. Whatever spell Miss Taylor seems to be slowly casting on me may be rubbing off on him, too.

"Lars?"

"Yeah."

In another life, Lars used to work as a medic, so I know he's reliable. He's seen to my injuries plenty of times, but I'm a little displeased that Parker thought of the idea and I didn't.

As I glance over at Megan, I'm reminded of the information that Lars shared with me not that long ago. Megan probably spent more time in hospitals as a child than any kid ever should. The petrified look on her face makes my decision pretty simple although I imagine Lars is not going to like it. He's a pretty inflexible son of a bitch.

"Fine, let's go to the club," I agree to Parker's suggestion. "But call Lars and give him a heads up."

"Sure thing, boss."

However, the whole drive back, Megan is quiet and almost a shadow of herself; her hands don't stop shaking.

The way she's curled into a corner of the car in an attempt to make herself as small as possible makes me wonder about what *exactly* happened to her.

And who the hell do I have to destroy to make sure that they pay for it?

Chapter 11

It's In My DNA

MEGAN

I feel sick to my stomach.

When the car stops at The Blue Whiskey, I rush inside to the bathroom and vomit, but I haven't had anything to eat since morning, so nothing comes out but yellowish bile. I can't get the memories that are playing over and over again in my head to subside.

The thin needle.

The probing hands.

The screams.

I sink to the marbled stone of the bathroom; my hands pressed against my ears as I try to drown out the screaming of the terrified little girl. There's a knock at the door and I just hunch further into myself as I hear the sound of the door opening. I want to say something, but no words come out, and then somebody is covering me with a jacket. I look up, expecting to see Mr. Middleton again, but it's Lars.

"What are you doing?"

He stares blankly at me for a moment, not saying

anything, and then he crouches down next to me. The warmth of his jacket is giving me a barrier to hold on to.

"Breathe," he instructs, his voice unusually kind. "Take long breaths."

I stare at him and follow his instructions. The breathing helps calm me down, and he tightens the jacket around me. "You're fine. You're safe."

Tears rush to my eyes at the words, and I press my lips together, bobbing my head up and down in understanding.

"Don't tell him."

"I won't," he says steadily. "Can you stand up?"

He helps me up when I nod. Wetting a hand towel, he wipes my face as I stand there dully. A man who I'm pretty sure looks upon me as a nuisance most of the time is taking care of me. I've never had a male figure in my life who's looked after me.

My panic is subsiding as he begins to talk to me, his voice quiet, "I had a daughter once. She would be around your age if she had lived. She'd probably be just as fiery as you, too."

It takes a few seconds for his words to register and for me to respond. "I'm sorry. What happened to her?"

"She died a few years ago." His hand pauses, and then he says, "She used to have panic attacks like the one you just did—bad ones. I'd get her ice cream when she had one, and then I would tuck her into the couch and put on her favorite movie, and she'd watch it until she fell asleep. She loved Jaws."

Lars puts down the towel, and I follow his movement, feeling hollow but better now.

"Why are you telling me this?"

He studies me. "I don't know. You just reminded me of her for a minute."

My heart tightens in my chest at this surprising glimpse of the gruff bodyguard, but it's only for a moment. His posture stiffens, and once again, his usual unpleasant demeanor returns.

"Why are you letting someone beat up on you?"

"I'm not beat up."

"Come, I'll fix you up in Mr. Middleton's office. He's waiting."

"It's just a scratch," I protest as he pulls out a small first aid kit.

"Actually, it's a bruise with some deep lacerations that you're going to have to keep clean, or they'll get infected. And you need to ice that ankle too. So it's either me or the emergency room. Your choice."

I huff in exasperation. Lars knows, by the way he just found me ten minutes ago, that I'm not stepping foot into a hospital. So I guess I have no real choice if I want to keep my job.

"Fine, let's go."

"After you."

When I enter Mr. Middleton's office, I notice that he looks a bit agitated. Maybe I'm just projecting my own unease.

"Are you okay, Miss Taylor?" He asks with a tight face.

He swiftly approaches and brushes the calloused pad of his thumb underneath my fresh bruise. My body shudders in surprise, and I stumble over my response.

"Yes, sorry, I didn't mean to-"

"It's fine," he says abruptly. He backs away from me and takes a seat at his desk. I notice how he flexes the same hand he used to touch me as if touching me was painful. Oddly enough, I find myself yearning for him to touch me again.

"I see Lars found you," he says with little effect. "Do

you have a problem with him patching you up? He has experience at that sort of thing."

It throws me off when I realize that he's being considerate, and I shake my head mutely. Two nice gestures from two very dangerous men in one day? That's a little hard for me to process.

Mr. Middleton watches intently from his desk as Lars cleans my bruise and applies a liquid bandage to seal the cuts. When he checks my ankle by slowly rotating it, I wince.

"Ouch."

I had known that my words would come and bite me in the ass, but I hadn't expected that Ashley would corner me in the bathroom after classes. It wasn't like I'd never been bullied in school when I was young, but I was under the impression that all of that nonsense stopped when you went to college. I mean, aren't we all grown?

So, when Ashley grabbed me by my hair and dunked my face into the toilet bowl, I was so shocked by it that I didn't immediately fight back. When I finally started to struggle against her, she smashed the side of my face into the marble edge of the toilet bowl.

"Stop chasing Ricky. He doesn't want you!"

Her words didn't make any sense to me. She sounded angry and threatened as if I held some power over Ricky. I don't. All I am is some girl he taped, sucking his dick and nothing more. Doesn't she see that?

At the time, though, I didn't know how far she planned on taking her assault on me, and I definitely didn't have any plans to sit around and find out. I kicked one of the girls holding me in the crotch and ran outside, twisting my ankle in the process. Fortunately for me, classes had just ended, and I managed to hide myself in the crowd of students who were leaving.

My plan had been to go home, take a shower, and then figure out what to do about my face. I never expected to run into my terrifying boss right at the entrance of the college although I don't really know why I'm surprised. Mr. Middleton does what he wants.

"So let me get this straight, Miss Taylor, you were willing to go to blows for that server who was flashing her tits at my table, but you let some college kid do this to you?"

"I don't owe you any explanations."

"Next time someone attacks you, either you fight back, or you tell someone who can fight for you," he drawls, his eyes glinting with a tight emotion.

I don't answer him. He would never understand.

Ashley and Ricky both come from prestigious, wealthy backgrounds. No matter how much I want to, physically touching her would mean that she can exert her family's influence and get my scholarship taken away from me.

Back when college had been a new start for me, a chance to fall in love and pursue my passion for art, I hadn't realized the den of snakes I was walking into. Ricky was the kind of guy who typically never gave a girl like me a second look, so when he showed an interest in me, I was flattered. He was very charismatic, gorgeous, and smart, and I quickly fell hard for him.

When he pleaded with me in that charming way of his to just get him off, I hadn't realized that he and Ashley were in their own very complicated and twisted relationship. I was simply a pawn, and they were laughing behind my clueless back. I just have to get through this next year or so and I'll be done with them both.

"You ready?"

Mr. Middleton has no intentions of putting off the shopping trip because after Lars wraps my ankle in an Ace Bandage, I'm packed into a dark SUV driven by Parker, and we drive towards the poshest part of Los Angeles.

When we stop in front of a chic-looking store with a gold and white design, the streets are crowded with mainly fashionably dressed women carrying designer purses. I feel so out of place in my faded jeans and beige blouse that it's almost laughable.

Mr. Middleton pauses at the entrance. "I have an appointment with Clark."

"Who's Clark?" I whisper to Parker, who grins.

"A stylist."

"What?" I ask, astounded, but we're already being ushered in.

"Mr. Middleton," I say in urgent hushed tones. "You can't hire a stylist to dress me. I'm just a manager. Steve wore the same thing every day."

Black slacks. Black button down.

"Exactly," he responds easily. "He didn't fit the part."

"This is feeling very Pretty Woman-ish," I whisper disapprovingly to Parker, remembering a previous exchange I had with Naomi.

"Trust me, it ain't," he replies. "The boss is no Richard Gere."

Clark is an exuberant man with silver hair, deeply tanned skin, and purple eyes. It's the eyes which throw me off first until I realize that he's wearing tinted contact lenses.

"Mr. Middleton!" He throws open his arms in welcome, and I freeze, wondering if he's planning to hug my stone-cold boss. I can't imagine anyone hugging Hunter Middleton.

But Clark stops short a few feet away, "So who have you brought for me to transform?"

When Mr. Middleton looks over at me, I wonder if passing out would let me out of this whole thing. I've never really enjoyed shopping, probably because I've never had any money. But it's a dizzying sensation to have to model outfit to outfit, from blouses to skirts to pants. I draw the line at underwear, though.

"Absolutely not," I hiss under my breath. "Nobody's looking at what I'm wearing underneath my clothes."

Mr. Middleton gives me a long, contemplative look, and I suddenly feel the urge to cover up. It's like he's undressing me with his eyes...one garment at a time.

"Whatever you want, Miss Taylor."

When we leave the store, I did not realize just how much he purchased. There are so many bags in Parker's hands that I feel faint.

"That's too many," I say out loud. "Did you buy everything I tried on?"

"No."

I don't believe him, but my feet are aching, and I'm starving. All I care about at this point is eating.

"Are we at least finished?"

My stomach chooses that exact moment to growl loudly, and without missing a beat, Mr. Middleton says to Parker, "Go to El Palo."

El Palo is one of those restaurants that you read about A-list actors eating at in a celebrity blog. It's a restaurant that's impossible for regular folks to get into, especially without a reservation. I think Jennifer Lopez got engaged to one of her husbands there.

"Wait, what?"

My head is spinning at all these new developments and

I'm still a bit rattled by what happened at school today. I really just want to go back home at this point and crawl into bed.

When we reach the restaurant, I stare at the decorative exterior before glancing at my boss. "My entire week's paycheck will not even cover a meal in there. I'm not comfortable eating here."

Mr. Middleton ignores me and simply gets out the truck and waits for me to exit the vehicle. It's probably the first time today that I've actually really looked at him. It's hot as hades today but he's dressed in a navy suit with a light blue collared shirt that fits like it was made for him. I don't usually go for guys that are corporate looking, but leave it to Mr. Middleton to make a suit look badass. He looks incredible.

"Can't I just get a hot dog?"

"No one should just eat a hot dog, and if we all did things we were comfortable doing, there'd be no personal growth."

"I just want something fast," I counter.

"Miss Taylor."

There's a warning in his voice, and I have no choice but to slide out of my seat. It's clear that I'm fighting a losing battle. The maitre'd who sees us immediately jumps to attention.

"Welcome back to El Palo, Mr. Middleton. We have your usual table ready."

I expect him to look at my clothes with at least some level of disdain but he doesn't so much as flinch, yet when we follow him past the other tables, the other well-dressed diners do raise their brows at me.

I'm not usually that easily embarrassed but I suddenly feel out of place. We are taken to a large corner booth which could probably fit a party of six easily but there is only a place setting for two. My ears feel hot as I slide in and he follows right behind me. Once we're seated, Lars and Parker go sit at the bar where they can keep an eye on us.

"Why are we here?" I ask him in a low voice.

He slides closer to me as if he can't hear me. "Come again?"

"I said, why did you pick this restaurant?"

He leans in, his lips dangerously close to my earlobe. "You were hungry."

My core becomes engorged with need, and the crotch of my jeans suddenly feels tight between my legs.

"I mean...aren't you hungry?" He suggestively licks the corner of his mouth.

On so many levels, the answer to that question is a resounding yes.

"I would've been fine with a hotdog or a pizza," I say miserably, feeling uncomfortable in my own skin.

"Have you ever eaten here before, Miss Taylor?" He questions. "Do you not like this place?"

Still sitting dangerously close to me, he hands me one of the thick menus already on the table.

"It seems really expensive," I mutter, squirming in my seat, unable to meet his gaze. The way he looks at me, especially when he's this physically close, it's difficult for me to hold it.

I'm not usually that type of girl, but with Mr. Middleton, I am. With each passing day, he intimidates me in a way that I don't recognize about myself.

"Well, it's on me," He tells me when the server actually hands us two additional menus. One is solely for wine and the other lists the specials of the day.

"Do you do this for all your managers?" I stare at the

main menu and almost choke on my own saliva at the prices.

When he doesn't answer, I turn my head only to find him still watching me. I have a feeling if I probe him more, I just might poke this temperamental bear, so I stick my head back in the menu and try to find the least expensive dish.

"Have you decided?" He asks after a few long seconds and I set down the menu.

"I'll have this," I point to the most complicated salad I've ever seen. There are a thousand ingredients, and it costs a ridiculous forty-five dollars, but it's the cheapest thing I can find.

He stares at me. "That's what you want?"

"Why?" I ask cautiously. "What's wrong with it?"

He sets down his menu to study me. "Miss Taylor, I hope you're not pinching pennies for my sake."

I press my lips together and look away. However, I can see from the corner of my eyes that he's struggling not to laugh at me.

"I love salad," I say, sinking deeper into the plush leather of the booth.

"Mr. Middleton?" A surprised voice comes from the side, and I thank the heavens for the interruption.

The voice belongs to a man in a pleated suit and golden-wired glasses. He has a stringy figure with a bald head and a pleasant smile.

"Dixon." Mr. Middleton nods at him, accepting the handshake. "I see you have time to roam around but not to return my call."

The words are almost gentle, but the threat behind them makes me shiver. Mr. Middleton's dark eyes deepen, and I see Dixon, the man, offer a nervous smile.

"I was busy with some personal matters."

Mr. Middleton smiles at him. "Well, it's fortunate that I saw you here then, wasn't it? I was considering paying you a personal visit."

I've never seen a man lose color so fast.

"I assure you that won't be necessary," the man stammers. "If you want, we can talk right now."

"I have a guest with me right now. As a matter of fact, it's a little rude that you didn't acknowledge her sitting here."

I give the terrified looking man an awkward smile, and he looks at me as if just noticing my existence.

"Good evening, Miss," the man says as he offers his hand to me across the table.

"Pull your hand back," Mr. Middleton orders in a deep baritone voice. I'm not sure which of us he's addressing, but I slowly put my hand back beside me and offer Dixon an awkward verbal greeting instead.

"Nice to meet you."

"I expect to see you tonight," Mr. Middleton tells Dixon. "Otherwise, I'll rearrange my schedule."

I wonder if this poor man is going to faint.

"I'll be there," he barely gets the words out.

I watch him leave, wondering if I'll see this Dixon person at the club later, and when I turn my attention back to Mr. Middleton, he's looking through the menu, totally unfazed.

"Why was he so scared of you?" I blurt out without thinking. "Are you going to hurt him?"

When he sets down the menu and looks at me, my heart nearly stops, and I quickly say, "I'm sorry. I didn't know my mouth was moving. It does that sometimes."

"One day, that pretty little mouth of yours is going to get you into a lot of trouble."

I gaze towards the door where Dixon exited and consider everything I know about The Blue Whiskey and just how little I know about Mr. Middleton.

At first, he was just a legendary fixture. A man who owns the place where I work but a man I never saw. I know that he has a lot of connections in Los Angeles, enough that he can make any awful thing that happens in the club disappear– even bodies. I also know that he's a well-known figure in the business community and filthy rich.

And then there's the other side of him.

The man with icy cold eyes at Table 21. A man who makes other grown men shiver in fear. Hell, I just witnessed it. The smart thing for me to do would be to quit this job. I've been the new manager for literally twenty-four hours, and already, I've seen this man more than I ever have in my six months of working there. What does he want from me? What does he expect?

I don't know, and I'm not sure I want to find out.

But, of course, things never go the way I plan.

It must be in my DNA.

Chapter 12

Is This A Seduction?

MEGAN

There's another new bartender when I arrive at work. I suppose they brought him in to replace one of the part-timers who left to move to New York. I had no idea he was coming, but I'm learning that if I'm going to survive in this new position, I will have to learn how to go with the flow.

"Gage Clayton." He shakes my hand, a quiet smile on his lips. "I transferred from the Chicago location."

The shift hasn't started yet, so I ask a question that I feel I should have already known the answer to.

"There are other locations?"

"It's not quite up and running yet."

"So Mr. Middleton brought you here instead? I already have a new bartender."

"And now you have another."

Gage is an attractive man with sandy blonde hair and gentle brown eyes. He reminds me of a younger Brad Pitt, and I know for a fact that the servers are going to be swooning over him.

"You look a little put off," he tells me as I watch him rearrange bottles behind the bar as if he's had the job for years.

"Sorry," I shake my head. "Mr. Middleton didn't tell me anything about you, and I just hired a bartender the other day. I'm going to have to ask him what's going on. I hope you don't mind."

"Sure, go ahead," Gage beams at me. He's so friendly that it's impossible to dislike him... or trust him. Ugh, I've become so jaded.

As I make my way to Mr. Middleton's office, I struggle with the buttons of my new silk blouse. For a two-hundred-dollar shirt, I don't know why they keep slipping open. I hiss in frustration when they don't shut, and I layer the cloth over them before knocking on the door.

"Come in."

When I enter, my boss is leaning against the edge of the desk, his tie lying on the couch, his sleeves rolled up to expose strongly muscled forearms with one definitive tattoo on the left one. It reads: PRESSURE.

My mouth goes dry at the sight.

After silently gawking for God knows how long, he finally murmurs, "Miss Taylor, you should stop looking at me like that."

There's something dark in his voice, almost hungry, and I snap back to reality.

"What? Oh, I wasn't looking at anything. I just came here to ask you something."

"It's funny how just a few weeks ago, you didn't even know I was in this office, and now you're just dropping by whenever you please, huh?"

He's holding a file in his hand, and I see his eyes raking over me from top to bottom. When he sets down the file and moves from around the desk, I freeze. How am I supposed to say anything in response when he's stalking toward me like this? His movements are controlled and deliberate, like the stealth of a great predator.

The whole atmosphere suddenly shifts, and my heart is pounding as he approaches me. *Get a grip*, a small voice screams at me from inside my head, but I can't move.

He's right in front of me now, and when his large, firm hand slides around my waist, near the top of where my brand-new pencil skirt begins, my eyes squeeze shut.

Then I hear something rip, and my eyes shoot open.

There is dark amusement in those grey eyes of his as he holds up a tag. "You forgot to take this off."

My lips part in shock, but he doesn't move back, standing so close to me that I can smell his expensive cologne. I don't know what to do. I want to move back, but my body won't let me. It's as if I'm stuck in a frozen solid state.

I've never felt this way around anyone, not even Ricky, but this older man who exudes danger and wealth and everything forbidden makes me want to do things that no nice girl should ever think of. Because if he told me to drop to my knees this very instant, I definitely would, and I wouldn't give a shit if he was recording it.

"I told you not to look at me like that," he practically growls.

"Like what?" I ask, hoarsely, unable to look away from his piercing gaze.

The look in his eyes holds dark promises that make me suddenly damp between my legs.

His hand comes up, and he caresses my cheek with one

finger before trailing it down all the way to my chin and tilting my head up, firmly, "Like you want me to splay you over my desk and fuck you until you scream."

The soft, needy whimper that escapes my lips is unintentional and Mr. Middleton's eyes become a furnace. My whole body is burning with need and confusion and desire are running rampant within me. I need to get a hold of myself, but I can't seem to think straight.

"I have rules though, Miss Taylor," he breathes, and yet his eyes are drawn to my mouth. "I won't break them for you."

His words are firm, but his body language is confusing me. He continues to hold me in place with his piercing gaze, almost as if he's daring me to be the one to break his rules first.

So let me go, I scream internally.

Turn your back, I say to myself.

Walk away.

But it's as if he is taking great delight in my torture. He moves closer until my body is pressed against his. Along with a delicious amount of desire moving through my body, there are also red, loud alarm bells ringing in my head.

DANGER!

As I gain my resolve and try to move away, the front of my shirt pulls open, and half of my chest is on display for Mr. Middleton to see. His eyes dart toward my breasts before he drawls, "Now, this wouldn't be an attempt to seduce me, would it?"

His taunting words are like a bucket of cold water thrown on me, and reality slaps me in the face. What the hell am I doing?

I step back, my hand instinctively seizing the parted top and pulling it together.

"I came to ask you...I wasn't trying to..."

I feel like a fool when I can't get the words out. My head is swimming in a mixture of emotions, and none of them are good. I'm angry, horny, and embarrassed. What the fuck is wrong with me?

"Forget it," I hiss. "I just came to. Never mind, it doesn't matter."

My body is trembling as I rush towards the door. This whole day has been one hellish blunder after another: my day at school, the shopping excursion, and the overpriced dinner. All of this special treatment was probably all a game to him. An opportunity to bag the mouthy, inexperienced college girl. A ruse, like Ricky, and like every other fucking thing in my life. And I almost fell for it... again.

I've barely reached the door when a hand on my shoulder whirls me around and slams me against the wooden structure, making me gasp.

"Where the fuck do you think you're going?" he growls.

His expression is tight, his eyes narrowed, and then he snakes his hand behind my head, grabs a fistful of hair, and yanks it back before he slams his mouth down on mine.

There is nothing sweet or tender about the way he kisses me. It's hot and dark and hungry. It's delivered with total dominance and wanton desire, and my body melts like butter as he forces his tongue into my mouth. It's almost as if he's punishing me...but in the best way possible.

A guttural moan escapes my lips as he presses his hard body against mine, and I can barely register the painful throb in my nipples as they harden into tight points. He's not gentle by any means, taking and taking my mouth until my head is dizzy and filled with just him.

He licks the inside of my mouth in a filthy manner and I want to open my legs and beg him to stuff his dick inside me because I desperately need some relief. I want to be used by him. I feel like I've been aching for him ever since we locked eyes that night at Table 21.

My scattered thoughts make no sense as they're filled with illicit desires and fantasies, all meshing into one. His other hand is sliding across my stomach, mapping out my waist, trailing heat on the covered skin.

Fuck me hard is what I really want to scream, but I only manage to utter his name in the breathiest of voices. "Mr. Middleton." I'm hoping he understands what I'm asking. What I need.

It's the hard knock on the door that has him going still and when he pulls away, his hand releasing my hair, I feel limp. I'm only standing with his support right now. My legs are like noodles, and my brain is complete mush.

"Hunter?"

Mr. Middleton hisses and then growls, "I'm busy!"

"You called me, asshole!"

The angry response of someone who has the audacity to insult my boss has me slipping back into my senses. I catch a glimpse of myself in the mirror affixed to a wall on the opposite side of the room and can't believe what I see. I look like someone who almost got her common sense completely fucked out of her.

My curls are all over the place.

My cheeks are flushed.

My chest is bare.

My dignity lost.

"Oh, God," I whisper, horrified at my behavior. "What did I do?"

"Do you have someone in there with you?" The same man's suspicious voice asks.

"Go away, Vaughn. I'm not going to tell you again!" Mr. Middleton roars, and I still myself.

I hear something unfavorable mumbled on the other side of the door before the footsteps fade away.

When it's just the two of us again, he takes a step toward me, and I immediately lift a hand to stop him in his tracks.

"No, that can never happen again."

He arches a brow, "I don't think you're-"

"I'm not going to be your little plaything," I say, suddenly furious with myself for my stupidity. "I should have known that you aren't different from any other guy out here. All these nice things that you were doing weren't because you suddenly wanted to take care of your employee. You just wanted to get in my pants."

Mr. Middleton's face grows cold.

"I assure you that if I want to fuck a woman, I won't go in such a roundabout way to do it. There's never been a lack of women to warm my bed."

The crushing sense of humiliation is familiar to me, and my hands clench into fists.

"Then go find one of them. I'm not going to be somebody's source of amusement anymore. I have more self-respect than that." His eyes turn into slits, and his jaw ticks, but I don't care if he's angry. "I'm not going to be some toy for you to play around with until you get bored, sir."

"You're making it sound as if I was the only participant in this," he says in a tone laced with venom. "You couldn't keep your hands off me. You kissed me back."

"That's what you're going to make me feel bad about?" My laugh is filled with bitterness. "That I kissed you back? You're an attractive older man. Why not?"

"Older?" he scoffs, shaking his head.

"I'm not blind, and I'm not delusional. I'm attracted to you, but this is where it stops. You had your fun, but you also supposedly have your rules. If this is why you promoted me to a manager, then I quit. I'll work somewhere else. I need this job but don't need it that badly."

"You're so extreme." His lips press together into a thin line. "Stop overreacting. It was just a kiss. It doesn't mean anything. You're a young, impressionable girl, and I don't have a habit of bringing inexperienced women to my bed. Trust me, nothing was going to happen beyond that kiss. You think too highly of yourself, Miss Taylor; you're not that special."

My nails dig into my skin, but I barely feel it. The coldness that seeps into me as I'm put in my place quite effectively, my pride and self-worth crushed under deliberately ruthless words, is like a wake-up call.

Of course, he thinks I'm worthless, too.

Just another piece of meat, a body to fuck or use.

Nausea curdles my stomach, my hands go limp, and my fists uncurl.

"It's good you know that I'm nothing special," I say quietly, my entire being numb. "Next time, don't touch me."

Emotional flashes of my past are overlapping with the present and the faces of my father and stepmother are darting through my thoughts, replacing Mr. Middleton's. I can hear their voices.

You're nothing more than trash.

"I'm going to go back on the floor now," I say in a monotone voice.

I've retreated into myself. I can see Mr. Middleton. I can hear his voice as he says something, but it's a droning sound.

Can't hurt me if I can't hear you or feel you.

I turn around and walk out.

I don't know what I came here for.

I've forgotten.

It's the familiar taunts in my head that are echoing louder and louder.

Filthy, useless bitch.

Why won't you just fucking die?

Nobody wants you. You're a waste of space.

I hear something behind me as I cross the hallway, but I don't register the sound until a sudden hand on my shoulder stops me. I look up to see Parker's confused face.

"Where are you going?"

I stare up, blankly. "What?"

He studies me, his brow furrowed. "Megan, what's wrong?"

"I'm going home," I say numbly.

His voice is distorted in my head, "But your shift just started."

"But I'm going home."

I shake off his hand, wanting to eliminate this cold feeling inside. Maybe once I get warm, the taunts in my head will die down. I thought I was past all of this. I haven't felt like this in a long time.

I use the other exit and walk out. It's now a chilly LA evening outside, especially in my silk blouse, but I don't truly feel it, so I keep walking in the direction of my home.

You're not special.

I know that I reply silently to myself.

I mindlessly walk past my normal bus stop, mainly because I don't want to stop moving. This is probably not one of my best ideas. I'm not really sure what time it is, but it's dark, and the road I'm on is an empty stretch. It's the heavy footsteps behind me that slowly cause me to become self-aware, my mind fighting against the torrent of memories.

Then, the hairs on the back of my neck rise.

The footsteps are rapidly approaching me, but before I can turn around and react, something heavy comes crashing down on the back of my head, and after a flash of blinding white pain, there's only darkness.

Utter darkness.

Chapter 13

Death And Despair

HUNTER

I'm staring at the tattoo on my arm and recalling its meaning. If you want to become whom you are destined to be in this world, you need to apply pressure to everything and every one until you get what you want...until you get what you deserve. It's a simple premise that has so far worked in my favor.

Apply calculated pressure.

Get the desired results.

The inspirational word, inked forever in my skin, is supposed to serve as a visual reminder of all that I've done to get where I am in life, but it must be losing some of its potency because I'm starting not to recognize myself.

My reactions to Megan are not how I normally respond to people who intrigue me, amuse me, or upset me. I've never lost control so easily when it comes to a woman, but when I saw that flash of heat in her eyes as she looked at me, dressed in that delicate silk blouse that stretched against her breasts and the figure-hugging pencil skirt outlining her curves, I felt my leash snap.

I could have simply told her from across the room about the clothing tag mistakenly left attached to her skirt, but at that moment, my dick did all the speaking for me. I was undisciplined and approached her, feeling almost like I was unable to help myself.

I started it.

It's good you know I'm nothing special.

The look in her eyes when she said that, the emptiness, haunts me. It was as if her internal flame, the vibrance that makes Megan who she is, was suddenly extinguished. She looked at me as if I finally saw her for whom she thought she truly was.

I had expected her to get angry, to lash out at my cruel words, but I hadn't expected this reaction. Now, I stare at the door, wondering if I should go back out there and seek her out. I may be a monster, but even someone like me has boundaries. I'm not usually cruel to women, and I was cruel just now.

There's a knock on my door, and I look up. A part of me wonders whether it's Megan, but it's Parker who enters. "Hey, boss, do you know what happened to Megan? She just left, and it's only the new dude out there."

"Left?" I stare at him. "Left where?"

"She said she was going home, but the weird thing is that she didn't get her coat, bag, or anything. She just walked out. The city is experiencing an unusually cold front, and it's fucking freezing out there. Maybe I should find her and drive her home?"

My blood grows cold.

Has she lost her fucking mind?

I stride across the room. "Which way did she go?"

"The exit down the hall," Parker replies, looking visibly confused. "Is everything okay?"

"Does everything look fucking okay, Parker?" I bite back.

Why the hell didn't Parker stop her? What am I paying him for? This is what I get for hiring amateurs as security. Vaughn tried to warn me. I should have hired someone with actual credentials, like a retired cop or something.

"I guess not, boss."

I throw open the door of the exit as I storm outside, angry with Parker but mostly with myself. I'm the reason why she's wandering the streets of LA without a jacket or her wallet or her phone, for God's sake.

"Miss Taylor, are you out here?"

I call for her as I look for her outside of the club, but she's not in the alleyway. There's a cold wind blowing, and if she gets sick because she's out here without a jacket, I may just kill her myself.

Cursing her for making me feel like a desperate idiot, Parker peeps his head out the club door as I roar, "Bring the goddamn car around!"

Parker hurries to obey as I continue looking for her. It may be one of the first times ever that I've wished that Blue Whiskey was located in a nicer part of town. This isn't an area that you're supposed to be taking evening strolls in. You're just supposed to come to the club, drink, get in a car, and go home.

I remember that Megan doesn't have a car and typically takes the city bus to and from work, so I walk quickly toward where I remember the nearest bus stop is located. Hell, it's been years since I've even stepped foot on a bus.

Fuck, she's not there.

I've covered over two blocks when I see a familiar curvy

figure in the distance, but Megan is not alone. At first glance, I think she's meeting with someone from her school, but as a car rushes past me, I see a hooded figure lift something that looks like a baseball bat and bring it down on her head.

"Megan!!!"

My heart is pounding a mile a minute, and my brain is working overtime as I run through scenarios of how I will catch and kill whoever dared to assault one of my employees in my own backyard.

Where the hell is Parker?

My gun is in the car.

I'm running towards Megan when I see her assailant pick her limp body up and throw her into the car, which has stopped right next to them, and climb inside. The whole street is empty, but I manage to get most of the license plate numbers before the car roars off.

Parker is a minute behind, and I jump into the car, growling, "Drive!"

I'm loading the piece I keep in a gun box underneath the passenger seat when I see the car turn right before it disappears around the corner. We follow after it, but when we reach the street, it's as if it has vanished off the road.

Parker stops the car, his face pale. "Who the hell would take Megan?"

I don't answer him, reaching for my phone and getting out of the car. I have a direct line to some of the most powerful people in this country, people who owe me favors. I don't care what time it is as I stand in the middle of the empty road; the phone is pressed to my ear.

The person who picks up on the other side sounds sleep-addled and I say, cooly, "Wake up, Commissioner. I need you to do something for me.

It takes two hours of police barricades over a 50-square-mile block radius, every car being checked and traffic cam footage being reviewed before the first sign of the car is found. It's in the system as a stolen vehicle, but one of the traffic cams caught it, turning it into an area that has primarily empty warehouses.

"We'll take it from here," I tell the police commissioner whom I dragged out of bed to accomplish this. The various cars surrounding the road and cutting off any escape routes belong to me now.

The commissioner, an older man with grey temples and crow's feet, looks uneasy. "My debt is paid, Middleton."

"Is it?"

"You've spent two hours of Los Angeles Police overtime and a plethora of resources to find one employee. We're done."

I've spent many years making shady deals and trades to have powerful people at my disposal, but the commissioner is probably right. This was a big favor I called in, and normally, I wouldn't have wasted it on searching for one of my employees, but...this is different.

This is Megan.

"Your attention on this matter is appreciated. Sorry I dragged you out of bed."

"Just try to make sure this doesn't make the news."

"It won't," I murmur. "It never does."

When the commissioner drives away, I signal to my men. It's all hands on deck. I have my entire team here, even Vaughn.

"There are a number of empty factories and warehouses

on this road, all slated for demolition. She's got to be here somewhere," I say. "Find her."

Lars and Parker organize the men while Vaughn and I enter the first warehouse. We're both armed and move softly, years of practice under our belts.

"It doesn't seem anyone's here," he says, quietly, his voice grim.

He's not wrong. There's nothing disturbed here, and the only sound I hear is of him breathing.

"Let's do one more quick sweep and then move on to the next one."

We find nothing at the first warehouse.

The next one is also empty.

But it's the third one where we hit the jackpot.

"There's a car here," Vaughn whispers, jerking his head towards a corner. It takes me a minute to see it since it's concealed by the dark shadows of the wooden structure above it.

"Keep a lookout," I instruct as I keep to the shadows and make my way toward the vehicle.

It takes me a few minutes to identify the license plate. It's definitely the same car.

"It's empty," I say, peering inside.

"She must be here somewhere," Vaughn mutters. "How many floors does this place have?"

"Looks like two."

We exchange a look and I nod. "You take the top floor. I'll take this one."

This warehouse clearly used to be a slaughterhouse.

God, I hate these places.

It smells of death and despair.

As I go deeper inside, having notified my team of the car via text, I hear a murmur of voices coming from the back of the cooling room where meat was probably once hung to drain. I move through the old, tattered tarps, careful not to make any noise.

I text my team as well as Vaughn that I think I've found something or someone but to still keep looking for clues wherever they are. Everyone knows that I can handle myself if I happen to find myself in trouble.

The murmur of voices grows louder as I reach the back where there seems to be an open area. There is a single-bulb lamp dangling from the ceiling and it's lit, casting light over a small area where I can see one folding chair and a person tied to it.

"Bitch!"

The sound of flesh striking flesh is not an abnormal sound to me, but my blood grows cold as I watch who is being hit.

Megan's face whips around by the force of the blow. She doesn't see me, but I can see her face, and it's the emptiness of her eyes that makes me tighten my hand on the gun. I've seen this once before. It's as if she's not present in the room. Almost as if she has to disassociate herself from the situation to survive it. It's a coping mechanism that only someone who's had their ass beaten repeatedly would know to use. The thought of that makes my chest tighten.

"What did you do?" A familiar voice snarls. "You little bitch, what did you do? You snitched to him, didn't you? That's how that bastard knew about everything, right? You wanted my position and used your tits and ass to get it, I bet."

Nothing typically surprises me, but I have to admit that I underestimated my former manager, Steve. I thought he was nothing more than a lazy jackass using an overworked college student to do his job for him, but now I see that he can get very creative when he wants to be, and he clearly has a taste for vengeance. That would have been nice to know a few months ago. Perhaps I could have used him in other areas of my work, but now he's really just pissing me off.

Even though every part of me wants to put a bullet through his head right now, I have to be smart about this. From my recollection, there was a getaway driver, so his accomplice must be somewhere in here.

I watch Steve's hand grab a chunk of Megan's hair as he forces her to look at him. "What did you do? Suck his dick? Did you crawl on all fours and let him fuck you? You always thought you were better than me, but you're nothing more than a little whore, you know that?"

Megan doesn't utter a word, and when he releases her after a stinging blow to her ears, her head falls forward, her eyes dazed. She's totally checked out. Gone is the fiery and brave girl who took on my entire table at The Blue Whiskey.

I grind my teeth, my hands itching to blow this bastard's brains out, but I watch carefully around the edges of the room where the light dimmed, and sure enough, I see a slight movement.

There's definitely someone else here.

So I wait.

Chapter 14

He Must Atone For That

HUNTER

"Look, you said she knew things about Middleton," a man complains from where he stands in a corner, and I see the flicker of a match as he lights his cigarette. "She's not even talking."

"She knows something," Steve tries assuring the man.

"I'm not sure if this is working out. The deal was that you were going to get me information that would be beneficial to me. This kid is nothing more than some who-gives-a-shit bartender."

"I'm telling you, she knows something!" Steve says desperately. "I've never seen him act like this before over some pussy. And she'll sing like a fucking canary if I rough her up some more. I promise you that.

The man's voice lights up in interest. "She's a pretty little thing, and there are different ways to get her to talk. Why don't you step out, Steve? Let me and the little lady have a few minutes together."

I'm going to rip this wanna-be gangster's balls off first, I think to myself icily.

"I'm not done with her yet," Steve says, his face getting angry. "She got me fired and insulted!"

When Steve lifts his hand to strike Megan again, I've had enough. I raise my gun and aim it at the center of his palm. I pull the trigger, and the howl of Steve's agony is beautiful as he bends over, clutching his wrist. The other man fumbles, reaching for his gun, but I shoot his left kneecap, forcing him to fall, and his gun slides across the floor out of his reach.

I walk into the circle of light, making a clicking sound with my tongue. "I warned you, Steve. I warned you to leave and never look back."

The asshole is screaming in pain and doesn't respond as I cover the distance to Megan and lift her face gently. Megan stirs, but she doesn't move. She has one large bruise over her right cheekbone, in exactly the same place she had been injured earlier today. Her lip is cut, but she doesn't seem to have any other injuries on her face. I'm tempted to lightly kiss some of the pain away for her, but I restrain myself.

"Are you hurt badly?"

She stares at me but offers no response, her eyes unfocused. I'm not done with either man, but I don't want to leave her side. The look in her eyes bothers me. Why are they so empty? How can she be so strong one moment and so broken the next?

I move to stand behind her, gently urging her head to rest against my thigh. I cover her eyes with my left hand, whispering in her ear, "This will all be over soon."

I shoot Steve again in the crotch. His screams are bloodcurdling, and when Megan hears them, she flinches, but I don't falter. The sight of his blood spraying across the chair and all over Megan's new outfit is irrelevant. This bastard put his hands on her.

He must atone for that.

I have a lot of experience in inflicting pain, and I know exactly where to shoot someone to cause maximum damage without killing them. This time, I move from his crotch to his collarbone. He curls into himself, pleas for mercy falling from his lips.

"What exactly did you think would be the outcome of this, Steve?" I drawl, watching him try to crawl away. "Did you think you could just put your hands on what's mine, and there'd be no repercussions?"

Mine?

I mean my employee.

It takes me a second to correct myself in my head.

I'm angry because Steve tried to harm an employee of mine and not for any other reason. My viciousness isn't because the staff person in question was Megan. I would carry out the same justice if he had so ruthlessly abducted any other employee to try to get to me.

Okay, I probably shouldn't have done the crotch shot. Steve is bleeding out rather fast on the floor, but what's done is done. I watch him bleed out dispassionately, which actually takes a lot of self-composure because what I'd rather be doing is using my fists to crush his skull.

The texts are flying in on my phone. At this point, everyone on my team has heard the gunshots and is probably wondering if I'm alive, but I give them direct orders to stay where they are. I'm handling this. This shit is personal.

Lars: Can we come in, sir?

Parker: Are you okay, boss?

Me: Stand down for now. I'm good.

The deviant in the corner who started all of this tries to slide across the floor and out of sight when he sees me focused on my ex-manager, so I turn and say in a casual tone, "You didn't think I would forget about you, did you?"

I recall his comment about the different ways he planned to get Megan to talk, and I aim the gun at his balls, too. His scream is ear-shattering, and Megan recoils into me.

"It's okay," I croon to her. "Keep your eyes closed."

She's frozen in place, and now I hear footsteps. There can only be one person who wouldn't take a direct order from me to stand down: my friend, Vaughn.

"Well, damn, Hunter," Vaughn says in a concerned tone. "You could've at least moved the girl out of the room. She's just a kid. You've probably fucking traumatized her with all of your cowboy shit tonight."

He's right.

I was abhorrently selfish about this.

Megan is an art student, not some seasoned woman who knows this life. Getting her to safety should have been my first priority, not exacting vengeance.

"Take care of this," I order Vaughn, suddenly realizing that I need to get Megan out of here.

"Stop snapping orders at me. I don't work for you. Call your team."

When I'm in auto mode, I start barking out orders to anyone around me. It's what I do. So, instead, I send Lars and Parker a quick text.

"They're coming," I tell him before I lean down to

whisper in Megan's ears. "I'm going to remove my hand now, Miss Taylor, but I want you to keep your eyes closed."

She nods her head in a jerky movement before I lift my hand. Her eyes are squeezed shut, and I take off my blazer, wrapping it around her, before leaning down and picking Megan up in my arms. She feels good in my embrace, almost as if she belongs to me.

Mine.

"Eyes closed," I remind her gently, and she just curls into my arms, burying her face in my chest, not letting out a single sound.

She weighs next to nothing, I think to myself. I'm going to have to take her out to dinner a few more times.

Lars and Parker are running inside the building as I carry her toward the entrance.

"You good, boss?"

"Keep them alive," I instruct them. "And wait for me. I'm not done."

Lars glimpses at Megan and then back to me. He flashes an unusual smirk, and I already know what that means. I'll probably come back to far more injuries than I've caused. Lars can be sadistic when he wants to be, and I think he may be forming a soft spot for our new club manager.

So be it.

"If you don't mind, Vaughn, can you please drive us back to the club? Lars and Parker are a little tied up," I say as politely as I possibly can, although I'm not used to asking anyone for anything. I am typically the ordering-around type.

"Fine, let's go."

"No." Megan stirs in my arms, and when I look down at her, she's not looking at me.

"I'd like to go home. Please."

I stare down at her before uttering, "You've been through more than any one person should go through today. I need to check your injuries. Make sure you're okay. He banged you on the back of your head really badly."

"He just beat me up a little," Megan says, her voice almost dull. She's trying to slide out of my lap, but I tighten my hold on her, unnerved by her flat response to what's happened here tonight.

"I'd still like to be sure," I say, but she turns stiff in my arms.

"I thought I wasn't special?" she retorts. This time, there's a hint of anger in her tone. "Will you just let me go, please? I can sit on my own, and I know how to treat my own injuries. I'm a fucking pro at it."

She throws the one thing I regret saying to her back at me, and now she refuses to look at me. I hate it. It's only when I release her that she scampers to the end of the seat, farthest away from me, hunching next to the door.

"I'm not going to hurt you," I say in the calmest voice I can muster, although it irritates me to no end that she's afraid of me, of all people.

She wraps her arms around herself and doesn't answer. For a moment, I wonder if she has a right to be afraid of me. I did just shoot two people repeatedly in front of her. Hell, I am a monster.

"Take her where she wants to go, Vaughn."

I tear my eyes away from her figure and look outside the window as Megan rattles off an address to Vaughn. I'm not accustomed to experiencing guilt. The amount of blood on my hands is endless. Guilt isn't something I can afford in my line of work. Yet here I am, feeling pangs of this useless emotion for having created havoc in the life of the young woman huddled in the corner of my car.

It's not like any of this was her fault. I've completely insinuated myself into her life, and this is the result. Not long ago, she was just a nameless, faceless bartender whom I didn't know at all. But I'm the one who had to know more about her and who approached her despite my own self-imposed rules.

Don't get involved with staff.

Don't date staff.

Don't fuck staff.

So when I tried breaking those rules, and she rejected me? Well, the sting of that rebuff made me lash out at her with very harsh words in an attempt to hurt her. It was immature and very unlike me, but I did it, and now I have to own the consequences of the choices I've made ever since I laid eyes on her.

As I take in my new surroundings, a moment of realization hits me, and I shoot Vaughn a sharp look. He meets my gaze in the rearview mirror and shrugs. The neighborhood is a familiar one to both of us, and apparently, it is where Megan lives.

Just when I thought this night couldn't get any worse.

Chapter 15

Little Do They Know

HUNTER

I don't say much of anything as Vaughn parks the car in front of what I suppose is Megan's apartment building. The building is run down, and the entire street only has two working streetlights. The last time I was in this decrepit neighborhood, I brazenly killed a man. It was a crime of passion, not intelligence, and almost did a lot of time for it. Luckily, I had a police chief in my pocket who made the whole thing go away for me.

After that unrestrained incident of violence, I promised myself that night that I would stay out of this neighborhood and never soil my hands with bodywork again. I would leave that for contract killers and other desperate souls. Of course, that promise to myself has gone up in smoke since I've met Megan. Steve had to be handled, and it had to be me to do it. The shit was personal.

I can see a few men loitering around and I internally roll my eyes to myself. This is going to be a problem. Their small group is across the street, gathered on the steps of a building, smoking and drinking as they watch us. I step out of the car, meeting their gaze. I can see them eyeing the expensive Bentley and when they walk over to us, I feel a hint of depraved amusement.

"That's a sleek ride you got," one of them comments, running his hand over the hood.

Here we go.

Megan is trying to get out of the car, but I block her path, casually standing in front of the open door. Vaughn gets out, too, looking formidable, standing next to the car with his arms crossed.

"It is," I agree.

The one who's talking, the leader of this ragtag group, I have to assume, has a mean look in his eyes and tattoos all over his face like some wannabe biker.

Unsightly.

"You should know better than to bring something like this in this neighborhood," he comments.

"Why?" I smile, my eyes tracking his every movement. "Do I have something to be worried about?"

Megan is trying to push past me and I put my hand on her shoulder, my hold firm, not allowing her to move.

The men sneer at me, and their leader grins, a disturbing look if you take his silver teeth into account, "Why don't you let me drive this baby around the block? I'll park it somewhere safe for you."

"Why don't you go back to where you were sitting, and I'll try not to dig your eyes out with my fingers?" I say lightly. "Does that seem like a fair deal?"

Megan flinches under my touch. The man's smile disappears, and I can see the ugliness underneath. He's quick to dig out a switchblade from his jacket's pocket, and I scoff at the sight of the tiny weapon.

From the corner of my eye, I can see Vaughn's body tense up, ready to spring into action. We've had many scuffles in our time, and the shit going on with his lady probably has him itching for a fight.

"Give me your wallet and the car keys!" The man brandishes the tiny weapon, and then he peers into the car, and his smile turns into a leer. "And I'll take that little girlfriend of yours too."

I was amused by this exchange at first, reminds me of old times, but when I feel Megan's hand clench the fabric of my pants at the man's words, an icy feeling settles over me. The man is still watching me, looking like he just struck the mother load, and his little group is watching in anticipation, clearly ready to jump at me and Vaughn at a moment's notice.

Little do they know.

I eat assholes like them for breakfast.

I exchange a brief look with Vaughn before quickly whipping out the gun, which I just shot Steve with. My first shot is aimed at the hand holding the knife, and the loud echo of the gunshot makes the men flinch. As their leader howls, clutching his hand in pain, I point the gun at his forehead, my tone eerily pleasant, "Why don't you repeat what you just said?"

It's clear from the expression on the faces of these corner boys that violence is second nature to them. However, they look taken aback because they hadn't expected it from me. All of them draw weapons of different forms and sizes on us, but only three of them are holding guns. It's the mouthy one clutching his hand who finally recognizes me, and his face grows white as a sheet.

"Fuck, you're—"

My next bullet lands in his shoulder, and he screams in agony, scrambling back. "Wait! I didn't know it was you. I'm sorry."

His cronies look to be a mixture of confused, angry, and scared.

"What're you saying, man?" One of them says to the guy I shot. "Why are you apologizing to this overdressed lunatic? He should go back to his own neighborhood. We got guns, too."

"Shut up, Brady!" The mouthy one howls, spittle flying from his mouth, his eyes wide with terror. "Let's go! Come on."

"Where are you going?" I ask, my gun still pointed at his forehead.

"Stop, Mr. Middleton!" Megan reprimands me through the open car door. I use the base of my foot to kick the door closed again.

"I thought you were going to look after my car... and the *girl* for me." I cock the gun and smile. Menace flowing through my veins at the thought of him even thinking about Megan. "Unless I was wrong?"

Even with two gunshots, the mouthy one is still able to respond. His fear of me is stronger than whatever pain he may be in. That's good.

"We'll guard it. I swear. Nobody will touch it. Or we can leave. Whatever you want."

He's stumbling over his words, and I study him for a moment longer before tucking my gun back in and saying, "Good."

I can hear his men mutter between themselves, but I'm not overly concerned.

Megan tries to dart out again as if she's in a rush to get

away from me or into her apartment. I allow her to exit the car, but then I grab her carefully. I don't know the extent of her injuries yet, so I don't want her walking. It's a bad habit I've picked up lately, worrying about her safety.

I knew it was coming, but she struggles against me when I pick her up in a bridal hold. "Let me down!"

"Wait for me here, Vaughn. I won't be long."

"You sure about that?" His eyebrow raises.

"Just watch the car." *Smartass.*

I glance over my shoulder at the corner boys who have now retreated a few feet away. It's as if they're waiting for my approval to get the mouthy one some help. I can see the recognition in one of their eyes when I give a simple head nod, and then they prop their friend up and start walking away.

"Keep still," I order a very wiggly Megan. "Or I'll throw you over my shoulder and carry you inside."

"I can walk," she says defiantly, but at least she's no longer fighting me.

"Which floor?" I ask, ignoring her comment.

She hesitates but finally reveals, "Fifth floor, but there's no elevator."

"It's broken?"

Of course, it is.

"It's never worked." She shrugs as if a non-working elevator is par for the course when you live in west hell. "Look, it's a long climb. You should seriously let me down."

"I'm stronger than I look, and you're not that heavy."

"I didn't say I was," she grits her teeth. "It's just inconvenient, and I asked you before not to touch me. It seems you have a hard time understanding directions."

"And here I thought you were scared of me," I say

lightly, carrying her up the steps. "But you're just holding a grudge." My hold on her grows tight as I watch her breasts sway with each step I take.

"Scared of you?" She sounds dismissive, but I can hear a hint of strain in her voice. "You had guns pointed at my head the first time I met you. I'm not holding a grudge. There's nothing to hold a grudge over. It would be stupid for me to hold a grudge against a man who can kill me at a moment's notice."

My body turns stiff at her words, and I stop walking, looking down at her. Her eyes turn away from me and I feel a flicker of anger within me.

"I've never once tried to harm you. If you're angry about what happened between us in the office, that's fine. However, I've done nothing to make you feel that you're in any danger around me."

It's true.

I've been unusually tolerant of Megan. Nobody has ever spoken to me the way she does or challenges me without hesitation. She's aware that there's a line, but she constantly flirts with crossing it. I've killed a man for less, but things are very different with her. I find her bravado, when facing me, almost amusing.

She doesn't say anything in response to my comment and continues to look anywhere but directly at me. Her whole eye contact avoidance thing irritates me, and I keep climbing.

Her apartment isn't hard to find since there are only three apartments on the fifth floor, but when we enter, I blink at the organized, colorful mess we walk into. I stand at the entrance, looking around, until I hear Megan clearing her throat.

"Is it possible to get the hell down now?"

Feeling a little intrigued by the organized chaos, I walk over to the couch a few feet away from me and gently lower a silent Megan onto it.

"You must be feeling better," I smirk.

In the light, her bruises look mottled, and I don't know why the sight of them angers me so much. She tries to get up, but my voice is hard as I snap, "Stay."

"I'm not a dog, Mr. Middleton," she bares her teeth at me. "This shit is getting old. Stop telling me to stay or sit. I'll do whatever I want in my damn house."

I've decided that an angry Megan is better than one with a dull look in her eyes. Mainly because every time I see that furious glitter in her beautiful eyes, I feel the urge to see how far I can push her. Perhaps because something about it always seems restrained, as if something still holds her back from going totally postal on me. Maybe common sense. Maybe something else.

"If I wanted that level of obedience from you, sweetheart, I'd just put you over my knee. And trust me, you'd enjoy it."

Her eyes widen, and her face flushes, but then she pretends to stick a finger down her throat as if what I said disgusted her. "Eww, what is wrong with you?"

"I've already had my tongue down your throat," I chuckle. "Let's not pretend that a good old-fashioned spanking wouldn't turn you on. Now, where's your first aid kit?"

My cell rings. It's Vaughn. I already know what he wants.

"Vaughn."

"Did your old ass arrive at your destination yet? I'm

getting a little tired of sitting down here in the middle of a war zone."

"I've done worse for you."

"Like?"

"Like listen to you whine about your wife."

"You shot someone in the middle of the street. Someone had to have heard those shots and called the cops."

"No one is calling anyone in this neighborhood. You know that."

"I'm hanging up now. Just hurry the hell up, Hunt."

I turn my attention back to Megan, who looks displeased. I turn the deadbolt on her door to lock it before I ask, sitting down at the edge of her aged coffee table, "Where did they hurt you?"

"I can do this myself."

"Or I can start removing your clothes to find out." I look her square in the eyes. Seeing the blush crawl over her neck like that is always fascinating.

I can see the frustration on Megan's pretty face before she says stiffly, "Mostly my face and stomach."

"First aid kit?"

"Under the sink," she huffs.

I locate and open the box and raise a brow at the well-stocked kit. Not commenting, I take out the alcohol pads and bandages. "Why were you walking out in the middle of the city without your belongings like that?"

A hint of anger colors my words, but she looks away. "I was going home."

"Or were you throwing a tantrum?" I ask softly, my words a caressing blade.

She snorts a small derisive sound, and her gaze is sharp enough to wound when she turns it in my direction.

"Do you really think you're the first man in my life to

tell me I'm worthless, Mr. Middleton? Don't give yourself that much credit. Do you think a few harsh words are going to make me sit in a corner and cry or wander into the city at night? Well, fuck you."

The fire is returning to her eyes, and that pleases me.

And apparently, it also pleases my dick.

Chapter 16

I Want More

HUNTER

I tear open the alcohol swab, my movements steady, silently wishing for my hard-on to settle down.

"You keep surprising me, Miss Taylor."

"Why?" She spits out. "Because I don't let you walk all over me? Or because I'm not ready to kiss your ass like everyone else?"

I smile lightly before turning to face her and gripping her chin. My hold is firm but gentle as I press the disinfectant on the cut on her cheek.

"Because the fact that I just shot and tortured one of your neighbors in front of you doesn't seem to bother you that much. I'm surprised you're sitting here talking back to me as if nothing has happened."

She falls quiet and then mutters under her breath, "Well, it's not like they didn't deserve it."

Vicious little kitten.

"True," I admit, my hand pausing as she hisses in pain.

The curve of her jaw is lovely, I muse to myself. Her

face is so delicately formed, her lips a little pouty, but only when she's angry. Her eyes have this endearing wariness in them whenever they land on me. She doesn't trust me, which is smart, but she also doesn't entirely fear me, which is ... interesting.

"Also, if you wanted to hurt me, you wouldn't be sitting here trying to patch my face up. The way I see it, there's nothing to fear."

She hasn't grasped the most important part. I don't do this for any of my employees. Hell, I don't do this for anyone. I lied when I said she wasn't special. All I see when I look at her is special. The shit is blinding.

Obviously, there's something about Megan that continues to draw me in like a moth to a flame. She's a college kid, whom I promoted to manager of my club practically overnight and whom I allow to speak to me in whatever disrespectful tone she feels like.

This is like the goddamn twilight zone. Anybody else would be dead three times over.

"Turn your cheek," I command.

Reluctantly, when she turns her head, she has to face me, and I see the flash of awareness in her eyes before she looks away. However, I still continue to make an inspection of her, taking in the bruises from this afternoon and also from this night. I don't like the sight of them. She looks like she's been through a bar fight... and lost.

"Next time you want to storm off, you tell Parker to drive you home. That's what he's there for." My tone is a little hard, and her eyes widen.

"But that would be *special* treatment," she says in a mocking tone. "And you've made it quite clear that you don't find me the least bit special."

"You keep mentioning that," I say through gritted teeth.

"Maybe my opinion matters more to you than you want to admit."

"Maybe," she shrugs casually. "Or maybe I'm just trying to understand why every time I turn around, there you are, trying to talk to my un-special ass, help my un-special ass, fix my un-special ass, sniff up my–"

My free hand darts forward, grabbing her by the neck and pushing her back as I loom over her. I can feel her blood pulsing through her jugular vein, and for a moment, I forget that she has bruises over her face or that she's been through a traumatic event.

I press her into the back of the couch, my eyes narrowed, my dick hard. "Do you really want to keep pushing me like this, Miss Taylor?"

I'm not hurting her.

I'm very careful of my grip.

But then she's also not scared of me.

There isn't an ounce of fear in those stormy eyes of hers as she gazes back at me. I see something else, though. Something that makes my cock strain against the zipper of my slacks. It's a trace of lust and submissiveness, tainted with defiance. Her small hands are curled around my wrist, but she isn't pushing me away. It makes me wonder for just a moment if something is stirring between her legs as well.

Her jaw is tight when she responds, "I don't know why you're so upset. I'm just repeating what you said."

I stare at her, my eyes drawn to her lips. Her lipstick faded hours ago, yet I want to taste them again. This defiant creature with a wary look in her eyes as if she doesn't quite know what she wants and that luscious mouth that never stops running.

"Don't," she hisses at me, her eyes sparking as if she's fully aware of what I want to do.

"Then push me away," I challenge, unable to tear my eyes away from her lips.

Fuck, what is it about this girl that's making it so hard for me to hold on to my own self-control? Why is it that whenever I'm around this damn art student, I feel like a horny sixteen-year-old kid?

I'm leaning into her, holding her in place by her swan-like neck, and she snarls at me, "You said-"

"I say a lot of things," I growl back against her mouth, my breath ghosting over her lips. "But it seems none of them ever apply to you."

And when I slam my mouth down on hers, she lets out a quiet gasp that I can feel in her throat.

Addicting.

She tastes addicting.

And I want more.

My other hand is itching to reach under her skirt, part her legs, and have a taste. I want to flip her on her stomach and bury my aching dick inside of her. I want to fuck her until she is hoarse from screams of pure pleasure. I want to put my marks in seen and unseen places on her body.

I kiss her fiercely, desperately, drinking her in, *wanting more.* Her hand is still holding on to my wrist, and when I give her neck a slight squeeze, a needy whimper escapes her, and her hands go limp.

Fuck, she has a submissive streak.

She likes this.

The realization sends all the blood from my head rushing to the one between my legs as I tighten my hand even more. When her hips arch up, I smile in satisfaction. Vaughn is going to be pissed if he's even still waiting for me downstairs because right now, I don't want to go anywhere.

As I devour Megan's mouth, I fantasize about what she

will look like, her pretty red mouth wrapped around my cock as she sits at my feet, painting a picture of both obedience and submissiveness. The mental image almost makes me groan as I hook my feet around her ankles and yank them apart.

Her skirt is riding up, and it takes every ounce of self-control I have not to push it up even further. The quiet gasp that leaves her lips at the quick movement drives me wild, and I can feel my control slipping. My hand is on her bare knee; the soft skin makes me want to mark it and leave something of myself on her so that it's visible for everyone to see. When that dark thought passes through my head, I snap back to reality.

What the fuck am I doing?

I abruptly pull away from Megan who looks dazed, her eyes hazy with pleasure. There's no trace of anger or embarrassment on her face, only want. I stare down at her, taken aback by the force of my attraction to this young woman.

This makes zero sense.

All the rules I have created for myself and my world exist for a reason. I put these self-imposed chains on myself because they were needed. And yet here I am, dangerously close to violating my rules for *this* woman.

This beautiful woman.

I see clarity seep into Megan's eyes and a slow look of horror.

"You – You asshole!" She pushes my hand away, and I immediately grab both her wrists, pinning them beside her head.

"Calm down."

"I'll calm down once you leave!" she snarls with fury. "This is the second time today you've put your mouth on mine. Just because I work for you doesn't mean that I'm some toy for you to play around with."

"I never said you were," I growl, the leash on my anger snapping. "You're the one who keeps calling herself that. You're the one who keeps minimizing whatever this is between us."

She falls silent as if stunned by my display of temper or the words I've just said. I'm not sure which. But Megan isn't one to be dissuaded that easily, so I'm not exactly surprised when she tries to kick me in the crotch.

I fend her off, watching her in amazement. "You really have zero self-preservation skills, don't you?"

"I didn't survive all these years," she spits out, "by letting people take advantage of me, at least not for long."

She's struggling so fiercely that I have no choice but to let her go. I don't want her to hurt herself. Her words are still ringing in my ears as she jumps to her feet, pushing me.

"I've had enough of this shit. Stop taking me shopping. Stop showing up at my school. Just stop. Either kill me or get out of my house! And by the way, I quit."

Her last statement stops me dead in my tracks. "Excuse me?"

She bares her teeth at me, "I quit this job."

"You need this job."

"Not *that* fucking much."

Anger curls inside of me, and I take a step toward her. "We'll see about that, Miss Taylor."

Suddenly, I notice that she looks shaken, and her hands tremble. Fuck, I may have crossed a line today.

I could leave and give her some privacy.

That would be the smart thing to do.

But I can't bring myself to leave her in this condition.

"Sit down," I decide to calm her down first. "Let me finish bandaging you up."

"No," she shakes her vehemently. "I don't want you in my home. Just get out."

She's trying to push me out, and I have to grab her by the upper arms, being careful not to hurt her. "Megan, I won't do anything to hurt you. I'm only trying to help. You have my word."

The tears in the corners of her eyes tighten something inside of me, and I curse myself for my recklessness. I know the brief moment between us on that couch was powerful, but she wasn't ready for it. I should know better. She's barely a damn adult.

"Look, I know you can do it yourself, but I just want to help." She tries to shake her head, but I release her, gently guiding her to the couch. "Come on, you've been through a lot today."

She doesn't put up much of a fight this time, and I imagine it's because of exhaustion. She looks tired. I work quietly and efficiently, trying to think past this sharp throbbing in my chest at the bruised look in her eyes.

A text on my cell phone goes off.

> Vaughn: Seriously? I'm about to leave you here. Call your damn driver or take an Uber home.

He's right.

I've been up here entirely too long.

Enough is enough.

I've got to leave this woman alone and screw my head back on straight.

> Me: On my way

I can tell that Megan is paying attention to what I'm doing, yet she doesn't meet my gaze as I press send on my text. I finish tending to her face and afterward toss the dirty alcohol swabs in a nearby trashcan. I'm pleased that the warm color of her umber flesh looks slightly better than it did.

There's no reason for me to remain here now, so in keeping my word, I get up to leave, but her strained question gives me pause.

"Why are you doing this?"

Chapter 17

Is He Dead?

MEGAN

Based on my past experience with people in general, but especially guys, I used to wonder if my father and stepmother fucked me up in the head. Now I know the truth. They fucked me up real good. Because how else can I explain the fact that I've allowed this grown-ass man to barge into my life and take it completely over? Why am I not afraid of him? He's a criminal and a very dangerous man. Dead bodies end up behind his club, and I wouldn't be surprised if he's the one who puts them there.

Having said that, I think that it's those dangerous parts of his personality that I'm drawn to because those are his qualities that keep me safe. I never expected to feel so utterly protected when he held me against him, covering my eyes as he doled out his brand of brutal justice.

Nobody has ever tried to shield me from violence the way this man did. I've never felt special or important enough to anyone even to deserve such protection. And yet, he flayed me with his tongue in a deliberate effort to remind me of my status in this world. But now he's here, bandaging me up, drowning me with care and consideration, and I don't know what's real anymore.

"Why?"

I've always been able to keep my emotions in check, even when I was humiliated by my own family or those elitist bullies at school, but this push and pull between Mr. Middleton and me has me bursting apart at the seams.

"What are you trying to achieve by all of this?" I ask him.

The words feel as if they are being torn out of me. I have to say them. I have to ask the questions that I'm dying to know the answers to. He doesn't say anything in response, but he doesn't walk out the door either.

When I lift my head, he's not looking in my direction. He's staring at the door. "I don't know."

I get to my feet slowly and approach him. "You don't know? What kind of bullshit answer is that?"

He turns his head to look at me and his eyes are flickering with a smoldering anger but I stand my ground, refusing to be intimidated.

"I am a student, Mr. Middleton," I say, deliberately keeping my voice even. "The only reason I'm working at your club and risking my life every day is because I need the money. I can't afford to get dragged into your world. I want to make something of myself. I want my own art studio. I may not deserve it but I have my own dreams, small as they may be, insignificant to you as they may be. So please stop treating me like this. You're fucking with my head, and I'm not going to be somebody's whore."

His eyes narrow at my words, yet I continue on ruthlessly, wanting to get this out of me.

"You were right in your office. I don't have any value.

I'm not special. So stop treating me like I am. Don't give me jobs I'm not qualified for, nurse my wounds, or scare the shit out of my neighbors when you have no idea what you want from me. If this is a game you like to play with your employees from time to time, I want it on the record that I don't want to participate. Let me tap out. Let me quit, and you can go play ball with some other young girl at the club."

"That's enough," he says with a sharp edge to his voice, but I'm not done.

"So then stop," I hiss, my hands curling into fists. "Let me just do my job, get through my college, get a decent paying job, and maybe find a nice guy for myself. Let me live the life I'm trying to live."

His eyes harden at my words and his voice becomes dangerously deep, "And just who do you plan to find for yourself, Miss Taylor? Some nice accountant who bores you to death and fucks you every Friday like clockwork or a politician's son who treats you like trailer trash and never lets you forget where you come from?"

"At least he won't be ramming his gun down somebody's throat and shooting them dead. I'm just asking you to leave me alone for, I don't know, like the millionth time! You made a compelling argument in your office today and I'm glad you put me in my place. That is what you wanted, isn't it? I got it. I learned my lesson. I'm not your problem. I never was."

For a moment, the flash of heat in his eyes makes me falter. If he touched me right now, I would melt. If he kissed me, I would die. I hate that I find myself wanting him to do it, but I do. I can't help myself. What the hell is wrong with me? I'm starting to think that the biggest game player in this toxic relationship of ours... is me.

Then, without a word, he turns and walks out of my

house, and the minute the door slams behind him, I feel my knees turn weak, and I sink to the floor. My heart is pounding, and I scramble back to lean against the back of the couch. My lips feel raw and tingly from the way they were so deliciously abused. I've never been kissed the way this man does, in this ruthless manner, taking everything from my mouth until there's nothing left and then demanding more.

"I have to stay away from him," I mumble to myself, running my hand through my hair and then wiping at my lips to remove his dark taste.

I bring my knees to my chest and wrap my arms around them, "I'm fine. I'm fine now."

My stomach still hurts from where Steve punched me. I still don't understand the animosity that led him to kidnap me like this. When I saw his face, I was shocked. Confusion had followed shock, ending with resignation. Steve had always been a lazy bastard, but he'd never been mean to me. The hatred I saw in his eyes tonight was something new to me. It only reinforces the fact that I am a bad judge of character.

Now that I'm home, within the four walls of my apartment, I can't calm down. Everything that has happened today comes crashing down on me at once. I had been this close to dying tonight or, at the very least, to being tortured. I stare at myself in a long mirror in my room. I rip open my blouse, buttons fly everywhere, and I unzip and step out of my skirt. A sob escapes me as I stare at my bruised body. I wish Naomi was home. She'd know what to do to get me to forget this horrible day. She always knows what to do.

It takes me an hour to crawl to bed once the sun is nearly out, and when I do sleep, I dream of a night long ago when my arms were drenched with blood, and I stare down at a face I once loved.

And then the dream shifts to a faceless man, hiding me in his arms as people scream around me.

***

I don't go to college for a few days. The bruises on my face are something I can't hide under makeup, even if I had Naomi's help. Fortunately, she's gone to visit her family for a week or two, so I don't have to worry about her freaking out over the complete downturn of my life.

I don't go to work as well.

Naomi promised to cover my portion of the rent this month, so to save the little bit of money I have left, I just ordered a carton of ramen noodles, which I cook every day.

I spend the entire week under my favorite fuzzy blanket, eating noodles and watching cartoons. There is no way I can step outside with my face like this. There is no way I can face the world with a broken spirit like this. I don't even have the energy to sketch.

It's on the eighth day that there's a knock on my door in the evening. When I open it, it's the last person I want to see. I typically go out of my way to avoid our landlord, Mickey, but when he shows up unannounced, I don't have any way of walking away from him.

He's a fucking creepy fifty-year-old man with a round face, small eyes that are too far apart, and thin pink lips. Mickey is also an alcoholic with a protruding beer belly and a formidable six-foot-frame.

He takes one look at my face and sneers. "Somebody went at your face, huh? What did you do? Piss off your ex or maybe a new boyfriend?"

I grind my teeth at the insinuation. "What do you want, Mickey?"

"Where's that crazy friend of yours?"

I open my mouth, about to tell him the truth, but something inside me warns me not to let him know that I'm alone. "She's a few minutes away. Why?"

There's an odd glint in his eyes. "I came to fix the kitchen sink. There's a drip, right?"

"It's working just fine," I say, not moving out of the doorway. "And I told you to let us know beforehand if you have to repair anything."

"Well, I don't have time to run after the two of you." He pushes past me into the apartment and looks around.

I wrap my blanket around me even tighter because I'm only wearing a sports bra and panties underneath. I never should have mindlessly answered the door.

"Get out, Mickey. I'm working."

"What're you wearing under the blanket?" He eyes me hungrily, and I have the urge to scrub off my skin.

"None of your business!" I growl at him. "Come back another time to fix the sink."

He's watching me, and then he takes another look around the place. "I thought I told you I don't want you girls bringing random men in here. I'm not running a whorehouse."

His words are deliberately provoking, but I'm not so stupid as to let him get to me. "We know the rules, Mickey. We've been living here for a while now."

"Then who were those two men last week?" He narrows his eyes at me. "I saw them."

Such a creeper.

"If you saw them, you should have asked me then. Why

are you asking me a week later?" I retort. "I don't have time for this. Like I said, I'm working."

"Because I wanted to be sure that your crazy bitch friend wasn't home when I came by."

His voice is sly, and a lousy premonition hits me.

He knows.

He knows that Naomi is out of town.

I glance down at Mickey's hand, and my voice is wary. "Where is your toolbox, Mickey?"

He's standing in the middle of the room, ignoring my question. "Since when have you started bringing around men in expensive cars?"

He takes a step towards me and my little voice is warning me quite loudly to remove myself from this situation.

"That was my boss."

"Bullshit," he responds, smiling at me, his yellow-stained teeth visible. "Why would your boss come to your apartment unless you're offering him something special? And here you keep crying about not being able to make rent."

"I've always made my rent," I spit out, tense. "I want you to leave."

"I own this place and rented it to you two without a credit check," he sneers at me. "If you were willing to suck dick to get by, you should have just told me."

I don't hesitate, picking up the ugly ceramic duck-shaped vase on the table next to the couch and throwing it at his feet, "Get out, you sick pervert!"

He slides his feet out of the way, and his sneer morphs into an ugly look.

"I'm not going anywhere. You girls are always flaunting yourselves in front of me, teasing me. You want this," he says, grabbing the small package between his legs. "Why else would you bring those men around for me to see?"

The sick feeling in the bottom of my stomach compounds as I realize a couple of things. First, that Mickey is a delusional psychopath, and two, that he's here to rape me.

In a heartbeat, I rush towards the door, and I'm about to pull it open when he's on me, grabbing me by my middle and throwing me to the ground as I let out a loud scream.

But I'm a fighter.

I scramble back on all fours and dart behind the couch. Mickey is so focused on my ass that he doesn't see me grabbing the hot mug of tea that I just made a few minutes ago. I toss the whole thing into his face, and as he screams in pain, I scramble over the couch and dart towards the door, pulling it open and running outside with bare feet and only the blanket around me.

I'm so busy looking over my shoulder to make sure he's not following me that I run smack dab into a wall of firm male muscle. Fear is rampant within me, my breathing uneven as I try to jump away, but the man grabs me by the waist.

"Leave me—"

Before I can get out the word alone, I look up and see Mr. Middleton staring right back at me. I'm in shock. He's the last person I thought I'd see again. After a week of no contact, I thought he was finally done with me.

"What's going on?" he asks, his voice tense. "Why are you running outside with no shoes on and a blanket?"

I look over my shoulder, terrified. "My landlord, Mickey, he came in and tried to; I think he wanted to—"

I can't get the words out. I'm shaking so badly.

"I've got you." Mr. Middleton's arm wraps around my

waist, pulling me into his chest, his other hand tightening the blanket around me. "It's going to be fine."

"He's still in there, though."

My ear is pressed against his chest, and hearing his steady heartbeat calms me down. I don't understand why I feel so safe in his arms; I'm pretty sure that I've gone from one monster straight into the arms of another one.

"Not for long," he reassures me, his voice calm.

I worry for a moment that Mr. Middleton may kill my landlord, but when Mickey emerges from the apartment building and starts verbally attacking me, I begin not to give a damn.

"You fucking bitch! How fucking dare you?!"

Mr. Middleton's voice is cool as a cucumber as he whispers into my hair, "I won't let him touch you."

I've never once relied on another person to protect me because I never had that luxury, even as a child. But why are those six words everything I needed to hear? Why does my body instinctively relax when he says them? All I want to do is to envelope myself inside his embrace, where it feels completely safe... and stay there.

Mickey comes to a stop when his pea brain realizes that I'm not alone. He's huffing for breath, his face an angry red from where I threw the hot tea at him. "Who the fuck are you, and what the fuck are you doing in front of my building?"

He squints his eyes as if he's finally getting us into focus. "Wait, you're that man from last week, aren't you? You need to get going, man. This bitch is mine tonight."

As Mickey advances, Mr. Middleton does not so much as move. Part of the reason may be because of a dark shadowed figure which moves past us and then tackles Mickey to the ground.

The front of the building isn't that well-lit, so it takes me a second to realize that it's Lars. Parker is right behind him, with a gun in hand. He smiles at Mickey sinisterly, who is struggling under Lar's chokehold. "You're an ugly little fucker, aren't you?"

"Let me go!" Mickey shouts. "This is illegal! You can't just assault me when I've done nothing. I'm going to press charges against all three of you."

Lars exchanges a look with Parker, who shrugs and brings down the butt of his gun on the back of Mickey's head. My perverted landlord collapses onto the ground like a sack of potatoes.

A panic overwhelms me.

"Is he dead?"

Chapter 18

Since Day One

MEGAN

Lars checks Mickey's pulse and then shakes his head. "Still breathing."

Parker cocks his gun and points it at Mickey's head, "You want me to kill him?"

I'm tempted to say yes after what the man just tried to do to me, but I shake my head, mutely. I've seen enough violence this week to last me a lifetime. Parker almost looks disappointed before putting his gun away.

"Take care of this," Mr. Middleton orders before turning his attention to me. "Did he touch you?"

"No," I mutter, unwilling to move away from his embrace but forcing myself to. My heart is racing so wildly that I feel a little sick.

I hunch down, trying to breathe past the sudden wave of crippling nausea, and I hear the alarm in his voice, "What's wrong, Megan?"

I shake my head, waving at him with my hand. "It's fine. Just give me a moment."

However, to my surprise, he crouches down next to me and rubs his hand along my back. "Take slow breaths. In and out."

I listen and realize that my hands are still quivering. Finally, when I feel a bit more like myself, I look at him and ask, "Why were you here?"

My question has him frowning. "You haven't come to work or gone to school in a week."

I sigh at the last part.

"You're checking my attendance at school?"

"No one at the university is breaking any privacy laws by telling me your business. I simply put Parker on in. He hasn't seen you on campus all week, and I thought you might've meant it when you said you would quit."

He helps me stand, and I study him. "So, you came here to do what? Drag me to work?"

Mr. Middleton shrugs but he doesn't meet my eyes. "To remind you that you have a contract with me for two years."

I get a strong feeling that he's not being entirely honest although I know that usually, he is, sometimes brutally so. However, I'm just grateful that he was here to help me...again.

"I was going to come back," I admit to him. "It's just the bruises – I couldn't hide them, even under theatrical makeup. They're a little better now. I'll come back to work tomorrow."

I glance towards my apartment window and hesitate. I don't want to go back inside. Although I know that Mickey is no longer a threat, I don't want to head in there by myself. Of course, there's no place else I can go.

Crap, how am I supposed to continue living here knowing what my landlord just tried to do. I cringe at the thought of what he might have gotten away with if Mr. Middleton hadn't been looking out for me as usual.

"Go pack up your essentials," Mr. Middleton orders as if he can read my thoughts.

"What?" I look up and into his expressive, stormy eyes.

He lifts a brow. "I'm not letting you stay here after what happened. Pack what you need, and I'll arrange a place for you. A safe one."

"But-"

"You don't have to fight every battle, Megan. Life will wear you down if you keep fighting everything that comes at you. Let me help."

There's no mocking edge to his voice this time, and I lower my gaze, suddenly feeling overwhelmed. He really is trying to do something nice, but fighting is the only way I know how to survive.

"Go pack up what you need," he repeats, and this time I do as he says.

There's not much I own that has any value except my art supplies and a framed picture of my mother. I don't even remember her, but it's nice to have a picture of a parent who might've loved you.

I quickly pack my art supplies, toiletries, and clothing, and when I enter the living room, I see Mr. Middleton looking into the cardboard box containing the Ramen noodles.

"Yeah, um. That's mine."

I lean down to stuff a few of them into my bag. "I was a little low on cash, and they're quite tasty," I say, trying to sound convincing.

"And full of sodium. Leave that garbage behind," he frowns. "You can't live on that."

"But I-"

"Leave it, Miss Taylor."

I look mournfully at the packets of perfectly good ramen before dumping them back into the carton. I try to sneak a few into my bag, but as Mr. Middleton gets up, he adds, "I saw that. Put them back."

Ugh.

"Is there anything else you need?" he asks sincerely.

I shake my head, looking around.

"Come, then."

I follow after him but when I'm about to lock the door, he says in a light tone, "Leave the key inside for your friend. You're not coming back here."

I think about Naomi for a moment, wondering how she'll feel about me just picking up and leaving, but I also know that coming back here would be dangerous after what's transpired tonight.

And while Hunter Middleton is far more deadly than Mickey ever could be, he's provided me with a sense of safety that I've rarely felt before.

It's not a hard decision.

"I can't stay here," I stammer, feeling overwhelmed as I take in my surroundings. This place is three times the size of my old apartment and gorgeous.

The apartment he brings me to, if one can call it that, has three bedrooms with king-sized beds covered in very expensive feeling bedding. The living room has a view of the whole city with windows that span the length of the floor to the ceiling. The kitchen is massive with gleaming marble tiles and equipped with appliances that belong on the back of some high-end catalog.

"Why not?"

Mr. Middleton trails in after me, looking somewhat amused by my reaction.

"Because I can't afford this place, which you should well know, because you don't pay me enough."

For the first time ever, I see what I think is a genuinely offended look on his face.

"You seem to keep bringing up how much or how little I pay you. Ask around, Miss Taylor, but I pay all of my employees quite well. But if you think that I pay everybody less than the market rate, I'll make sure to reevaluate the salary structure. I don't remember you voicing a single complaint when you signed the contract."

That's because I didn't read it.

It was difficult for me to insist on reading it from front to back, with him watching me like a hawk. Hell, I couldn't concentrate.

"Besides," he murmurs, his eyes meeting mine, "I won't charge you. I own this building."

My mind goes blank. "What?"

He points towards the ceiling. "I live on the penthouse floor."

"Oh," I mumble, taken aback. "So, I don't have to pay rent?"

He smiles at me with that small smile of his, which makes it difficult to discern what's going on in his head.

My first instinct is to reject the offer. No one gets anything for free, but this is Mr. Middleton, I say to myself. He's different. For whatever reason, I think he genuinely gives a shit about my safety. Plus, it's just temporary.

"Thank you," I say awkwardly. "I mean, thanks for doing this for me."

His smile disappears, and after a beat, he steps toward

me. I freeze in place when he invades my space and then tilts my head back with a finger under my chin. I can feel his breath on my face, and his cologne has an addictive woodsy scent that makes me slightly light-headed.

I have never been so wildly attracted to a man who is so much older than me, but there is something about this man that makes me quiver yet feel completely safe in his presence.

This intense attraction has been there from day one. It's clear that he's also aware of it, and he's made no secret of the fact that he does want me, but I refuse to be swayed. Yet, I'm concerned about my ability to keep holding out. How long can I refuse to give into this attraction when he protects me the way he does and performs gestures like these?

It's intoxicating.

"Have you been applying a cold compress to your cheek?"

"Um, yeah," I stammer, unable to tear my eyes away from his.

"Well, the bruise is fading," he releases me. "You'll settle in here today, and you'll come to work tomorrow."

I nod mutely, wishing he would step away from me so that I can think more clearly.

"All right, then," he says, moving back, and I immediately miss the warmth of his touch. "Go back to school tomorrow as well. I'm sure you've missed a lot of work."

Based on his tone, it's not a suggestion but more of an order, and again, my natural instinct is to bare my teeth at him, so I have to force myself to control myself.

Not every battle, Megan.

For some reason, his words are reverberating within me.

When he turns around, I find myself saying, "I didn't

mention this before, but I have a roommate, and she's a friend. I'm worried about her staying there, too."

"Naomi Turner?" he states plainly.

Of course, he knows.

"Yes," I mutter.

He looks over his shoulder at me, "Would you feel better if she stays here with you?"

I nod.

"You have three bedrooms. Do what you want with them."

"Would she pay rent?"

"No."

"This is temporary, of course," I remind him. "I don't expect to live anywhere for free forever."

"Of course."

He's about to leave when I speak up again, wondering why I keep finding excuses to make him stay. "What's going to happen to Mickey?"

His eyes darken. "Don't ask questions you can't handle the answers to."

I fall silent, but it seems he also has some questions.

"Is this the first time he's come after you?"

I try to shrug, but the movement is jerky because the look in Mr. Middleton's eyes makes a shiver of fear run down my spine.

"He's wary of Naomi, so he's never pulled something like this before, but he watches me sometimes, which is why I try never to keep a routine so that he doesn't know when to wait for me."

Even if he's never pulled something like this, my instincts always warned me about him, and I trust my instincts. They've never failed me before. I'm still here, and I'm still in one piece.

"I see," is the only reply he gives me.

He's about to leave the apartment when I call out, "Mr. Middleton-"

"I think we've been through enough together that you can call me Hunter outside of work," he interrupts.

"I can't call you that."

"I'd prefer it."

But I don't.

Using his first name would strip away the boundary of boss and employee between us, and the ground becomes uneven for me with that barrier taken away from me.

There's a glint in his eyes as he approaches me, and I'm rooted in my spot. This time, his massive hand envelops my cheek, and his voice feels like a velvety caress against my skin, making my lower muscles tighten in need.

"It seems as if I don't like your tears for some reason."

"I'm not crying," the words stumble out as shock envelops me at his statement.

"You were about to," he murmurs. "You held on to me, and your eyes were terrified. People rarely seek protection in my arms, Megan, except you, it seems."

"I was desperate," I force the words out, my heart beating so wildly that I'm afraid he'll be able to hear it.

His words are whisper-soft and hold a hint of menace, "I'm a different kind of monster, Megan, but you're the first person to see that and still hide behind me. Those kinds of actions have consequences."

I want to say something, but I swallow the words that are on the tip of my tongue.

"You have me questioning my every rule." His tone is calming, and my heart trembles.

"I didn't make you."

"Ah, but you did," he counters softly, his words piercing

me, his gaze holding mine. "You make me lose my self-control at every turn. I can see in your eyes that you want me, too. How long do you think you'll be able to hold out? Days? Weeks?"

My eyes narrow at his words. "Is that why you brought me here to this impressive apartment you own? Easy access?"

"Of course not," he scoffs. "I brought you here because if one more motherfucker tries to put his hands on you, I'll slit their throat in front of you next time."

A normal person's blood would grow cold at his calm statement but strangely enough, it makes me feel warm and tingly all over.

"Why?" The question is out of me before I can stop myself.

He takes a long time to answer before he simply replies, "I don't know."

I stare at him, stunned.

"I'll see you at work, Megan."

When he releases me and walks out, leaving the key on the kitchen table for me, I just stare after him, feeling both lost and confused.

Tomorrow, then, *Mr. Middleton.*

Chapter 19

You'll Never Guess

HUNTER

"We got some information."

I look towards Parker as I step into a secluded room in the basement of the club, which is covered from top to bottom with plastic. Parker and Lars moved Steve and his kidnapper buddy to this location almost a week ago, and now they're hanging by a rope that is tied around their wrists in the center of the room. Their clothes are a bloody mess, and Steve's head is lolling forward, which lets me know that he's out.

Parker strips himself of his blood-stained gloves and throws them into the trash bin, a cheerful smile on his face. "It took a damn week, but I got it. You'll never guess whom your old manager works for."

"Who?"

"He works for Johnathan." I toss Parker a look of confusion and then stare hard at Steve as I continue to listen. "Steve was planted in the club to report everything he saw."

Johnathan.

I haven't heard that name in a long time.

"But he barely knows anything," I say, damn near speechless. "And I'm surprised Johnathan would be this bold to make a move like this."

Parker shrugs. "The man had the balls to steal twenty million from you and walk away. Why does he spying on you even surprise you?"

"I wasn't out for that fucker's blood the first time around," I say, my tone hard. "But that's all changed now."

The betrayal I faced at the hands of the man I once used to trust implicitly still stings, but I haven't destroyed him for two reasons. First, I blame myself for being asleep at the wheel and allowing this to happen. And second, because I haven't been able to find the motherfucker. But planting a snitch in my club after he's blatantly stolen from me? I can't let that ride. This time, I want Johnathan's blood on my hands.

I hear footsteps and then see Vaughn step in, staring at the sight of Steve. "Well, is he dead yet? Bullets in the groin never end well."

"No," Parker replies lightly. "But he might as well be."

"Did he admit how Johnathan approached him?" I ask Parker.

"Johnathan?" Vaughn says, his voice shocked. "That fucker came back?"

"Steve met some woman around three years ago. Johnathan sent her. She drugged him, probably fucked him, then made him an offer he couldn't refuse. Your boy here said she's been at the club more than once."

"Who is this woman?"

"We looked at some footage, but we need more time. We didn't find anything yet," Lars says.

"He said that she asked him for information on your

business dealings and personal life, and, most importantly, she wanted to learn everything she could about any weaknesses you have."

Vaughn snorts, "Weaknesses? Hunter?"

However, I realize this is not at all funny when I see the still look on Lars's face.

"What is it?" I ask him.

"He wanted to get a sample of your DNA, boss," Lars answers, his Danish accent thicker than usual today.

"My DNA?" I go still, my attention turning to both Parker and Lars. "For what?"

"It took me an hour of working him to get it out of him, but Johnathan wanted to compare the sample with someone else's. Some girl. Steve said he managed to see a picture once. He said that the girl was pretty young," Parker says.

I freeze, and my voice is careful as I ask, "What else did he say about the picture?"

Lars watches me carefully, then replies, "He couldn't recall her features aside from her ashy blonde hair, but he did say that there was a distinctive scar on the inner side of her right wrist. He remembered because she was holding something in her hand–"

I'm no longer listening. My mind has gone blank.

A scar on her inner wrist.

It's not possible.

A memory of a burning room, the flames shooting to the sky, the screams of the only two people I held dear to me echoing in my ears.

That night from fifteen years ago is still etched in my brain, no matter how much I try to forget it. My hand curls into a fist as I mutter, "It's not possible."

But what if it is?

The reason Johnathan's betrayal had been so particularly painful had been that we had grown up together on the streets. We hustled people and ran scams together as children, trying to feed ourselves, simply trying to survive. We joined the organization together and worked our way up the ranks. It had been a bitter pill to swallow when he, my most trusted right hand (really more like my partner), had stabbed me in the back. But if Lena – If Lena survived, would it be so far off to imagine that he would try to use her against me? She would be my one weakness.

"Wake him back up," I snarl, fury and hope flickering through me. "I want information on that girl."

Both Parker and Lars nod in understanding.

"And get the doc back here to patch him up again so he doesn't die."

"What about the other one?"

"I don't care about him. Just make sure Steve doesn't die, then get ruthless if you have to. I want information. If he still doesn't talk, then tell me. I have other methods of making people talk. Squeeze every bit of information you can get about Johnathan's whereabouts. That bastard wouldn't send someone in here if he wasn't completely assured of his loyalty. And find that damn woman!"

I storm out, trying to get a hold of my raging emotions.

Then I think of Lena.

Precious Lena with her sweet, angelic smile.

"If that is you, I'll find you," I vow to her silently.

Vaughn follows me, "Hunter."

"Not now," I growl.

But he steps in front of me, snapping, "It has to be now. Who is that girl Parker was talking about? If Johnathan has her or knows something about her and she's a weakness, then I need to know. If you fall because of her, we all fall with you."

He looks tense, and I glower at him. "I wouldn't let that happen. I'll handle it."

I'm about to walk away when he says, tersely, "Are Lars and Parker on tap to eliminate this girl in case–"

I won't let him finish his sentence. Whirling around him by the front of his shirt, my voice icy cold. "No one touches a hair on her head. Not until I know for sure."

"Then tell me who she is!" He shoves me, furious. "This is the second time I've seen you lose control like this. I'm just trying to help you."

I open my mouth, but then I snap it shut, recalling Johnathan's betrayal. I have a hard time trusting people now, but Vaughn knows me too well, and he steps toward me.

"I'm not him, Hunt. You and I are like blood brothers. You should be able to trust me. I've never given you a reason not to."

I stare at him, trying to sort out my emotions, and then I say with great difficulty, "I can't talk about it today. Give me a few days."

I expect him to argue back, but he takes a step back. "Fine. Take a few days. I'll stay with Parker."

"Maybe you should go home to your wife."

"If you're not talking to me, then I'm not talking to her."

I shake my head at Vaughn's lame attempt at a joke. Grateful that he's not pushing me, I take the elevator to the top floor of the club and walk directly into a private room that overlooks the bar. From the one-way mirror, I see a familiar figure behind the bar, talking to Gage.

It's her.

Chapter 20

You Said Where?

HUNTER

Bringing Gage Clayton here to work has been a strategic decision. The man has been with me for years. I picked him up from the streets. He used to be my runner, somebody I trusted to dispose of bodies and do all those sorts of tasks that required discretion. But the man has a more useful skill of getting people to talk to him, which is why I regularly move him through all the country-wide branches of my operations. With the current situation brewing in LA and Steve's betrayal, I brought him here because he comes off as friendly and the right guy to act as my eyes and ears.

It's been several days since Megan returned to work, and I'm not surprised to see a massive shift in the work environment because of it. She has a very personal touch with both coworkers and customers alike. Although she and Gage have worked together for just a few days, he has been singing his praises of her. It still takes me aback that this woman, who is so combative with me at every turn, is so well-liked by the employees and patrons of the bar.

Since I moved her into the apartment a few floors down, she hasn't swiped her claws at me for a while. In fact, she's been oddly polite, albeit a little wary around me, but I've got to admit, I've been avoiding her as well. If I'm Megan's Superman, she is my kryptonite. Nothing good can come from us spending more time around each other than we need to.

Having said that, my eyes are still glued to her. I can't help but watch her moving through the customers toward where the female bartender she hired, Diana, is working. I notice how Diana smiles as Megan converses with her. However, the look on her face when Megan turns her back catches my attention. It's a cold look of distaste. Megan doesn't see it because she's already walking away, but I do, and I tuck it away in the back of my mind to deal with later.

As I watch Megan work her magic through the crowd of grinding and writhing bodies on the dance floor, I think about the farfetched possibility of my sister being alive, and then I recall the events of that night. I remember it like it was yesterday, although I wish I didn't.

Johnathan had been with me, holding me back from running inside the small apartment, which had been ablaze. The men who set the fire dragged us away and threw mementos of my mother and sister at my feet, describing to me in explicit detail how they had tortured them before setting the fire and watching them burn.

It was the cruelest tale any human being ever told.

What kind of scum are capable of killing a child?

But now I'm wondering if it's possible that they lied.

What if the screams I heard were from someone else?

What if my mother and sister escaped? What if they were never inside, to begin with?

I'm quick to discard the thought, though. I'm sure that my mother would have found a way to track me down if she had escaped, plus our sweet Lena had only been three years old when this happened. She wouldn't have survived a life on the run and on the streets.

When I returned to the burnt building, it had been flattened to the ground, and I wasn't able to find any remains of them. The authorities were clearly bought off and ruled it an accidental fire. So, barely a man myself, all I had been left with was the knowledge that my family had been tortured and murdered because of me.

I touch the glass, not knowing what to do with the flickering ember of hope. Now that I know that Johnathan is somewhere close, it's going to be easier to find him. The streets of Los Angeles are my turf, and he'll make a mistake eventually. Finding him shouldn't be too hard because we're bound to sniff out the stink of someone so rotten.

The sound of the door opening makes me look up, and I notice Megan's startled expression when she sees me. She was hoping to avoid me the rest of the night, but I think we need to finally end this cold war. It's silly.

"Sorry, I thought this was empty," she says.

She's backing out of the room and about to close the door when I call out, "Wait, come in."

She hesitates, and I can tell that coming in here is one of the last things she wants to do, but I'm finding that no matter how good an idea it may be for us both, I don't like it when she avoids me.

"I really have to go."

"Come in and close the door, Megan."

She looks torn, and I narrow my gaze. "If you try to run,

I'll just throw you over my shoulder and carry you inside, and I won't care who sees it."

She quickly enters, and I almost laugh.

Megan looks pretty tonight in her soft sky-blue blouse and black pencil skirt. She's wearing natural makeup, which pleases me, too, especially because it means that her bruises no longer show that much.

"Take a seat," I order.

"Why?" she gripes. "I have to get back to the floor."

"Sit," I point to the seat.

"Seriously, Mr. Middleton, I have work to do."

"Megan," I give her a steady look, and she reluctantly slips into the seat. "And I thought I told you to call me Hunter."

"You said to call you that outside of work, and last time I checked, we were at work."

She places her hands on her hips to emphasize her point.

Damn, those luscious hips.

"Gosh, you're so bossy," she complains under her breath, and I narrow my eyes.

"I am your boss."

"And you never let me forget it."

"Are you having any problems with any of the staff?"

"What?" Her head jerks up. "No, everything is fine."

"What about the apartment?"

"What about it?" she asks carefully.

"Is it comfortable? Are you enjoying it?"

"Yes, and yes."

"The roommate, too?"

"Yep."

I know that my questions are vague, but I'm feeling restless right now. All these thoughts about my mom and sister have me off-kilter, and for some reason, Megan's presence is calming. I don't like that she feels the need to avoid me, and I consider what I need to do to change that.

"What happened to that class of yours? The one for which you drew my picture. Did you get a grade yet?"

I see her reflection go still, and a strange expression crosses her face, "I don't know yet."

"Now, why don't I believe you?"

She's silent.

"Tell me what happened."

"It's stupid," she mutters, but I can see the anger flashing behind her eyes.

"Megan-"

"Look," she takes a deep breath. "I don't want to talk about it if you don't mind. Work is work, and school is school, and I'd like to keep the two separate."

Her fingers are picking at her skirt, and I know she isn't telling me everything, but I won't press. It seems that every time I see Megan, she's under some sort of duress. Giving her the apartment had been a random act, but I also hoped that it would relieve some of the financial burdens she may be dealing with. Between paying her bills, dealing with those shitty kids she goes to school with, and working here—she's got to be stretched thin. I remember being young, broke, and struggling. It sucks.

I look at her gorgeous face and ask myself if she's ever experienced any pure joy at all. I wonder if she's ever just gotten on a plane and traveled. Yet even as I ruminate over that, I already know the answer.

She hasn't.

"Go home and pack an overnight bag," I blurt out.

"What?" She blinks at me.

"The weekend is about to begin. You don't have any classes, do you?"

She shakes her head, confused.

"Good." I tuck my hands in my pockets. "After your shift ends, I'll take you home, and I want you to pack an overnight bag. Just pack a few essentials, nothing more. You won't need much."

"And where am I going?" she asks mockingly as if my request isn't serious.

"A place that every art student like yourself should visit."

"And where's that?"

"Paris, we're flying out to Paris tonight."

The stupefied expression on her face is well worth it.

"Wait, what?"

Chapter 21

No Strings Attached

HUNTER

Watching Megan try to hide her excitement as she looks out the small window of my private jet is worth me taking a pause in my own life. I think it's safe to say that she and I are making small increments of progress with each other. After all, I would think that visiting Paris is on every art student's bucket list.

It's cute how she's so horrible at hiding her emotions, and it's clear that she wants to stay awake for the whole plane ride, but she's tired and falls asleep next to me pretty quickly. She's probably exhausted from the arguments she threw my way about not going, yet I have to say the pushback wasn't as hard as it has been in the past. So, yeah, I definitely think we're making progress.

I tell the attendant to dim the lights and cover Megan with one of the cashmere blankets I keep stocked on board. It's not like I expected her to completely agree to hop on a plane with me without hesitation, but it's easy to wear her down if you know which buttons to press. It's either mental warfare with her or straight-up kidnapping. I chose the legal route, although I'm not averse to doing the other when necessary.

Even in the dim lights, I can see the exhaustion on her pretty face. She desperately needed the rest. I curl a strand of her hair around my finger and watch her lax expression as her head leans into the window.

I don't know why I'm doing this.

I've met plenty of beautiful women in my life, but there's something about Megan that draws me in like a moth to a flame. Like a faulty pilot light on a stove, there's a fire within her that keeps trying to go out, yet she makes it blaze again with just her willpower. She refuses to call it quits, even with the whole world against her. She's fierce and beautiful, and while she's still young, she can go far in life if she doesn't ever give up. But the world is a cruel bitch, and it's going to try its best to crush her. A part of me doesn't want to see it happen.

She shifts in discomfort in her sleep, and her head slides in the opposite direction to rest on my shoulder. She mumbles something.

I freeze.

The innocent way she snuggles into me and the warmth radiating from her is so addictive. It's something I fear I could get used to. Even as I tell myself not to, I gently pull her closer to make her more comfortable until her head is resting on my chest and her arm is draped over my stomach.

She smiles in her sleep, burrowing into me, and I feel a strange sensation under my ribs. The cold, empty hole in my chest, where my heart used to be until it was ripped out by the fire that took my family from me all those years ago, throbs.

"You're a dangerous little thing," I murmur, pressing my

lips to her forehead, knowing she won't wake up. "You might just be my undoing, Miss Taylor."

I've been to Paris multiple times on business but I've never looked at the city quite in the way that Megan does. Her eyes are wide with excitement as she looks around when we land, as if she's desperate not to miss a single thing.

I have an apartment in the city, so we drop off our things and go for breakfast. There's a charming little café with a view of the Seine River near the apartment, and I take Megan there. To me, food is just something to consume for energy. I do enjoy certain foods, but once again, clearly not with the enthusiasm that Megan does.

I find it adorable how she keeps trying to contain her excitement and fails so miserably. Her eyes are shining as she takes in the sights. I've come to this café quite a few times over the past few years, but I don't think I've ever enjoyed a simple breakfast of coffee and croissants more.

"So, why are we really here?" Megan asks, sipping her coffee.

Her nerves have died down now that her belly is full, and I can sense a hint of that familiar wariness that she displays around me.

"You're an art student, right?" I shrug before gesturing around us. "You should be able to appreciate all the art Paris has to offer."

Her hand holding the coffee cup falters. "So this trip is for me?"

"Yes."

"But why?"

"Because I wanted you to have this experience."

I expect her to blow up at me as she has done so before.

I expect some level of accusation of me trying to get into her pants, but she surprises me once again.

"No strings attached?" She asks quietly, looking at the waterfront with a wistful gaze before shifting her eyes back at me.

At this moment, even if I did have some ulterior motive, it vanishes. I am the seasoned adult in this relationship, and right now, she looks like a child who has been given a toy but is scared to touch it for fear of it being taken away from her.

"None," I say calmly, sipping my coffee and watching her.

She swallows, and I can see the struggle on her face.

"So, you're just being nice to me?"

"I wouldn't say that," I murmur.

"Well, this is what one would call a grand gesture. What else would you call it?"

"I get to spend time with you."

The words are out of my mouth before I can stop myself, and her eyes turn wide, and she blushes fiercely.

"What?"

Now that it's out there, I can't exactly take it back, so I take another sip of coffee and allow her to process what I've just admitted.

"I don't get it–" Megan cuts herself off, a tight smile on her face. "No, you know what? I'm not even going to ask. Because the answer is probably something that I don't want to hear, this might be the only chance I get to come to Paris. I willingly got on the plane. We're here. So, I'm going to enjoy myself."

She sounds so determined that it's adorable, and I smile into my cup. "Go crazy. I won't stop you."

She takes out her phone and starts searching for something.

"It's the weekend, so some museums and art galleries have free entries. You have to wait in line, but we can still get in, and–"

"I assure you I can afford to get you a fast pass into any museum in the city," I say, feeling a little insulted, but Megan isn't listening.

"There's a coupon for a lunch menu in–"

"Megan!" I growl at her, and she looks up.

"I brought you here on a private plane. I'm funding this trip. Stop looking for coupons and free entries. It's a waste of time and energy when we only have a few days here."

She frowns now. "No, that'll make it seem like I'm using you for your money."

"Not when I'm offering it." I stare at her. "Plus, I have plenty of it."

She looks back down at her phone and continues to scroll whatever tourist discount site she's on.

"I don't like you because of your money, and I don't want you getting that idea."

Her words are thoughtless, and I blink, absorbing them and their meaning.

"Come again?"

"What?" She gives me a distracted look.

"You said you like me."

I don't know why her words make me feel so taken aback but also, dare I say, they make me feel good?

This time, when she blushes, she shrugs a deliberate movement.

"Well, you're nice to me a lot, even when I yell at you. And you haven't shot me even once, although you shoot other people. And you took care of me, twice by my count, even though I can sometimes be a complete bitch."

"I never once thought you were a bitch," I say with a smirk, wondering why her words sound so pleasant.

"But you're still my boss, and I'm not shitting where I sleep or whatever the saying is," she promises with narrowed eyes over her coffee cup.

"I'm not your boss here," I say plainly.

She deliberately looks down, refusing to meet my gaze. "Yes, well, you'll still be my boss when we return."

I don't know what compels me, but I am leaning forward. "But we're not back yet. We are in Paris. And I'm not your boss in Paris."

"Then what are you?" She looks a little hesitant, as if she knows that she's treading in dangerous waters but can't stop herself.

I shrug, giving her a small smile. "We'll find out."

Approaching Megan is like approaching a wary kitten. I can't win her over until she trusts me. This trip had been an impulse, and I was second-guessing my own actions during the plane ride here. But seeing her here like this, so filled with life and excitement and away from the pressures of Los Angeles, all my doubts fade away.

It's also a good distraction for me. This weekend will give me the chance to sort out my head and come back to tackle the whole situation going down with Johnathan with a clearer mindset.

Resting my cheek on my palm, I watch Megan attempt to plan out an entire itinerary. I really did try to stay away from her, but it never seems to go my way when it comes to this woman. That one week that she stayed home drove me wild. I couldn't forget the taste of her lips. The soft sounds she had made still echoed in my ear. I lived with a hard-on for her most of that week. It was both disturbing and intox-icating.

I don't know what I'm going to do with this fiery little kitten, but staying away isn't an option. Fucking her sense-less would be my favorite option, but something tells me that if she figures out what's running through my head, she'll run straight for the hills. I need to find a way to either get her out of my system or just keep her around me until I get tired of her.

Damn, I hope I get tired of her.

'I don't like you because of your money.'

Although words are the most meaningless thing in the world to me, Megan's statement has me smiling. There are only a few people in my life, a mere handful, who have looked past my bank account and really at the person I am.

However I thought this trip would go, Megan continues to prove me wrong. Where I assumed she would want to at least shop at some of the famous flagship stores and enter the most vied-after boutiques, I see that she genuinely isn't interested in any of them.

She refuses to use the private car so we mostly walk around the city. It's nice for me, too, because I don't need security in Paris, so Lars and Parker are home keeping an eye on things in LA.

I'm free.

Instead of going to Galerie Viviene, which is a paradise for shopping for expensive clothes, she drags me to a labyrinth of alleyways that is home to small Parisian markets and stalls. She takes pictures but not once does she buy anything. Every time I catch her with a wistful look in her eye, she moves so quickly that I don't even know what she's looking at. She doesn't let me splurge on an expensive restaurant lunch but instead insists on buying me a sandwich. We sit on the waterfront, eating a baguette with ham, tomatoes, and cheese, and it's the most satisfying meal I've had in a long time.

"Take a video of me." She thrusts her battered cell phone into my hand and quickly steps back towards the entrance of Notre Dame. "Press record when I jump!"

Amused at her eagerness, I do as she says. However, I don't expect the scolding that follows.

"No, when I jump!" She tries to teach me. "When I do this, you have to hit this button. The one that says slow."

I have no idea what that means, but I've never enjoyed being bossed around this much by this tiny woman. After a few tries, I managed to get it right to her satisfaction.

However, as the afternoon fades and we make our way to the art galleries, I see a transformation come over Megan. I tuck her arm in mine when we enter one of the galleries on her list, and when she looks at me in surprise, I pretend not to notice. However, she's far too distracted by the stunning pieces of work to protest.

"I used to love painting when I was a child," she says in a quiet tone, as she looks at a dark blue ocean that is framed in black with a small inscription on the side. "I was never allowed to buy paints but I had this teacher in school who took a liking to me. She would always bring extra paints for me.

"She lived a few blocks away from us, and when she stopped being my teacher, I would always find excuses to visit her home. While I always had some raw talent, she taught me how to paint and refine my craft. She also taught me how to use charcoal. She was one of the kindest people I knew, and our relationship always reminded me that there were actually nice people in the world."

"What happened to her?" I ask, noticing the faraway look in her eyes.

The soft smile fades from Megan's eyes, only to be replaced by a bitter look.

"My shitty life happened. My stepmother found out what she was doing, so long story short, I was not allowed to go to her house anymore, and then she was fired from her job."

"Fired? For what?"

She shrugs. "I don't know, but I can bet my parents had something to do with it. They went to the school to make a fuss about her inappropriate behavior outside of school with a student."

The more I hear about Megan's parents, the more I despise them. Some people shouldn't be parents. Some people shouldn't be breathing.

"Did you ever see her again?" I ask.

"Once. It was just before she died. She got liver cancer. When I found out, I sneaked away after school to visit her. I doubt she recognized me because she was in a lot of pain and on a series of medications, but the last time I saw her, she had tubes sticking out of her, and she looked withered and frail. I heard from another student that she died a few days after."

There's a dull acceptance in Megan's voice as she tells me about this part of her past and I look down at the top of her head. She's still staring at the painting, her expression lost.

"She was the one who got me fascinated with art. She had me convinced that I was good at it."

"You are," I tighten my hold on her arm and she looks at me, a small smile on her face.

"I'm not great yet, but maybe one of these days I'll

manage to get my work displayed at a gallery like this, and it'll be through my own hard work, and no amount of bribery will be able to rip that opportunity from my hands."

Her tone is fierce, and something dawns on me.

"Is that what happened?" I ask calmly. "Did somebody steal an opportunity from you?"

"You can't steal something that was never mine."

"Megan." There is a hint of reproach in my tone, and she glances at me, frowning.

"It's no big deal. I'm not on good terms with some of my classmates, and after it was announced that my work was going to be one of the pieces on display for homecoming, the teacher took me aside and told me that there was a mixup." She makes a derisive sound. "As if I didn't just see Ashley slip her two tickets to whatever show."

"What does displaying your pieces at homecoming mean for a student?"

"You know how some universities have boosters who support their sports teams? Well, there are graduates who come back to our school who work in major art spaces or who are collectors, and if they see a piece they like, they'll often buy it or even offer the artist a position at a gallery."

My expression turns dark. "So you were cheated out of a major opportunity, then."

Her face tightens. "It doesn't matter. There will be other opportunities, and even if it doesn't happen for me, I'll save up money after college and figure out another way to get noticed. I'm not going to let some stuck-up daddy's princess bring me down. Fuck her and her money."

The last parts are spoken with a sneer.

My brave little soldier.

I want to fight all her battles for her, but I'm slowly realizing that she can fight them on her own.

I pat her hand. "Your time will definitely come. I saw that drawing you made. You have an amazing talent, which I doubt this Ashley girl does. Otherwise, why would she have to pay her way to get approval?"

As I hoped, my words cheer her up. "You're right. Fuck Ashley."

Without doing a deep dive into Megan's personal business, or at least beyond what Parker and Lars have already reported back to me, I'm starting to piece together this whole school situation.

Megan is being bullied by one or maybe several privileged brats who are bored with their mundane lives and have nothing else to do but fuck with her. Who else would she have been fighting with at school? Probably the same girl who bought her way into the homecoming art show.

I suppose there wouldn't be any harm in taking a deeper look at this little shit, Ashley. I want to make sure that Megan's doing fine, of course. Not because I'm irritated that the little bitch had the audacity to take something which was rightfully Megan's. That would be overstepping.

I send a quick text to Parker.

Chapter 22

Can I Tell You A Secret?

HUNTER

Megan and I walk around the gallery, and at some point, she whips out a small sketchbook from her purse and gives me a pleading look. "You don't mind, do you?"

My lips twitch, "Of course not."

I sit down next to her on the bench, watching her as she tries to copy the painting she's looking at. It's a dull scene in my opinion, but she seems to be fascinated by it.

And I'm fascinated by her.

She sinks her teeth into her bottom lip, concentrating on the broad strokes of the dark-looking pencil in her hand. Her soft hands are moving with quick precision, her eyes focused.

"If you still have that charcoal drawing of me," I muse, watching her, "I'd like to buy it from you."

"I didn't get it back yet," she says. "But I could make you a new one, though. You have really distinct features. Great for sketching. If I could just convince you to sit still for a painting, that would be so fucking awesome."

Her enthusiasm is unparalleled at this moment and I have a feeling she isn't completely aware of what she's saying because all I heard was she thinks I'm attractive.

"Maybe you'll figure out a way to convince me." My lips curve.

My eyes catch a glimpse of her sketch, and it's already evolving into something impressive. I don't try to initiate any further conversation, not wanting to distract her. There is something calming about just watching her work in silence. I don't realize how much time has passed when her pencil suddenly stops.

It's only when she lets out a shuddering sigh that I ask, "You're done?"

I lean over to take a look, and I can't help but be amazed. She's managed to capture a lot of the detail of the painting in this half-hour.

"Like I said," I say, feeling a little proud for some odd reason. "You've got incredible talent."

She smiles at me, her cheeks high at the praise, and it occurs to me that I've never seen her look this happy. If she's beautiful in her anger, she's breathtaking in her happiness. My heart stutters, and I stare at her, unable to process the swift emotion moving through me.

"What?" Megan asks.

"Nothing," I say, shaking my head. "Let's get this framed. Come on. I'm sure we can find a place. I want to keep this one."

As I pull her out of the art gallery, she laughs. "It's just a sketch, and it's not even cleaned up."

"I like it," I tell her firmly. "Don't change it."

I see the pride in her eyes when we manage to find a

small local shop that frames the picture for us while we wait. Even with the rush of cars and bikes in the city, business is still slow and easy in Paris. Shop owners don't rush things like they do in the states. So we wait. And for once in my life, I don't mind waiting because the wait is with her.

"I'm buying this from you," I tell her as the shop owner hands over the framed sketch. The glitter of pure happiness in her eyes makes me want to snatch her up in my arms and kiss her, but I hold myself back.

"You like it that much?" she whispers in awe.

"Of course," I say calmly. "I don't say things I don't mean."

Her lips part, and then she holds out the framed picture. "If you like it that much, then it's yours. I can never repay you for this experience that you gave me, but I can give you this. I hope it's as valuable as you think it is."

I look down at the carefully sketched picture and I don't insult her by demanding to pay her. Megan has a lot of pride and I won't make the mistake of trampling over it again.

"Thank you."

She's exhausted, but I can tell that she's not had her fill of the city yet, so I take control of the rest of the evening. I make reservations for dinner on a cruise boat. It'll allow Megan to rest but still take in Paris at night with all its lights and glory. However, the downfall of pouring rain has me canceling the plan, and we move dinner to the apartment, where I order from one of the best restaurants in the area.

The food is exquisite, but the time I spend with Megan is precious in its own way. This was not what I imagined when I decided on this impulsive trip. My rigid personality is loosening, and we sit on the large wooden coffee table in the living room while Megan tries out different dishes, preparing me a plate as well.

When was the last time I was this intimate with someone? I don't remember. I don't remember sitting together with a woman and actually enjoying myself without any ulterior motives from either party.

It's different, but it's nice.

Seems like Megan is determined to get drunk on the champagne I ordered with dinner and after the first three glasses, I reach out and take the bottle from her.

"All right, lightweight, that's quite enough. You'll thank me in the morning."

She makes a face. "I'm not done yet."

"Yes, you are," I tell her firmly. "You're going to have a bad hangover tomorrow if you keep this up."

"I'm a freakin' bartender. I know when someone's had too much."

Her decolletage is flushed with heat from the alcohol as she reaches forward for the bottle and tumbles straight into my lap. I expect her to come to her senses almost immediately, but she lets out a giggle before wiggling herself on my lap to make herself comfortable and then flinging her arms around my neck.

"You're very handsome," she says, smiling at me.

It takes every ounce of my self-control not to touch her.

"Thank you." My smile is strained as I can feel in my cock the painful position I'm now in.

"But you're grumpy all the time." She grins in an unabashed manner. "And very controlling. Too controlling. You're always bossing everyone around and me around. I mean, I guess it's kind of hot sometimes, but as a rule, women don't like that."

Intrigued with our conversation, I carefully wrap my

hands around her waist and settle her in a more comfortable position in my lap.

"But you like it?"

"Well, when you use this kind of voice, I might just like it," she mimics my deep tone.

She buries her face in my neck in a fit of shyness that is simply the most endearing thing I've seen all day. It seems that drunk Megan likes to talk, joke, and snuggle. I've got to admit, I'm starting to like drunk Megan.

"Should I care about what other women think of me?" I ask her mildly.

"Nope," she says in a muffled voice and then pulls back to look at me. "How come you don't have a girlfriend, Mr. Middleton?"

"Mr. who?"

"Okay, why don't you have a girlfriend, Hunter?" She grins playfully.

"My line of work makes that difficult."

"Oh," she frowns, and I can feel her fingers playing with my hair. "Well, you can be a little scary, but you've always been nice to me. You saved me two times. Nobody's ever looked after me like that. I didn't think anyone would come to find me when Steve took me."

My smile fades. "Why not?"

She moves her shoulders. "When bad things keep happening to you, you kind of expect them to."

It's a dark and pessimistic statement coming from her, and she's too young to feel that way, as jaded about life as she does. That's for evil men like me.

"I'll always come and save you," I tell her.

"No, you won't." Her laughter is somewhat drunken and amused. "The minute you figure out a way to get in my pants, you'll throw me away."

My smile fades as something cold forms inside my chest.

She taps me on the tip of my nose. "You thought I didn't know that, do you? Remember, Hunter, you told me yourself that I don't have any value."

I hate that she's saying this while still smiling. "I didn't mean that. I said it out of anger."

"It's fine. It's the truth. But one day, I'll make something of myself, and then everybody who looked at me and said I was worthless will regret it."

My hands tighten on her waist as my heart clenches in an almost painful manner. "They will regret it, but they don't matter, anyway. You're not worthless. You never were."

"You don't have to feel so bad." She pats my cheek. Then she lowers her mouth to mine and gives me a tender kiss before saying, "I don't take anything people say about me to heart. Not even you."

The kiss and her clipped words work at cross purposes. "I think it's time you go to bed before you do something you regret."

Her smile is wicked and filled with mischief. "Can I tell you a secret?"

I have a bad feeling about this right now. I'm feeling a little helpless against her, so I nod. She leans forward until her mouth is next to my ear, and her warm breath hits my neck.

"I really want you to fuck me."

Chapter 23

Are You Drunk?

MEGAN

I usually stay away from champagne, but this entire day has been like something out of a dreamy Netflix special, and I want to indulge. Suddenly, my boss is no longer this fearsome entity. He seems almost human with flesh and bones and... feelings.

I've never seen this side of him, not that I've known him for that long. But this past month, every time I have interacted with him, I've never felt that I can ever stand on the same footing as him.

However, right now, as the bubbly champagne flows through my bloodstream and straight to my sensory zones, I feel light.

Hunter Middleton isn't that bad.

I mean, he's violent, and he shoots people without considering the gravity of his deeds, but then I come from a household where violence against me was commonplace. He's been arrogant, bossy, and maybe even a bit nasty at times, but then he's also protected me. But at least he doesn't hurt me.

During the candlelight dinner that he's arranged, I wonder if all of this was just a plan to get me into bed. Something inside me stirs in warning at the thought, but I push it away, feeling pleasantly inebriated because I'm not going to lie–it's nice to be wanted by someone like him. Hell, it's nice to be wanted, period.

When was the last time I had sex?

I don't even remember.

But the more I look at Mr. Middleton, the more I wonder if it would be such a bad idea. How many men am I going to meet who are going to whisk me away for a trip to Paris just because?

Being here in this city is like a dream come true, and even if he walks away from me after one magical night in bed, I could treat it like another part of the Paris experience. As long as I remain professional afterward, he wouldn't have any reason to throw me away. This is why when I fall into his lap, I decide to make myself comfortable. My head feels loopy, and I'm not completely drunk, just tipsy enough to misplace my filter.

Mr. Middleton is watching me with a wary gaze as if he doesn't quite know what to make of me. It's a different look on him. He's always so confident and so sure of himself that seeing him like this is interesting.

I don't care if he throws me away after this. I'm a survivor. I've survived worse things than being tossed aside after a one-night stand. And I make no qualms about letting him know this.

His large hands are around my waist, holding me, and his grip is firm, and all I can think about is how good his hands would feel on my bare skin. I bet those hands aren't just good at pulling a trigger; I bet those big ole' hands are magic hands. I wonder how fast he can make me come with them?

I giggle to myself.

French champagne is a hell of a beverage.

I can tell that Mr. Middleton is being cautious with me right now, but it's his reluctance and my growing desire for him that makes me want to see how far I can push him.

"I really want you to fuck me."

I whisper the champagne-laced words into his ear, and my eyes close in wicked satisfaction when his hands tighten around my waist, a low growl leaving his chest,

"Megan."

"What?" I ask innocently, pulling away and looking at him.

However, I feel my smile slipping when I glimpse the heat in those smoldering eyes of his. I'm treading dangerous waters.

"You're pushing it," he says harshly, but even as he says it, I can feel his fingers digging into the side of my waist.

I shrug, leaning forward. "I want what I want."

"And what about the consequences?" he asks thickly.

This time, I brush my lips against his.

"What happens in Paris stays in Paris," I whisper, ignoring the warning bells ringing in the back of my head. "Right?"

He doesn't say anything, letting me kiss him softly.

His eyes are still open, watching me, but I don't care.

"How drunk are you?" His question has an air of finality.

I smile almost sinisterly. "Enough to know what I want, Mr. Middleton."

His jaw tightens, and he removes one hand from my

waist, running it up my spine. I shift at the sudden sensation of his touch. My lips part in a quiet gasp as his hand finds its way into my hair, and he yanks my head back roughly, forcing me to look at the ceiling, his hot mouth trailing against my neck as he whispers, "It's Hunter, not Mr. Middleton. But since you like saying it so much, you can call me Mr. Middleton when I have you under my desk at the Blue Whiskey, sucking my cock."

Wetness floods my panties as the mental imagery of me on my knees between his powerful thighs consumes my thoughts. His tongue darts out and slowly licks along a slight blue vein in my throat, and I whimper at the blatantly sexual act.

"You'd better be sure about this, Megan. You can't take this back."

My hands tighten around his neck as he licks and sucks along my jaw, leaving small bites. "It's just one night, and afterward, we don't ever have to talk about it again," I tell him.

His chuckle is both raw and holds a tinge of anger. "So you just want to use me?"

This time, he pulls down the strap of my blouse and bites down on my shoulder hard. I make a distressed moan, but his hand is still in my hair, and I can't move.

"That would be convenient for you, wouldn't it?" I ask through labored breaths.

It's difficult to keep my voice steady when he's asking me questions while simultaneously using his mouth to explore my body.

"Convenient?" His voice now has a dangerous quality to it. "And since when have you decided what is convenient for me or not?"

My fingers clench in his hair for a moment in a flash of

irritation, but when I try to look down at him, he refuses to let me move, holding my body prisoner.

"If you don't want this, you can just leave. I'm hardly putting a gun to your head." I say the brave words, fueled by champagne kisses and Parisian moonlight, but I definitely don't want him to leave.

"I see." I feel his lips curve against my neck. "So, it's my choice."

"Of course."

Hunter presses an open-mouthed kiss against my jaw. "And tonight is all I get?"

"Like I said-"

"Yes, I heard you."

He pulls down the other strap of my blouse, and I can feel the breeze on my bare cleavage. "I don't like ultimatums, Megan."

Before I can respond, a few things happen at the same time. I feel him move his arm and the sounds of dishes crashing to the ground echo in my ears. Then, he releases me and turns me around, bending me over the small dining table, my chest against the cold smooth wood, his body pressed against mine.

My heart is thudding in my chest at the sudden change in position as he bends over me, his tongue tracing the shell of my ear. "We'll do this, but on my terms."

I don't get a chance to ask him what he means because his hands are pulling down my blouse until it's bunched around my waist.

"Wait-"

"What's wrong?" He presses a kiss on my back, and my mind is fogging over with every touch. "This is what you wanted, isn't it?"

He's not wrong, but he's so overwhelming right now

that I'm feeling both confused and yet so turned on. I want him but I didn't think it would be like this.

"Yes, I mean, I don't know what to do," I stammer. "I can't see your face."

His chuckle is deep, and it holds a hint of darkness as he yanks my hair back, once again with a fistful of my hair, turning me enough to kiss my mouth, a filthy, open-mouthed kiss that has me pressing my legs together. When he pulls away, he says in a low voice, "You just have to take what I give you."

There's nothing delicate in the way he's touching me, and while I'm nervous, there's a part of it that thrills me. When his mouth descends on mine, his free hand undoes my bra so quickly that I barely register him yanking it off of me and tossing it aside.

He's a pro at this.

But he should be. He's a grown-ass man.

Quickly releasing me, he orders me to "Turn around."

The deep tones delivering the order make a shiver run down my spine, and I hesitate, feeling super nervous. I've had sex before, barely, but do I really know what I'm doing? Can I keep up with a man who has probably been with dozens, if not hundreds, of women?

"I won't ask again, Megan," Hunter murmurs in a tone that demands obedience.

He's not touching me anymore, and I slowly turn around to face him.

"Have you ever slept with a man?" He asks, watching me (and my nipples) quite intently.

It's difficult to answer that question without blushing. I seem to have lost all of my bravado when I'm standing bare-chested in front of him.

"I asked you a question."

I don't know why my knees feel so weak when he uses this particular tone.

"Once, a boy from-"

"I'm talking about men." His voice is dark as he puts his hands on both sides of me on the table, effectively caging me in. "I'm not going to make love to you, Megan. I'm going to fuck you just like you asked me to. So, I want to know if you've been fucked before."

I don't know the difference between the two, but I do know that my previous partner never made me feel... like this.

When I stare at him, he cups my breast with one hand, and my nipples pebble painfully hard at the touch. He rolls one of the nubs between his thumb and forefinger.

"Clearly not."

He pauses before suddenly pulling at my nipple and making me gasp at the sliver of pain.

"So, let me teach you a few things."

His fingers immediately soothe the aching flesh, and he lowers his head to lap it before taking it into his mouth. I can't stop the sounds from slipping out of my mouth. This rush of electricity wherever he touches my skin is driving me insane.

He lets go of my nipple with a plopping sound and then murmurs, "I'm not going to treat you like a piece of china. I'm going to break you. I'm going to fuck your mouth and then your pussy, and you're going to like it. I'm going to make sure that you don't even remember your own name when we're done."

His hand takes mine and pulls it toward his pants. "Take out my dick."

My hands are shaking with his promises, my legs rubbing against each other as I feel the dampness in my panties. I don't know what I've gotten myself into, but I can't bring myself to turn back now. I know I'm about to experience something life-changing, and I'm all for it.

What happens in Paris stays in Paris.

I fumble with his zipper and then he stops me, before taking my hand and guiding me to the armchair. He sprawls onto it first, his posture relaxed, looking every bit of the businessman that he is. His suit jacket is neatly folded and resting against the back of the armchair and the sleeves of his white shirt are rolled up.

I stand in front of him, clueless about what to do next as he studies me.

"Take off your pants."

As we toured the city today, I wore a cute spaghetti-strapped blouse with tiny pink flowers and dark blue pencil pants. I felt very Parisian in it. I slowly unzip and push the pants to the floor, feeling a little dizzy from the champagne. I almost tip over but then catch myself. Now, the only thing between me and Hunter is a pair of white lace panties.

"Fucking beautiful," he compliments me under his breath.

He continues to stare at me as I press my lips together, unsure of what to do now.

"Are you drunk, Megan?"

"No."

"Are you sure?"

"The only thing I'm sure of is that you seem hesitant about doing this. Are you afraid of me?"

He grins. "I'm just making sure I have your consent."

"I think I just gave it when I pulled down my pants just now."

He chuckles lightly. "You're a funny girl when you want to be."

"Yeah?"

"Come closer."

I step forward, standing right in between his knees, which are spread open. I can see a large bulge begging to break free between his legs, even in his loose trousers. I never considered the size of his penis before. It's probably as big and angry as the rest of him.

He unexpectedly slides two fingers between my legs to feel the crotch of my underwear. I close my eyes as everything feels sensitive down there, my clit especially.

"You're definitely wet." He rubs his length through his pants. "That means you're ready. I want to use your pretty mouth first, Megan. Get on your knees and slide down my zipper with your teeth."

When I stand there, frozen, he arches a brow. "Don't tell me you scare this easily. We haven't even started yet."

It's the mocking tone that gets to me. "I'm not scared."

"Then prove it." His burning gaze runs over me. "Put your hands behind your back, slide down my zipper, take out my dick, and put it in your mouth. Let's see if that pretty little mouth of yours knows how to give head."

His lust-filled words go straight to my pussy, and I feel them clench with want and weep from emptiness. I want to be full of Hunter Middleton by the end of this night, and I'll follow every direction he gives to get me there.

"On your knees, Megan," Hunter orders, his voice slightly bored now, as he rests the side of his face on his palm, watching me.

The man is sexy as sin, the smirk on his face making me realize that I may have started this, but he damn sure is going to finish it.

I'll do whatever he wants.

So I sink to my knees.

I'm not scared.

The large bulge that is growing in his pants is eye-catching, though, and I hesitate.

Do I even know what I'm doing?

When I lean forward, he calmly says, "Hands behind your back."

I grind my jaw and do as he says. It's not easy, but I manage to get my teeth around the small zipper, and I pull it down.

The dick that springs out is huge. It has a wide girth and the top of it is already damp with pre-cum.

"It's too big," I stammer.

Hunter smiles and reaches out to cup my chin in his palm, forcing me to look at him. "You can take it."

He rubs my lips with his thumb in a slow, caressing manner, and my lips part as I hold his gaze. When he pushes his thumb in, resting it on my tongue, I immediately begin to suck it, and the pleased expression on his face makes me shiver.

"You do know what to do, after all," he mutters as his dick begins to bob up and down on its own.

He pulls his thumb out of my mouth and then gestures towards his cock with his eyes. "Go on. Taste it."

My performance fear is slowly decreasing, and I ask cautiously, "Can I use my hands now?"

He presses his lips together as if fighting a laugh. "Yes."

Leaning forward, I grasp the base of the veiny shaft in my hands, and my tongue darts out to lick the plum-like head. When I don't hear any sound of displeasure, I take the head into my mouth and suck on it."

From the corner of my eye, I see Hunter's hand clenched on the arm of the sofa, and I feel a little empowered by that. Being able to elicit even this much of a reaction is a win for me. I start licking along the sides of the cock and then use one hand to cup his sac and fondle it lightly.

As the sex tape made of me without my permission would suggest, I've done this before, so I'm not completely without knowledge. But I've never sucked a dick like this one. I should get a medal for even trying something to swallow something so large.

Running my tongue down his fat dick, I push it towards his belly and then give his balls wet attention. This time, I get an actual groan.

He likes this.

Feeling more confident, I stroke his dick while sucking his balls, and Hunter growls under his breath.

"Suck my cock," he commands greedily. "I want to see it in your mouth."

I'm still a little unsure of myself, but I wrap my lip around the thick tip and try to swallow as much as I can. However, I can only get a small portion of it inside. It feels weird having something so big stretching my jaw.

Hunter isn't saying anything as I try to bob my head up and down. I put my hands on his thighs for support to try to lower my head down the shaft some more, but then his hand slides to the back of my head to hold me still.

"I think that's enough," he says in a harsh tone. "It's my turn now. Relax your jaw."

When his hands tighten in my hair, I do what he says, feeling a little pensive. My mouth is stuffed with him.

I nod.

He pumps his hips up slowly, and I go still, feeling his dick slide in and out of my mouth as he uses it like some hole. I can feel something wet slide down the inside of my thigh as this new sensation of utter sexual thirst ripples through me. My nails dig into his thighs, and I don't move as he uses my mouth to get himself off. But why am I getting so turned on by being used like this?

Things become so much worse (or better) when he picks up speed. The faster he goes, the more my lower belly is clenching. I can hear wanton moans ringing in the room and can't believe they're coming out of my mouth. My pussy is dripping with need, and I'm feeling both helpless and frustrated.

His face is tight as he thrusts into my willing mouth, and my eyes widen as he forces his entire shaft down my throat. "Breathe through your nose. Take it slow."

I'm gagging and trying not to, and it takes me a few seconds to push away the panic, my eyes watering. He pulls out and then plunges all the way in, his voice firm. "Your throat needs to be trained to take me. To please me. I'm being gentle right now. Flatten your tongue."

It takes a few tries for me to get a little more used to it, but I have discovered a different problem now. Every time I nearly choke on his fat dick, my clit pulses, and an orgasm starts to slowly climb down my spine like a slithering snake.

I'm nearing my own release as he fucks my mouth in steady, deep strokes, his grip on my hair holding me in place. I can't see my expression, but I feel wanton and desperate, and I want more.

Suddenly Hunter pulls out, hovering his throbbing dick just over my lips, smirking, "Look at you, Megan. You look so hungry. Do you really like sucking dick that much, or is it because it's my dick?"

I make a slight whimpering sound, my legs rubbing against each other like a cricket, my juices running down my inner thighs.

"Please," seems to be the only thing I can think to say.

I'm begging for more of him, for a release, for any damn thing that he will give me.

"So greedy," he chuckles.

He holds his stiff dick and guides it towards my lips, smearing my lips with the pre-cum. I'm not a fan of the salty taste, but I obediently lick it off my lips, looking up at him. He smiles, stroking my cheek with his other hand.

"Should I make you drink it or cover you in it?" His voice is soft and caressing, and the tone doesn't match the dirtiness of the question.

"Whatever you want, Hunter."

This is not me. This total submission. But when he looks pleased with my response, I feel a hint of gratification.

"Open your mouth and stick out your tongue."

I do so immediately.

Hunter strokes himself, and I watch, hypnotized by the precision of his movements. It doesn't take long for his face to tighten from the orgasm that hits him. I watch with rapt attention as he emits a quiet groan that escapes his lips as his come lands on my waiting tongue. I flinch in surprise but am also pleased with myself. I made him come like that.

"Suck the rest out," he growls, forcing his dick back into my mouth.

I don't hesitate, bobbing my head up and down with a little help from him. I feel the bitter liquid hit the back of my throat, and I swallow. My legs are shaking, and I carefully suck hard as I feel my own orgasm engulf me.

When I finally pull away, I'm trembling.

Hunter's hand is stroking my head now, his voice oddly gentle. "You all right?"

I nod, feeling both shaky and satisfied.

"Do you still want to go on?"

"Yes."

Chapter 24

Stay On Your Knees

MEGAN

My voice is hoarse, and my throat feels deliciously raw from the way he just fucked it. He studies me as if not quite believing me, but then a slow smile forms on his lips.

"Stay on your knees," he orders.

I watch him from the floor as he stands and slowly unbuttons his shirt, folds it, and places it on the back of the chair. The same goes for his pants and boxer briefs.

I'm in awe. Hunter Middleton is a beautiful specimen of a man. He doesn't have one ounce of body fat. His waist is shredded. His chest and arms are defined but not bulky. He is perfect and would be the ideal nude model for a painting class.

A girl can dream.

He sits back down in the chair and pats one of the arms with his hand. "Climb up. Knees on the armrests."

Suddenly, our positions are reversed. I'm high up on my

knees, my pussy directly in front of his face, just where he wants it.

"You're dripping wet," he growls, and I whine when he runs a finger over my slit. "You're like a fucking tap. I wonder if you can come for me like that again."

When I don't answer because I don't think I'm supposed to, he easily slides one of his thick fingers into my pussy, and I gasp.

"I think you can," he says, sounding wickedly delighted. "You came from sucking me off, so I can only imagine how you'll respond when I fuck you with my tongue."

I don't get the opportunity to say anything in response because he presses down on my clit hard, and I nearly scream. I'm still reeling from my previous orgasm, and as I shudder, I feel him using two fingers to spread me apart for his mouth.

"Oh, my God." My eyes roll up in my head as a wet appendage forces its way inside of me.

I've never had my pussy eaten. None of my previous boyfriends were interested in that, although it's not like I pressed the matter. They didn't offer, and I didn't ask.

But right now, Hunter has his face in the most sensitive part of me, his tongue flicking my clit back and forth as he alternates between that and pushing it in and out of my pussy. The sensation of being eaten out is overwhelming. I never realized what I was missing.

"Hunter," I moan in exquisite pleasure, wondering why people aren't doing this lewd act all day, every day. I would rather be doing this than eating, sleeping, or painting any day of the week.

His hands are holding onto my ass, and when I try to move, he pulls one of my thighs over his shoulder without breaking momentum, giving him open access to me.

"Please," I plead with him as he brutally fucks me with his tongue, moving in and out at a steady pace. I can't think, the pleasure blinding me. I can hear someone sobbing, but all I can see is white heat.

Is that me begging for mercy?

The sensation of Hunter piercing me with his tongue as he licks and curls it inside of me is driving me insane. I fall forward, my hands against the wall behind the chair, as I grind my pussy against his face. I've never done this before, but it almost comes second nature to me.

Fuck his mouth, Megan.

Fuck it good.

I cry out his name as I beg him to stop, go on, go faster, and slow down. Nothing makes sense as he drags orgasm after orgasm from me. My moans are long and drawn out, and just when I think I can't come again, ever, he pinches my clit, making me come one final time. "Fuck!!!"

This time I go limp, my legs feeling weak, and he pulls away, patting my butt. He gently unhooks my leg from his neck and peels my floppy body away from his.

"On your knees."

I sit back on the floor of the hotel room on my knees, still reeling from the force of my last orgasm. I watch as he opens a bottle of Evian water and pours it into two crystal glasses. He drinks his entire glass in one shot, then hands me mine.

"Drink."

My entire body is flushed with heat, and the water feels good going down my sore throat. When I'm finished, he takes the glass and sets it down.

"You look so beautiful when you come, Megan. Prettier than any picture you could ever sketch. I want to see more."

He picks me up and carries me to the bedroom. "We are far from finished."

I doubt I can come another time.

But that assumption about my body is put to the test when he tosses me onto the bed and pulls me toward him by my knees, and flips me over. I'm still trying to get my bearings when I feel him come up behind me, and his hand rubs me between my legs and over my pussy.

It just takes one touch from the man to get me wet all over again, and I let out a needy sound when he sticks those two fat fingers back inside me.

"H-Hunter!"

He chuckles and pumps his thick digits in and out of me, and I clench the bedsheets and raise my hips higher every time he thrusts into my hole.

"I already warned you," his voice is low and husky, making me arch my back. "I'm going to have you all night."

"Please," I look over my shoulder, begging him. "Just put it in!"

"Put what in?" He asks idly, inserting another finger inside of me, and a short cry escapes my lips.

"Your dick! fuck me, already!" I howl, wanting more, my body needing the real thing.

I hear a soft laugh, and when I look into the wall mirror in front of him, I see the hunger in his eyes.

"Since you asked so nicely."

He pulls his fingers out of my pussy and then offers them to me, "Clean them."

When I don't obey fast enough, his hand comes cracking down on my ass. The sudden pain makes my eyes turn wide, and he repeats the request.

"Suck my fingers like you just sucked my cock. If I have to ask again, I won't be happy."

My mouth parts, and I clean my juices off his fingers. His eyes are twinkling with satisfaction, and I wonder why I am enjoying this. Every time he talks to me like this, I want his approval. This feeling of wanting to please someone, to please a man, is so foreign to me that it terrifies me.

"Good girl." He caresses my ass lovingly. "So, you know when to not talk back to me."

I can't reply because I'm obediently sucking his fingers.

"Maybe next time you try to fight me on something or run your mouth off at me in the office, I should feed you my cock," he muses. "I think you like it."

I moan at his naughty words.

"You'd like that, wouldn't you, Megan?" He whispers against my skin as he presses a kiss in the middle of my back. "Maybe when I've had a stressful day, I'll call you into my office and have you get on your knees and fuck me with your mouth under my desk."

His fingers, on one hand, muffle my answer, and he thrusts two fingers from the other harder into my pussy, which is drenched now.

"You'll stay there for hours, and I bet you'd like it. People partying on the club floor while my dick is in your mouth. How does that sound?"

What is he doing to me? I wonder, dazedly. Why do I find that idea so appealing? Why do I pray that he makes that fantasy come true?

"Maybe we take a risk and keep the door unlocked. Who knows who might walk in and see you on your knees, ass up, sucking me dry."

My mind is growing blank. All I can think and feel is Hunter Middleton. All I want is him in Paris... and after Paris.

He removes his fingers from my mouth, and I lie there,

my cheek resting against the bed, feeling hollow. I dimly hear something tear, and then I feel his fingers slide easily out of my pussy, only to be replaced by something harder, something bigger, something hot.

I howl as he thrusts halfway inside me. He doesn't let me get used to his size, but it doesn't hurt much since I'm so wet. I try to hold on to the headboard, but he grabs both my hands, pulling them behind my back as he uses them to control his pace.

"Hunter!" I beg with a sob, his name the only thing I know for sure.

I feel so full right now as he pushes himself in and out of me, scraping against my inner walls, using my pussy as he pleases like it's just another hole to him. The dirty thought of how he's using me makes my pussy tightly contract, and I scream when I come.

"I knew you could come again," he snarls, increasing his pace.

I sob and try to twist away from him and closer to him, lost, wanting more. I hear him groan when he comes, and I mewl his name out with a hoarse sound, coming once again.

My body is limp when I collapse on the bed. I feel so deliciously used, the after-effects of the orgasm running through me. He lays next to me, a little out of breath as well, but he's smirking when I look at him.

"I hope you're not planning on sleeping." He runs his hand along my spine before spanking my ass lightly. "I'm not done yet."

My eyes widen.

It's the sun hitting my eyes, which makes me stir. I groan and huddle into the sheets, my whole body aching. I've just pulled the blankets over my head when I hear the sound of the door opening.

"We have to be at the hangar in six hours, Megan," comes a familiar voice, and I feel the person sitting down next to me. "We still have some things left to see on your itinerary before we leave."

"I'm so tired," I moan. "You're a monster."

I hear a chuckle. "Get up."

"I don't want to." I burrow myself into the blankets.

There's a long silence, and then the voice has a suggestive tone to it. "I can always join you."

"No!" I sit up straight, my sore vagina horrified by the very idea and coming face-to-face with my boss.

"If you touch me again, Mr. Middleton-"

"Hunter," he corrects, his eyes laughing at me. "We're *still* not at work."

I take a deep breath. "If you touch me, Hunter, I will throw the first thing I can find at you. Everything hurts!"

Of course, I'm messing with him because my body isn't in terrible pain but rather is suffering from an all-over delicious ache. However, my response elicits a look of concern on his face.

"Was I too rough? Should I take you to a doctor?"

"No," I lean forward, resting my head on his shoulder and closing my eyes. "I need painkillers, coffee, and a massage– not a doctor."

His quiet laughter vibrates through his body. "Well, if that's all, that can be easily arranged, but you have to get out of bed first. Go take a shower. You'll feel a little better."

Complaining under my breath, I climb out of bed, not caring about my nakedness. After all the positions this man put me in last night, letting him see me naked is not a problem anymore. The modesty ship has sailed. He's seen more of me than my gynecologist.

I'm about to enter the bathroom when I hear him say, his voice thoughtful, "I don't know why I thought that you would be a little shy this morning or that you might want to avoid me."

I look over my shoulder at him. "What happened last night was my choice, and I started it. Wrong or right, I know how to take responsibility for my own actions. I don't blame you. I was drunk, but not that drunk."

He stares hungrily at my bare ass, and I walk into the bathroom, locking the door behind me.

Staring at my naked body in the mirror, I see the marks left all over my body, courtesy of Hunter's mouth and hands. I refuse to feel ashamed because I'm not. I had the best sex of my life, and I'll never forget it. The only thing to do at this point is to enjoy the next six hours in Paris, and when we land in Los Angeles, Hunter will become Mr. Middleton once again.

My dangerous boss.

My smile is forced as I look at myself in the mirror. "Keep it together, Megan. You knew what you were doing. If you want to keep your job, you're going to get your shit together and not treat this like it's anything more than just a one-night stand. It could never be anything more."

As long as I keep it professional, Mr. Middleton has no reason to fire me and I'll get to cherish the memory of this one weekend with a handsome man in the most romantic city in the world.

The hot shower does help some, and when I come out, there's a cup of coffee waiting for me from the cafe downstairs. Hunter is reading an American newspaper, already dressed in a casual dress shirt and pants that probably cost him my entire year's salary.

"I booked you a massage after we eat," he turns the page of the newspaper.

"Oh," I wince as I sit down. "My butt."

He looks over the top of the newspaper to study me. "I've never heard a woman complain so much after sleeping with me."

I glare at him, picking up my coffee. "How would you know? I doubt you keep them around long enough to find out."

"That's true."

His two-word answer reminds me that this was a one-time thing. Casual is what he does.

Wake up, Cinderella.

"Where's my ibuprofen?" I get up and shuffle toward my bag. "Oh fuck, my back."

"Maybe we should get you that massage first," he offers, clearly pleased with his bed acrobatics.

An hour later, I'm lying on a comfortable massage table with a woman named Francine, giving me the first massage I've ever had in my life. She's releasing knots in my muscles that I didn't even know existed. I enjoy listening to her chatter in French about her methodology as I doze off, pleasantly content.

"I forgive you," I tell Hunter when I walk into the café next door after my massage, where he's been waiting for me.

He raises a brow. "I'm sure, however, some context would be nice."

"For nearly breaking my back," I sink into the seat across from him, beaming.

He gives me an amused look. "You do know that every time you say that, you're giving me a compliment?"

I shrug, feeling all loose and fluid again. "Francine fixed every part of me. I feel like a new woman. Your feelings are insignificant to me right now. I have been reborn."

I add the last part with a dramatic gesture to myself, and Hunter's lips quirk up. "Good to know. Order some breakfast now, or at this point, I guess it's lunch. I was waiting for you."

"You waited?" I give him a surprised look. "I was in there for over an hour."

He doesn't respond, sipping his coffee, unaffected. "This place has a very nice selection of pastries. Your roommate likes croissants, doesn't she? You should get a dozen to bring home."

I blink at him. "What?"

"And get some souvenirs, too," he adds. "For both of you."

It takes me a long minute to digest his words, and I repeat my question loudly in an attempt to get clarification. "What?"

"Did Francine damage your hearing?"

"No – I mean," I stare at him. "Why do you want me to get souvenirs?"

"You went to Paris. You should be able to brag about it. You walked into the most famous art galleries in the world. You should have something to remember from your trip."

For a moment, I feel like he's patting himself on the back for taking the poor girl to Paris, but then I realize that isn't it at all. I sink back into the bistro chair and look at him. "Can I ask you something?"

"What is it?" He's looking through the newspaper that he brought down from the apartment.

"Why did you really bring me here?"

He pauses and then sets the paper down. "I'm not quite

sure, Megan, but I don't regret this trip, and I hope you don't either."

"Do you have business in Paris?"

"Sometimes."

"Can I ask you another question?"

"Go ahead."

"If you have the money to fly us privately to Paris and fast-track us through the galleries like you're some kind of VIP, why did you open a club in one of the riskiest areas of the city?"

"That's a complicated question."

"So, what's your answer?"

"I serve a particular clientele, and they like it there. Just because I'm wealthy doesn't mean I only want to accommodate wealthy people."

"Sort of like you never want to forget where you come from?"

"Something like that."

"Last question."

"I'm waiting."

"Have you ever taken a date to Paris before?"

I can't quite read the look on his face right now. Normally, Hunter is painfully honest, but he's hesitating as if he doesn't want to hurt my feelings. I don't even know why I asked the question. Of course, he's taken women here before.

"Forget it," I say abruptly. "I shouldn't have asked."

"Was this a date, Megan?" He asks, repeating the word I used in my question. His face is unreadable.

I swallow the tears inside of me down my throat like a bitter pill. I can't show any emotion. The very definition of a one-night stand is that it happens one time. That's what adults do. Being emotional about his response would only reinforce what he's thinking anyway, that I'm some immature college kid who doesn't know her ass from her elbow.

"Absolutely not."

"Right, so let's not overanalyze a good time to death." He gives me a quiet smile. "Just enjoy yourself."

His words aren't harsh, but they aren't exactly what I wanted to hear, either. In fact, I guess they were the glass of cold water that I needed to wake up from this Parisian fantasy. At the end of the day, Hunter Middleton is not my lover or my boyfriend– he is my boss. I can't look at him and see potential because there is none.

I can never forget that even if for some reason he favors me, and is attracted to me, Hunter Middleton is a dangerous man and there's a reason for everything he does. He admitted it himself. There's a part of him who's a monster.

A big part.

Picking me to be the manager of the Blue Whiskey was not because he thought I was up to the task but because I was the only one who would even dare step up after firing that wacko, Steve. I'm not exceptional.

Taking me to Paris was a kind gesture to flaunt his wealth and his cache, and it may or may not have been an opportunity he used to sleep with me. I'm not special.

I may not know all of his business dealings, but I know that he's a man who can shoot a man without any qualms and walk away from it. I'm not fucking crazy. I should just do a good job at managing his club and expect nothing more. It's really the best offer a girl like me could hope for and the safest option, too.

The man sitting before me now, with the kind grey eyes, is not the man who was sitting at Table 21 a month ago. In Paris, he's a man who's quiet yet kind, domineering yet gentle, a giver and a receiver in bed, and I'm going to leave that man behind in Paris.

He's not real.

He's a warm, wet dream.

"What're you thinking about with that look on your face?" he asks, retaking a sip of his coffee.

I smile at him, feeling a slight twinge in my chest. "Nothing important, just marveling at how strange life can be."

"Is it strange?" he questions, watching me.

I look around at the busy roadside café and try to memorize everything I see to never forget it. This is a city I want to keep with me for a lifetime. It's just the feelings I want to forget.

"Let's go get those croissants," I say softly, not looking at him any longer.

Hours later, when we're settled on the plane home, and I watch him working on his laptop, I realize that Mr. Middleton is back and our trip is behind us.

I take out my sketchpad and draw a beautiful café alongside a cobbled street, with a couple sitting there. I don't sketch the girl's face, but just a silhouette of her back and relaxed shoulders. Her body language says it all. She's happy. But the man, his eyes, when he looks at that woman, reflect a quiet passion and kindness. It's important that I sketch the man's face in detail so I can remember him.

The man I left in Paris.

Because there's no monster in this picture.

Chapter 25

Art Appreciation Day

HUNTER

"You look better," Vaughn comments from the sofa as I enter my home.

I narrow my eyes at him. "Why are you still here? I thought I changed the code to the keypad lock."

He shrugs, turning his attention back to the movie playing on the screen. "I already know all the possible password combinations you'd use. Only took me five minutes to break in."

I place my suitcase against the door, muttering, "Of course you did."

Vaughn turns off the television and studies me. "Steve's dead."

My vacation from reality with Megan is over. For a few moments in time, it was wonderful not to have to think about all the messy shit in my life.

"Did Parker do it?"

"It wasn't Parker." His tone is grim, and I go still. "And it wasn't Lars."

"What the hell do you mean, it wasn't them? Did Steve kill himself?"

Vaughn shakes his head. "This happened just a few hours ago. Lars had to make a run, and Parker was taking a break, so I was the only one outside the room when the fire alarm went off. At the same time, I received a notification from the alarm on your office door. Somebody was trying to break in. By the time we realized that someone had just pulled the alarm to keep us distracted, it was too late. All the security footage had been wiped, and Steve's throat was slit."

"And you're sitting here on your ass watching movies? Why didn't you call me right away?" My voice is stern as I step towards him.

"There was no point," he replies calmly. "I just got back myself. All the staff were interviewed. All the customers were drunk, of course. Nobody saw anything."

"Who breached the security room?"

"No one. Both guards were sitting there. The monitors just turned black. Based on how quickly it happened, I suspect a cyber-attack. I just sent all the staff home and was waiting for you."

"I should have stayed here!" I growl, furious with myself, but Vaughn cuts me off.

"No, you needed a break, and it looks like you got a nice one."

I think about Megan for a moment, and an unfamiliar warmth fills my chest.

"It was relaxing," I admit.

"Good," Vaughn smiles. "Listen, we weren't prepared for this because we weren't expecting somebody to attack the club. It's neutral ground. It's a fucking death wish to come at you like this."

I sink into my favorite armchair. "What about Steve? Did we get anything useful out of him?" "Actually, yes." Vaughn looks pleased. "His death wasn't a complete loss, and let's be real. They couldn't keep him alive forever."

The new doctor I have on the payroll since my old one was dumped in the alley basically said as much before I left for Paris.

"According to him," Vaughn continues, "it seems that Johnathan hasn't met the girl he's looking for. Steve overheard him talking to a private detective about finding her, but she was in LA somewhere. Also, Johnathan is working either with or for someone, which explains a lot if he's responsible for pulling something like this off at the club. He isn't smart enough to have done this by himself."

"But why did he come back?" I comment, leaning back against the chair and studying the ceiling. "He stole from me, and I let him live."

"Yeah, it's confusing how you decide whom you're going to annihilate on any given day."

I ignore Vaughn's snide comment and try to work out this situation in my head.

"I assumed he was on the other side of the world spending my money, but he's returned? He had to know that if he came back here, I'd want him dead. He may not be a criminal mastermind, but he's smart enough to know not to come back here without a plan or without muscle."

"Right now, you're at the top of the food chain in LA. If you're removed, there's a large gap that needs to be filled almost immediately. Johnathan knows this, and he might be aiming for that."

I'm quiet for a moment, thinking over his words. "Did you take care of Steve's body?"

"Lars handled it."

Lars is meticulous about these things, so I feel better now.

"I think I should have a word with Nick tomorrow. Get in touch with him and tell him to come to my office at noon."

Vaughn glares at me. "I'm not your secretary, you know. I have my own company to run."

"Considering you're up under my ass lately, you can at least make yourself useful. Hasn't the whole thing with Shelly been resolved?"

My friend's expression turns dark. "Well, it's funny you asked. I haven't heard from her in a few days since she kicked me out. I'm starting to worry."

"I can't believe you let her kick you out of your own house," I say in disgust. "That's your house. If she wants to leave, she should be the one walking out." I shake my head. "And now you're worried."

Vaughn is quiet, and then he sighs heavily. "I don't know what I'll do if I find out she's cheating on me. I don't think I can take that."

I don't say anything because I'm not really sure what to say. Out of the few friends I have, Vaughn is the one with the softest heart. His hands are not clean by any means, but unlike me, he has some shred of humanity left in him.

"Christian is coming back tomorrow," he adds. "He wants to see you. His apartment is getting repaired, so he said he'll crash here."

"Fantastic," I mutter. "Fucking fantastic. We'll pop popcorn, eat Twizzlers, and make a fucking slumber party out of it."

"I could do with some junk food," Vaughn jokes. "You know, if you take the stick out of your ass every once in a while, it might be easier for you to breathe."

"Maybe I should just shoot you and solve all of Shelly's problems," I say darkly, but Vaughn just ignores me.

"So, do you ever plan on talking about how you just took that hot little bartender with you to Paris?" He grins. "It's not like you to whisk a woman away for a romantic weekend."

My eyes narrow at his description of Megan. "She's not just some random hot bartender; she's a manager at the Blue Whiskey and deserves your respect."

"Ohhh," he exaggerates his tone, simultaneously chuckling. "My bad."

"And it wasn't a romantic getaway."

"Then what was it?"

"None of your fucking business, that's what." I kick his legs, which are resting on my coffee table, off of it and make my way to the bedroom. "And stop breaking into my house. I'm changing the entry code again tonight. You won't guess this one."

He ignores my threats.

"Maybe I should just visit the studio and tell Nick in person that you want to have a word with him. I might see Shelly there."

Vaughn then turns on the television, and I scowl at the door. "Whatever, man."

I don't tolerate people easily, but there are a few who have stood by me for years and have proven their loyalty over and over again. Both of my friends, Vaughn and Christian, come from different backgrounds than me. Vaughn grew up on a pumpkin farm up in Seattle, which was lost during a property dispute with another family member. Christian comes from a wealthy family who has turned their backs on him for many reasons I have yet to fully understand.

I met each of them separately over a decade ago when I offered them help to deal with their personal difficulties. In return, they paid me back in kind. They are two of my most trusted friends. I would almost call them family, which is why I want to murder at least one of them once a day.

As I unpack my suitcase, I pull out the framed sketch that Megan gave me. I know that she's only a floor below me right now, but for some reason, she seems very far away. I stare at it and reflect on our time together. The trip was impulsive, and I hadn't expected to enjoy it so much. I didn't anticipate anything that happened between us. The side of Megan that I saw isn't something I'll be able to forget. She looked and acted like a completely different person.

Happiness suits her, I muse.

When was the last time I was this comfortable and at ease with a woman? When was the last time that someone looked at me without a trace of fear in their eyes? When was the last time I had a woman in my life who didn't want something from me?

Megan made me feel almost human, and then she let me drown in her. I feel my dick harden at the memory of her bouncing on top of it, begging me for more, screaming my name. I've had plenty of women in my life. The sex has always been satisfying, but with Megan, it was much more so.

God, I crave the taste of her.

But that was yesterday, and this is today–the real world. Now that she's back in her own space and hopefully out of my system, I don't have anything distracting me.

I should throw this away, I tell myself, looking down at the framed sketch. I have far more priceless paintings in all of my offices. Collecting art is a pastime reserved for the types of people who have that kind of money to blow. When I purchase them, it's all about the look for me. It tells people that I'm a powerful player and that I've got money to burn. I never much cared what kind of art it was. Half of the time, I don't even know the names of the artists.

And yet, I find myself hesitating when it comes to this piece. The look on Megan's face when she handed this sketch to me makes me falter.

I glance around my room and see a small painting of the French Riviera I purchased at an auction a few years ago. It cost me a few thousand dollars, and it's been hanging in my bedroom ever since. Without hesitation, I work diligently to remove the painting from the frame and carefully replace it with Megan's sketch.

It looks good up there.

I wasn't lying when I told Megan she had skills. It's obvious to the naked eye that she has talent.

'I'm going to make something of myself!'

Her fierce words resonate within me, and a small smile curves my lips as I speak to the empty room, "I can't wait to see that day."

Putting away my clothes, I step in to take a shower and wash away any remaining remnants of our Parisian holiday.

Unfortunately, I still have work to do.

Chapter 26

Vengeance Plan For Two

HUNTER

The monthly Zoom board meeting with the shareholders of the Middleton Financial Group goes relatively well and once the quarterly goals are discussed and negotiated, our virtual connection ends, leaving behind only Vaughn and me in my office in the club.

I relax and unbutton my suit jacket. "Did you reach out to Nick?"

Vaughn yawns and gets up to prepare a cup of coffee for himself. "Yeah, I dropped by there on my way here and ran into Shelly."

I scowl into my cup of coffee, not wanting to hear of Vaughn's long, drawn-out drama with his wife.

"So, she's alive?" I ask sarcastically.

"Yeah, and she was surprisingly nice to me," Vaughn comments, his voice thoughtful. "She told me that we should have lunch tomorrow."

Shelly Parson is a bitch through and through. The only

time I've ever known her to be nice to Vaughn is when she wants something. Usually, Vaughn is a sharp man, but when it comes to his wife, he's blind as a fucking bat.

"You can't be this stupid," I tell him. "Lunch with her?"

He just scowls at me, walking over with a coffee and sprawling into his seat.

"Maybe she's had a change of heart."

"The devil doesn't have a heart," I remind him lightly.

Our conversation is interrupted when there's a knock on the door. "Mr. Middleton, there's a Mr. Nick who is here to see you."

Vaughn and I exchange a look before we get up.

Mr. Nick always has a fidgety look about him, and no one would ever suspect that he runs one of the most successful Hollywood studios in the country. Normally, somebody like him would never have come under my radar, but three years ago it was he who approached me to help him out with a problem, and once you associate yourself professionally with me, you can never get rid of that link.

"How can I help you, Mr. Middleton?" Nick leans forward in his seat, cautiously eager to hear why he's been summoned.

"I'm looking for a girl," I study him. "Ashy blonde hair and an old scar on her right inner wrist."

"Ah, may I ask why?"

I give him a pleasant smile. "No, you may not."

He looks both puzzled and a little nervous as he glances toward Vaughn, then back to me. "How am I supposed to find a girl like that? Have you tried a private detective?"

"If I needed suggestions, I wouldn't turn to you," I say coldly. "Approach your casting crew and tell them you're finding a girl with that description. Make something up about why. The girl should be eighteen."

Nick rubs his hands on his thighs, looking agitated. "You know I don't like getting involved in these sorts of things."

"That's interesting," I smile lightly. "From what I remember, you have a thing for young girls."

"Not like that."

"You were also the one who approached me to handle your business partner. You didn't seem to have a problem with my help back then. Now, I'm asking you to return the favor."

I can see the sweat beading on Nick's forehead. "I know, but I'm a changed man. If you just tell me what you want her for so that I don't feel guilty for putting her in harm's way."

I give him a long look, not knowing whether to feel impressed by the man's courage or disappointed in his stupidity.

"Mr. Nick," I steeple my fingers together on my lap, leaning back in my seat. "I told you back then how things work. If you ask for my help, then you are to make your resources available to me whenever I require it, as long as I don't harm your place of business or your profits. Your morals are your problem, not mine. You knew exactly what you were doing when you agreed to my help."

The man's face is turning white as a sheet and I wait for a response. "If–" his voice is unsteady. "If you can, just give me an assurance that you won't harm the girl."

"You're forgetting your place," I say icily. "I don't have to make assurances of any kind. If you refuse to help me, it's very easy for me to crush your little studio and all of your business investments. I have enough dirt on you to put you right back where I found you."

The defeat in his eyes is satisfying. "Okay. Fine. I'll help."

He stands up, his shoulders slumped. "It's like looking for a needle in a haystack, and it'll take a few weeks, but I'll keep you updated if I find anything."

After he leaves, Vaughn asks, "You think he's going to flake out?"

"No, that studio is precious to him. If he was willing to bend his so-called morals to ask me to dispose of his biggest competitor, he's not going to have a problem now."

I turn to look at Vaughn. "Did the security footage from across the road capture anything?"

He shakes his head. "I was reviewing it this morning. People are leaving, but nobody who catches my attention in particular."

"Conduct deep background checks on all the staff," I tell him grimly.

Vaughn sits up, his expression alert. "You want me to do it?"

"I want an external investigation. I find it hard to believe that a customer would be able to get in and out of the basement so quickly not unless they had help."

"Inside help," Vaughn adds, his expression heavy. "I'll run facial recognition software over the video. I need a list of your regulars as well. Could be staff or somebody who's in and out of the club regularly."

"You can talk to Megan," I tell him. "She seems to know mostly everybody who comes in."

Vaughn runs an information brokerage company. His services are used widely, and he's made a name for himself. Despite his easygoing demeanor, he's not someone to be taken lightly. I typically use in-house resources to gather information on potential clients, but shit has just gotten real, and now I need to use someone I can trust 100%. Vaughn can be a dangerous opponent if crossed. After all, information is the most dangerous of all weapons.

"I've got access to traffic cams all around the city. So far, I haven't seen a glimpse of Johnathan, but then, with all that money, he could have gotten surgery to alter his features. That's what I would've done."

"Check into the deaths of any prominent or small-level plastic surgeons, starting from the day he ran," I say. "If he used one, he's not stupid enough to have left them alive."

Vaughn nods, "Got it."

When he doesn't leave, I stare at him. "What else?"

"So, who is she? This girl we're looking for."

My fingers tap on my desk, and after a long silence, I say quietly, "My younger sister. There's a possibility she survived the fire fifteen years ago that I thought killed her."

Vaughn's eyes widen, but he doesn't say anything else. He's not that stupid. Instead, he gets up to leave. He makes his way to the door before pausing and looking over his shoulder. "What're you going to do if it is your sister?"

"Bring her home."

I'm not surprised by his question. After all, my reputation as a heartless monster precedes me. The people closest to me know that rather than having a weakness, I'd rather eliminate it altogether. It's why I've never had a serious relationship like Vaughn does.

I get up and walk over to the large window, and look outside at the busy Los Angeles traffic. From this floor, the cars passing by look almost like tiny Matchbox cars. As I take in the sight of them, my eyes are unfocused.

It wasn't easy to be raised in the streets. My father abandoned us after my sister's birth. I was old enough at that time to still remember his face, even now. The bastard took every cent my mother saved up and left us while she was in the hospital, leaving us broke and homeless (although it wasn't like we were well off before then.)

I tried my best to take care of them, but I was young and had few resources, and ultimately made the biggest mistake of my life, a mistake that cost me them. I became a runner for a small-scale gang in my area which was part of a larger crime organization. They gave me good money, which allowed me to put a roof over my family's head, but the good times were short-lived. I was framed for a local murder I didn't commit, and the gang decided to torch my house to teach me a lesson. It was only later they discovered I was innocent. But it had been too late.

So I waited.

I waited for years until I had the money and the power to hunt them down one by one and murder them in the most vicious manner possible. It hadn't brought my mother and sister back, but wiping out that entire gang with such meticulous precision and watching them cower in fear, not knowing when I would strike next, had been satisfying.

I close my eyes in regret. I should have kept at least one of them alive. Maybe I'd know the truth about my sister if I had.

With a sigh, I open my eyes and see the hard glint in my eyes reflected in the window's glass. It will be challenging to weed her out, but if it is truly her, then I have enough resources to scour the entirety of LA with a fine-tooth comb. It's just going to take some time.

The same goes for Johnathan.

There is nowhere he can hide from me. I just have to be patient. I might have let him off easy for stealing from me because of our history, but attempting to find my sister and use her against me is unforgivable. I'll make him pay in blood for even entertaining that thought.

I will have my vengeance.

Glancing down at my watch, I check the time, and a cold smile settles on my lips. I have to settle another score in the meantime. I recall Megan's words.

I'm going to make something of myself, and they'll regret looking down on me!

I take the elevator into the garage, where Parker and Lars are waiting for me. It's time to give my fierce-eyed kitten a little vengeance of her own.

Chapter 27

I Need An Explanation

HUNTER

"Mr. Middleton, what brings you here today?"

The man sitting behind the desk jumps to his feet at attention when I stroll into his impressive-looking collegiate office.

"Mr. Darwin," I greet him before sitting down without invitation on the luxurious leather couch that you'd typically find in the law firm's office, Lars and Parker, standing behind me. "Do I need to have a reason to visit State Arts College? I am, after all, one of your biggest donors. Is this a new couch?"

John Darwin, the Dean of State Arts College, looks like he's seconds away from passing out.

"I – I wasn't implying that you're not welcome here, of course!" he stammers, dabbing his dewy-looking forehead with a handkerchief that appears in his hand like magic. "I'm just... I mean, you hardly take any interest in... what I'm saying is I meant no disrespect."

The last part is added hastily when I narrow my eyes at

him. When he finally shuts up, I say casually, "Yes, well, I decided to visit the institute I keep throwing my money at."

"Of course."

"Parker, please go get me the Head of the Accounting department. After seeing this couch, I want to see where my money is being spent. I'm not sure five-figure redecorating expenses were in the budget."

As Parker nods and leaves, Mr. Darwin looks terrified. "Sir?"

I give him a pleasant smile. "I'm sure that's not a problem, is it? After all, I should know where my money is going, and it's annoying waiting on those quarterly statements you send over. I'm more of an instant gratification kind of guy."

I can already tell from the fear oozing out of his pores that payment for this couch didn't come from his own pocket. However, I'm not here to pick on the small things. Today, I'm here to tackle a big fish.

"I heard there's a student gallery showing in two weeks," I continue when he just gives me a strangled look. "I'm sure you won't mind me seeing the pieces that have been selected to be displayed."

Mr. Darwin is desperate to get me out of his office, and he quickly darts towards the door. "Of course, we are so proud of this year's selections. They were created by some of the most talented students that the college has ever seen. Right this way!"

He's half shouting with excitement, and I sneer. Does he think that I'll overlook the liberties he's taken with my money if he tries to show off the progress of a few students? However, I'm here for a specific purpose, and I don't care what happens to the money that I invest in this college. It's just to support my image as a philanthropist in the eyes of the world.

I follow after him, strolling at a leisurely pace, my hands in my pant pockets with Lars following a few steps behind. The room he brings me to is a large art space that seems to be only used for sorting and mounting artwork. There are some select pieces already displayed on the walls, while there is a heap of what looks like some new ones on a table.

"This is what we're putting on display," He gestures toward the artwork displayed on the wall. I take a cursory glance at it.

They're fine, nothing spectacular.

A few of the pieces are eye-catching, but my eyes wander toward the signatures of the artists. As expected, I don't see Megan's anywhere.

My smile grows colder.

Mr. Darwin takes my silence as encouragement to continue. "What's unique about our university is that all pieces at our gallery showings are for sale. The students get a percentage of the proceeds from their work, but what's also exciting is that we give the student who sells the most pieces an opportunity to produce three pieces for sale in a very popular upcoming commercial art exhibition in New York. Their work will be displayed alongside some very prominent names in the art world, and they will also get a piece written about them in the arts section of The New York Times. As you can imagine, our students are vying for this honor."

The anger inside me grows at his words as I'm realizing that the opportunity stolen from Megan is clearly far more precious than she had let me know.

"I see," I say softly. "And what were the selection criteria?"

Mr. Darwin is babbling on, but I tune him out, my attention turning to the heap of artwork that has clearly been tossed aside in a careless manner like trash. What kind of professors have no regard for their students' hard work?

I walk over and go through the pile. My hand stops when I see a familiar charcoal sketch. I pick up the paper from the pile and stare down at the signature on it. Mr. Darwin hasn't noticed what I'm doing, and he is still prattling on. I look through the pile and find four more works with the familiar, neat little signature at the bottom.

I'm no art expert, but it's clear that Megan has a unique and exquisite touch to her work. Her strokes are broad and clean. And I notice how she captures small details well as I study a painting of a red-haired woman with her back towards the painter, as she sits on a beach, the sky depicting dusk. The emotions of loneliness and longing are captured so eloquently that I can see Megan's potential. She's truly gifted.

"Mr. Middleton?" The hesitant voice of the dean makes me look up. "Those are the rejected works," he explains carefully.

"I'm aware," I respond, picking up one of Megan's paintings and holding it against a mediocre-looking sketch hung on the wall. "I'm just wondering if the professors you hire are so incompetent that they can't differentiate between something of quality and something that looks like a ten-year-old did it."

Mr. Darwin's face pales. "Sir?"

"You have eyes, don't you?" I glance at him. "Tell me which one is better." I gesture towards the one with the name Ashley scrawled at the bottom.

I remember the name of the girl.

Mr. Darwin looks a little puzzled now, and it's a point in his favor when he studies the two paintings side by side and then says, "This one is better, without a doubt."

"Then, I'll ask again." I meet his gaze. "How competent are your hires?"

His face flushes. "I'm sure there must have been a reason behind this. The staff here is composed of highly accomplished professionals. Maybe they saw something we can't."

"I'd love to know what it is," I say coolly. "Why don't you call over the person responsible for choosing the artwork? Maybe he or she could educate me."

Mr. Darwin clears his throat and says in an obvious attempt to protect his staff, "I don't think that's—"

"Mr. Darwin," I interrupt, still studying the crappy artwork on the wall. "I don't think you realize just how many prestigious universities are looking for donations in these difficult times. I could easily change my decision to support this program of yours, but trust and believe that if I decide to withdraw my sponsorship, I will also demand a full-fledged investigation into how my funds were utilized. Speaking of my funds, I wonder what's taking Parker and your accountant so long?"

"You can't do that,' Mr. Darwin gasps, the reality of the situation hitting him. 'I mean, the university really values your contribution, Mr. Middleton."

"Make this easier on all of us and call the instructor in charge." I give him a cold smile. "You've got five minutes."

Chapter 28

Gotta Rattle A Few Cages

HUNTER

The instructor is a short, stocky woman with an outdated haircut who arrives within a few minutes of me making my threat. She looks wary as she looks between me and the dean, her eyes zeroing in on my face for a few seconds as if she finds me familiar.

"Mr. Middleton, this is Professor Wanda Hillsman. She's the one who chose the artwork which will go on display at the art gallery this month. Professor Hillsman, this is Hunter Middleton and one of the school's most generous donors."

Wanda's eyes glint when she understands who I am, and she steps forward to shake my hand. "It's a pleasure to make your acquaintance, Mr. Middleton."

I can smell the greed coming off of her. However, I don't let my feelings show when I return the handshake. "Likewise."

"Wanda, Mr. Middleton wants to understand the

criteria you used when you chose the student artwork for the gallery display."

Wanda immediately brightens up, and her tone is a little pompous. "Well, having had work showcased in several gallery showings myself, I know what to look for in my students' work. It's all about brushwork, strokes, and the story the artist manages to get across. I chose my top five students. They have produced excellent work ever since they entered this college."

"Really?" I drawl. "I find that hard to believe, Miss Hillsman."

Her eyes narrow at the thinly veiled insult.

"I beg your pardon."

"What Mr. Middleton is trying to say is that he disagrees with a few of your choices." Mr. Darwin hurries to soothe the tension. "He was going through the rejected pile and he found a few pieces that he found much more eye-catching."

It only takes me a minute to come to the conclusion that Wanda Hillsman has an ego that blinds her to common sense. Her voice is tinged with disdain as she says, "No offense, Mr. Middleton, but as an artist, I'm better qualified to differentiate between what is good art and what is great art. I'm sure you might disagree, but you're hardly a professional."

"Wanda!" Mr. Darwin hisses, horrified at the tone she's using with one of his super donors.

I lift a hand, cutting his protest off. "No, no, let her continue. Why don't you explain the difference in the quality of these two pictures, then, Miss Hillsman? After all, you're such a professional."

My voice is dripping with sarcasm as I hold out Megan's painting, and I watch her face grow pale when I hold it next to Ashley's painting. She tries to hold on to her confidence by saying, "It's all about the brush strokes."

"The brush strokes, huh? You know," I drawl. "If I didn't know any better, I'd say that there's another reason for your choice. The inferiority of this student's work is obvious to even me."

She grows red in the face and quickly darts a look towards Mr. Darwin, stammering all the while. "I – I don't know what you're trying to imply, but this student has a history of being tardy and –"

I hold up the charcoal sketch of me, which I had placed at the bottom of the pile in my hand. "And what do you think of this picture? Does this also have irregular brush-strokes?"

I enjoy witnessing the moment of realization in Wanda's eyes as she recognizes my face from the sketch.

"It's you."

"Well, clearly, there's nothing wrong with your eyes," I say sarcastically.

I can see the growing panic in her eyes as she realizes my intention for this whole scene.

"I'm not sure what's going on here."

She doesn't know what to say, and Mr. Darwin finally realizes that something is alarmingly wrong.

"I don't understand. Why is there a sketch of you in this stack, Mr. Middleton?"

"I was approached by one of your students to pose for it, and I allowed her to do so. She informed me that her work had been selected for the gallery showing based on the quality of her submissions. It was only later that I discovered she had been replaced in the showing by another student. I found the whole thing a little odd, especially because I have a habit of purchasing this particular student's artwork. I like her style."

I meet Wanda's eyes, which are terrified. "Now, I don't usually get involved in these things, but I would like an explanation. If this other student's work were of superior quality, I would have been fine with the decision change. But it seems like something has been happening behind closed doors. Would you like to tell me what you received in exchange for swapping the winners, Miss Hillsman? Especially when this can potentially affect the student's entire career?"

"Wanda?" Mr. Darwin sounds tense. "Is there any validity in what Mr. Middleton is saying? Did you pick this student's work first, then change your mind at the eleventh hour?"

"Th-that's not the case!" Wanda stammers, her eyes darting left to right. "I don't know what Miss Taylor said to you—"

"Miss Taylor didn't tell me anything," I say smoothly. "As a donor of the arts, I just looked into when the exhibition would be because I intended to purchase the sketch and perhaps a few others. It was only then that I found out about the switch, so I felt the need to come here and see for myself what phenomenal artwork was so good that it knocked Miss Taylor's pieces out of the showing."

"Are families paying you under the table for a spot at these showings every year? And is Professor Hillsman the qualified and tenured staff that you speak so highly of, Mr. Darwin?" I demand answers. "How many times has this happened? How many other deserving students have lost out on opportunities because of the greed of the instructors?"

Mr. Darwin looks white as a sheet as I shoot my questions at him like darts toward a dart board.

"I assure you, Mr. Middleton, that I'll get to the bottom of this matter."

"Don't bother," I snap. "This is something that you should have caught long ago as the leader of this university. Instead, I'm going to officially request a review of the entire staff of this place, including you."

"Mr. Middleton, let's think about this." The dean looks ready to throw himself at my feet. "A formal review will ruin the reputation of the school. Please let me handle this. I'll make sure to set everything right."

Wanda is shaking but remains quiet, probably pondering what lies she's going to say to absolve herself from any wrongdoing. I pause, letting the silence sink in. They need to feel the magnitude of this fuck up. There's no way in hell I'm going to allow the self-important assholes of this place to kick around my Megan like she's a piece of trash.

Wait, my Megan?

"Since I don't want to rip away the opportunity for the students who actually earned their spots in the showing, I'll give you an opportunity to fix this on one condition."

"And that is?"

"I'll be sending over my own impartial art critic to choose the work to be displayed. I want a report about how you handled it emailed to me by the end of the week."

"Yes, of course!" The relief on the dean's face is immense. "But I think it's safe to say that Megan's work will be put back in the show. It's clear that she is one of the more talented students in this class."

"Yes, well, we can let the critic help with that," I say, of course already knowing that Megan will not only be in that showing but her work will be prominently displayed in the front of the gallery and she will be highlighted in the New York Times piece.

I carefully set Megan's sketches down, satisfied with the outcome. Sometimes you've got a rattle a few cages to remind the animals that they don't actually run the goddamn zoo.

Parker finally shows up in the room with a man I can only assume is the head of accounting. Both the dean and Professor Hillsman look as if they want to puke.

"You've got a wonderful program here," I say to the room, smoothing the lapel of my suit jacket. "But I intend to take more of a hands-on approach from now on. You know, if you want any more of my money."

The look on everyone's face is fearful when I leave, especially Dean Darwin. It's a wonderful fucking thing.

"That was fun, eh?" Lars says as we walk back to the car. "What took you so long with the accountant, Parker? Were you tickling his balls or something in the washroom?"

I laugh out loud. Lars doesn't talk much, but when he does, he's got the timing of a dirty stand-up comedian.

"Very funny, idiotic viking. Those pencil pushers gave me the longest runaround. Pretty sure that dean sent a text or something telling them to stall."

"Every business is hiding something," I tell them. "And universities are some of the most gangster businesses out there. They charge these kids ridiculous amounts of money that they'll probably barely make back in their lifetime. It's insane."

"Then what did we do all that for back there?"

"Because Megan's only dream is to be an artist," I answer, asking myself what I'm doing all of this for.

"Then you're going to like this," Parker says, quite pleased with himself.

"What?"

He pulls out a manilla file folder he was hiding underneath his shirt. It's full of university spreadsheets and interoffice memos that Parker must have lifted from the accounting department.

"A fucking dreamcatcher for Megan."

Chapter 29

Now That I've Had A Taste

HUNTER

"I knew the asshole was embezzling money," I comment as I study the copy of the account ledger during the drive back.

"I've never seen you be so strategic about something like this, boss," Lars looks at me through the rear-view mirror as Parker drives. "You're going to be more active in Megan's college now?"

"Yeah, they obviously cheated our girl out of a spot in the gallery show. In instances like this, you usually shed blood first and ask questions later," Parker grins, looking over his shoulder at me from the passenger seat.

"That's not entirely true," I turn the page, raising a brow at some of the expenses. "Sometimes you have to let people walk into the fire first. Makes it easier to control them."

"And you did this for the girl?" Lars asks, and my hand tightens on the papers even as I keep my voice casual.

"I can be nice at times."

Parker makes a scoffing sound, which I ignore.

"Drop me off at home. I'm going to shower and sleep before I come back to work."

Parker doesn't say anything, simply turning the car around. Instead of getting out in the underground parking lot, I decide to use the main entrance. I am at the elevator in the main lobby, and just as the doors are closing, I hear a familiar voice shout, "Hold the elevator!"

I oblige by sliding my hand in the middle of the doors to keep them from closing, only to see Megan run at full speed, struggling with three shopping bags. When she enters the elevator car and sees me standing there, she gasps. "Thanks, Mr. Middleton."

Megan looks so shocked to see me that I have to wonder if she forgot I lived here too. She's wearing a short-sleeved pink sweater that looks like it's had better days and a pair of tight jeans with slits at the knees. Her hair is in a messy bun and looks fucking gorgeous.

"We're not at work," I remind her.

"Right," she blushes. "Thanks for holding the door, Hunter."

"What's that?" I ask, gesturing towards all the bags.

"Groceries and a few art supplies. There was a sale at Target, so I rushed there after class. Then, there was a farmers' market open next to Target. They're usually only open on Sundays when the pickings are slim, so I took advantage of it and got a lot of groceries. I'm going to make tandoori butter chicken. I got the flour, see?"

She points towards a white-looking bag. I don't know why I thought the next time she saw me, she'd be a little shy. After all, we spent a steamy night together in Paris, but Megan looks completely unaffected.

It bothers me for some reason.

"You look like you're in a good mood," I say, begrudgingly.

The smile she gives me is brilliant, and I blink at the sight of it, feeling a little dazed.

"You know the competition I told you about, where five students were selected to display their artwork? Well, evidently, the professor in charge of the selection process was fired, and they're getting some professional art curator to come in and reselect the winners. The results will be announced tomorrow." She grins.

"You're happy about that?" I ask, feeling an odd sort of satisfaction.

"Happy?" She grins. "You should've seen the look on Ashley's face! You remember her, right? She's the girl I was telling you I have a little beef with."

I feign ignorance.

"Anyway, I know it's petty, but she looked crushed. I heard that she went to the dean's office to talk to him about it but he wouldn't even let her in. Also, the dean refuses to reveal who the new evaluator is."

My lips quirk at the glee in Megan's eyes.

"Sorry," she says, giving me a sheepish smile. "I know you don't care about stuff like this."

"Who said I didn't care?"

"I'm just happy because it means I may have another chance to be included in the gallery showing, which is a really high honor in my school."

"So, how did you hear about all of this good news?"

I literally just left that idiot's office.

"Oh, it's all anyone can talk about at school. I was in a workshop class, but as soon as I got out, a friend was waiting at the door. He couldn't wait to tell me all the gossip."

"You said he."

"Uh-huh."

"A male friend was waiting for you?"

She stares up at me with those gorgeous doe eyes of hers and waits a moment to answer.

"Yes... I have male friends."

I stare her down with a look of disapproval. Now that I've had a taste of Megan, I don't feel comfortable with some kid waiting on her after class like they're a part of an after-school special.

But I let it go.

She's not my woman.

And this moment of joy she's having isn't about me. I don't want to ruin it for her by bringing up things that are none of my concern.

"It's good to know that you're getting a fair chance," I tell her. "I hope they select you."

"Yeah," she agrees, beaming at me before leaning down to pick up her three bags as the elevator doors open. "I hope so, too. Oh, Naomi is also coming home today, so I won't be alone any longer. Which reminds me–" She tucks two of the bags under her arms, struggling with the third one. "I didn't get a chance to say this before, but thanks for letting Naomi move in with me. It was a really generous offer."

I take all three bags out of her hands. "I'll carry these for you."

"Wait, no." She tries to take the bags from me, alarmed. "I can carry them!"

"Not before falling and cracking your head open or damaging any of your precious supplies," I tell her. "Come on. Let's go."

She looks reluctant but follows my lead, grumbling the entire way to her front door. "I can carry my own things. I didn't need help."

I roll my eyes. "Of course you could."

Unfortunately, she catches the gesture and scowls. "I could totally carry those bags. You just snatched them from me before I could adjust myself."

"Yes, yes," I say soothingly. "It's my fault."

"You can be really patronizing, you know?" She gives me a dark look, and I press my lips together to keep from smiling.

"Open the door, Megan."

The bags are surprisingly heavy, and I frown at their weight. Did she just carry all this stuff by herself to the apartment? Why doesn't she have a car or, at the very least, take an Uber?

"You need to invest in a car," I tell her matter-of-factly.

"I need to do a lot of things." She unlocks the door by punching four numbers into the keypad, then holds open the apartment door for me. "Getting a car is not at the top of my list, Daddy Warbucks."

I scoff at the Annie reference and enter the apartment, silently absorbing all the changes that have taken place inside since the last time I was here. I can see that Megan has been quite busy making the space her own. All the furniture has been rearranged, most of it facing the window, and there are small sketches and paintings hanging on the walls. I'm pleased.

I place all the bags on the kitchen counter before wandering over to one of the charcoal sketches. It's of a busy street with a child standing in the center of it, with a forlorn expression on her face.

"A little depressing, wouldn't you agree?" I study the sketch, entranced by the sense of loss in the child's eyes.

"The world often is," Megan says from the kitchen counter as she unpacks everything.

I look over my shoulder at her. "A little dark coming from somebody your age."

"My generation is more in touch with our mental health." She grins playfully. "Your generation likes to pretend that this too shall pass."

"How old do you think I am, Megan?" I laugh.

"Probably a question I should have asked you before Paris, but I don't think our age difference really matters at this point, does it?"

I am enjoying Megan's good mood, and I take some pride in the fact that I had a hand in making it happen. I was quite busy this afternoon, shaking things up at her university, and I don't feel an ounce of regret meddling in her affairs.

"Do you paint in the living room?" I look around for any paint stains like the ones I'd seen in her old apartment.

Her phone rings, and I watch her fumbling through her purse, looking for it. "No, I set up the third bedroom as my art studio. You can go take a look if you want."

"It's not a third bedroom. It's supposed to be your walk-in closet," I correct her.

"How can any one person own enough clothes to fill a whole bedroom?" She chuckles. "It's ridiculous."

I can think of ten women offhand who could easily fill a room with clothes, but her philosophy about 'things' is so refreshing. I can tell that she would rather have experiences like Paris.

I walk towards the room as curiosity guides my feet. Opening the door, I step inside, and the first thing I realize is that the entire floor is covered in plastic. There's an easel in the middle of the room with a small stool and an unfinished painting. A bunch of fluffy cushions are piled in the corner, and an empty coffee cup is next to them on the floor.

I rented this place to Megan, which is fully furnished, but the bed and all the furniture have been pushed to the side, clearly to ensure that nothing is damaged. Where the dressing table used to be, a rusty-looking wooden table is where it is, and a bunch of art supplies are carefully arranged there.

The place looks a little disorganized, but it has charm and Megan's artistic footprint all over it. I wander over to the unfinished painting and, on closer view; I see the rough outline of a river and an old couple walking alongside it. Only the sky is scattered with the paint, depicting hues of pink, orange, and blue. It reminds me of Paris, and I wonder if she's drawing inspiration from her visit.

Hearing Megan's voice on the other side of the door, I exit the room just in time to listen to her hiss at the person on the other end.

"I told you I'd send you the money when I get it. Threatening me isn't going to make me pay you any faster!"

Chapter 30

Who Was That Man?

HUNTER

Megan sounds both upset and angry, and I frown. Rounding the corner, I see her hunched over herself, one hand on the marble counter, her expression tight.

"That's not my problem, and I don't live there anymore!"

The hand that's holding the phone is shaking. She doesn't see me since her back is towards me, but her posture reveals her fear.

"What do you want from me?" she half shouts, struggling to keep her voice low. "I sent you more than half my fucking paycheck! I don't have the kind of money you want. "

I've heard enough.

Walking over to her, I pluck the phone out of her hand, my tone icy. "Who is this?"

"Wait, Hunter. " I silence Megan by grabbing her by

her shoulder, whirling her around, and covering her mouth with my left hand.

She struggles with me as I turn my attention toward the person on the other end of the line. It's a man's voice on the other end.

"Who the fuck are you?"

"I believe I asked you that question," I respond, unfazed by Megan's attempts to escape my hold as she makes muffled protests against my hand on her mouth.

"That little bitch sleeping with you?" the man sneers. "It figures. She was always like her mother, spreading her legs for every Tom, Dick, and Harry."

"Do you know how easy it is for me to track your phone number and find your ass? It'll take me less than a few minutes."

"What?" the man growls, suddenly angered. "You threatening me, you son of a bitch?"

"Threatening you?" I chuckle angrily. "I don't make threats, Mr. whoever the fuck you are. I have a reputation for carrying out whatever I promise, and I don't like what you just said to my friend or to me. Maybe I should pay you a visit and slit that dirty mouth of yours from ear to ear since you like talking so much."

"What?" My cold words rattle the stranger. "You put Megan on the phone, you crazy bastard!"

"Mmph!" Megan tries to push me off of her, but I ignore her struggles.

"I'm afraid she's not available."

"Listen, you piece of shit, I don't care if you want to fuck her or whore her out, but you tell that bitch, if she doesn't send me my goddamn money, I'll make sure those pictures of her are sent to the police. You tell her that. Trust me, she'll make herself available to talk real fast!"

I abruptly end the call and set the phone down on the counter, slowly absorbing the words.

A moan leaves Megan's lips, and I finally release her, causing her to stumble forward. All the laughter that had been in her eyes just a short while ago is gone, and she trembles with fury and horror.

"What have you done?"

"Who was that man?" I ask her, an icy snowstorm brewing inside of me at the callous and disrespectful way that man just spoke of Megan.

Sparks shoot out of Megan's eyes and in my direction. She's pissed, although I'm confused why all of her venom is directed at me.

"You had no business taking that phone from me!"

I stare at her, and my tone is soft when I ask, "No business?"

"Yes," she grits the word out angrily. "That was a personal call."

I run my tongue over my teeth, struggling to contain my temper. "He was threatening you."

I see the way her face shutters at my words. "You misunderstood the conversation."

"Did I?" I take a step toward her, and she immediately takes one back.

"Yes, you did." Her voice is hard.

I'm seething mad and simply furious at how she lets other people treat her, not to mention refusing to ask for help. It's not like she doesn't know I won't help her if she asks. But the fact that it takes a crowbar to pry anything out of this woman is driving me insane.

The man's vulgar words are still ringing in my ears as I walk backward against the refrigerator, only stopping when her back hits the metal and she realizes that she has nowhere to go.

"I'm usually a very patient man, Megan," I say tightly.

"Could've fooled me," she retorts.

"Regardless," I ignore her provocation and continue my anger brewing. "It seems that when it comes to you, I'm very quick to lose my patience."

"Why?" She bares her teeth at me, and the show of defiance infuriates me, and I grab her hair, yanking her head back to face me, pressing my body against hers.

"I may give you a free pass now and then, but don't you ever forget who I am," I growl at her. "I'm not some puppy you can tame, Megan!"

She shoves at my chest furiously. "I never said that you were. And what free pass? I'm not doing anything to you. You're the one butting into my life, making my business your business. That was a private phone call, and you had no business taking that phone from me. You are my boss, or maybe my boss with benefits, but you have no right to interfere in my personal matters."

The more she talks, reminding me of the chasm between us, the more it infuriates me. *I am just her boss?* Is she serious? Did she just come home from the same Parisian trip I did? The one where I fucked her senseless?

She should be the one pining for me, the one who should be unsure of how to act around me, and yet I'm the one acting like a fool, unable to stop interfering in her affairs, damn near begging to keep her safe and offer her my protection.

Unable to take it anymore, I smash my mouth down on hers in a punishing kiss, wanting to hurt for making me feel like this. But as soon as the taste of her floods my mouth, I feel a gnawing hunger inside me. It's swift and familiar, and my cock hardens at the scent of her light perfume.

I release my hold on her hair, grasping both her hands and slamming them beside her head on the refrigerator, pinning her to it. She tries to fight me off for a few seconds before dissolving into me with a helpless moan.

I thrust my leg in between her legs, deliberately pressing my thigh against her hot pussy and moving it enough to give her the kind of friction that'll drive her wild.

And it does.

She's straining against my hold, trying to get closer to me. Her cheeks are flushed, and her eyes are ravenous.

I want more.

I want to strip off her clothes and take her on the marble counter. I want to lap at her pussy until she begs for forgiveness for the words she just spat at me. I want her screaming my name as I pound all the defiance out of her with my dick.

Sliding her hands up, I pin her wrists together, grasping them in one hand as my other lowers to where her chest is thrusting out, the buttons of her blouse protesting.

"Bastard," she whispers against my mouth, her eyes opening to reveal a dazed expression, and a wanton moan escapes her lips as my hand curls around her breast, squeezing it and rolling the hard nipple between my finger and forefinger.

She's thrusting against my thigh, her face twisted in pleasure and need, and I run my mouth over her jaw and her cheeks before descending onto her lips in a now tender assault. I can feel it when she's on the edge because she tenses up, so I pull away, abandoning her aching pussy.

Trembling, she gives me a confused look, her eyes clouded with need, and a whimper escapes her before she nearly crumples onto the ground. I catch her in time, holding her up by the waist and whispering into her ear as she pants, "I will never be just your fucking boss."

With that, I let her find her balance, and then I walk out of her apartment, stuck with a painful hard-on that not even a cold shower manages to ease.

I hope I left her in just as much pain.

Chapter 31

What Kind Of Voodoo?

HUNTER

"You do realize that you have a nice home office in that building you live in, right?" Vaughn asks, lounging on one of the sofas lazily. "Why do you keep coming here?"

"I guess for the same reason you do—a change of environment," I say shortly, my eyes straying from my laptop and through the window towards a familiar figure on the ground floor.

"Change of environment or because you want to keep your eye on your little bartender?" Vaughn sneers.

"She's a manager," I correct him, my eyes narrowing as I see a man try to cop a feel of Megan's ass.

"I don't blame you," Vaughn says carelessly. "She's hot. You should keep an eye on her."

"Why the fuck are you here?" I ask Vaughn icily, annoyed he's even looking at Megan in that way. "I thought I gave you a task."

"Watch your tone, man. I'm doing you a favor, remember?" Vaughn scowls. "Plus, I'm waiting on your little bartender to give me the employee files. These things take time."

Since I started personally overseeing the operations here at the Blue Whiskey, instead of staying holed up in my office, the kind of crowd that usually visits has lessened. The small-time thugs who had become frequent visitors now no longer dare even to step inside, making Vaughn's assignment all that more difficult. Who would have had access to the club and know enough about my business to know I had Steve in the basement?

I see Gage slip away for a break, and Megan instantly covers for him, efficiently dealing out drinks. Her eyes flicker toward a man seated at the bar, and my face grows hard when I see her smile at him. It's not her usual dismissive smile, which is aimed at most customers. She's enjoying this conversation. My hand curls into a fist as I see her throw her head back and laugh. This must be a really amusing motherfucker.

The stranger reaches forward and wraps a strand of her hair around his finger. The quiet fury that fills me is both surprising and deadly. *Should I knock him out with the butt of my gun, or should I have Lars do it?*

Just then, Megan's smile slips, and she steps back, immediately creating distance between herself and the man. My tense form relaxes—for just a moment. But when the man leans forward again, I'm out of my seat. Before I can move, however, he quickly turns his head, looking up at the one-way glass, and shows his middle finger, grinning. Megan looks confused, and I scowl once I see the man's face.

"That bastard."

"You're gone, brother." Vaughn is behind me, howling with laughter. "I can't believe you got so worked up. What the hell kind of voodoo did she put on you in Paris?"

I see my friend Christian, with his dark hair and green eyes, smirk at me. Obviously, he and Vaughn thought this juvenile prank was funny.

"Do you want me to shoot the two of you?" I threaten as Vaughn continues to have the time of his life, still cackling.

A few minutes later, the door of the office opens, and Christian walks in, grinning from ear to ear. "How was I?"

"He fell for it." Vaughn is still howling with laughter. "Jumped out of his chair and everything. If he had been downstairs, you might have gotten a bullet in your back."

"Are we in high school?" I glower at the two of them. "What the fuck is wrong with you two?"

"Hey, man." Christian lifts his hands in a peaceful gesture. "It was his idea. Besides, I didn't even know you were seeing somebody."

"I'm not *seeing* anybody," I say harshly.

Christian and Vaughn exchange a look before Christian asks him, "I thought she was the one he took to Paris?"

"She is," Vaughn assures him.

"So, what's the deal?" Christian shrugs, taking a seat on the long couch. "She's a little young for you, but she's fucking gorgeous."

"I swear if neither of you don't shut up. "

Both my friends gape at me, and Christian lifts a brow, his face astounded. "You already slept with her, didn't you?"

I've had just about enough of these two and decide to step out for a smoke. It's either that, or I'm going to punch both of them in the jaw. As I descend the stairs, my hand goes towards the box of cigarettes in the inner pocket of my suit jacket. It's still unopened. Using the private exit, I enter the alley. Wishing I had grabbed my electronic cigarette, I make do with what I have and take out one of the cigarettes from the back, clenching it between my teeth.

I savor the smell of the tobacco and how the filtered tip feels between my teeth. I'm tempted to withdraw my lighter and have a real smoke, but I've been trying to break that habit. It's been two months since I've smoked a real cigarette, and I miss the ritual of it—now more than ever.

Hands in my pockets, I lean against the alley wall, closing my eyes in an attempt to empty my head. My self-control has been slipping these past few weeks. I'm furious with myself for letting this damn art student get under my skin like this.

Megan is... well, *she should have been*...like all the women who have come and gone in my life. And yet here I am, trying to stop myself from taking a smoke because she's got me all worked up.

The door to the alleyway opens, and I see a familiar figure step out. I'm hidden in the shadows, and Megan doesn't see me. She quietly closes the door behind her and sits down on the edge of the steps, a sandwich and a cup of black coffee in her hands. I should slip away and allow her to enjoy her break, but my body is frozen as I watch her. She sighs heavily and then bites into the sandwich unenthu-siastically.

She looks weary.

It's an expression I haven't seen on her face in a while, as if the weight of the world is on her shoulders. I thought I took care of that weight for her. The look wasn't on her face when we went to Paris, and I didn't see it when she told me the good news about what happened at college two days ago–but I see it now. She looks lost in thought as she mindlessly chews her sandwich, staring blankly at the ground. I can't seem to tear my eyes away from her, my chest feeling suffocated. Then I hear the sound of her ringtone breaking the silence.

"Hey, Naomi," she answers, her voice soft. "Is everything okay?"

I've not yet met her roommate. I decided to give Megan a wide berth to invite whomever she wanted into her new home without my scrutiny, although I knew it would be her.

"Yeah, they selected it." Megan sets down her sandwich and takes a sip of her coffee. "Nah, I'm happy. Of course, I'm happy. Why wouldn't I be?"

She doesn't sound happy.

Naomi says something to her, and Megan shrugs her shoulders. "I sent it this morning. Thanks for loaning me the money. You didn't have to do that, and I appreciate it."

After another brief pause, she sighs and says, "I don't know. He's not going to stop. I just have to graduate from here and then I'll be out of his grasp. I'll leave the city, no maybe the country. He won't find me."

I have a dark feeling she's talking about the man on the phone from the other day.

"I get a day off this weekend. Let's go get drunk. I need to get wasted. I heard Pallo's is having a ladies' night on Saturday. We can get in early, and drinks are free before eleven."

I know of Pallo's. It's an upcoming club in Los Angeles where many younger Hollywood celebrities like to hang out and take pictures for Instagram.

I wait for her conversation to finish, and then I stir. The

shuffling of my shoes makes her shoot her head up, and her voice is cautious. "Who's there?"

When I walk into the dim light, she's on her feet, and when she sees me, her whole body relaxes—and not in a good way.

"Oh, it's you."

Chapter 32

My Dick Won't Allow it

HUNTER

Megan's expression when she sees me is irritating the hell out of me.

"I'm going to go inside," she says flatly.

The way she's trying to avoid me and pretend as if nothing ever happened between us is pissing me off and making me want to smoke this damn cigarette.

"So that's what you're going to do now?" I ask, my voice mocking with anger. "Run away every time you see me?"

She pauses on the steps and stares at me. "I'm not running. I'm doing what you wanted and what we agreed upon, which was what happens in Paris stays in Paris. Plus, the last person who did the running was you when you stomped out of my apartment."

"I never agreed to any what happens in Paris arrangement," I correct her coolly. "You used me, not the other way around."

"What do you mean you didn't agree to it?" Her face drops. "You know what, I'm not getting into this with you right now. I need to get back to work. If you remember, I manage your club."

I take a step closer to her, my voice silky, "From what I remember, since we've met, it's been you who was insistent on not sleeping with me because you were sure I was going to take advantage of you, but then look what happened. You turned the tables on me in Paris and took advantage of me, and now you're not talking to me?"

From the look on her face, she clearly didn't expect me to say what I did. The guilt in her eyes is adorable as I feign the injured lover.

"That's not what I meant to do," she stammers.

"But you did," I reply smoothly. "And now that you've had your fun, you want nothing more to do with me? A little hypocritical, wouldn't you say?"

I wonder if I've taken things a little too far when I see the panic settle in her eyes, her hand clenching around the sandwich in her hand, crushing it.

"I didn't mean to send out any mixed messages, and I definitely wasn't using you. Paris was your idea, if you recall, and honestly, I didn't think you gave the trip or any nights after that a second thought at all."

I feel a hint of satisfaction as I gain more ground, but then she adds, "Plus, I'm pretty sure I remember you saying once that you can have any woman you want, so why are you so worried about whether or not I'm talking to you? It's no different from you not having much to say to me on the plane ride home."

My brows knit together at her offhanded comment. Is that why she's so pissed at me? I barely recall what was said or not said during the flight home.

"Listen, Mr. Middleton, you've been nothing but nice to me most of the time. A month ago, my life was shit, but now

I have a nice apartment and a stable job, which you and I both know I wasn't next in line for. I know it's just because you're trying to help me, and I'm grateful. I swear I am; I'm just trying my best not to be a nuisance to you."

"A nuisance?" I repeat her words, uncomfortable with where this conversation is headed.

"It seems harmless enough for us to play around with each other as we did in Paris, and even in the apartment the other night, but once you've had your fill and decide to get rid of me, your life will be unaffected. I'll be the one to pay the price, and I'm not ready to pay that price.

"You were right to distance yourself from me first. We're in totally different places in our lives. So now that we're both sober and back in the States, let's just let what happened go. That was drunk sex and nothing more."

I stare at her, stunned by the firm conviction in her words. No woman has ever talked to me like this, at least not ones I've had in my bed. They always wanted more.

"Nothing more?"

While this is probably one of Megan's smarter decisions about me, I don't know why her regret about what happened angers me so much. I'm not sure whether it's just my arrogance or something more, but I want to punch something and punch it hard. However, I wouldn't be standing where I am today if I were that impulsive person. Cooler heads always prevail, even when it comes to matters of the heart.

I stare at the voluptuous beauty before me with hungry eyes. I've not yet had my fill of Megan. My craving for her proves to be a steady distraction, and the very thought of her is enough to make my dick throb right where I stand. I don't know why I can't get this tiny artist out of my head, but until I do, I have no plans to back off.

My dick won't allow it.

I take a step towards her, covering the distance between us and leaning down, my lips right next to her ear. "That was a very cute speech, and I was willing to play nice... before, but you broke the rules, so now this doesn't end until I say it does."

"What rules?"

Megan's body stiffens as I grab her jaw in my hand, forcing her to look at me.

"You're fooling yourself if you think I can't see the desire you have for me every time I'm within five feet of you. What happens in Paris, stays in Paris? Hell, what happened in that hotel room is sitting between us like an elephant on our chests, and it can't be ignored."

"No—"

"Why do you continually deny yourself pleasure? Remember how you've fallen apart for me under my touch?" I ask, cutting her off mid-sentence. "I know your body better than you do, and I damn sure know what it wants."

"And what's that?"

"Your pussy quivers when I stroke it, when I talk to it, when I eat it."

I release her jaw but leisurely slide my hand down to her collarbone and trace it lightly with a finger. I can see her nipples pebble underneath her blouse. She's so fucking responsive to the slightest touch from me.

I love it.

"You were able to hide it better before, but not anymore," I tell her. "Not after Paris, and not after falling apart so hard for me under my touch."

Her jaw tightens, and I can see the frustration in her eyes as I whisper in her ear, "Don't worry, I won't force you.

I prefer it when a woman comes begging to me on her knees. And you will beg, kitten. I promise you that."

I toss the unlit cigarette onto the ground and grind it into the concrete with the bottom of my shoe as I walk confidently past a speechless Megan and back into the club.

If she wants to run away because she's frightened of how good I can make her feel, I understand it, but I won't make it easy.

Megan is quickly becoming my favorite distraction, and this thing between us is far from over.

Chapter 33

The Rumor Mill

MEGAN

My heart is racing at the words Mr. Middleton whispered in my ear. It's been quite a few days since my life-changing trip to Paris and the heated moment between us in my apartment, but ever since then, I can't seem to distinguish between Mr. Middleton, my boss, and Hunter, the man.

Hunter was a considerate man who patiently amused me as we explored Paris. He was also a passionate lover who drove me wild and made sure I was the center of attention in bed. Mr. Middleton is my boss, a dangerous man who leads a complex life and doesn't blink an eye when it comes to taking someone's life.

I'm not sure which man just left me standing here with a dumb look on my face, nipples at attention, and damp panties. Trembling, I sink against the closed door, rattled. The man can turn me on with a single word, no matter how much I try to fight it.

I should be angry with him. I should be horrified. *He's*

going to make me beg? The nerve. But under the shock of his words is a thrum of anticipation and need.

That one night between us is imprinted in my brain. I thought I'd had sex before, but after being fucked by Hunter Middleton, I realize I hadn't even come close, and I desperately want more of it. Try as much as I can, I haven't been able to replicate that sensation. My fingers aren't good enough, and neither is my silver bullet vibrator.

I let out a shaky breath before getting to my feet. The way he kissed me a few days ago, touching me in all the right spots, driving me insane, making me toss and turn every night. It was pure evil of him to leave me hanging on purpose. I'm headed down a slippery slope with this man with no end in sight.

I pick up my ruined sandwich and cold coffee and walk inside, only to see Diana standing there. She blinks when she sees me, and I wonder if she is eavesdropping on me.

"Were you outside with Mr. Middleton just now?" she asks me.

"What?" I question her. "Why are you back here? This area is restricted to management personnel only."

"I got lost." She shrugs. "So what were you talking about with the boss man? I didn't know you two were close."

For some reason, I'm not too fond of the look in Diana's eyes, and my tone with her is a little harsh. "I think it's best that you return to the bar. You're not supposed to be back here."

She gives me a quick grin, ignoring my order. "Are you and him together?"

I already take enough shit from kids at school, and I certainly don't need any conflict at work, but Diana's insinuating question makes me uneasy, so I take a step toward her. "Listen, you and I are not close enough to talk about our private lives. Go back to work and stop asking useless questions."

Her face flushes at my curt words, and I can tell that she wants to bite back, but she wisely holds her tongue.

I'm not usually very harsh with the staff because I've been in their position literally a few weeks ago, but I also cannot let them talk to me like this, especially Diana, who's just started. When I hired her, I never expected her to have such a nosy personality, but lately, I've seen her poking her nose into matters that are not her concern.

I head to the kitchen to check the schedule and run into Billy. The uneasiness of my encounter with Diana is still lingering in the back of my head, so I ask him, "What do you think of the new hire?"

"Gage?"

I shake my head, turning my attention toward the schedule board.

"Diana."

When Billy doesn't say anything, I look over my shoulder at him. He's wearing an annoyed expression on his face.

"I don't like her. I don't get a good vibe from her. She's far too friendly for my liking, like she's trying too hard."

I don't comment because I've been getting the same vibes.

"She asks a lot of questions as well," Billy continues. "She's very curious about you, your background, how you got promoted so quickly, and all of that."

My lips purse. "Has anybody on staff been talking to her?"

I don't quite like the look on Billy's face, so I press the issue. "What is it?"

"Well, Dan works with me on the stove, and he's cool

with you. The male servers have no issue with you. I mean, you're an upgrade from Steve, and you know all of our situations, and you're cool about it. So if anyone's going to talk a little smack about you to Diana, it would have to be the girls. They've been a little uptight lately."

"Uptight?" I echo. "All of them?"

"Well, Allie and Mia have been the most vocal. Apparently, Sally was their friend, and when she was asked to leave, they blamed you."

I recall the incident with Sally and the men at Table 21, which sparked this whole situation that I'm in now.

"I saved her ass," I hiss. "And I warned her. What the hell are they blaming me for?"

Billy doesn't meet my eyes. "You know how women can be. Apparently, you're on good terms with the boss, and you also get along well with Gage. All the girls have a crush on the man. He's not as friendly with them as he is with you."

I gape at him, and Billy continues in a rushed manner. "Rumor around the Whiskey is that you slept with the boss to get your position and get Steve fired. Now they're worried you're going to sleep with Gage, too."

"What?" I croak. The shock of the rumors hit me like a ton of bricks. "They think I did what?"

"Of course, I know that it's just bullshit," Billy hurriedly tries to reassure me. "You're not the type of girl to do something so stupid."

Well, he's half right, I think to myself miserably.

The kitchen door opens, and a brunette in a waitress's uniform enters. I meet Mia's eyes, and she sneers in my direction before heading off to the back of the kitchen to take her break.

"How long has this been going on, Billy?" I ask, keeping my voice low.

"Ever since you became manager," he replies. "But listen, kid, you can't worry about shit like that. People will always talk about the people in charge. The talk will die down soon. Besides, the ladies will soon realize that Mr. Middleton isn't the kind of dude to sleep with people like us."

"Us?"

"Employees, I mean. Have you seen the kind of socialites he likes to be seen with? Google him. He's been with some stunners."

I unlock my phone and type in Hunter Middleton in the search bar. I haven't done an enormous amount of Google research on him because I assumed I wouldn't find much based on his underworld ties. I've never been more wrong. There are literally dozens of pages of online images of him and a variety of beauties in formal attire posing on the red carpet.

One picture stands out.

He's wearing a very expensive-looking tux with a random brunette on his arm. She reminds me of a younger Nicole Kidman with dark brown hair. She's statuesque, with ivory-white skin and a sexy red dress on, and they're both attending an event held last year in Paris.

Paris, of all places.

I glance at my tired reflection on the shiny metal counter and wince. Billy's not wrong, but I feel a slight throb in my chest at the reality he's just shoved in my face.

"You're right," I murmur. "But if you get the opportunity, can you track down where the rumor started? This is a workplace, and like it or not, I am the manager. If stories like these start affecting the waitresses' job performance, it will be an issue for me. I need to nip it in the bud."

Where I would have once ignored something like this,

I'm no longer on an equal footing with the staff. I have to make sure that they at least respect me; otherwise, getting them to follow my orders will be a pain in the ass.

Billy nods in agreement, but before I can leave, he says, "I actually have to talk to you about something."

"What is it?"

He looks a little sheepish. "My brother-in-law invested in a steakhouse down in Ohio. He wants me to go fifty-fifty. It's a great opportunity, and with the baby on the way, it'll help a lot, especially since we'll be staying with my mother-in-law there. Brianna doesn't want to raise children in LA. Says it's not safe enough."

I blink.

"Did you just say, mother-in-law?"

Billy grins, holding up his hand and showing me a gold band around his finger.

"Yeah, we eloped last week. I'm not going to find anybody better than her."

I smile and step forward to hug him.

"Oh, Billy, that's fantastic. Congratulations!"

He's beaming when I step back.

"Thanks."

"So, when do you plan on taking that offer?"

"Next month," he says hesitantly. "I didn't want to do you wrong and leave you hanging, so I thought I'd tell you now. That'll give you time to hire somebody, and I can train them."

Billy was the club's main cook long before I was hired, and he's one of my closest work friends. Seeing him leave will make me a little sad.

"I'll talk to Mr. Middleton," I promise. "Write down your duties for me, and I'll create a job description."

The look on Billy's face has me pausing. "What is it now?"

"I may already have somebody in mind," he says. "She's quite young, but she comes by the soup kitchen that Brianna works out of. She helps out sometimes, and I met her a couple of times. She's a good cook."

When I don't respond immediately, Billy adds quickly, "Look, when this place started up, Mr. Middleton gave me an opportunity. I was pretty much broke. I applied on a whim. I never expected to get the job. He may be a stone-cold bastard, but he looks after his people, and he isn't afraid to give people an opportunity. I would never recommend somebody who wouldn't be a good fit. This job got me on my feet, and the kid I'm thinking about bringing on needs the same chance."

I trust Billy, but I must talk to Hunter before doing anything.

"Give me a day," I tell him. "Meanwhile, get me that girl's resume, and I'll talk to Mr. Middleton."

I check my watch. I still have a few hours of work before I can go home. It's not like I don't have the time to talk to Hunter today, but I don't want to approach him right now. My head is still a tangle of emotions.

I'll wait until Billy gives me her resume.

Chapter 34

Really, Ricky?

MEGAN

"Here, hun', these are two tickets that you can give to your parents to attend the gallery."

I stare at the elegant writing on the thin slips of paper.

"Thank you."

The woman looking at me smiles. "You have a lot of potential, Megan. If you don't mind, I would love to introduce you to some people at the exhibit."

Something warm flares in my chest, and I hold the two tickets close to my chest. "Really?"

"Yes." Miss Maverick beams at me. "I know you don't place a lot of focus on digital art, but I have a few connections who are always looking for brilliant students to offer internships. I invited a few of them to the showing. They usually offer internships for students who work on digital platforms, but your work has so much depth that they might give you an opportunity."

I press my lips together to hold it in the excitement.

"This is why I personally wanted to meet you to give you the tickets," she explains, smiling at me kindly. "You have to make a good first impression with these folks, so make sure you dress appropriately for the event. I would recommend classy attire and muted tones. Let your art be the only thing that stands out."

I look down at the tickets, trying to contain my happiness, and before leaving the room, I'm careful to tuck them deep into my bag. Classes are already over for the day, and the hallways are empty. I hurry to my art supply locker only to see a familiar face waiting for me there.

"What do you want?" I ask coldly, stopping in my tracks.

Ricky, the asshole, smiles at me as if we're simply old pals.

"Megan, I wanted to say congrats."

The biggest mistake of my life, Ricky, is majoring in digital photography and specializing in film. While his work is not subpar, he didn't make it as a gallery finalist.

Neither did Ashley.

I don't smile, my hand tightening on the strap of my bag. "Thanks."

When I stare at him, he shifts in his spot, clearly uncomfortable.

"So, did you get the tickets?" he asks me.

I don't respond. His toothy smile, which months ago used to make my heart skip a beat, makes me feel sick to my stomach now.

"Do you want something, Ricky?" I ask, my tone is frigid.

He takes a step forward.

"Look, I know you don't have a plus one, and it's not like you have any parents to attend the exhibition." *Asshole.*

"Plus, I've been thinking for a few weeks now; I know I messed up, but I want to give us a second chance. So, I wanted to ask you out to the exhibition."

I purse my lips, suddenly finding the humor in the whole thing, even as a sliver of anger cuts through it.

"If you're asking me out, shouldn't you be the one providing the tickets?"

He gives me a boyish smile, taking yet another step forward.

"Well, you already have them, so what's the point of me buying them?"

I offer him back an insincere smile of my own. What an ass.

"It shows commitment. The showing is a fundraiser; each ticket is at least a thousand dollars. If you're suddenly so desperate to give *us* a chance, the least you could do is pay for the privilege."

I can see his expression falter, and his smile slips.

"Don't be like this, Megan. You know that having a plus one will help with nerves at an event like this, and aside from me, you have no one."

"Really?" I drawl, my anger curling around me. "You don't know shit about what I've got."

The next step he takes puts him directly in my face and he looks down at me, his eyes glinting, his cheese puff breath hot on my face.

"I know you still have feelings for me. If you didn't, you wouldn't have done all the things you have for me." He grins.

My eyes tighten in fury as I fully understand what he's insinuating.

"You son of a bitch."

I thrust my hands at his chest, and he grabs them, slamming me into the locker. All the breath leaves my body at his rough handling of me, and I feel enraged, more than scared.

"Be grateful I'm giving you another chance." He spits defiantly. "Considering the reputation you have at this place, you don't have much chance of ever landing a plus one. Nobody wants to date a slut."

I push at him again with all the force I can muster.

"You mean the false reputation that I got because of you and Ashley? You have some fucking balls coming to me and asking me for a date just because you want to attend the exhibition. In fact, you have some nerve talking to me at all."

"Nobody forced you to get down on your knees in front of me." He slams his hand on the locker right next to my head, making me flinch. "You're lucky that wasn't a full-blown sex tape. Everyone would have seen that birthmark on your ass."

Even as my body starts to shake in a combination of anger and fear, I refuse to give him the satisfaction. "You must be on crack if you think you can just stroll up to me and get me to take you to that exhibition. Why don't you spend the evening with Ashley or buy your way into the event like you always do?"

Ricky's eyes turn into slits once he realizes that he's not going to get his way, and his voice lowers a decibel. "You don't know how easy it would be for me to ruin your life, Megan. You don't understand the kinds of connections I have. I still have the video. All I have to do is edit it and circulate it online. In a matter of hours, your reputation, your scholarship, this exhibition, and anything else that matters to you will disappear."

My face pales at his threat. I've never seen Ricky so venomous.

"So, you had better do what I'm fucking saying or—"

"Or what?" Comes a dark, familiar voice I wasn't expecting.

My eyes widen in recognition just as Ricky is tossed a few feet away from me with such casual ease that I'm left staring blankly at the man in front of me.

"Mr. Middleton?"

My boss steps in front of me, studying my shocked expression. As always, his is like a cold, impregnable fortress.

But his eyes.

His eyes are blazing hot.

I've never seen him look crueler.

"Are you hurt?" he asks, his hand reaching out to caress my cheek, and I shake my head, feeling both frightened and so completely safe.

"Then what's my name?"

"Hunter," I answer softly, and he seems pleased by my response.

Ricky is groaning on the floor as he tries to stand up, and suddenly, Hunter's attention goes toward him. It's as if I'm no longer there.

"Why don't you repeat what you just said to her?" Hunter asks, using a voice he typically reserves for people he's angry with.

Ricky stumbles to his feet, and his face has a twisted expression on it. He glares at my protector.

"What the fuck is your problem, dude?"

Hunter tucks his hands in his pockets, and I can't see his expression because his back is towards me.

"What exactly do you think a boy like you can do to Megan?"

I shudder at the undertones of cold fury in his voice, even as it remains affable.

"Listen, asshole," Ricky snarls. "This has got nothing to do with you, so why don't you go take a walk?"

Hunter just studies him. "You didn't answer my question." He takes a step forward. "An insignificant boy like you should know his place, so why don't you repeat what you were saying to her to me?"

"Who the fuck are you?" Ricky scowls, and I see his eyes dart toward me before turning back to Hunter as he sneers. "Oh, shit. I remember you now. You were the dude in the suit who showed up that day to pick her up. So is that what you're doing now, Megan? Fucking old guys? Is he like your sugar daddy or something?"

"Hey!" I snap before I can stop myself. "Watch what you say about him."

"Why?" Ricky just snorts. "What're you going to do? Do a mediocre job of sucking my dick again?"

As the last word falls out of his disgusting mouth, Hunter punches him fiercely in the mouth, making Ricky fall to the ground with a groan.

"Oh, shit!" I gasp in shock as I rush towards the man breathing fire standing before me.

"Hunter, you can't do that. Not here."

I look over my shoulder, terrified that security is on its way. There are cameras all over the campus. It might just be a matter of time before the arrive.

"You can't assault a student on school property, especially because you don't know who his family is," I say, keeping my voice low.

Hunter's gaze lowers to mine, and the fury clouding them is thick.

"Go to the car, Megan. Parker is waiting."

I'm shaking right now at the power radiating from him, but I force myself to stand my ground for his sake and mine.

"You don't understand what I'm saying. If you do anything more to him, it'll come back to me. I have to go to school here."

"No, you don't."

"I want to finish school. I've come so far."

"He insulted you." Hunter looks at me, his voice tight. "I heard him threaten you."

"So?" I respond, trying to keep my voice even but failing.

"How much more of this shit are you going to take from him and that girl? I won't stand for it."

"I'm not saying he isn't an asshole. He is. But this is not your turf, Hunter. If you attack a college student, there will be consequences, no matter who you are. His family is very well-connected. I don't want you to have to deal with any unnecessary drama just because of me. I'm not worth it."

"Say that shit again," he threatens in a deadly voice. He looks so angry that my voice gets stuck in my throat. "I don't think it's up to you to decide whether you're worth it or not," he says coldly now. His words are phrased like an insult, although I know they're clearly not meant that way.

"Please," I grab his wrist, which feels hot to the touch. "Even if you think you can face the consequences, I can't. I didn't put up with all this hell from them to lose my scholarship because you got angry. Don't do this, not when things are finally going well for me."

He hesitates at the last part of what I say, and I can see his jaw move before he finally says, "Fine, I just want a word with him."

Before I can protest him having a final anything with

Ricky, he's already walking past me and crouches next to a terrified Ricky.

"You don't know me, but trust me when I tell you that it would only take me a day to find out who you are, where you live, and who your parents are. It will take me less time than that to slit their throats while you watch. I'm not the kind of man you want to fuck around with, little boy."

I swallow thickly at his threat, and if I'm this terrified, I cannot even imagine what Ricky is feeling.

I hope it's sheer terror.

He deserves nothing less.

"Go near her again, and I will methodically strip you of every bit of happiness that you have, starting from your life here in college to your money and ending with your family. Don't touch her. Don't look at her. Don't think about her. Megan Taylor doesn't exist for you or the little whore who you run with. Am I clear?"

Ricky's face is as white as a sheet, and I can see a large bruise forming on his left cheek. He's quaking when Hunter bends down, grabs his jaw, and says, "This is a good look on you. Remember who gave it to you."

Then Hunter stands up and shoots a mocking look at Ricky. "One last thing. It doesn't matter who touches her: you or one of your other little art friends. If word gets back to me, I'll come for you. It would be smart to ensure that nobody tries to treat her the way you just did."

When he turns and walks towards me, my heart is lodged in my throat as I stand there frozen in a mixture of shock and awe.

"Come, Megan."

Chapter 35

Ulterior Motives

MEGAN

Hunter places his hand on the small of my back, guiding me toward the exit of the building. My body moves forward on autopilot, and it's difficult to even utter a single word. It's almost as if my brain is frozen.

He opens the car door for me, and when I sit down, he reaches over to buckle me in. The familiar scent of his cologne has my legs tightening, and when he pulls away, his face hovers above mine, meeting my gaze.

My eyes dart toward his lips and then back to his eyes, my heart racing. His proximity to me feels dangerous, especially when I'm in such a vulnerable state. That one moment between us makes it difficult for me to breathe, and there's a knowing look in his eyes as he straightens up and closes the door on my side.

I meet Parker's eyes in the rearview mirror, and he asks carefully, "Is everything okay, Megan?"

I press my lips together and shake my head. Fortunately,

he doesn't pursue the topic when Hunter takes a seat beside me, anger still rolling off of him.

He doesn't say anything, yet I keep waiting for an explosion. Finally, he firmly orders Parker, "Put up the divider and keep driving until I tell you otherwise."

I watch as a dark mirror suddenly springs up from behind the headrests of the front seats, and it locks into the roof. He's never used this before. I didn't even know he had one of these and now I can no longer see or hear Parker.

"What's going on?" I ask warily.

He turns to face me.

"That was your ex-boyfriend back there?"

"What?" I ask, taken aback by his question. "No! He was–He's–We never exactly dated."

His hand darts out and grasps my jaw, his thumb tracing over my lower lip.

"Then what exactly was your relationship with him? Has he touched you? Have you touched him? Did you wrap your pretty little lips around his cock like he alluded?"

My lips tremble, mainly because of his last particular question.

"It's not like that."

"Then what is it like?" He asks, his tone deadly.

The memory of a small bathroom stall hits me like a ton of bricks, and I push Hunter away, suddenly feeling dirty and used.

"You wouldn't understand."

"Try me."

"It was a dare, all right?" I snap, humiliation flooding over me. "I was new, and he was nice to me. I was the scholarship girl without a single friend. His friends wanted to see how easy it would be for him to screw me, to screw the desperate scholarship kid from the hood. And I fell for it because he was nice to me, and being at the receiving end of kindness is a fucking luxury to me."

My hands are shaking, and I wrap them around my middle, remembering everything from that afternoon down to the cold bathroom floor that hurt my knees to the way he grabbed my head and tried to get off on my mouth. Then, there was the shock and betrayal of seeing myself on video.

Hunter doesn't seem to be phased by my embarrassing revelation, so I continue talking, but I don't look at him as I tell him this part.

"He tried fucking me for weeks, but I would always find a way to subtly refuse. Finally, he persuaded me to give him a blowjob and somehow made it feel like I was the one who initiated it."

I look up at Hunter after my admission.

"Do you know why I don't trust people, especially when they're nice to me? Because every human being on the planet has ulterior motives—everyone. People use you to get what they want, whether it's getting a good laugh, furthering their career, or for money. People like Ricky and his friends like to put people like me in their place, to crush us under their shoes until you're a fine powder."

I can't control the words as they tumble out of my mouth like a tornado, spinning out of control, probably because I've never said them out loud before—even to Naomi.

"I was stupid enough to let him get into my head, and I said yes, but I was nothing but a joke to him. He took me to a nearby bathroom after classes ended. I didn't know that he'd set up a camera there. How would I? People don't usually do that type of thing without another person's consent, right? It felt wrong, like totally wrong, and I did a horrible job. He didn't get off, and I felt like a whore. But this is the worst part. Afterward, I went home and cried in Naomi's arms because I feared I had disappointed him."

Remembering that now makes me want to go back in time and slap myself.

What an idiot I was.

"The next morning, the video was circulating all over the school," I spit out, my hands clenching my jacket. "The visual art program is small, and I was easy to identify on campus since there aren't many students who look like me. When I was accepted into this program, I thought my life would be different, but after the video, people wouldn't look me in the eye when I walked down the hallway. I heard giggles and snickering behind my back. I was completely humiliated."

I can't calm down. I can't stop the tears of frustration I've been feeling for weeks and months from spilling down my cheeks.

Suddenly, I'm being pulled into a firm chest, my face resting against a strong shoulder as I'm dragged into Hunter's lap.

"Stop crying," he orders roughly.

But try as I might, the tears don't stop.

All this anger and injustice that I had been storing inside of me for the past few months, as well as overlooking the years of abuse I'd suffered in my childhood, is all coming out whether I want it to or not.

I'm shaking, and I want to break something or at least hit something. I want to lash out at the world that has only ever been cruel. I want someone to feel an ounce of the agony that I live with. That makes even something as simple as breathing difficult.

"Why didn't you report it?"

"He didn't put a gun to my head," I say into his chest. "It wasn't rape."

"He taped you without your consent and shared it with your peers. There has to be some rule against that at your university."

"I didn't have to report what he did to the administration," I tell him. "The Dean found out. He blamed me for leaking the video and said it went against the moral clause of the school. When he threatened to expel me, I told him that I didn't have any idea that I was being taped and mentioned the names of the other students who were involved.

"Once he heard the names, I could see him closing off any understanding of my situation. Ricky and Ashley have strong ties to the university. Their parents donate to the school and are important people in the community. To add insult to injury, he then said he was going to take away my scholarship for my part in the fiasco, and I realized at that moment that nobody else who'd put me in that position was going to suffer any consequences."

"Then what happened?"

"I didn't back down. I told him that I'd go to the media or the police. The threat shook him for a moment. He called the parents of the kids I said were involved, but they came to an agreement with the university. They would take the video down, nobody would get in trouble, and I'd get to keep my scholarship. Of course, almost everyone in the program saw that video, so they couldn't completely remove it, but the important thing was that I got to keep my scholarship and stay in school."

Hunter's hand tightens in my hair, not painfully so, but as if to remind me how angry he is about this.

"I see."

His tone is dark, and he lightly pulls at my hair so that I look up at him. I don't care if my face looks a mess, and apparently, neither does he.

"But you still talk to this boy?" he asks, confused by what he just witnessed. "Why?"

I sigh and attempt to explain to Hunter what is truly unexplainable.

Chapter 36

Waste No Tears

MEGAN

I rest my hand on one of Hunter's forearms, and through his jacket, I feel cords of sturdy muscle.

"I do what I have to do to survive in there. If I act like I've moved on from what happened, they'll get bored and move on, too. I can't have everyone thinking that those elitist kids broke me."

"You shouldn't have stopped me earlier then. Don't tell me you still have feelings for him."

"Don't insult me," I snarl furiously. "Once is enough to make a fool out of me. If I ever had the opportunity, without facing any consequences, I would embarrass the fuck out of Ricky. I would put him in the same position I was in and then make sure the whole world sees it."

A pleased expression crosses Hunter's face at my vicious words.

"Good, hold on to that anger. He's not the only one who has backing. Remember who you belong to. Don't ever forget that. As long as I have your loyalty, you are under my protection. From this moment on, nobody will dare lay even a finger on you. I know you don't trust many people but trust that."

I stir in his arms, conflicted by his possessive words.

"I don't belong to you. I work for you."

His mouth is inches from mine when he murmurs, "I think you and I both know that you most certainly belong to me, and I don't like the fact that any part of that boy's body touched your mouth. I want to erase every memory you have of him from your body and your brain."

His tongue darts out to lick at the seam of my lips, and my lips part without hesitation, almost instinctively.

Then I pause.

"I'm not doing this with you," I tell him, trying to remember my resolve.

"So, tell me to stop," he responds, his eyes boring into mine.

I hear nothing but the tires rotating under us as Parker drives us aimlessly around the city. Nothing but heat surrounds me as Hunter looks at me with hunger and ownership.

"You are—"

His kiss is surprisingly gentle as he covers my mouth, cutting off any more conversation. There is no fierce explosion of electricity, just a smoldering heat, which makes it difficult to think. He gently forces his way inside as his tongue curls around mine, taking from me whatever he wants.

Everything.

This differs from every other kiss we've had. I want to sink into him. I want to ask for more and plead for him to give me everything.

I unhook my seatbelt with my left hand and curl into his

body, sliding my arms around his neck. Our kiss grows deeper but not pornographic. It's intense but not dirty.

His arms gently slide around my waist, and when he palms one of my ass cheeks, I can't help but emit a small groan. The attraction between us is palpable. There's no denying it. I feel something different for this man, and it's not just lust.

I want him to consume me.

I just don't know how to tell him that I do.

Suddenly, the kiss ends, and he pulls away. Without thinking, I mumble the words, "I hate you."

"No, you don't." He smiles down at me, amused, but his eyes are burning with something so intense that I can't hold his gaze, my heart beating wildly. I don't know what this emotion is or if it's shared between us, but it terrifies me.

"You should be careful of whom you chat with for appearances' sake, Megan," He breathes against my neck, his mouth pressing an open-mouthed kiss on the side of my neck. "I seem to get a little homicidal when I see other men around you."

It's difficult to form a coherent response with his mouth peppering kisses on my neck. "Well, that's a pity, considering that I work with chatty, drunk men at the club all the time."

"Maybe I should change your position," he offers, and my eyes widen in horror.

"You can't be serious. I just got the management role."

A glint in his eyes spells trouble, and he presses another kiss to my neck.

"Maybe I should hire you as my personal assistant. The kind of work I do is so stressful. It would be nice to be taken care of."

It takes me a few seconds to realize what he means, and I slap him on the chest.

"You are a perverted old man!"

"Only for you."

He steals another kiss, deeper this time, while he traces my collarbone with his fingers, which always wreaks havoc on my panties.

"We discussed this before," he continues, teasing me with his words and mouth. "There's nothing perverted about it. I can work at my desk, and you can be my little cock warmer."

I should be offended.

Any woman would be.

But when Hunter talks dirty like this, it only makes me want him more, so he keeps talking.

"You don't think. You don't speak. For those few hours, you're on your knees like a good girl, licking my cock like a lollipop. Tending to it." His thick voice in my ear makes me let out a whine, and I feel his chest rumble. "You just become mine for those few hours. You don't have to worry about anything. I'll take care of everything. Your job is to exist for me."

My core aches for him.

What kind of control does this man have over me? I think in dazed shock. My entire head is filled with visions of me on my knees, serving him, just like he said.

"Not today, however." He chuckles lightly, and my cheeks flush in shame. "Today, I still need a manager."

"You jerk!" I hit him again.

He roars with his amusement. His laughter is a low, soothing sound filled with wickedness.

"Good, you're no longer crying."

My hand automatically goes to my cheeks, and I realize

they're indeed dry. Even with a smile on his face, his eyes turn dark and dangerous.

"I don't even like sharing your tears, Megan." He swoops some of my stray hairs back into their ponytail. "Don't ever waste your tears on a man who isn't me."

I blink, not believing the words coming out of his mouth.

"What?"

"You heard me. Not one more fucking tear."

Chapter 37

You Overestimate Yourself

MEGAN

"Out of all the conversations we've ever had, this has got to be the most toxic."

"Yes, well," he studies me, unbothered. "Nothing I say should come as a surprise to you."

I give him a long, judgmental look and one of introspection.

"I'm not going to sleep with you again," I say as if I've just decided something profound.

"We'll see about that."

I glower at him, annoyed by his confidence.

"I mean it."

"I'm sure you do."

"Maybe I should write it on my forehead in permanent marker so you remember," I mutter under my breath.

"You'd be writing that onto your skin for your own benefit." He grins. "Thinking if the ink sinks into your pores, maybe you'll stay away, but you won't. You can't because your body and mind are not in agreement."

"Well, fuck my body and my mind," I growl, scrambling off his lap.

Hunter reaches over to tap on the black divider and it comes sliding down a moment later. He then tilts his head to study me, his expression dark and his tone back to business.

"Why were you at school so late? Did he do anything else to you?"

It was then that I remembered the tickets. I immediately open my bag and take them out, breathing a sigh of relief. For a moment, I thought that Ricky might've managed to swipe them.

"I had a meeting with Miss Maverick. She's the new evaluator the university brought in. She wanted to give me my friends and family tickets for the showing. Ricky–" I hesitate, my hands tightening around the precious slips of paper. "He wanted me to invite him along. I refused. I would rather stab myself in the eyes with a spoon than take him."

The corner of Hunter's lips turns up, and he plucks the tickets from my hand, making me blink.

"So, who're you going to take with you?" he asks, studying the slips of paper.

"I don't know. Naomi, maybe."

"That still leaves one ticket."

"I don't have to use it."

"You're going to need a plus one," He states as if it's obvious. "Someone who can help you mingle and network. These exhibitions can help your career if you work it right."

"I know." I shift in my seat uneasily. "Why do you think everyone wants to be selected?"

"It would be useful to have someone by your side who

can help draw attention to you," he continues casually. "And to your work."

In the rearview mirror, I see Parker's lips twitch, and a suspicious thought forms in my mind as I glare at Hunter.

"Are you inviting yourself?"

He shrugs. "I don't need to use your invitation. I receive regular invitations for most artistic or fundraising events in the city, including this one. But considering that you have a sketch of my face up there, I think it would be the polite thing to invite me."

"You're unbelievable."

"Thank you. I've heard that many times."

"It's not a compliment." I grit my teeth.

The quick smile he shoots my way makes me melt and then get angry over my reaction. *Come on, mind and body, and work with me here.*

"I'm the obvious choice to go."

"How so?"

"I would be of benefit to you."

"I don't like to use people," I say coolly.

"Well, sweetheart, you need to learn," he smirks. "You won't get far in life if you let your misguided moral compass dictate all your choices. Sometimes you have to climb on people's backs to achieve your goals in life."

"Or annihilate them?" I ask, thinking about all the people I imagine Hunter has dealt with in his work.

"That too," he replies without skipping a beat.

"You're a terrible role model," I say quietly under my breath, although his offer isn't all bad. If I go to this once-in-a-lifetime showing, I should make the best of it. That's the entire point of going.

I shoot him a cautious look. "What do you get out of it?" I press when he moves his shoulders in an elegant shrug, remembering that Parker is listening. "I'm serious, Mr. Middleton. You don't seem to be the kind of person who hands out favors expecting nothing in return."

"I gave you a job."

"That I'm kicking ass at."

"I took you to Paris."

I look down to hide the blush on my cheeks.

"I thanked you for that."

He adjusts himself, smoothing the wrinkles in the front of his slacks.

"Sometimes I do things just for personal satisfaction," he comments, and I snort, refusing to believe it.

I try lowering my voice so that Parker doesn't overhear us, which is impossible since we're all in the same car. I wish he had kept the divider up.

"I'm telling you now. What happened in Paris isn't going to happen again if you come with me to the gallery and work the room."

The look he shoots me screams dark confidence, and he leans forward, his lips brushing against my ear, making my lower abdomen tighten.

"Trust me, you'll be begging me to fuck you by the time the exhibition is over."

His arrogance should piss me off, but all it's doing is turning me on harder.

"You overestimate yourself," I counter, feeling unbearably hot, my clothes feeling tighter around me.

He chuckles and hands me back the tickets. "You have some time to decide, but don't take too long. My calendar fills up fast."

I tuck the tickets back into my bag, refusing to respond. Other students will have their parents there, pridefully gushing with each other over their work. It would be nice to have someone, too.

"What were you even doing at the university today?" I ask him since it suddenly occurs to me that his presence was unexpected.

"I was dealing with some business matters," he replies. "You're lucky I was there."

"What business would the owner of The Blue Whiskey have at a fine arts college?" I stare at him. "And I would have eventually kneed Ricky in the balls. Nobody was around, so I might have gotten away with it."

His slight smile vanishes.

"Next time somebody tries to come after you at school, defend yourself violently and worry about the consequences later. And if you can't defend yourself, you call me or Lars or Parker. But if I ever see another bruise on you, which has not been made by my hand on your ass, you won't be able to stop me a second time."

My cheeks feel hot, and keeping my voice steady is a physical struggle. "First of all, I keep telling you I don't plan to jeopardize my scholarship. I can't hit anyone. They have a zero-tolerance policy for violence."

"And what about those kids touching you?"

"Let me rephrase that. The school has a zero-tolerance policy for violence you can prove."

"What if I can guarantee that your scholarship will not be taken away from you and they will not kick you out of school?"

I hesitate to answer. "I don't... I don't think you can do that."

"Can't I?" He responds in an amused voice, his hand reaching out to curl a strand of my hair around his finger in a possessive move. "I keep having to remind you of who I am. I have enough influence to protect your scholarship and your position there. And even if you lose your scholarship, I can create another solely for you."

My jaw drops at his casual statement, and I struggle to retain my composure.

"Yes, but—"

"So, next time, either put them in their place, or I'll do it for you."

He yanks at the strand of hair wrapped around his finger, which forces me to lean in closer. My eyes meet his, and even as his piercing gray gaze robs me of my breath, I wonder what I've gotten myself into.

Hunter Middleton is a complicated man who is far more experienced in life than I am, and it feels like he is systematically trying to possess me, body and soul. But once he decides that he's done with me, will I be able to walk away unscathed?

Chapter 38

Afraid Of Falling

MEGAN

"He punched him?" Naomi looks at me from where she's chopping carrots for dinner, her face reflecting shock. "Like in the jaw?"

I nod from where I'm sprawled on the couch, wearing my Tweetybird character pajamas.

"I know I shouldn't think about it like this, but it was fucking hot, and if I hadn't stopped him, I don't know what he would have done to Ricky."

"That is so hot."

"Every red flag about this man drives me insane."

"Hot ass red flags." Naomi grins.

Naomi's hair is tied in a slick bun, and not a single hair moves out of place when she brings the knife down harder than necessary on the cutting board, her voice filled with satisfaction.

"I'm glad somebody finally stood up to Ricky. I mean the fucking audacity to think that you still have feelings for someone who humiliated you like that. The guy might be good-looking, but he's a certifiable douchebag."

I close the art history book, leaning against my raised knees as I prepare for an upcoming test.

"I'm kind of still worried about what he said, though. What if he edits that video and rereleases it before the exhibition?"

"Didn't Ricky and Ashley's parents make an arrangement with the Dean? There would be some consequences if those two tried that dumb shit again."

"Yeah, an agreement was made, but then their parents donated to the school. A large donation. So, I'm still in a precarious position."

"Are you, though? Sounds like your boss handled him."

"I mean, Hunter definitely frightened him but–"

"Wait, a ding dong minute. Did you just call that grown-ass man Hunter?" Naomi looks up at me, her brows so high up in her head that they are at risk of disappearing in her hairline. "Since when did Mr. Middleton, our benevolent landlord, your boss, become Hunter?"

My eyes lower as I sink deeper into the couch. "I don't know. In my head, I started calling him that." I don't want to tell her everything.

When Naomi doesn't say anything, I peek over the top of the couch to see her staring at me.

"This calling him Hunter in your head started after Paris, right?" she asks suspiciously.

I shrug, trying not to give away much.

"Girl, you told me nothing happened in Paris. You said he was a perfect gentleman."

I grimace. "Well—"

"Megan!" Naomi rounds the island counter and strides

over to me, her eyes blazing. "You pretty little liar! I knew it. Something freaky happened, didn't it?"

I sit up, the book falling against my chest as I scramble away, but she's already hovering over me.

"Spill it. What happened between the two of you? I want all the details."

I have no choice but to reveal the truth. I can never hold things from Naomi for too long. "We slept together."

Her eyes widen. "You and your boss? The billionaire? Our landlord? You had sex with him?" The shock immediately transforms into suspicion. "Wait, did he force you?"

"No." I shake my head vehemently, horrified by the suggestion. "I had a little too much to drink, and it was my idea. He tried to put me on pause."

"Ha," she scoffs. "I bet."

I swing my legs around until they dangle from the seat, pressed into the carpet, sighing.

"I fucked up, okay? I was convinced that Paris would be a one-time thing and that he wouldn't look at me after we slept together. Honestly, he was acting like that on the plane ride home. Like, perhaps he regretted what happened."

"Wait, hold up." Naomi perches herself on the edge of the coffee table, facing me. "I don't understand how this all unfolded. I thought he was just some rich dude looking out for you because you remind him of his little sister or something, and I assumed him punching Ricky out today was him just acting like a cool big brother, albeit a hot one. But now you're saying you slept with him, liked it, and you're hoping it might turn into a relationship?"

She gestures with her hand alongside her temple that her mind is blown. This is precisely why I didn't want to tell Naomi any of this. I was afraid she would make a big deal about it, and I was right.

"I didn't say anything about wanting a relationship, okay? Hell, I barely know him. I can't even tell when he's serious or playing games with me. He says *I* used him, and I think he may actually believe that."

"Then we'll move out. Fuck it. We can find somewhere else to live."

"No, I don't think he meant that I used him for this apartment. He insinuated that I used him for sex and said that we're far from finished, whatever the hell that means." I mutter that last part.

"Got it." Naomi makes a slight sound of understanding. "So your tall, dark, and sexy boss, who's also way older than you, wants your ass."

"You think so?"

"He doesn't believe for one second that you were using him for his body. He's just fucking with you."

"I don't know, Naomi. Hunter doesn't often say things that he doesn't mean."

"I'm telling you this is all a seduction. And how do you feel about that? What did you tell him when he said you two were far from over?"

My head springs up. "Of course, I said no. But I don't think anybody has ever said no to him. And whenever he gets his hands on me, it's as if my brain stops working. I don't know what to do. As you said, he's my boss and our landlord, and evidently, he's acting as my personal security."

Naomi laughs. "That man is trying to be your sugar daddy. Actually, he ain't trying. He already is. Look at how quickly your life has turned around since you met him. You're a nightclub manager, we live in this luxury apartment, and you've spent the weekend in Paris!"

"I don't want a sugar daddy and–" My voice stutters to a stop as Naomi studies me.

"And what? What else is stopping you from enjoying whatever is happening?"

I rub a spot on my chest that has been throbbing every time I think of Hunter.

"I'm afraid of falling in love with him, Naomi." I bring up my knees to my chest, hugging them. "I've never had a man treat me like this. I've never felt so protected by a man I'm attracted to. Every time I have a problem, he's ready to fix it. I practically melt into a puddle whenever he stands close to me. Not to mention that he smells delicious at all times."

Naomi chuckles, "I'm jealous."

"But I'm not under any delusions about who he is," I continue. "Hunter lives in a dangerous world, and that kind of anxiety is the last thing I need. Working at the club is drama enough."

The words are pouring out of me, and Naomi envelops me in a hug. "Okay, you're panicking, honey. Breathe in and out. It's okay. You don't have to do anything you don't want to do."

Her voice is soothing as she hugs me tighter, forcing me to relax. Naomi doesn't talk much about her family but has alluded to having difficult relationships with some of them. Living her life on her own terms is a motivating force for her.

"Why haven't you said anything to me about this?" she asks, not letting go. "You're clearly worked up over this."

"I don't know," I sigh, pulling away from her to look at her face. "You know what The Blue Whiskey is like. Remember, I told you that I'd rather not share all the stuff that happens there to keep you safe?"

She has no idea what happened to Steve.

God, I can never tell her what I suspect.

"But this is about you and Mr. Middleton, not the club." She frowns. "This is about something personal, and you should be able to tell me anything. What if something happened to you? I wouldn't have had all the information I needed to help."

"You're right." I give her a small smile. "I guess I was reluctant to share because I feel like I'm way in over my head. I try to be respectful around him because he's my boss, but he's also this man I've been intimate with. When he took me to Paris, he was like this whole other person, and for a moment, I forgot that he was my employer. When we were there, he was just Hunter."

"So, what's the problem?"

"The problem is that you can't compartmentalize people like that. He is a complicated person. And now that we're back from that fantasy trip, I thought things would return to normal, but they haven't. He keeps trying to push his way into my life in the most wonderful damn ways. I don't know what will happen if I give in now and get my heart broken later on."

"Why are you so sure that he'll break your heart?" Naomi asks quietly.

This time, my smile is a little sad.

"Because that's what men like him do to women like me. I am nowhere on equal footing with him. He's the one who holds all the power: age, wealth, and experience. Even when I try to keep my distance from him and tell myself that this is not going to go anywhere, there he is. Mr. Wonderful. If he keeps this up, I won't be able to push him away much longer."

My friend studies me and then sits down beside me, flinging her arms around my shoulders. "Thank you for sharing that. I know that was hard."

"I should have told you sooner. You're my sister." I rest my head on her shoulder. "If not by blood, then by choice."

"Yeah." She presses a firm kiss on top of my head. "Listen, I know your head and heart are at war, and you also know I never give good advice." I snicker in agreement. "But I've never seen you talk about a guy like this. And as for him, you have to mean something to him, even if he doesn't know it yet, because no man will go to the extremes he has for no reason. He wouldn't keep you next to him unless there's something else there. He can have meaningless sex with anyone."

The thought of Hunter having sex with anyone else makes my stomach churn.

"I suppose that's true."

"So my advice is don't look for love. Don't hope for love. Enjoy the physical. Enjoy the gifts." She twirls around in our state-of-the-art kitchen to make her point. "Enjoy sweaty sex and the steamy kisses and whatever the fuck else you guys do. If you get your heart broken, that's fine because I'll be right here to pick up all the pieces and put you back together. I'll set you up on so many first dates that you won't even remember Hunter Middleton afterward. Just live in the now and enjoy it. You're young. You should have at least one hot, forbidden relationship under your belt by now."

I absorb her words, and while I know they come from a place of care, Naomi doesn't see the harm in taking risks, but I'm fearful of them. The riskiest thing I've ever done was take a job at that club.

"But I recommend you talk to him upfront about your job, this place, and his expectations if that worries you. Don't beat around the bush. This is your peace of mind we're talking about."

My friend has made some excellent points tonight, and I burrow myself into her, grateful to have someone like her in my life. I didn't grow up with any friends so it's finally nice to find a good one.

"Fine, I'll stop worrying incessantly. I'll talk to him."

Just then, there's a knock on the door, and I stand.

"I'll see who it is."

When I open the door, I see Parker standing there with a few rectangular boxes in his hand.

"Um, hi."

"Who is it?" Naomi calls out, but I don't reply because I see Parker taking in my pajamas. When he grins, I blush in embarrassment.

"I got these on sale. Stop judging me."

"They're cute," he chuckles. "Here, this is for you. The boss sent them."

I look at the large boxes and then back at him. "What is it?"

He shrugs. "Not for me to say."

I extend my arms to take them, but he shakes his head no.

"Where do you want them?"

"Put them there." I point to the coffee table.

He enters the apartment, and Naomi waves from the kitchen.

"*Heyyyy.*"

"Naomi, this is Parker. He works for Mr. Middleton," I introduce them. "Parker, this is my roommate, Naomi."

"You're the one who beat up our old landlord, right?" Naomi smiles in appreciation.

Parker glances at me before saying in a low voice, which means it's only for my ears, "I didn't do much to him. Mr. Middleton dealt with him personally."

I blink.

Really?

However, Parker doesn't offer more than that, putting the boxes on the coffee table.

"That's definitely a dress box," Naomi points out, glancing at me. "Why don't you open it while I get Parker something to drink?"

"Oh, I'm not staying."

"I'll make you a coffee." Naomi beams. "I make amazing coffee. Sit down. It won't take long."

Parker looks a little unsure as he watches Naomi hurry toward the kitchen. When he glances in my direction, I shrug my shoulders.

"Do what you want. She does make good coffee."

I reach over and open the smallest box on top, and my heart nearly stops at the prism of lights reflecting off what's inside.

"Please tell me those are fake." I stare down at the diamond stud earrings cushioned in a red velvet cloud.

Parker looks away.

My heart is pounding in my chest as I open the next box, only to reveal a necklace with a similar design. It's a beautiful 18k white gold chain with a stunning diamond pendant attached, and now I'm terrified to open the following two boxes.

The next box contains a pair of black stiletto heels, size 8. My size. I don't recognize the brand, but they look expensive. However, when I open the dress box, I freeze.

It's a black classy backless number with a low-cut neckline.

It's beautiful.

And the box is from a renowned design house.

"I can't wear this," I say, holding it up against me.

"Sure you can," Naomi calls over from the kitchen, having caught a glimpse of the dress. "You'll be turning heads in it. It's gorgeous."

"It's a good dress," Parker says with an afterthought.

"Why is he sending me a dress and freakin' diamonds?"

"He thought it would... I don't know. I don't speak for him."

"Clearly," I retort. "Where is he?" I carefully put the dress back in the box and glare at Parker.

"Upstairs."

"I see."

I walk over to the front door and march outside, ignoring Naomi's calls. I don't stop until the elevator opens in front of a large door that looks different from the front doors of all the other units in the building. It takes two loud raps for someone to answer.

But it's not Hunter.

"Hi, is Mr. Middleton here?"

The dark-haired man stares at me blankly before his eyes gleam with laughter. "You must be Megan."

He looks familiar, and then a head pops up from behind him. "Is it the pizza?"

My brows knit together at the sight of the man who had been shamelessly flirting with me at the bar the other day.

"What're *you* doing here?" I stare at him.

"Hi, Megan." He winks at me.

"She's looking for Hunter," Man number one tells him.

The flirt turns his head and bellows, "Hunter, your girlfriend is here!"

"I'm not his girlfriend," I replied irritably.

"And she looks adorable in her pajamas!" The man who opened the door for me adds loudly with a broad grin. "Very retro."

It's then that it hits me that I'm still wearing my Tweety pajamas. It's bad enough that I'm coming to pick a fight with Hunter, but doing it while wearing oversized children's sleeping attire was not one of my brightest moves.

"I'm going to change and come right back," I say with less confidence than when I arrived.

My words are interrupted when the man at the door flings his arm over my shoulders, pulling me inside, looking way too happy for my liking. "Oh, no need. You look adorable, just as you are."

I hear the sounds of hurried footsteps, and even as I try to escape the firm hold on my shoulders, I fail. I look up to see Hunter walking into the room, his hair wet, a towel wrapped around his waist, with droplets of water still dripping down his body.

"Get your hands off her, Vaughn, or I'll slice them off," he says cooly, striding forward and yanking me towards him until I'm pulled against his wet body. I press my hands against his firm abdomen as he wraps his arm around my waist in a proprietary hold.

Flirty guy wolf whistles from another part of the room. "I think he means it, Vaughn."

"Your name is Vaughn, but what's your name?" I direct my question to flirty guy.

"It's Christian," he chuckles. "I never gave you my name the other night?"

"No, you didn't, and now I understand why."

Hunter pulls me tighter as if annoyed by the exchange between me and his friend, and I struggle to free myself.

"Ick, get off me," I fuss. "You're getting me wet."

He releases me reluctantly.

"Now that all the unnecessary introductions have been

made, what're you doing here, and what're you wearing?" Hunter asks me.

I quickly cross my arms over my chest in an attempt to hide whatever part of my pajamas that I can. I hadn't really been expecting anybody else to be here, but I can't back down now."

"I don't want your diamonds," I say, swallowing my embarrassment.

"Excuse me?" Hunter lifts a brow.

"What?" Vaughn and Christian echo simultaneously. "You gave her diamonds?"

"Don't you two have places to be which is not here?" Hunter gives them a dark look, which would have anyone shivering in their shoes, but not these two. They're used to it.

"Nope," Vaughn wanders over to a couch on the right and settles down, watching us. "I'm basically homeless right now."

"And my apartment is being renovated, so I've got no place to be," Christian wanders over with a tub of ice cream in his hand to perch himself on the arm of the couch.

I can see Hunter's irritation increase, and then he says in that particular tone, which never fails to bring down the temperature of the room by a few degrees, "Get out before I toss you both out of the goddamn window."

I see the eyes of both men smile, and then they get to their feet.

"Fine," Christian snaps. "But the ice cream goes with me."

He grabs his wallet off the counter and wanders out while Vaughn grabs his coat.

"You live downstairs on the seventh floor, right?" Vaughn asks.

I blink, confused by the timing of the question.

"Yes."

"And your roommate is home?"

"Yes, but–"

"Great, we'll be there."

Wait, what?

But they're already gone before I can stop them.

I whirl around to face Hunter, demanding to know, "Are they seriously going to my apartment?"

"It seems so," he replies casually.

"Don't they have money to go somewhere else?"

"Absolutely, but they refuse to go home. Some people actually enjoy my company."

"And some people smoke crack."

"Funny." Hunter chuckles and then fully opens his towel before adjusting its tightness around his waist. I reactively widen my eyes in admiration of this man's package and can't believe that giant monstrosity was ever inside of me.

He notices my response and flashes his teeth behind one of the most self-satisfied smiles I've ever seen.

"Now, tell me, Tweety Bird, what's wrong with the diamonds?"

Chapter 39

We Could Have Been Killed

MEGAN

After casually asking me why I don't want his extravagant gift, Hunter begins to walk away, so I trail after him.

"Why are you giving me diamonds? They're expensive. Where am I going to wear them? On the bus?"

I realize that I've followed him to his dimly lit bedroom when he picks up a large towel from the bed and rubs his hair with it, watching me the entire time. "They're for the art exhibition."

"It's far too extravagant of a gift." It's difficult to stand my ground when he looks so sinfully delicious. "I can't accept them."

I try to distract myself by looking around the bedroom, which looks like a luxurious hotel room rather than an average bedroom. There's a slanted skylight right over the bed and since it's just two hours to midnight, the moon is shining on his black bedsheets.

"You have a skylight in your bedroom?"

"Yeah, do you like them?"

"Everyone on the rooftop can see what you're doing."

"Everyone, like who? The rooftop is reserved for the inhabitant of the penthouse, which is me."

It must be nice.

"And are those Egyptian cotton?" I ask awkwardly about the sheets because I don't know what else to say at this moment. I feel so out of my element.

"Come here." He gestures with a crook of his finger.

Even as my brain screams at me to stay put, I find myself moving toward him.

"What?" I ask tentatively.

He suddenly hangs the wet towel around my neck, and when I grimace, he grins.

"Stay still."

"I'm not your towel rack," I complain, but I don't take it off because it smells exactly like him. His sudden smile throws me off guard.

"Why are you smiling like that?" I ask, feeling a little breathless, something tightening in my chest. The look in his eyes is gentle but alluring if that even makes sense. I want to close mine or make a run for it.

"Smiling like what?"

I swallow thickly.

"Stop looking at me like that. It's not fair."

Before I can take a step back, he lifts his hand and slides it into my hair.

"Well, then, next time, don't show up at my apartment looking so fuckable."

Fuckable? I think to myself incredulously. My hair is in a messy bun, I'm wearing Tweety bird pajamas, and I don't have a trace of makeup on my face.

"Are you going blind in your old age?" I ask facetiously, peering up at him.

His hand tightens in my hair in punishment as he growls, "I may be older than you, but I am far from an old man."

"Don't tell me you have a thing for Tweety?" My eyes squint. "Is that some kind of fetish?" I jest. "Of all the things to have a kink about."

"What?" He stares at me, baffled. "What're you going on about now?"

I pinch at one of the pictures of the yellow bird on my top, forcing him to look.

"This."

Hunter narrows his eyes at me. "You'll say just about anything that pops into your brain, won't you? I don't have a kink for some damn cartoon character. Just the woman wearing it."

I hate that I hang on to his every word. This man could sell sand in the desert.

"I don't want the dress or the diamonds," I enunciate, jumping back to the entire point of my coming up to his apartment.

"Well, too bad, Tweety." He shrugs, leaning down to brush his lips over mine. "I already bought them."

"Then you wear them!" I retort without thinking.

He chuckles against my mouth. "Are you sure you're not the one with the kink?"

He seems to be in a good mood for some reason, which confuses me even further. Most days, he's super serious, and then there are other times when he's pretty playful.

"I'm serious," I try to get my words out as he kisses me hungrily, his other hand reaching for his towel. "I didn't come here to—"

I go still when I see something move in my periphery. It's a shadow, breaking through the moonlight on the bed. For a moment, I think I just imagined it, but just as I turn my head to look at the bed more clearly, I see it again. Something is partially blocking the reflection of the moon.

This time, my eyes move toward the skylight.

"Megan?"

I see the dark figure, and then I see the heavy-looking gun aimed right at Hunter. I don't hesitate, my instincts kicking in as I shove him back, screaming, "Get out of the way!"

He stumbles backward, and I see the momentary surprise in his eyes before they turn sharp. The bullet ricochets off the floor and into the bed frame, which scares the hell out of me. I jump backward, falling onto the ground.

There's a brief silence, and I exhale, thinking that it's over. But the hail of bullets that begin, all of them targeted at Hunter, has my heart leaping out of my chest. Any person with half a brain would realize this had nothing to do with me and would run out of the room.

But I can't leave Hunter alone.

My brain and the adrenaline coursing through my body are working at cross purposes as I crawl towards the bedside table.

"Get out, Megan." Hunter snarls. "Now!"

However, I'm moving deeper into the room, my body cold with both fear and determination. I can't see what Hunter is doing right now, but I can hear movement. It sounds like he's finally got a hold of his gun. The bullets keep coming, however, which is why I'm crawling so close to the bed. Hopefully, I can crawl under it.

I let out a short scream, covering my ears with my hands when the sound of shattering glass fills the room. The rapid exchange of fire that ensues is deafening, and I force myself, trembling and all, to move. I have to get to the cell phone on the bedside table.

"I told you to get out, Megan!" Hunter roars as he returns fire, his voice furious and filled with a tinge of something that I can't really identify. However, hearing him gives me the courage to move faster.

I ignore the pain that the shattered glass is causing against my wrists. It scrapes along every exposed part of my body as I crawl across the floor, and I bite my cheek in pain. Reaching the table, I slide half of my body underneath the bed for cover as I dart up my hand and feel for the cell phone.

"What are you doing?" Hunter demands angrily.

Then I hear an empty click and fear he's out of ammunition. Unfortunately, the shooter on the roof seems to realize it, too. As the barrage of gunfire continues, I quickly fiddle with the phone, my fingers sliding and slipping over the screen because of the blood on my hands. I manage to find the flashlight application, and then I immediately roll over onto my back, flashing the shooter in the eyes.

I hear a cursing sound, and the shooting stops for a moment.

"Get out!" I yell at Hunter, who jumps over the bed, grabs me by the middle, and then carries me out of the room within a second. He doesn't even put me down, striding over to the coffee table in the living room and reaching under it. When he pulls out another handgun, I look horrified. There must be hidden guns all over this apartment.

"You don't plan on staying and fighting, do you? That guy is clearly trying to kill you. He's got some sort of bazooka or something. Call the police, and let's get out of here."

"If it were a bazooka, we'd both be dead. I need to call Lars and Parker. I'll get my phone."

I soon realize that I dropped his phone on the floor when he pulled me out, and my hands tighten on his arm.

"You can't go back in there. He'll kill you. What if he's in the apartment as we speak?" I whisper.

Hunter gives me a cold smile.

"We'd be dead already, and trust me, I'm not that easy to kill. Now, go do what I said."

Hunter's words are barely out of his mouth when the front door bursts open, and four men charge in, armed to the teeth. For a moment, I forgot that they were in the building, but Vaughn and Christian enter the apartment with Lars and Parker already behind them. Each man has a unique but grim expression on their face.

"The alarm tripped," Parker explains. That's how we got here so fast. "What the fuck happened?"

Parker notices my bloody arms. "You okay, Megan?"

Then Lars moves forward towards me, his eyes concerned. "Were you shot?"

I look at both of Hunter's loyal security guards blankly. I think I may be going into shock. Hunter suddenly tightens his hold before turning me around to face him.

"Wait, were you shot?"

"What?" I look at all the concerned male faces in the room. "No, it was the glass on the floor from... the skylight. Oh my God, the shooter was on the skylight," I whisper, as if the man who just unleashed a gazillion bullets into Hunter's bedroom would just be in the other room, eavesdropping. It just hits me that he must be either gone or dead because the shooting has stopped.

Lars gives me one last look before he and Parker rush

inside the bedroom. "We'll check it out and get you some pants, boss."

"Shouldn't we call the police?" I say to Hunter, but he isn't listening. Instead, he has a strange expression on his face as he continues to study the cuts on my palms and arms.

"Hunter?" I ask again. "Shouldn't we – Wait, were you shot?" A hint of fear creeps into my heart. "Are you hurt?"

I can't control the way my eyes fill up, and the look on his face gets harder, and his voice is deep and gruff. "Stop crying. I'm fine."

"I'm not crying," I sniffle, wiping my tears with the backs of my hands and wincing at the movement as the shards of glass still stuck to my wrists move in deeper.

"Stop moving," he orders angrily. "Why don't you ever listen to me? I told you to get out of the apartment."

"And leave you there?"

"It's my job to keep you safe, Megan, or is having a man protect you a foreign concept?"

I think about what he just said. *It's his job to protect me? Does he mean that as my boss or as something else?*

"He's gone!" Lars's voice comes as he exits the room with Parker on his heels.

"Yeah, it's all clear, boss," Parker adds. "We'll go check the roof."

"I'll go with you," Christian says.

"I'll stay here," Vaughn adds.

I plop myself down to the floor of the living room as the adrenaline levels slowly subside in my bloodstream.

"Go put some clothes on, man," Vaughn tells Hunter. "I'll work on sweeping up some of that glass."

It's only then that I realize that Hunter lost his towel a

long time ago and has been stark naked since the shooting started.

"Come," Hunter sticks out his hand, and I grab it. "Let's see about cleaning you up."

Then, the weight of everything that just transpired hits me like a ton of bricks.

We could have been killed.

And I fall apart.

Hunter sweeps me up in his arms and pulls me into his very tight, naked body, telling Vaughn as he carries me, "We're going to be a while. You got this?"

"Take care of her," he says. "I got you."

Chapter 40

I Won't Go

HUNTER

Megan has never looked younger than she does right now, sitting before me on the closed toilet seat as I carefully pluck out the tiny shards of the glass stuck in her arms and hands. She's trying to be brave, but every time she flinches, I have the urge to put my fist through something. Lars offered to do it because he had the training, but as gentle as his touch was, I could see the pain in her eyes, so I told him I'd rather handle it.

Her wrists are so delicate as I hold them. It would be so easy to break her in two. For a woman so tiny, she has this fierce spirit inside of her, which is like a flame that refuses to damper even when it's on its last flickering ember.

I expected her to run.

I expected her to scream and escape like any sane person would have done.

But once again, she defied my expectations.

What she did was a dangerous move, but I'm pretty sure it saved both of our lives. However, she shouldn't have put her own life in harm's way. I can't even imagine the hell I would unleash on this city if something more violent had happened to her other than the glass in her hands.

It doesn't take long for my security team to swarm the building, looking for any clues as to who the assassin might be. Christian is on the phone with someone while Vaughn has disappeared. Both have their roles to play in helping me right now.

As do I.

But for now, I'm sitting in the master bath, plucking shards of broken glass from the beautiful, quivering woman before me.

"You need to try to hold steady," I chastise her, the sight of her blood irritating me. I'm typically not that affected by the sight of blood, but hers bothers me far too much.

"I'm in shock!" she snaps back. "And stop yelling at me."

"You're the one who's yelling," I remind her.

I sigh when she gazes back at me with mournful eyes filled with a sense of injustice. Without so much as a warning, I reach out and lift her up by the waist before turning around and carrying her to the guest room. I sit down in the middle of the made bed, settling Megan in between my legs and wrapping myself around her as I proceed with my task.

"There, this is much more comfortable. Now stop shaking."

I can feel her body tense at this closeness, but then she relaxes into me and complains, "It hurts."

"I know." I can't help it when my voice turns a little soft. I hate that she's hurting like this because of me. "Just bear with it for a little longer."

"Do you have any idea why that person was trying to kill you?"

My hand goes still, and I look down at the top of her head. So far, Megan has made it a point not to ask any questions about my business, which I guess is why it's been so easy to incorporate her as a part of my life at the club and home, too. Her easy acceptance of the violence she has faced at the club has been odd for a mild-mannered art student slash bartender, but I hoped, since she tends to look the other way, that she'd continue to.

"So you want to start asking questions now?" I ask her, my voice low, as I carefully pluck out another shard of glass. "I'm sure you have an understanding of the kind of life I lead."

She's silent, and then she burrows deeper into me as if seeking warmth. "A dangerous one, but besides that, I know next to nothing about you. I mean..." She hesitates and then says abruptly, "Never mind."

I let out a small sigh, then respond because I know I should after all that she's been through. I owe her that much. She almost died in this apartment.

"Megan, as long as you keep your head down and pretend to know nothing, you will be fine in my world. The key to survival is silence."

She stiffens. "So a man tries to annihilate you, and you don't want to involve the police?"

"I don't use the police for protection. I pay them to mind their business. This is my mess to clean up."

"Is that why no one's responded to the gunshots?"

"My team made a few calls. The police are aware that we have the situation in hand."

It doesn't escape me how different I am with Megan. I'm telling her things about my business that I've never told a woman before, and it makes me feel uncomfortable, to say the least. I've only known her for a couple of weeks, and she's gone from an intriguing woman in my bar to the object of my desire; and now she's in my apartment, whimpering as I try to patch up the injuries she received because she chose to save me rather than herself.

Ever since the night of the fire, when I stood in front of my blazing house, screaming myself hoarse as I was held back, something within me froze. When I realized that the two people who'd meant the world to me no longer existed, that they had been torn from my side in the most vicious manner possible, my insides turned glacier cold. I vowed to myself that I would never be in that situation again. I would never make myself vulnerable again.

To love.

But as my jaw tightens at the sound of the small woman in my arms, I realize I've left a small crack in my impenetrable shield open. I want to break her, own her, and consume her every thought. I want to possess this woman in a way that frightens even me.

"Fine," she tells me. "If the entire Los Angeles Police Department stays tight-lipped, who am I to ask any questions?"

I hold out her wrist in the light to see if I've missed anything.

"Good, because you know too much already. The less you know, the safer you are from the people who want to hurt me."

"Well, this is a fun conversation," she says under her breath, and despite the grim reality of the situation, the corner of my lip twitches. "If that's the case, shouldn't you just leave me alone?"

"Why are you so desperate to walk away from me?" I demand, knowing full well that she's completely right, no matter how much I hate to hear it. I should leave her alone.

The smart thing to do would be to distance myself from her as far as possible. But I don't always make the intelligent choice when it comes to her. "Do you have another lover lined up?"

"What?" Her voice is genuinely surprised, but I ignore it, fury pumping through my blood at the mental image of her with any other man.

"Are you fucking someone else?"

Her eyes widen, but her lips still don't move.

"I will say this once." I lower my head and whisper in her ear for effect. "If you let another man so much as touch you, I'll slice off his hands and gift them to you in a pretty red box. You belong to me, Megan."

"I'm not your property," she hisses, her voice defiant. "I'm going along with whatever this is between us because you're a pushy bastard, but that's pretty much it."

Amusement and anger run side by side within me at her response. She pushes all of my buttons, even the good ones.

"If it was just about me being pushy, I think you would have walked away from me a long time ago." My tongue darts out to lick the rim of her ear, and I smile in cold satisfaction when she shivers. "You want me so desperately; I can feel it in the air. I just have to touch you, and your delicious pussy immediately gets wet for me. So, don't act all pious for my benefit when we both know you'd love nothing more than to have your legs in the air while I fuck you raw."

I can see the hard indents of her nipples against the soft material of her pajamas. Just the effect I was hoping for.

"You're an asshole," she finally snarls, her voice slightly weak. "We almost died, and you're still being an asshole."

"And you're in dire need of having this attitude spanked out of you," I growl back, my hands itching to bend her over and whack that plump ass of hers. My dick hardens at the mere thought.

If she wasn't injured and if someone didn't try just to kill us both twenty minutes ago, I'd have her face down and ass up on this bed so damn quick.

Now my dick is hard as a rock, which she can no doubt feel. Her face is twisted in conflict as she tries to climb off of me, but I lock my ankles around her legs and wrap my arm around her waist.

"And just where do you think you're going?"

"How are you going to take the glass out of my arms and want to spank me in the same breath?"

"Sit still, Megan. We're not done," I order firmly, but of course, my authoritative tone just slides over her. She has a deep resistance to it that I find fascinating.

"What's going on?" Christian's surprised voice comes as he enters the room, watching Megan struggle fiercely in my arms. "No means no," he says to me with a smirk on his face.

"I want Lars to fix me," she whines to Christian.

My friend blinks at me, stunned by the scene before him.

"What did you do?" he asks me, laughing.

"Nothing," I say through gritted teeth. "Get out," I tell him. "Megan, I swear, if you don't stop right now, I'll tie you to the headboard."

She's still struggling when Christian tells her, "He will tie you up. He's not kidding."

She finally stills.

Christian just looks entertained. "You picked a real handful, didn't you?"

"The handful can hear you." She rolls her eyes at him. "I'm right here."

He gives her a grin. "Sorry, it's just that I've never really seen anybody resist Hunter's orders to his face and live."

"Lucky me."

I'm about to tell Christian to step outside again when I pull up Megan's right sleeve and see a huge shard stuck in her forearm. It sliced right through the fabric into her skin. She must not have noticed because of all the other cuts on her. *How did I miss this one?*

"Dammit, you're going to need stitches," I say, studying her wound.

When I meet her gaze, I see the look of stark fear in her eyes, and she shakes her head almost desperately.

"Lars can do it, right?"

"No," I tell her, hating the way the flicker of hope dies from her eyes.

"It's not that bad," she says, studying it. "So I'd like him to try. I'm not going to the hospital."

She tries shoving the long gaping wound in my face as if to prove it to me, but she's shaking all over again. My chest tightens in anger at the sight of the tears welling up in her eyes. This courageous woman has no problem facing death square in the eye, but the thought of going to a hospital terrifies her.

I look toward Christian, but he shakes his head. "We're still looking for a replacement."

Isaiah's death is an inconvenience. Losing a personal physician who didn't ask questions but was a master of his craft was a huge loss to me, and our backup doctor is not going to work long-term. I wouldn't want to pull him in on something like this.

"Megan." I gesture with my head to let Christian know it's okay to leave. When he walks out, I gently turn her around.

"I won't go."

"Listen." I grip her jaw, forcing her to meet my gaze. "I'll be with you the entire time. You'll never be alone. Nobody will touch you without my permission, and if anybody tries, I'll put a bullet between their eyes. You have my word."

She presses her lips together, giving me a tearful look, her voice choking up. "It'll get better by itself. I want to go back to my apartment. Naomi will be worried about me."

She's never this distraught. The last time she got even close to this upset was because of the hospital as well. The cut isn't bleeding that much, and it's begun to clot, but she still needs it looked at if it's going to heal correctly.

"The skin must be stitched, or it won't heal properly." I recognize that force or even strongly worded commands from me won't work here, and I can't bear to push her when she's already so upset. So, I try reasoning. "If Lars could do it, I would call him," I tell her, stroking her face and hair. "But I promise I'll be there. I won't leave you for even a second."

She looks so unbearably young at this moment that for a split second, I question what I'm even doing with her in my bed.

She's too immature for you, idiot.

But once again, I don't listen to that little irritating voice in my head, not when I have this fireball of a woman in my arms. There's a reason why she's so frightened, and I owe it to her to at least try to help her through this. She can't avoid hospitals forever.

"Do you trust me?"

"Yes," she hesitates before slightly nodding her head. "I probably shouldn't, but I do."

She's right about that shit.

I barely trust myself right now.

Her voice is a little hoarse, and I use the pad of my thumb to wipe the tears dangling from her lashes.

"Good answer, but I promise you can trust me now. Whatever it is that has you so terrified of hospitals, it won't touch you. I'll make sure of it. You'll always be safe when you're with me."

"Like I was safe today in your bedroom?"

This woman.

Damn, she pushes all of my buttons.

How could I be so off my game and allow someone to get that close to me? To her? If he had been a half-decent shot, he would have killed either of us, and the mere possibility of Megan no longer being on this earth is fucking unacceptable.

"That shit will never happen again. I promise you that."

Or I'll die trying.

Chapter 41

He's Thrown Down The Gauntlet

HUNTER

Half an hour later, with Megan relatively calm, I exit the car in front of the entrance of the hospital. I fix my eyes on her as she gets out and I see the rising fear in her eyes replaced by confusion.

"What is this?"

There's a long line of black cars with tinted windows waiting in front and behind us in a long procession, and just as we exit, so do the occupants of those cars. In their pristine black suits, their earpieces, and the grim expressions on their faces, anyone would be intimidated.

I scoop her up in my arms, ignoring her gasp.

"This is all for you. I brought in my full security team and placed them here, hoping their presence will be sufficient for you to feel safe?"

Her eyes are wide and watery when they turn to me as if she doesn't quite believe what I've done for her.

"I didn't–" she stammers, her eyes darting between me

and the security team. "I mean, you really went for the shock factor, didn't you? I look like a visiting dignitary."

I'm not surprised to hear the snarky quip. In fact, if anything, it makes me feel a bit relieved because if she's comfortable enough to snipe at me, she won't have a panic attack once we get inside.

"Ready to go inside?"

"I can walk."

"I'd rather carry you," I say calmly, not ready to let her go.

Her injured arms and hands are loosely bandaged, and I can tell she wants to hold on to something from the way her fingers flex, so I secure my hold on her, and she gives me a stiff nod. She looks like a soldier about to go to war, and while the thought is amusing, my amusement fades when I see her expression fade as we stride into the hospital, flanked by Lars and Parker.

"I need a doctor," I tell the wide-eyed nurse who greets us when we reach the station.

She looks at both men watching her intently, and then when she glances at me, she does a double take, recognition dawning in her eyes.

"What exactly is the issue, Mr. Middleton?"

I raise an eyebrow at the fact that the nurse knows my name. Perhaps we've met before, or maybe I'm more notorious than I thought.

"My fiancée," I lie, enunciating the last word and tightening my hold on Megan. "She had an accident and fell on some shattered glass. Please get me a female doctor."

"I apologize, Mr. Middleton," the nurse says uneasily. "But you'll have to wait a minute. We're quite busy tonight."

I smile at her, annoyance flashing in my eyes. "I don't

think you want to ask me to wait. My patience is running thin, and she's in a tremendous amount of pain."

I can see the nurse trying to stand her ground, clearly for the patients who are in the waiting room, but they are not my concern. This is why I need a permanent surgeon on my payroll.

"Nurse Paula." I glance down at her name badge before continuing in a pleasant tone of voice. "If I don't get a doctor with female pronouns within the next three minutes, I will shut down this hospital in five minutes, whether it's by setting fire to the building or buying it out with cash. I don't care which method."

"Hunter!" Megan quickly disapproves of the threat in my ear. I shush her with a soft pat on her thigh.

The nurse pales before stammering, "P-Please go to room four. I'll send a doctor in to see your fiancée immediately."

I see her try to glance in Megan's direction, but I narrow my eyes at her, and she scampers off. The room we wait in has a surgical bed, and I advise Lars and Parker to stand outside the door in case she tries to send security to deal with me.

"I'm not your fiancée," Megan hisses, her face still pale as she scoots closer to me when I place her on the bed. Her actions don't go unnoticed by me.

I carefully unwrap some of her bandages. The wounds look red and inflamed. It's probably a good thing I insisted on this hospital visit because I'm not sure I did the best job of pulling the glass out.

"Well, I'm too old to call you my girlfriend, and if I described you as the woman I'm sleeping with, you'd probably throw something at me."

"I've never thrown anything at you," Megan says indignantly, but her hands are cold to touch, and when I meet her eyes, I can tell she's trying to hide how terrified she is.

"It'll be over before you know it," I assure her while cupping her cheek, wishing that she'd relax. I don't know why I feel so uncomfortable in the face of her crippling fear, but I choose not to overanalyze it. This isn't about me.

The doctor, who arrives a few minutes later, is a middle-aged woman with her blond hair wrapped into a tight knot at the top of her head. The nurse has clearly already briefed her as she treads carefully around me, her voice painfully cheerful.

"Hi, I'm Dr. Yasmin. So what's going on today, Miss Taylor? I see you have some injuries to your arms."

I don't miss the hint of curiosity camouflaged in a pleasant tone from the doctor. She's skeptical about the nature of Megan's injuries. I guess it's common to assume the worst in a city like Los Angeles. I'm sure the physicians here have seen their fair share of abused women walk through the doors.

"Yes, I had an accident at home."

Megan, who hates relying on people, leans into my chest, damn near hyperventilating as Dr. Yasmin slowly rolls up her sleeves and then her pajama bottoms to inspect her injuries. I realize I didn't check her legs, but I can see that her knees are cut up a little as well.

Dammit.

My hands itch to inflict punishment on the man who crawled onto my skylight like a goddamn roach, and not because he tried to kill me, but because he hurt Megan. I shouldn't have my best men here at the hospital. Parker and Lars should be out with the rest of the team looking for that asshat. Hell, when we get out of here, I might have to join the hunt. I'd like to personally send him on his way to the underworld where he belongs.

"Well," Dr. Yasmin comments after a brief examination. "It looks like most of the shards have been plucked out already, which is good. But there are still a few remaining, and we'll need to treat you for any possible infection. I can have a female resident come in and take care of this quickly."

"We'd like you to do it," I tell her plainly.

"I understand your concern," she replies. "But this is how our residents get the training they need. We are a teaching hospital."

"Not tonight," I counter firmly, doing my best to keep my composure. I'm exhausted, and I have a shooter to catch. I don't have time for some uppity doctor who thinks she's too good to pull the glass out of someone's arm.

We have a brief stare-off, and then the doctor finally addresses Megan. "I will have to disinfect your arms and legs before I proceed, and it might sting a little. Are you ready?"

Her voice is kind, and the usually mouthy Megan nods, her face buried in my chest. Seeing her turn to me for comfort and protection is satisfying, even if it kills me to know that I'm the reason she's like this.

She doesn't flinch quite as much as the doctor removes the shards from her skin and puts them in a stainless steel bowl. By the end of the procedure, Megan is still leaning into me, but some of her fear has faded. I wonder if she simply had a bad experience with a doctor once, although my instincts tell me that it might not be that simple.

Dr. Yasmin carefully cleans the wounds with a saline solution and pat dries them with clean gauze. However, the moment she brings out a dark thread and needle, Megan begins to shiver and I immediately grasp her tightly, glaring at the doctor.

"We need to close your wounds," Dr. Yasmin gently tells Megan as she looks at me hard.

"I know," Megan finally speaks. "And I apologize for my behavior, but I know it will hurt badly."

Dr. Yasmin frowns. "Not with the numbing cream."

"W-What's that?" Megan asks.

I see the doctor pause, and then, after a moment of silence, she asks carefully, "Have you ever had stitches before?"

Megan nods mutely.

"Can you tell me the process? As in, what steps did the doctor take?"

Megan shivers again. "I knew somebody who was a nurse, and she'd always stitch me up."

I practically bite a hole into my tongue as Megan briefly pauses before she finishes her story. Why the fuck has a girl as young as Megan had a lot of experience with getting stitches?

"She would bring me to the local hospital to stitch me up, but since it was a favor, she'd tell me to sit still and not make any noise, or she'd get fired. There wasn't any numbing cream involved. Just a needle and thread. I didn't even know there was such a thing."

Dr. Yasmin stiffens, and her voice remains steady as she picks up a tube and shows it to Megan.

"Well, I'm going to use this prescription-level numbing cream on you so that you don't feel any pain, and your sutures will dissolve into your skin in two weeks, so you won't even feel that either. You also need three stitches on your forearm and two on your leg, but again, the same process."

I continue to hold her close but remain silent so that Megan can independently navigate the rest of our visit to the Emergency Room. The entire process is quick and efficient and while Megan's breathing is unsteady and her eyes glaze over at times, she doesn't say a word. Dr. Yasmin is professional throughout and when we're about to leave, she takes me aside for a quick word.

I reluctantly hand Megan over to Lars and step away to hear whatever she has to say.

"Make this quick, please."

"Somebody put a needle in that girl without anesthesia and, based on her story, it feels like it was done on purpose to harm her. If you can provide it, I would like that nurse's name and report her for malpractice. Your fiancee has been traumatized."

I study the doctor, and with a longer glance, I realize that she's not as middle-aged as I thought. The lines on her forehead are probably from stress or too much time in the sun. If I had to guess, I would say that she's only a year or so younger than me. With that realization, an idea strikes me as I give her a meaningful smile.

"I'll let you know."

"Don't smile at me like that, Mr. Middleton," she says curtly before turning around to leave. "It creeps me out."

I smirk.

And she has a backbone.

She'll do nicely.

As I return to Megan, who insists on walking on her own, I look at Lars as I brush past him. "Find out everything you can about Dr. Yasmin Torres."

"What about the shooter?" he asks, worried.

"Parker can take the lead on that."

I know he'd rather be hunting down the shooter, but

Lars nods discreetly before slipping away to handle what I've asked.

"How are you feeling?" I ask Megan as I help her into the car and adjust the seatbelt so it locks in comfortably across her chest.

"She was right. I don't feel anything but tightness from the sutures. The miracles of modern medicine, huh?"

"I don't know that numbing creme is a modern miracle. It's been around for a long time."

Megan simply shrugs her shoulders, and while I want to dig a little deeper into the fact that someone in Megan's past tortured her, I can feel someone watching me. I turn my head and look back at the hospital building.

My eyes narrow on a dark figure standing in the shadows, quite a distance from us. He's at least six feet tall, wearing a puffer jacket, and they pull the furred hood up. His hands slide into his pockets as he watches me. I stare back, realizing that he's far enough away that giving chase would be pointless. I'd never catch him, and neither would Parker. After a few long seconds, he turns around and retreats into the side of the building.

My smile is dark.

The events of the last few weeks are all crashing around me and have no doubt led me to this very moment.

One dead doctor, another dead Steve, and a hail of bullets in my home can only mean one thing.

My enemy has thrown down the gauntlet.

And I accept.

The one fact he seems to have forgotten is that you can't hide when I run this entire city.

I will find him.

And when I do, I will destroy him.

Chapter 42

Jealous As Fuck

HUNTER
One week later

I casually cross my legs, somewhat bored, as I address the man hanging before me in the club's cellar.

"Have you considered my offer, Craig? Once you do, I can make this all go away."

His face is bloodied, and he spits at me, "Fuck you!"

"You're a thief," I reply calmly, lifting my hand to gesture toward Parker, who grins and then yanks at the chain linked to the man's wrists.

Craig lets out a painful groan, and I click my tongue. "You shouldn't have taken what wasn't yours to begin with. Your business partner's son died because of your messiness, and you know mothers and their sons. She's understandably upset."

"What happened is not my fault; she's a stupid bitch!"

"Parker," I say calmly, cutting my captive off, and there's a loud crack in the air as the man howls in agony.

I check my watch. The midnight shift has just started

which means my favorite little manager is on duty. I need to wrap this up if I'm going to spend any quality time watching her from afar like I do most nights.

"But it absolutely was your fault," I say mildly, unconcerned about the man's broken teeth and his bruised face. "She trusted you, and you stole the funds meant for her son's treatment."

It seems that Craig doesn't have an ounce of remorse within him or a sense of self-preservation. He sneers at me and says, "If she's so broke, then where did she get the money to hire a low life like you? She's a lying bitch."

"Oh, I have a soft spot for mothers and children. I usually take cases involving them pro bono. Even men in my line of work like giving back to the community every now and then."

I tap my fingers patiently on my thigh as my mind wanders back to Megan. I'm wondering if she's taking things easy as I instructed her to. She tends to jump in and "handle" things when the employees aren't completing tasks at the high level she'd like.

She's adorable like that.

These scenarios are all the same. Craig's face tightens in anger as he struggles in his restraints, still refusing to admit his guilt.

"What you're doing down here to me is fucking illegal!
"

"Illegal?" I chuckle. "That's funny, coming from you, considering what you did. Now, listen, I think we've fucked around down here enough tonight. Don't you think so, Parker?"

"Yes, boss." He grins.

Parker enjoys toying with these lowlife types as much as I do. Lars, on the other hand, isn't into mind games as much as we are. If I left the interrogation in his hands, poor Craig would already be dead.

"Exactly, so you can either return that money you stole and leave LA alive, or we can take the money by force and arrange to dispose of you in a very inconvenient car crash. The choice is yours."

Craig mutters something obscene, and I sigh in disappointment. It's always the same. Men are either blubbering idiots or super tough guys when they find themselves in the basement of the Blue Whiskey. It would be nice if one day someone would surprise me and be a man about it and admit their guilt.

"Go ahead, Parker."

It's a half hour later that I finally exit the basement. It seems that Craig chose to be a tough guy. As I'm leaving, I run into a grim-looking Vaughn.

"We found something. Six months after Johnathan disappeared, there was a murder of a high-end plastic surgeon in Chicago. His entire family was murdered. At the time, it was considered part of an ongoing serial home invasion. A few families in the area had faced similar fates. The surgeon, Tate Meyers, was the third victim."

He hands me a file and I look at it. The picture staring back at me is of an ordinary-looking man. No one remarkable.

"Smart," I say. "He probably got some work done on his face and then made the doctor his third target. The police would have focused on the first or the last one."

"Explains why we haven't been able to find him."

"What do we know about this Doctor Meyer?"

Vaughn hands me another file out of his jacket. It contains the biodata of a rich brown-skinned woman with a pretty smile and kind eyes.

"There isn't much to say about the poor doctor at this point, but this is one of the nurses at the clinic Meyer worked at. Her name is Rose Grant."

"Young, probably easy to manipulate, especially if you have a handsome face." I study her bright eyes. "Easy to garner sympathy from as well."

"Yeah, that's what I was thinking." Vaughn agrees. "Interesting thing is that she quit her job a few months after the murders. Then, she landed in New York City and worked in a hospital. From what I managed to gather, she was dating somebody, although none of her ex-colleagues knew anything about her boyfriend except that they seemed to think he was well-off."

"They never saw him?"

"No."

"And you say they're her ex-colleagues?" I keep staring at the picture of Rose. They're two completely different-looking women, yet something about the look in her eyes reminds me of Megan. "Is she dead, too?"

"She went missing two years into her job. Just straight-up vanished. No communication, no credit card activity. The only thing I've managed to uncover is some security camera footage from a bank near her apartment. On her way to work, she stopped by the bank and withdrew a lot of cash. I corroborated it with her bank statement on that day. She emptied her account. She had a few thousand dollars in it."

I look up at Vaughn. "You think Johnathan took a fancy to her, and they moved to New York? Is he this nurse's rich boyfriend?"

"We weren't looking for a couple, we were always just looking for his shady ass. Maybe this Rose was his cover. No one gives a couple a second glance ."

Johnathan is strategic enough to pull something like this, I think to myself.

"So, she ran," I say. "Nice girl like this probably discovered something and made a run for it."

"And either Johnathan found out and killed her, or she is still out there hiding," Vaughn finishes.

"If she's still alive, then she's our biggest lead. She knows what he looks like."

"Exactly."

"If she's hiding, she wouldn't take another job in the same industry. He would be looking for that. Two years with him would have made her a little smarter."

"So what are you thinking?"

I look at the picture again, willing her to tell me where to find her.

"Look at her family. If she's scared, she may have managed a way to contact them. And also check out the homeless community in New York. Get in touch with our usual contacts there, and I'll reach out to a few as well."

Vaughn is about to leave when he says, "You didn't ask about the clinic or Johnathan's files."

"If she still worked there after the surgeon's death, then she probably stole those files and erased them from the system."

"That would make her complicit."

"Johnathan wouldn't leave evidence like that around, but you're right; I don't think the nurse willingly helped him commit murder. I'm not sure what we're looking at here, but there's something. Put the files in my office."

I have a lot to think about. However, I decide to check on Megan before I go to my office. It's been a couple of days since the incident at my place, and apparently, she's bounced back. Any normal person would be traumatized from being shot at, but Megan has the ability to recover from life-or-death situations quite quickly. It says a lot about how she values her life if I think about it. At first, I thought it was an impressive show of resilience, but now I'm thinking that a certain level of apathy like hers can be pretty dangerous.

Oftentimes, I see a dull acceptance in her eyes that bothers me, like how she deals with those idiots at her school. It's almost as if she's complacent about her life, but then she gets back up and keeps on fighting. How can I not be drawn to that spunk?

I open the door which leads to the main floor of the Blue Whiskey and I'm hit by a blast of dance music. Ignoring the gyrating bodies around me, I cut through the dance floor and meet Gage's eyes who is conversing with a customer. He gives me a discreet nod and then gestures with his shoulder towards the corridor where Megan's small office is.

As I enter the corridor, a tall figure bumps into me, and a sultry voice murmurs in surprise, "Mr. Middleton!"

I look down at the woman, and it takes me a second to recognize the bartender Megan hired. She's still pressed against me, showing no indications of moving back. I stare down at her, oddly repulsed by the look in her eyes, which is an invitation, clear as day.

"If you're quite done, step back," I say coldly.

Her eyes flicker, a flush crawls up her face, and she quickly moves back. I look around before narrowing my eyes at her.

"And what are you doing in this part of the building? This is for managerial staff only."

She toys with a strand of her hair, a coy look in her eyes. I can't believe this type of act works on other men.

"I got lost."

"You've been working here for nearly a month now," I say icily. "If you're this incompetent, I can always hire somebody else."

"Wait, what?" She asks worriedly.

"What's going on?" I hear Megan's voice as the door to her office opens.

She blinks when she sees Diana and me, and then, interestingly enough, I see a flash of a darker emotion move through her eyes as she sharply questions me, "Hunter?"

My lips curl in satisfaction at Megan's first clear display of jealousy and the fact she called me by my first name.

"I told you to stop coming back here, Diana," she quickly reprimands the bartender as she strides forward, her gait a little slower than usual because of her stitches. She inserts herself between Diana and me, who is now wearing a curious expression on her face. "This area is off limits. This is the second time I've had to tell you."

"Sorry," Diana says, her voice a little hostile. "I got lost."

"As you did last time." Megan's voice is cold. "Return to the bar. Now."

My lips curl again.

And my dick approves.

Look at my little, badass, managerial Megan.

Jealous as fuck.

Chapter 43

What If Someone Walks In?

HUNTER

I watch the bartender leave, but not before she shoots me a look with a coy smile. Persistent little thing. It's too bad she doesn't understand that before Megan came into my life, I wouldn't have ever entertained sleeping with an employee of the club. She's lucky I'm in a good mood. I would have fired her on the spot if this were even six months ago.

"Bitch," I hear Megan mumble softly under her breath, and my brows lift in utter delight.

"What was that?" I ask facetiously.

"Nothing," she growls before turning to face me. "And what were you doing just standing there with her?"

I can't seem to wipe the smirk off of my face.

"Listen, if you want to start looking around for someone new to play with." Megan's slim, bandaged finger drills a hole in my chest.

I take her finger and lay it lightly against my chest as I

stare intensely into her eyes. "I'm not looking to play with anybody but you, Miss Taylor."

"Oh," she mutters in a softer voice. "Okay, then."

I can see the rapid confusion on her face at her own actions, and I wonder if she even realizes that she was acting out of jealousy. I doubt it. But I don't need her to understand it right now. I'm just happy that she reacted at all.

That's progress.

"Why were you here, though?" She looks at me strangely. "Your office is on the other end of the hallway."

"I came to see you."

Obviously.

"For what?" she asks warily, and her familiar, suspicious tone amuses me.

"Do I need a reason to visit my favorite Blue Whiskey employee?"

"Favorite, huh?" she repeats skeptically. "I guess since you're the owner, you don't really need a reason to be here at all, so come on in, Mr. Middleton."

I tossed out anything that belonged to Steve and stripped down the office to the bare basics so Megan could make the space her own. So far, it's sparsely decorated, although I can see that she's hung up some random sketches and artwork on the walls.

"When are you going to order a new desk or something?"

"That's a waste of money."

"My money."

"Actually, it's Blue Whiskey money, and spending it wisely is part of my job." She knocks on the surface of the desk. "This old oak desk works just fine."

It's funny how it was easier to get her to accept a trip of a lifetime to Paris than to let me buy her a simple desk for work. When I glance at the surface of the desk, I can see that she was busy working. With a single hand, I shift through the stack of papers on her desk and look at her laptop screen.

"What are you working on?"

"I'm creating a digital system for your suppliers," she replies, coming over to stand beside me. "I know you're old school, but enough is enough."

"Impressive," I chuckle.

"I figure if I make myself useful, you won't want to fire me once this thing between us is over."

I give her a steady look. "Thinking long term, are we?"

She shrugs but doesn't quite meet my eyes.

"This is a thing, right?" she asks tentatively.

"It's whatever you want it to be. I simply find it interesting that you're thinking beyond whenever you think this *thing* of ours is going to end."

"Well, I have to."

"And why is that?"

"I'm not going to wait around until you get bored with me. "

This again.

She's actually serious.

"What do you have planned once I'm out of the picture?"

My tone is significantly cooler now. It irritates me that she's planning a future where I don't exist because she still doesn't trust me.

"Oh, don't be so sensitive," she scowls, meeting my gaze. "It's unattractive."

"Don't let anyone in the club hear you talking to me like that," I say incredulously, half surprised at myself for tolerating the insult.

"Yes, well." She looks a little guilty in the face. "I wasn't trying to be rude." Her eyes shoot up. "But you're going to get bored sooner or later, and I won't always be able to depend on your kindness. I need this job if I'm going to pay my way through school and eventually get my own apartment. So, my master plan is to prove my worth and make myself indispensable to you."

I don't know why she's so damn convinced that I'm so fickle, but it's probably smart of her to assume so. I tend to only stick with a woman for a night or so, and I'm sure that reputation has gotten back to Megan from some of the other workers here or the internet. What she doesn't realize is that I've broken half of the rules in my own handbook when it comes to her.

I cast a cursory glance over her computer screen and peep at the software she's working with, and it's interesting enough to impress me. "Are you taking coding classes?"

"No, but I took one a while back." She shrugs. "I'm not that great at it, but it used to help me make some pocket change when I was younger."

"Younger?" I ask flippantly.

"Yes, younger," she responds as one corner of her delicious mouth turns up.

"I see."

She pauses. "It's good that you dropped by. I want to talk to you about something."

"Go ahead."

"One of the kitchen staff, Billy, is leaving, and he gave me a recommendation for a potential employee I want to check out. From what I know, the girl is young and homeless, but he asked me to test her cooking before I turned her down. I know you're a little skittish about new employees after the Steve fiasco, but I think we should try her out."

I sprawl out across her couch and pray that the traitor Steve never did anything disgusting on it during his time here. Now that I think about it, I should have thrown this out, too.

"Come here," I tell her.

Megan gives me a narrow-eyed look. "I'm talking about work right now."

"No reason you can't do it from my lap," I smirk suggestively at her. "You might even be able to convince me of a trial run for the new girl if you play your cards right."

She hesitates, and I pat my leg, my voice firm. "Come."

When she moves towards the door, I tell her, "No, leave it unlocked."

"What if someone walks in?"

"Then they'll know you're off limits," I smirk, unbothered by her concern. However, she walks across the room and locks the door anyway.

"I have a reputation to maintain. Half the servers already think I got this position by screwing the boss. I don't need to confirm their suspicions."

"What suspicions?" I ask pleasantly, but my eyes aren't smiling.

"Does it matter?" She scowls, walking over to me.

I reach out, grab her by her slim waist, and lower her luscious ass onto my lap until she's straddling me. I immediately harden underneath my zipper, but that's par for the course whenever I'm close to this little fireball.

"To be fair, you've only ever screwed me once, and even then, I was the one doing the fucking. If I recall correctly, all you did was plead and scream for more."

Megan's hand covers my mouth, her eyes full of embarrassment. "Quiet."

I grin against her hand, amused by her sudden bout of shyness, and then lick her palm.

"Hunter!" she cries out in disgust, pulling her hand away from my mouth and wiping it on my suit jacket. "That's disgusting. Why would you do that?"

I have to laugh at her response. "You know I've licked you all over your body, right?"

"It's still disgusting." She contorts her face, and I laugh even harder. "I haven't washed my hands in hours."

"I suppose in your head that makes complete sense," I chuckle before cupping her face in my hands. "Let's try this then."

I bring her face down to mine and kiss her softly on the mouth, enjoying the sweet sensation of her soft lips moving against mine. She sinks quickly into our kiss, and when she moves closer to me, I momentarily break away, warning, "Careful, you still have stitches."

"Oh, yeah," she says through shallow breaths, her eyes cloudy with desire. It's fascinating to see how easily she gets turned on with the simplest of touches. I kiss her neck and her jaw, enjoying her sweet taste. She smells like jasmine on a summer evening.

Normally, sex for me is fast, rough, and transactional, but I don't want to have sex right now. I mean, obviously, I wouldn't mind it, but presently, I'm more than satisfied that Megan's pressed against me. In fact, there's nothing more I'd like to see than her rub against me and watch her release. It's a beautiful thing to watch.

And I wouldn't care who walked in and saw us.

Chapter 44

There's No Shame In Asking

HUNTER

I slowly move my hands underneath Megan's blouse and cup one of her breasts, pulling up the bra and kneading the soft flesh in my hands. Her small but dense breasts fit so perfectly in the palm of my hands. I swallow her soft moans, relishing the sound.

The way she squirms against me is tantalizing, and that jasmine scent is driving me crazy. I use the other hand to push up her skirt and cup her mound through her panties. She lets out a soft gasp, "Hunter."

"What?" I press an open-mouthed kiss against her jawline. "Do you want something?"

I steal another kiss from her, sucking on her tongue and making her press down into my hand. A dissatisfied sound escapes her.

"It's polite to ask for something you want, Megan," I bite gently down on her shoulder through her blouse.

"Stop rubbing me and do something," she groans.

"Like what?" I hide my self-satisfied smile on her neck.

I can see the visible struggle on her face. She's dying to tell me what she wants but is battling with herself. I assume all she's ever been with are little boys who probably rut themselves inside of her without a moment's consideration for her pleasure. She's never had to voice her desire because no one's ever cared.

Well, I fucking care.

"Megan." I pinch her nipple in a punishing manner to get her full attention. "There's no shame in asking to be fucked. You can always use your words with me."

I part the bottom lining of her panty and rub against her hardened clit, which is damp with her juices, another part of her that drives me wild. She gets wet so easily with just a few words or some strategic touches. I can only imagine what she'd be like in bed if she could fully get out of her head and just let go.

"Why are you such a condescending asshole?" She glowers down at me and then immediately throws her head back when I thrust a finger inside of her.

"Language," I remind her mildly. "No name-calling."

I watch with delight as she tries to fuck herself on my finger, but she can't move her leg that much, and she gives me a look filled with frustration.

"Fine, you win!"

"I win what?"

"Please, just fuck me already."

"With what?" I ask sadistically, enjoying her suffering.

"Your fingers, please." She mouths the last word against my ear in a soft, submissive-sounding whisper that makes my dick harden instantly.

I slide in another finger, and she lets out a wanton

moan. Then I press a kiss along her bared throat, stretching my fingers inside of her, making her writhe. However, my patience is fleeting, and I withdraw my fingers, reaching out and undoing my zipper.

I relish the smell of her as I take out my cock, which is painfully hard, lift Megan by the waist, and position her straight down my stiff length.

"Hell!"

Her scream is loud and so very satisfying, but I can't have half the staff running back here to see what's going on, so I quickly cover her mouth with my hand, letting out a quiet groan of my own. She's so wet and tight. I want more of her. When I use my hands to lift her hips and slam them down on my dick again, she lets out a sobbing cry and wraps her arms around my neck for leverage.

"Hunter," she exhales harshly.

The original plan was to take things gently and slowly, but it seems impossible when I'm inside of her because I just want to fuck her so hard that she can't walk. I move in and out of her sweet pussy, trying not to jostle her too much and be mindful of her stitches. And yet, this slow pace is torture for both of us.

"Faster," she pleads, her words mindless. "Do it harder. I need harder!"

I want to.

God, I want to.

But I don't.

"You'll take what I give you, kitten," I whisper against her mouth. "As slow or as soft as I give you."

I continue to fuck her in slow, long, deep strokes, and I can see the unfocused look in her eyes as she tries to control the pace and fails. Her face is twisted in desire, and as her warm flesh tightens around my cock, I feel my self-control slipping. My pace increases as I chase my own relief when she orgasms around my dick, crying my name, "Hunter!"

When I come with a painful grunt, it pushes her off the edge once more. She's wrapped around me so tightly that I don't even get the chance to pull out.

"Well, fuck," I sigh, rubbing my hand on her back as she trembles in my arms. "You really did it this time, sweet Megan." But she's too far gone to care about our misstep.

A while later, as I clean her up with some tissues, she becomes a bit more lucid. However, she doesn't seem very fazed by what happened.

"Don't worry. You're safe," she assures me in a hoarse voice.

She tries to stand up but stumbles, muttering under her breath, "You're bad for my health. I can't even walk."

"Are you on the pill?" I steady her. This is clearly something I should have asked about a long time ago, or at least ten minutes ago, but when it comes to this woman, my behavior has been irrational and irresponsible from the start —some might say obsessive.

"I should have told you that I test regularly and that I'm clean," I tell her.

"I'm not on the pill," she mumbles, not meeting my gaze. "It's just that I can't get pregnant."

"What do you mean?" I frown.

"I had an accident when I was young. It damaged my uterus. So, you're fine."

"Hey." I grab her arm, forcing her to look at me. "What are you not telling me?"

Her smile is sharp as she looks at me and her eyes dull in that way when she retreats into herself.

"Let it go."

She adjusts her skirt, but I can see her taut jaw. She's shutting herself off from me. It's an infuriating habit of hers, this refusal to give me even an inch.

An inch that I never knew I wanted so badly.

The more she holds herself back, the more I want to dig in deeper. I find myself wanting to know everything about her.

"That's not going to happen." I reach out and button up her blouse as she glowers at me.

"So, it's okay for you to have your secrets, but I'm not allowed to have mine?"

"Exactly."

"That's very hypocritical of you."

I smile at her, pulling her down until she's back on my lap. "I never said that I was fair, Miss Taylor."

She gives me a long look. "I see. So, what's your plan? Try to pry all my secrets out of me and then get me to fall head over heels for you. And once that's done, you leave me behind brokenhearted?"

I know they're fueled by insecurity, but my eyes narrow at her sarcastic words. "Watch it, Megan. Even I have my limits."

"What part of what I said was wrong?" She scoffs. "Or even offensive?" I watch her retreat to her desk, all passion erased from her face. "Understand this, Mr. Middleton. I don't trust anybody, especially not with my heart. I appreciate all the kindness you've shown me and the great sex, but I'd never be stupid enough to fall in love with you. If there's ever a day I think I may be falling, though, this entire arrangement ends."

Her voice is suddenly and strangely cold. It's almost as

if mind-blowing sex has the opposite effect on her. Instead of feeling closer to me like most women would, she immediately puts up a barrier, forcing me out.

I don't like it.

And I'm not going to allow this behavior of hers to stand.

Chapter 45

Let Me Remind You Of Something

HUNTER

"I don't think you understand how this works," I say softly, my eyes tracking her every facial movement.

"I think I do. Look, you want to fuck me? That's fine. I can admit that we seem to be on the same page with that. You don't treat me like shit, and I appreciate that, but I'm not going to put myself in a vulnerable position because you want to know every little thing about me."

She sits in her chair and places her palms on the desk, seemingly trying to center herself.

"First, it was that phone call. Now, it's you trying to get me to talk about my past. I don't want that. Those types of questions are for people wading into relationship territory. You don't want a relationship, and neither do I. In this arrangement, you get what every man wants: sex without strings attached. Isn't that what you want from me?"

My hands curl into fists at the rudimentary way she's describing our relationship. Sex without strings? The more she shoves it in my face, the more I realize that I don't like the sound of it. She takes my silence as permission to continue. Her voice is still eerily calm as she speaks again.

"This attraction between us will last a few weeks or maybe a few months. We'll both have a good time and if I'm lucky when it ends, you won't fire me or kick me out of the apartment before I find something else. You'll eventually go on to find some gorgeous model girlfriend, and I'll end up finding some nice, quiet artist, and we'll both go live our separate lives. So let's not make more of this than it is."

So, she already plans to leave me and find someone else. A fucking artist? I'm not even in the running as a possibility for her future.

That thought infuriates me.

I'm on my feet before I know it. Crossing the room to her, I put my hands on either side of the armrests of her chair, relishing in the sudden mixture of shock and fear I see in her eyes.

"Don't presume to know what I want, Megan. The only reason you get away with this much is that I let you, but the line you're treading is thin."

However, instead of being intimidated, she bares her teeth at me. "What part of anything I said was wrong? Go on, tell me."

A growl leaves my throat, frustration at this slip of a woman who is driving me insane. "All of it!"

"Excuse me?" This time, her expression goes slack. "What do you mean?"

My leash has snapped.

"You think you're going to still work in my club while you date a nice, quiet artist?"

"So you do plan on firing me."

"Why would you want to work for a man you *used* to fuck?"

"Because... because this is casual," she says tentatively.

"You keep pushing and pushing me with these insane assumptions about the future. My future. I think you forget who I am. This isn't over until I say it's over."

Her eyes widen, and she tries to move, but I force her back, furious with her and myself for my lack of control over this woman.

"Let me remind you of something. I fix problems for people by getting rid of their problems, which often means that I make people disappear. Also known as I kill them. That's the kind of man you're casually sleeping with for as long as it suits you."

I'm trying to shock her, but the fear is no longer present in her eyes. Instead, there's a mocking look in them as she pushes me back, getting to her feet.

"You think you can threaten me? Do you think I'm afraid of what you can do to me? What's the worst you can do? Kill me? I'm already living in hell. Do you think you're the cruelest person I've ever met? I already know what it's like to be tortured, so fuck you!"

She picks up a ceramic vase of seasonal flowers on her desk and throws it past my head at the wall behind me. It shatters on impact, and she's shaking, not in fear, but with rage.

"I never said I'd kill you," I say, trying to remain calm. "That wasn't my point."

"Then what was your point? What do you want from me, Hunter?" She spreads her arms, her face twisted in anger. "What is it?"

"You!" I roar, my anger exploding. "I want you, you infuriating woman!"

"You're already fucking me."

"I want more!" I reach over and grab her by her upper

arms, pulling her into me. "I'm not one of the boys from your university. I'm a grown-ass man whom you're driving crazy with all these damn plans you're making for once we're over, as if you just can't wait for me to leave! Don't you get it yet? I'm not going anywhere, Megan. I don't want to."

Her expression changes, shock overtaking her features. Suddenly, the coldness vanishes, and I'm looking down at the heartbreakingly beautiful woman who has me all twisted inside.

"What do you mean, you want more?" she almost whispers.

"I may be a cold-blooded monster in many areas of my life, but with you, I can be different. I've never once said that I would throw you away or that I'm using you. And I definitely never said that this was temporary."

I continue, "All of these are just your own words and assumptions. Do you think I go around acting like this with other women? Knowing how desperate you are to push me away, I can bet you've not even done your research on me. I don't date women. I fuck them once, and then we're over. But you're different. You've been different from that first day when you talked back to me at Table 21."

A heavy silence follows my words, and her eyes tremble as she meets my gaze. "I don't–I don't want to fall in love with you."

The doubt in her eyes makes me feel like I'm suffocating, and suddenly, I'm the same boy standing in front of that burning house, on the verge of losing everything. My voice lowers to a hoarse whisper. "Why? Would it be that bad?" I ask, vulnerable as hell. "Do you loathe the idea of loving me that much?"

I can see her searching my eyes, and her voice is hollow.

"I've never been in love before, but I have a feeling that if you break my heart, I won't survive it. I don't want to take that risk."

I hate that this isn't an innocent college student talking to me. It's a woman who's experienced far too much pain in life and has lost faith in people. I can see inside of her how tattered and broken she truly is. It only makes me want to hold her even closer.

"What if I promise not to break your heart?"

She shakes her head disbelievingly. "You can't make that guarantee, Hunter. No one can. You're taking a gamble, and my pain is the price."

I study her, an urgent feeling seizing my chest. I can't let her run away from this. I won't. It's too late for running.

"You, of all people, should know that everything in life is a gamble. You getting a scholarship into an art institute was a gamble. You coming and working here was a gamble. Sleeping with me was a gamble. Everything you've achieved in life has been through hard work, but it's also been a coin toss. So why not us?"

Chapter 46

Whenever, However and Always

MEGAN

Why not us?

I stare up at the man whom I'm already falling in love with.

My heart is racing.

He's usually so calm and composed, not a hair out of place. Even in his anger, he's like a frigid glacier, an immovable mountain. And yet right now, in front of me, he looks worked up, furious, his grey eyes boring into mine, demanding an answer—willing me to tell him exactly what he wants to hear.

I've spouted lie after lie at him, hoping that he bought my deceit and believed that I was content with a physical relationship. I hoped that if I said it fiercely enough, with just the right amount of conviction, even I would begin to believe it.

I never expected this reaction.

"So..." I choke on my salvia, feeling disoriented. "Do

you want to date me?" I finally ask after a long moment, and I can hear the disbelief in my voice.

"That's a start," Hunter says with a tight facial expression.

"Why?" The question slips out of me before I can reel it back in. He stares at me, and his hands finally loosen their grip on my arms.

"Other than the possibility of being hurt, which is the chance all humans take, I need to know why you're so afraid of falling in love with me. After all, while you may know about some of the darkest parts of me, you can also see that there's some light, too."

My heart crawls up my throat as he puts me on the spot. I don't want to answer his question, and I can tell that he knows it. I'm just not sure that I have any more lies left in me.

"You have five seconds," he warns.

"I don't know how to explain it," I try bullshitting him.

"Try."

"It doesn't make any sense."

"It will to me."

I lower my eyes from his. I'm not sure that I can look at him as I say the words. "You make me feel safe."

"Is that it?"

I raise my eyes back to his. The disappointment in his gaze is crippling, but if he wants more of an explanation, I'll give it to him.

"Ever since you walked into my life, everything has changed. I feel hopeful about my work, where I live, and even my life at school. You've been kind to me, and you protect me. It's a nice feeling to know that someone has my back, and when I'm around you, I can see a better future, a happier one than the mediocre one I imagined."

I look away, disconcerted by his gaze that is stripping the truth from me.

"I can't get you out of my head," I tell him. "And it terrifies me."

The words are raw; this time, his head lowers to nuzzle my cheek. "Is that all?"

My eyes slip shut as his show of gentle affection creates a physical vibration within me. "That's all you get."

"Then will you believe me that I feel alive around you, too?" he asks, and my eyes flutter open to meet his. "It's been a long time since I felt that way. Truthfully, I'm not sure if I've ever felt something like this."

I'm silent, not knowing what to say because how could someone this fantastic have never fallen in love?

He lets out a heavy sigh, "You don't believe me, do you?"

"Seems a little unbelievable." I give him a wary look. "I'm hardly ever nice to you."

"I disagree." He gives me a slightly amused look. "You saved me from an armed gunman in my own home. It's almost as if you actually want me to stick around."

"So, where do we stand?" I ask, still feeling hesitant. "Are we—"

He covers my mouth before I can finish my question, his brows knitting together. "If you say fuck buddies one more time, you won't like the consequences."

I abruptly push his hand away. "Stop threatening me with whatever these consequences of yours are. What are you, my principal?"

His grin is wide, and seeing that expression on his handsome face always makes my heart stop.

"That's something we can try," he teases. "I'm open to role-playing."

It takes me a second to process his meaning, and when my hand automatically lifts to playfully hit him on the chest, he immediately grabs it.

"Careful, Miss Taylor, you're still injured. I wouldn't want those stitches to pop. Since we're going to do this." He doesn't let go of my hand. "I would like to date you properly."

"I think your idea of dating and mine might be very different," I say hesitantly, still trying to grasp what is happening between us.

Hunter arches a brow. "Well, what do you call dating?"

"I don't know. It's been a while since I went out on a real one, but usually dinner or movies or something like that."

He pauses, and there is an odd undertone to his voice. "You want me to take you to the movies?"

I study him, suddenly finding the mental image in my head a little too funny.

"Why're you smiling?" he asks, almost defensively.

"I was trying to imagine you in one of those seats," my lips twitch. "I just can't see you watching a blockbuster movie in a crowded theatre."

"You're right." Hunter stares at me. "I can think of plenty of other creative uses of my time and yours."

"I'm not saying we have to do that," I say, hoping it's not apparent that I'm blushing.

"The advantage of dating me is that I can take you to the best restaurants or fly in the most talented chefs to cook us a gourmet meal at home."

Hunter steps closer to me and continues, "I can fly you to Venice or Switzerland for a weekend where you can watch the snowfall and ride in the gondolas. I can take you shopping in whichever part of the world you desire. That is my idea of a date."

"Of course, it is Richie Rich," I mutter under my breath.

"What was that?"

"Nothing. Look, I don't know, okay? Let's just go slow. I still need to process the fact that you just admitted to being a mass murderer."

He frowns. "It's not like you didn't know."

"I didn't!" I scowl at him. "Not really."

"So you pretended not to know?"

"I'm the manager of the Blue Whiskey. Whatever else it is you do is none of my concern."

"You're the manager because I needed to replace the old one," he reminds me.

"Did you kill Steve?" I practically whisper, praying that Hunter gives me the right answer.

"Would it bother you if I did?" he asks, his expression suddenly going blank.

I consider the question carefully before I answer it.

"I was exposed to violence at a very young age. Nobody ever protected me. Not until you. You may be a monster to the world, but not to me, and right now, that's all that matters."

I stand up, move past him, and clean the broken vase.

"Megan, I'm not a villain. These are not good people I deal with in my business."

"I never said you were."

"I have my own code, and I've never once hurt a woman or a child," he explains.

I toss some of the broken shards into a nearby wastebasket.

"I'm glad." I look up to meet his steady gaze. "Seriously, I'm happy to know that."

"But all this honesty between us also means that if you ever decide to leave me, you won't be able to," he explains, leaning against the edge of the desk, facing me. "I can't unsay what I've said in this room tonight. There are a select few people who know what I really do. I maintain my image as a business owner to protect my real identity as a professional fixer."

"Yes, of course," I say, dryly. "I figured you had a dual thing going on, but I just thought I'd pretend not to know. Helps with staying alive, you know."

"Megan." Hunter strides across the room. His hand reaches out to caress my cheek. His voice is deceptively soft. "This is what I was trying to say earlier, albeit badly. I'm not some crazy control freak. What I meant to say is that if you decide to leave me, you will still have to work for me—in whatever capacity because it's the only way I can keep you safe. I hope you understand that."

I let out a deep breath, trying to steady myself. "If you think that saying this to me makes me feel comfortable about dating you, it's not. Threats in the bedroom can be both creative and enjoyable. Outside, I have an issue with them."

"These aren't threats."

"Humph. Last time I checked, I'm the one who saved you from a certain death by gunfire." I pat my stitches as a reminder. "So, maybe you're the one who needs to be careful about walking away from me. It seems to me that I'm the one who keeps you safe."

He leans forward, brushing his lips over mine. "I can't decide whether your reckless side stems from bravery or stupidity."

"It's a healthy mixture of both," I inform him, kissing him back.

Then, I reach out and pat his cheek, smirking, "Now, since you've forced me to break my vase of pretty flowers, you have to get someone to finish cleaning it up."

He backs me into one of my office walls.

"In a minute."

Hunter slides his hands back under my skirt.

"Sex again?" I ask facetiously as I slam my head against the wall in excited anticipation.

"Sex with you whenever, however, and always."

Chapter 47

What Are You Doing?

MEGAN

"You look nice," Naomi says with a strange grin on her face.

"What do you mean by that?"

"Nothing, it's just that I've never seen you dress up for him before."

I look at myself in the long mirror affixed to the wall in my bedroom. It's framed by an intricately etched gold border, clearly, an expensive piece that Hunter's interior decorator probably purchased when he or she decorated this apartment.

Naomi's right, I never dress up, but I've also never dated a grown-ass man before. Hunter and I have been coexisting peacefully at The Blue Whiskey for almost a week since our "come to Jesus" moment in my office, and he's invited me out for an actual date tonight. I thought I should dress the part.

"Do you think it's too much?" I ask her, turning to look at my profile. I'm wearing a simple black halter dress with a single split on the side. It glides along my curves, showing off my back and my left thigh.

"It can never be too much." She hands me a liquid lipstick from her handbag. "Here, put this on."

The color is stiletto red.

"I never wear red," I tell her.

"But tonight, you should."

"You sure you don't want to go on this date instead of me?" I ask sarcastically.

"If I was sleeping with a hot, older man who gave me an apartment and a trip to Paris, I'd wear nothing but a trench-coat and this damn red lipstick."

I laugh because I know she totally would.

"You're hysterical."

"I'm dead ass serious. You should be naked in that little office of yours at the club every night. I would certainly be if he was my boss."

I am many things.

A club manager.

An art student.

A cynic.

But I stare back at an image of not just the sum of those things but a woman in the mirror who is... dare I say... happy for once?

A knock at the door leads me to pick up my purse on the bed.

He's here.

"That dress," is all he says after I've opened the door.

"What about it?" I ask, trying extremely hard not to blush.

"Did I buy you that one?"

"Absolutely not. I took the clothes you had delivered here the other day back to the store."

That was probably the hardest thing I ever did because he had some personal shopper send over a few fabulous outfits. But I've taken enough from Hunter.

A job.

A home.

I can't allow him to give me too many things or I may possibly lose myself.

"Well, regardless of where you purchased it, it's a stunner on you."

"That's what I told her!" Naomi chimes in through the door of her bedroom.

Hunter emits a slight chuckle. I think he finds Naomi entertaining, although he only briefly interacts with her.

"Let's go," he announces. "We've got a dinner reservation."

"Good night, Naomi," I call from the living room.

"Good night, red," she says back, and I can hear the smugness of her response.

In Paris, Hunter and I visited small cafes and out-of-the-way restaurants because those are the places that are popular in the city. However, in Los Angeles, I can see that Hunter likes to do things in a totally different way. Dinner was incredible. We dined on a rooftop with spectacular views of the city. While we weren't the only people there, we clearly had the best seat in the house, which was somewhat isolated from the other diners.

"Have you been here before?" I ask the typical question a woman sleeping with a man will ask when she wants to know if she's special or just more of the same.

"No, I'm a complete workaholic. I don't usually make time for dinners out, but I heard this restaurant had a new chef cooking here who was talented. I thought you might like to try it."

From appetizers to dessert, everything was top-notch, and, of course, the view of the Hollywood sign at sunset was the icing on the cake. I was pissed that I missed a great opportunity and didn't think to bring my sketchbook so that I could capture the moment, so I did the next best thing and took a flick with my cell phone. I'll be sure to sketch it later.

After our meal, we stay a little longer and have another cocktail. I choose an apple martini, and Hunter orders a lowball of his favorite whiskey. Then he does something crazy and grabs my hand across the table as we sip on our respective drinks.

"What are you doing?" I ask, a bit shell-shocked.

"The same thing you're doing."

"I mean with my hand."

"I'm holding it."

I look around at the other tables. No one is holding hands.

"It's weird." I try pulling it back.

"Pull your hand away from me again, and you'll be sitting on my lap the rest of this evening."

"There you go with the threats again."

"I can't help it. You bring the worst out of me."

"Agreed."

"Agreed?"

"You bring the worst out of me, too."

"Then we're a perfect match."

I think about everything we've been through together since we met. Steve, Paris, the shooting at his apartment, and I am more convinced than ever that we're probably the total opposite of being a perfect match. We're bad luck for each other.

Yet here I am.

Holding hands with a man who makes the engine inside

of my chest roar to life and makes me feel safer than I ever have in my entire life.

After he pays the bill, we head home. My plan is to peel off this dress, crawl into bed, and read another chapter of an angsty romance I've recently been into until I drift to sleep.

But Hunter has other plans for us.

He slides his key card into the elevator of our building and hits the PH button, never once asking me if I wanted to end our date in his home. Hell, the last time I was here, both he and I were almost shot by a sniper who is still out there for all I know.

"I didn't say I was going to your house."

"It was assumed."

"You assumed that I was going to put out simply because you bought me a lobster dinner?" I say incredulously.

"You've already put out." He smirks. "Repeatedly."

"Don't remind me."

"Oh, I'm definitely going to remind you."

"The elevator doors glide open directly to Hunter's penthouse, and I suck in a breath at what I see.

"What did you do?" I ask in awe.

There are candles.

Dozens and dozens of ivory-colored candles of varying heights, strategically placed throughout the apartment, all lit. All for me.

It's beautiful.

Like a fairytale.

He presses a button on the wall that I thought was a security panel but seems to control the entertainment system in his home. Soft music plays, like the kind you'd hear on an old 70s station. I think they call it yacht rock.

I'm speechless because this is a very calculated plan of

seduction. Is Hunter trying to seduce me? This isn't like him. This is...different and maybe kind of nice.

"Have you ever danced to slow music?" He asks as he pulls me into his body in the middle of the living room.

"Well, not really. They didn't play a lot of slow songs at school dances. In fact, they didn't play any."

"You went to school dances?"

He's so damn perceptive. Of course, I didn't go to any dances. I'm only saying what I believe an ordinary woman my age would say.

"No."

"Why?"

He places my arms around his neck, and he wraps his around my waist.

"I didn't live with the kind of people who supported that. A dance means I would have needed a ticket, maybe even a dress. No one in my house was paying for that. Not for me."

"When will you tell me more details about your past?"

"I'm not giving those people any energy. Talking about the past would do that."

"And who are *those* people?"

Both he and I have complicated pasts. He has a few ghosts from his past, whom I think he's desperately eager to find, and I have several I'm determined to avoid. I wonder if he's already started fishing around in my past. He's got the resources to do it. I'm just not sure if he's that interested in me to go digging.

"I'd rather not get into any of that. They're nobody."

Hunter grunts in response but says nothing else. It's clear what I've told him has angered him, but there isn't any point in getting worked up about the demons of the past. I've learned that lesson many times.

"This is an interesting song," I say. A man with a soothing voice is singing about sailing.

"Interesting, how?"

"He sounds like he knows what that feels like, to sail on a boat."

"I think it's a metaphor for love, but yeah, I'm sure the singer has been on a few yachts in his lifetime. He was pretty successful in his heyday."

We continue swaying to the music. I think I'm doing all right. I've never danced to a slow record before, not like this.

"Nice," I say wistfully.

"Would you want to sail one day?"

"Me?" I say incredulously.

"Yes, you."

"I mean... if you're offering."

His lips bend toward my ear.

"I'm offering you whatever you'll accept from me, Megan."

I look up at his serious eyes and suddenly suspect just how much trouble I'm really in. I'm falling for my boss, my landlord, my protector, my own personal genie in a bottle.

And I'm falling hard.

Chapter 48

That Was Epic!

MEGAN

I initiate a kiss that starts soft but grows into a passionate exchange between us that finds us in his bedroom. When he lifts me and places me on his massive bed, I look up at the skylight. It's been replaced, and it looks like nothing ever happened in this room. It distracts me from Hunter for a moment with its view of the full moon.

"Where are you right now?" Hunter asks.

"On the moon," I answered wistfully.

"And what are you doing on the moon when you're right here with me?"

"I bet it's quiet there."

"Probably."

"I bet no one could hear me there," I say, unzipping the size of my dress.

"Let me do that," he tells me in a deep, thick voice. "Let me do everything."

Within moments, my dress and bra are on the floor and

Hunter begins to worship the skin right underneath one of my breasts. Feathering kisses. Whispering incomprehensible sweet words into my skin.

"Lay down," I tell him. I don't want to stare at the moon any longer.

Only him.

He shockingly obeys me, and I unfasten his designer belt and unzip his slacks, tugging them down his strong legs.

The bulge in his boxer briefs struggles to push through the fabric as I straddle him. He tries to push them down on his own before I get settled in, but I grab a hold of his wrists to stop him.

"No."

I start to grind my freshly bare pussy into his hard mound, dry-humping his stiff dick, as I chase a quick release. My orgasm comes quickly as I've been thinking about fucking Hunter since dessert.

"That was torture," he tells me through gritted teeth.

I smile as the power dynamic between us finally feels like it's shifted my way.

"I haven't done something like that since high school," he claims.

"You didn't like it?"

"I didn't say that. You looked like a goddess, riding me to orgasm. You looked fucking beautiful. But I can only imagine how that pretty face of yours would contort with my enormous cock inside of you as you ride me a second time."

My mouth waters at the thought.

"Rise up," he tells me.

He slides down his boxers and kicks them away. His dick is huge and angry and points straight in my direction as if it's calling me out for being a tease.

"Take it," he orders.

I'm still sensitive from my orgasm as I slowly slide myself down his huge length.

"That's it," he groans. "Take all of me. Damn, you're tight."

Once I'm stuffed to the hilt with him, he places his hands on my hips and orders me to fuck him. "Now ride me."

I start rotating my hips to adjust to Hunter's size, but he isn't going to make this easy as he juts up and rams himself further inside of me.

"Shit!" I scream.

He grabs both of my breasts in his hands and holds them tightly as he continues to work my pussy from the bottom.

"You're not moving enough, Megan."

"I can't! You're...you're–"

"I'm fucking you!" He roars.

Suddenly, he flips us over. I'm on the bottom, and he's on the top as he sinks his dick into me deeper and deeper.

"Hunter," I moan. "Dammit."

"It's good, isn't it?"

"Fuck, yes."

"Your sweet, juicy pussy is meant only for me. Look how wet it gets whenever I'm around. Open wider, Megan. I need more of you."

I spread my legs as far as they can go as he takes several more deep, punishing strokes. I'm screaming his name when he suddenly stops.

Then flips me over.

"Head down. Ass up. I want to see your pussy before I take it again."

I clench the sheets with my fists as he takes me from

behind. From this position, it feels like he's grown another two inches as he pounds away at me. I damn near feel him in my throat.

"Oh my God!" I exclaim as my orgasm creeps up and threatens to strangle my throat.

After a few more strokes, Hunter slaps one of my ass cheeks, and that's all she wrote. My head spirals as I fall into the abyss. This orgasm feels damn near spiritual.

"Yesss!!!"

He emits a guttural groan as he comes to his release. Then we both fall over and spread out on his 800 thread count sheets, completely spent, with grins on our faces. He smooths back strands of my hair from my sweaty face as we lay on our sides, spooning each other.

"Are you still on the moon?" he asks after a few moments of silence between us, his thumb lightly brushing against one of my nipples.

"No, I don't think so."

"You don't think so?"

"I think I've found my quiet here, with you, at least for now."

He peppers soft kisses on the back of my neck.

"So stay a while."

His hand moves from my breast and down my body until he reaches between my legs. He languidly plays with my clit. He alternates between gently rubbing it and then squeezing it hard between his fingertips and continues doing so as I gasp in pleasure.

"Stay," he says again.

"Naomi will worry," I whisper in between gasps.

"You're only a few floors away."

"But I always come home."

"Not tonight." He squeezes my clit again.

I let out some sort of sound that's part pleasure, part plea.

"Okay," I submit. "I'll stay."

"Good girl."

He slides two of his thick fingers inside my pussy and carefully fucks me with them.

"That's it," he spurs me on as I push my hips forward, fucking his fingers back. "Come for me again."

I bite my lip and squeeze my eyelids shut as my pelvis and Hunter's hand duke it out for my next orgasm.

Then my cell phone rings.

"Ignore it," he tells me as my aching pussy begs to be satisfied. "Ignore it, and I'll let you come," he chuckles with self-satisfaction.

My phone rings a second time, and I get a foreboding feeling that I can't quite shake. People rarely call me back-to-back like this. Not even Naomi. She'd leave a hostile text. And even though the night has been magical and frighteningly normal between us, there's always trouble when it comes to me and this man. Why should tonight be any different?

"I think I need to take it," I exhale harshly, frustrated that someone is interrupting what was probably going to be another epic orgasm.

His fingers still.

"If you take that call, I'll make sure that you won't be able to walk during tomorrow night's shift."

"I've got to take it," I say, standing my ground. I don't recognize the number, but my gut tells me I should pick it up.

Hunter storms out of the bedroom and walks into his living room as I take the call. He's completely nude, and I get a glimpse of his tightly muscular butt as he walks away.

He's a beautiful man, and I could stare at him all day. I wonder when he finds the time to work out.

I press the home button of my cell phone and regret it as soon as I say hello. When will I learn that my gut can rarely be trusted?

When Hunter returns to the bedroom, his entire expression softens once he sees mine, which looks queasy. I can tell that it disturbs him as he rushes to my side.

"What is it?" he asks cautiously. "Who was that?"

"It was a nobody."

"Which one?"

"My bitch of a sister. She's here."

Uh-oh, I can't wait to see what happens when Megan's sister comes to town. Ready to learn what happens next?

Hunter and Megan's story continues in **Submission**, and girl, it's going to be a wild ride!

All He Fears Is Losing Her...

SUBMISSION, the latest installment in the pulse-racing series, self-made billionaire Hunter Middleton finds himself at war with unseen enemies who threaten to take away the only thing he's ever wanted—Megan. As dangerous forces close in, their forbidden age-gap romance intensifies, and Hunter is forced to confront the lengths he'll go to possess her, heart and soul. But can their love survive when the world is determined to tear them apart?

Thank you SO much for reading Obsession. If you've enjoyed the story so far, please leave a review at the retailer where you purchased it. —Lisa

Acknowledgments

This trilogy features one of my new favorite couples, Hunter and Megan, and was first drafted exclusively for my phenomenal Romance Ninja Insiders over on Patreon.

Ladies, without your support, I would not have been able to indulge my muse and write stories outside of my usual romances. I love y'all!

NINJA ADDICTS

Beejay Johnson
Tressa Stevenson
Breaking The Epigraph
Leslie S.
Queen Bee
Dawn Gilmore
Tahkeiya White
Hazel Honey
Lisa Lopez
Victoria Nogales
Pat Chrisp-Langston
Cheryl Cutaia
Lisa Adams
Melissa A Pratt

NINJA GROUPIES

Chafonta Whatley
Char B.
Dorothy Morris
Loc Prncess
Ashelt

NINJA SUPPORTERS

Taylor Eaton
Karen Niles
Norma
Louise Jeffcoat
Laurie Edwards
Katy
Martha
Margie Schmelzer
Erin Marshall
Nikki Afetian
Tatyana
Serena Fritz
Kate Doyle
Edana Walker
Dee Puffer
Johanne Levesque Murray
Jazman Diggs
Valeria Collins
Michele Handal
C Kennedy
Angie Lauridsen
Dolores Shortt Mawhinney

Special Invitation

Do you love stories like this one? Would you like to read the next new romance I write before everyone else? I write new books like this one exclusively for readers in my Romance Ninja Community over on Patreon. I can't wait to see you over there!
—Lisa

Learn More Here

Also From Lisa Lang Blakeney

****Discounted Book Bundles****
Ultimate Masterson Book Bundle
Ultimate King Brothers Book Bundle
Ultimate Nighthawks Book Bundle
Ultimate Alpha Book One Bundle

The Masterson Series
Devour this addictive series about the possessive bad boy,
Roman Masterson, who falls hard and fast for the girl he's
promised his family to protect.
Masterson
Masterson Unleashed
Masterson In Love
Masterson Made
Joseph Loves Juliette

Masterson Next Generation Series
The crazy hot fruit doesn't fall far from the tree. Dive into
this second generation of Masterson men!
Knox - Knox & Gigi

Bronx - Bronx & Karma
Seven - Seven & Sasha

The King Brothers Series

Dive into this series of interconnected standalones featuring 3 alpha hot brothers and the women they lay claim to without apology.
Claimed - Camden & Jade
Indebted - Cutter & Sloan
Broken - Stone & Tiny
Promised - All King Brothers

The Nighthawk Series

Sexy & sweet sports romances set in the professional world of football. All standalones.
Saint - Saint & Sabrina
Wolf - Cooper & Ursula
Diesel - Mason & Olivia
Jett - Jett & Adrienne
Rush - Rush & Mia
Freak - Freak & Willow
Brick - Brick & Kaya
Dak - Dak & Katrina

Valencia Ice Mafia Series

Hot hockey romances set on the college campus of Valencia City University.
Neo - Neo & Violet
Shane - Shane & Kennedy
Bass - Coming Soon!

The Middleton Series
(Club Blue Whiskey)

Dark, age-gap, romantic suspense trilogy, set in the underbelly of Los Angeles featuring dangerous billionaire Hunter Middleton and the object of his obsession, Megan.

Obsession

Submission

Possession

Where You Can Find Me

MY VIP LIST (Get the nitty gritty)

I have a VIP Reader mailing list. I only send free books, new release, sales or special giveaway information to this group. No spam. You can join here:
http://LisaLangBlakeney.com/VIP

MY READERS GROUP (Casual fun)

Join my online Readers Group on Facebook also known as my "Romance Ninja Warriors" where I share all things new going on, celebrate birthdays, post teasers, yummy pics, giveaways and just chit chat.
http://LisaLangBlakeney.com/community

ROMANCE NINJA INSIDER (Early access!)

For exclusive serials, early access to all my releases, and more goodies become a romance ninja insider over at my Patreon community.
Get started with this 7 day free trial!

About the Author

Lisa Lang Blakeney is a USA Today Bestselling author of contemporary romance sold in more than 28 countries. Worried that her fellow PTO moms might disapprove, she wrote and published her steamy debut novel Masterson under a different title and pen name in August of 2015.

Thanks to strong reader support of her alpha male character, Roman Masterson, she was encouraged to continue with the series and published the entire Masterson Trilogy the following year. She hasn't looked back since and continues to write novels featuring strong alpha men and the smart women they seek to claim.

A romance junkie for sure, you can find Lisa watching a romantic comedy, reading a romance novel, or writing one of her own most days of the week. If she's not doing that, she's outside in the garden tending to her roses.

Lisa is the wife of one alpha (whom she met in college), mother to four girls, and two labradoodles. Get news on releases, sales and giveaways when you become one of Lisa's VIP readers at : http://LisaLangBlakeney.com/VIP

facebook.com/authorlisalangblakeney

x.com/LisaLangWrites

instagram.com/LisaLangBlakeney

amazon.com/author/lisalangblakeney

bookbub.com/authors/lisa-lang-blakeney

goodreads.com/Lisa_Lang_Blakeney

pinterest.com/lisalangwrites

tiktok.com/@lisalangblakeney

patreon.com/lisalangblakeney

www.ingramcontent.com/pod-product-compliance
Lightning Source LLC
Chambersburg PA
CBHW030731310726
48969CB00005B/1186